Bloodwalker

Alex Emerson

To my wife, who has supported this project since the first time I brazenly told her I was going to write a novel, and who has subjected herself to painstaking rounds of edits, provided invaluable commentary (and occasional reassurance), and never ceases to amaze me.

<u>Chapter 1</u>

Samantha Nightshade's mobile phone buzzed an alert, breaking her concentration, a blessed relief. She had been staring at her laptop screen for hours. Days, it felt like. The house had been silent until the vibration on the tabletop; she'd been too dejected to even put on music.

Snatching up her phone, she pressed her thumb against the biometric scanner to unlock the screen. She was horrified to see that it wasn't even 10:30 in the morning yet. A text bubble manifested, sliding down from the top of the display like a thick drip of water from a leaking faucet:

Hey. I need to stay a little late tonight. Find any good jobs today?

Unconsciously, Sam growled. Why did it feel like every aspect of her life came back to finding a job? She didn't want to define herself by her vocation, the way so many of her peers seemed to do. Even Jack had taken to introducing himself to people by his job title. She dug an irritated fingernail into the palm of her hand before tapping the water drip text bubble to type her response:

Nothing. I'm so frustrated. Job market sucks. I hate this!

She scrolled through a list of cartoon images, first tapping on a face with a deep frown on it, then a red face that looked like it was swearing up a storm. She added a second message:

Ugh. Why do you have to stay late?

In her head, it was said in a whiny voice, one of the things she hated the most about herself. She always felt so childish when that tone came out of her. Sam scowled and returned her focus to her laptop and the digital job board she had been scouring.

The day started out so well, but her frustrations had boiled over. Sam knew she should message Jack back and ask about his day, or anything else to lift the damper she had put on the conversation, but she was feeling stubborn and willing to let her annoyance win.

Her memory flitted back to the beginning of the day, to the way Jack's alarm had sounded: an incessant digital beep obnoxious enough to wake the dead. He got out of bed quickly, stopping the noise with the press of a button, and glanced at Sam just as she was opening her eyes. Snug under the blankets, she had smiled up at him. "Go back to sleep, beautiful," he had softly whispered in her ear before giving her a quick kiss on the forehead.

"I love you, Jack Nightshade," she had said, lightly scratching her fingernails along his neck.

"Can't wait to come home to you tonight, Sam Nightshade" he replied.

Sam had watched him lazily as he stripped off his pajama pants and put on his work clothes. His freshly-pressed khakis fit perfectly on his muscular legs, snug in all the right places. She giggled as Jack's button-up somehow folded in on itself on his back, sticking to his undershirt. "You are helpless, Jack," she chided, reaching up from the bed to adjust his shirt.

He smiled at her. "Well, it's a good thing I have you to take care of me."

"Always."

Sam forced herself to stop reflecting on the morning and to get back to the grind that had frustrated her so much. Sighing, she pulled a stack of papers closer, brushed her short blonde hair away from her face, and picked up her pen. She looked over today's To Do list, even though she had it memorized. It had been the same list for months.

She knew how fortunate she was that Jack had managed to land this web development job. He was making more than enough to support them, even with their new house, but she hadn't gone through years of schooling to become a housewife. She had studied Psychology because of her "intrinsic desire to help people, to fix problems, and to make the world a better place," as she had written toward the end of her college career. Whining at her husband, even in a text message, was definitely not fixing a problem. Washing dishes at The Watering Hole, a dive bar a few miles from their house, was far from her dream, but at least it would be something while she waited to hear back from the hospital and the clinics she had applied to in the past few months. But even The Watering Hole hadn't offered her the job.

As she scrolled down the page, looking at the postings, Sam absentmindedly spun her wedding ring around her finger with her thumb. Married six months, a couple for seven years. She was 23, admittedly with no real job experience, but she had a college degree, she had graduated with honors and letters of recommendation, and why was it so hard to find a job? It was stupid! Or maybe she was stupid. She snarled as the frustration she had been feeling boiled up again, shoved herself away from the table, and stood to make herself lunch. It was early but she didn't care and needed the distraction.

Tomato and mozzarella slices on crackers were light enough to not dull her mind but she challenged herself to see just how identically she could slice the tomato, which proved to be something of a salve for her mood. The crackers disappeared far too quickly, however, and Sam found herself dreading the inevitable return to the job hunt.

An hour or so passed. Sam had found a few positions for which she applied, but nothing exciting or relevant to her area of study. She brushed her hair out of her eyes again, reflecting on just how much she hated attaching her resume, then being asked to fill out little text boxes detailing all of the same information that was in the resume she was required to attach.

The phone rang, startling her out of her reverie. Sam glanced at the clock. 12:15. Jack called almost every day at this time, preferring to speak rather than a simple text message exchange. At least she would have a chance to apologize.

A sound like wind and static came through the phone. It made Sam uneasy and made her picture being in one of those tunnels that were cut through a mountain instead of going around. She pulled the phone away from her ear and noticed the display said Unknown Caller. "Hello?" she answered, feeling slightly foolish, as if she were addressing the wind. The wind grew sharp, high-pitched. She thought it almost sounded like a woman screaming across a great distance. "Hello?" she repeated, but the call went dead. Puzzled, Sam set the phone back on the table.

Jack did not end up calling. Most likely, he was in a work meeting. That happened often enough, and she did not want to bother him if he was in a meeting. Sam tried to convince herself that he wasn't avoiding her because of her childish outburst earlier.

Some hours later, Sam stretched her arms above her head. Her hands were painfully cramped, and it was getting close to dinner. Her stomach growled, though whether in anticipation or as an autonomic response to her desperate need to perform literally any other task, she was unsure.

Thinking of Jack, and her desire to apologize to him after her whiny interaction that morning, she put a pot of water on the stovetop and turned on the gas burner. After several small clicks, the blue-white flame gave a soft, satisfying pop as it flashed into existence. She opened the refrigerator and took out a few cloves of garlic, half of a loaf of French bread, and a stick of butter. From the cabinet she removed an unopened box of spaghetti. Making his favorite dinner was a good start to the apology.

Sam pulled out a small bamboo cutting board and got to work. First, she peeled the garlic. The bread was next, cut in six-inch pieces before being split in two. She plucked a few of the bigger crumbs from the cutting board and popped them into her mouth before drizzling olive oil over the bread. Then she pressed the garlic with the flat of the knife, reveling in the scent as it wafted from the crushed bulbs. When the doorbell rang, she was so startled the knife slipped and sliced open her left index finger. The doorbell rang again as she was wrapping her finger in a paper towel to try to stem the bleeding.

"Just a second!" Sam yelled irritably, then felt immediately embarrassed. The vestiges of frustration just wouldn't leave her today, it seemed.

The first thing she noticed upon opening the front door was the set of blue and red lights oscillating in her yard. Then she saw the man standing on the doorstep. His complexion was dark; he was somewhere in his late 50s, his hair as grey as it was black and shaped tight to his head. He was overweight but not obese, the weight of age more than overeating. She had no idea who this man was. She had not met all the neighbors, but he didn't seem familiar. Then Sam's brain processed what she saw. The man was wearing a uniform, and behind him was the source of the blue and red lights: a police car. Sam's heart skipped a beat and she felt her hands go clammy as the pieces all clicked together.

"I'm sorry to bother you, Miss," the police officer said quietly, his baritone voice sounding like a distant roll of thunder. "Is your name Samantha Nightshade?" She nodded, slowly. "And your husband is Jackson Nightshade?" Sam nodded again. She felt her heart racing in her chest, as if she knew what he was about to say, but at the same time she felt as if it was someone else's chest, someone else's heart.

"I'm very sorry to tell you this," he began, and Sam felt her legs weakening. She could not hear his words anymore, at least not all of them. Sam heard the word "accident" and fell to her knees. The police officer stood back, but Sam didn't notice. Between her streaming tears, Sam stared at a bloodstained paper towel which lay crumpled on the floor. She felt like a caricature, like an overreacting character in a movie, but she could not stand up. She could barely breathe. The paper towel had been so important, but she could not remember why. As Sam began a sputtering cough, the police officer crouched in the door frame. "I'm very sorry, Mrs. Nightshade," he said softly.

"Can I see him?" Sam asked in a gasping voice. She tried to ask, at least. Air itself seemed to fight her; distantly she realized she was hyperventilating. The police officer instructed her to breathe, slow and deep, to try to calm herself down. Sam felt panic roaring inside, but she did as he said, forcing the drumbeat of her heart to decelerate, forcing her breath to slow. Eventually she was able to regain enough control over her breathing that she asked again, more clearly. "Can I see him?" The panic in her chest reared up, but she forced it down.

The officer hesitated, and his eyes shifted away from her face. "I'm, uh, not entirely sure you'd want to see him, Mrs. Nightshade," he said, sounding uncomfortable. "I've been doing this job for a long time, and it never gets easier. Your husband's accident was – well, I would rather spare you the details." He sighed before continuing. "But if you want to see him..." Sam nodded, her heart thumping, wondering how bad Jack must look for the officer to be so uncertain. The tang of salt on her lips was strong, and sobs wracked her body, but she needed to do this. The police officer reached out and gently touched her forearm, as if a reminder she was not alone, then stood and took a few steps back.

"Before I drive you to the hospital, Mrs. Nightshade, is there anything you need help with?" he asked, gesturing to the bloodied paper towel that lay crumpled on the floor. Sam shook her head slowly as she slowly rose to her feet. "Do you have something cooking, Mrs. Nightshade?"

The memory of the minutes before the police officer arrived crashed over Sam like a tidal wave. She remembered the dinner she had been preparing, how much she was looking forward to Jack getting home, to apologizing to him. Her sobs redoubled as she realized that the last words she ever said to her husband were of anger and frustration. Methodically, Sam put one foot in front of the other and turned off the burners on the stovetop. In an odd, disconnected part of her brain, she knew she would never be able to eat spaghetti or garlic bread again, and that even the smell of it would make her sick to her stomach. She vomited into the sink. The dish towel she used to wipe her mouth went directly into the trash as she stumbled out of the kitchen.

The next hour was a blur. The police officer, who re-introduced himself as Robert Webb, helped Sam into his squad car and drove her to the hospital. Sam couldn't remember the ride, or even being in the car. In her memories, it was as if she went from her house to the hospital with no intervening time. She was sitting in the waiting room, dimly aware of Webb speaking with the receptionist at the front desk. She was at the same hospital that had the opening for a Psych Evaluator, the one she had been waiting to hear back from for weeks. Why was she there? The waiting room had a steady buzz, a din of coughing and the flipping of magazine pages acting as irregular beats to the muted buzz of a television displaying network news. But Sam stared ahead, seeing nothing, lost in her mind. A hand on her shoulder made her gasp.

"I've checked you in, Mrs. Nightshade," Webb said quietly. "Come with me. I'll take you to your husband." Sam's breath caught as knowledge, tucked away to protect her, flooded back. She followed the police officer down the hall to the elevator as if in a trance, only numbly registering her footfalls on the tiled floor or the sounds of the hospital around her. Sam stared at the backs of Webb's shoes a few feet ahead, shambling more than walking. The elevator bell chimed, and she heard it in the way someone might hear a distant splash from a bullfrog leaping into an unseen pond on a hot summer's day.

The elevator was bright and sterile, a nondescript metal box full of glowing buttons and quiet, wordless music. It made the back of Sam's mind itch, and a tiny sliver of her brain tried to recognize the song, but she did not actively notice it. Webb pushed a button and the door slid shut, enclosing them in steel. The gears whirred and the elevator hummed with electricity and movement on the outside, but inside neither Sam nor Webb stirred. In a flash of conscious thought, Sam realized the moving elevator with her standing statically inside of it was a perfect representation of how she felt at that moment, physically moving through a series of external pressures but feeling nothing inside out of necessity. The thought quickly became lost, unconsciously discarded as her mind rebuilt its walls to protect her from what she was about to see.

When the elevator jostled its final few inches and halted, Webb turned toward her and put his hands on her shoulders. "Mrs. Nightshade," he said softly. "We can go right back to the lobby. You do not have to do this."

Sam looked into his deep brown eyes and took a breath. "Yes, I do," she said quietly. The air passing her lips felt foreign, and she realized she hadn't spoken in hours. At least it felt like hours. She wasn't really sure what day it was anymore. Sam raised a finger and touched her lips, as if reassuring herself they were her lips, on her face, and not the face of some stranger. She saw her reflection in the doors as they slid open, pulled and distorted, and did not recognize the shape that looked back at her. Then the metal disappeared and Sam saw the wall in front of her. There was a sign reading Mortuary, a stark black arrow pointing to the right. Subconsciously, Sam grabbed her left wrist with her other hand and squeezed, a nervous habit from grade school.

Webb watched her for a few seconds, then sighed. "Well, if you're sure," he said, "follow me."

Awareness continued to ebb and flow through Sam as she followed the officer down the hallway. She noticed how loudly their shoes echoed on the tiled floor, but not the color of the walls. Standing outside of the mortuary door, the unmistakable taste of formaldehyde coated her tongue, making her throat convulse. Sam felt a rush of saliva in her mouth, which mixed with the sudden acid burn of bile.

Webb stopped in front of the mortuary door and turned to face her once again. "Are you absolutely positive you want to go through this door?" he asked. "This is one of the worst car accidents I've ever seen. There is nothing wrong with remembering him how he was, Mrs. Nightshade."

Sam nodded solemnly. She needed to see Jackson one more time, even... Part of her brain still resisted the idea Jack was dead. Part of her brain believed that maybe the police were mistaken, that maybe they had misidentified the body. She did not want to see Jack because she believed they were wrong; it was simply something she needed to do.

Webb took a deep breath before pushing the door open. Almost everything in the room was painted an odd shade of green, so dull it seemed grey, except for the wall-length stainless steel cold chambers. Sam felt her heart skip a beat when she realized her husband was in one of the frigid tombs. A fluorescent bulb flickered somewhere in the dark recesses of the room. In the distance, Sam saw the coroner, sitting at a desk. She looked to be in her early 60s, her hair in a tight grey bun on the top of her head. She wore a white lab coat and was hunched over a desk, studiously scratching away with a pen. At the sound of the door opening, the coroner looked up. "Good evening, Melissa," Webb said, addressing the older woman. "This is Mrs. Samantha Nightshade. She's here to identify the body."

The coroner put down her pen and stood, shaking her head. "Melissa Ford," she said by way of introduction, walking towards Sam. "I'm so terribly sorry for your loss." Sam murmured something unintelligible; even she did not know what she said. "I'm not sure how much Robert has told you about the condition of your husband," the coroner said carefully. "I would strongly suggest you do not see him."

Sam shook her head. "I need to," she responded. For the first time, she met the coroner's eyes. Sam clenched her teeth, stopping herself from screaming.

The coroner sighed. "I know that look on your face, Mrs. Nightshade," she said. "I do have to warn you, though, his body is not fully intact. The accident caused," she trailed off, as if trying to find the right words, "substantial damage. The impact of the collision - " she stopped, then visibly steeled herself before starting over. "Mrs. Nightshade, the First Response Team was unable to locate his right arm, and there was significant trauma to his head and chest."

"I need to," Sam repeated before clamping her mouth shut. Her teeth ground together loud enough for both the coroner and the officer to hear, but she didn't care.

The coroner hesitated for a moment before walking over to the bank of refrigerated drawers. She stopped at number 11, read the paperwork in her hand again, then shook her head before pulling open the door to the cooler. A dull blue sheet completely covered the unmistakable shape of a human body. Sam's heart raced in her chest. She had seen movies and television shows with scenes like this, but she never expected to be experiencing it personally. It was horrifying, nerve-wracking, and surreal. Sam needed to see if it was Jack under the cloth, but now that she was so close to the moment, her resolve was flickering. Her knees were locked, but her feet dragged her forward almost of their own volition. When she reached the silver gurney, Melissa moved her hand toward the top of the sheet. Sam's mouth was dry; she felt like she was about to gag, or dry heave. The coroner looked at Sam and waited for her to nod before pulling down the sheet.

As soon as the body was revealed, Sam closed her eyes. The millisecond after the sheet was pulled down would forever be carved into her memory. It was not just the fact the body was clearly Jackson Nightshade that made her close her eyes, but the unbelievable damage to his head. Almost the entire right side of his face was missing, but his shaggy brown hair, now matted with blood, hung down as if trying to pretend nothing was different. She saw teeth - mostly broken - where his upper lip had been torn viciously. The left side of his face was almost completely battered and bruised. Even though the sheet hadn't been pulled down very far, Sam had noticed the wound at his right shoulder where his arm had been. Eyes still closed, she turned away. She heard the coroner slide the stainless-steel gurney back into the refrigerated drawer and the door snap closed. Sam felt a hand on her shoulder, gently pushing her away from the morgue and back toward the hallway. Dimly, she heard the coroner's voice, but she did not understand the words. In her mind, all she could see was Jack's battered face, her husband, the love of her life, dead in the basement of a hospital.

"I'm sorry." The phrase echoed unspoken in her head, pleading and futile. Guilt and panic twisted her words like a desperate mantra. She didn't know if someone had said it to her, or if she was saying it to Jack, or to herself, but the words wouldn't stop repeating.

The smell of the morgue hung in her nose even once she was out of the room and back into the hall, the strong chemical tang heavy and thick. Webb ushered her to a small bench. "That's never an easy thing to see, Mrs. Nightshade," he murmured softly. "Not a sight you're likely to forget. But

13

try to remember what things were like before today and try to think about what he would want for you."

The coroner appeared at her other side, holding a bottle of water. "Water helps get the taste out of your mouth," she said, offering Sam the bottle. "All these years later, I'm still not used to it myself." The coroner sat next to Sam on the bench. "You're welcome to stay here as long as you want, dear," she said softly.

Time passed in a strange mixture of agonizing seconds and blurred minutes. Webb remained in the hall with her the entire time she sat on the bench, slowly, mechanically, draining the water bottle. Sam did not have many conscious thoughts during the time she spent in that hallway, though she would later look back at the time as oddly peaceful, in a remarkably morbid way. The damage was so severe that at least there was no way Jack suffered. Sam sat staring downward, her eyes unfocused toward the mottled floor tiles. She jumped in surprise as Webb's hand gently touched her on her shoulder.

"Do you have anyone you can stay with, Mrs. Nightshade? A friend or a parent you can call?" he asked.

The words sounded strange to her ears, and it took her a moment to understand what he was asking her. "Oh," she murmured slowly. "I hadn't even thought about it. I need to call my mom."

Webb showed her down the hall to an unused office and said she could make the call from there, and that he would wait outside in case she needed anything. The office was small and nondescript, with an old wooden desk in the corner. An overly-bright fluorescent bulb illuminated months of dust. A small placard near the phone reminded users to dial 9 before attempting to call a number outside of the hospital.

Sam lifted the phone from the cradle and punched in her mother's number. The digital chiming of the phone felt unnaturally loud as it attempted to connect, and Sam had to pull the phone away from her ear a little. The ring cut off abruptly. Sam expected to hear her mother's voice, but instead she heard what sounded like a deep, steady thumping, accompanied by a strong wind, or a distant scream. It seemed to echo, stretching to infinite depths, and then the phone chime resumed. Sam's hands shook, and she could feel the blood drain from her face. When her mother answered the phone, it took Sam a minute to compose herself.

"Mom," Sam said in a whisper. "Jack is dead."

Over the course of the next three days, Sam found herself trying to juggle life without Jack. Officer Webb had driven her from the hospital to her mother's house. Her mom had been waiting in the driveway for her, dried streaks of tears plainly visible on her cheeks. Sam didn't think she had more tears left in her, but when she saw her mother, she sobbed until she struggled to breathe, then sobbed some more. When the tears abated, she called Jack's parents and told them what had happened. They lived on the other side of the country, retired and enjoying the warm weather. She remembered a lot of small details from the past few days, such as seeing her face in the bathroom mirror and noticing a rogue eyebrow hair pointing in the opposite direction of the others, but much of the time stuck in her memory as an indistinct mess.

Jack's parents arrived the night before the funeral, and the tears began anew. Sam had never been particularly close with his parents, but she had known them for so long that seeing them break down was enough for her to lose control again. Jack's father's face was like a mask, perpetually pale with wide, glossy eyes. Unsurprisingly, no one was interested in talking, or eating, or anything besides staring at nothing in particular.

Sam awoke on the day of the funeral to the sounds of songbirds outside her childhood bedroom. She still had not gone back to the house she shared with Jack. She didn't know if she'd ever be able to go back. She envied the birds for their song, their carefree exuberance for the bright morning sun. They were still singing as she pulled on the black dress she would be wearing when she buried her husband. She stared at herself in the mirror, not recognizing her own pallid face. Her red-rimmed eyes looked hazy above smoke-grey bags. Sam wasn't sure she had slept more than two hours straight since that night.

The funeral itself was something that, despite her best efforts, Sam simply could not prepare for in any way. Sun shining brightly through the windows, Sam's mother drove her to the funeral home well before the service was scheduled to start. As they walked through the door, Sam's mother squeezed her hand and whispered, "I'm going to talk to Mr. Silas for a few minutes so you can..." Sam's mother trailed off, unsure how to end the sentence. Sam simply nodded and continued into the large room where the service would be held. Her feet dragged her body where her mind did not want to be, to force her to face what she didn't want to see.

Sam's eyes immediately fixed on the pinewood coffin in the center of the room. Her husband was inside that box, and there was nothing she could do about it. Due to the severity of the injuries he suffered in the car accident, it would be a closed-casket service. The visuals from the hospital were still vivid and raw in her mind, and Sam would never tell another living soul what she saw beneath the sheet. On either side of the coffin were photos of Jack: some alone, some with family, and many with her. Sam left a path of tears as her feet pulled her toward the casket, the intensity doubling with each step, and at that moment, she wanted nothing more than to be the one inside the coffin instead of Jack.

Her hands shook violently by the time she finally reached the coffin. The feel of the varnished wood under her hands, hard and calloused, was how she felt toward the world since seeing Jack's body in the hospital. She put her head on the lid of the casket and sobbed. So quiet as to be almost silent, she began a steady stream of whispering, repeating herself as if in a mantra. "I can't do this without you. I can't do this alone."

As family and friends arrived, each comforting word or supportive hug felt progressively emptier, a hollow husk of skin and useless words of sympathy. A few people got up to speak about Jack. Sam did not hear any of it. Time stood still during the service, and she felt like she was not actually there. The visitors began to leave, some stopping by to offer more condolences. She stared forward with unfocused eyes, oblivious to the world around her. Eventually, only Sam and her mother were left in the room. The coffin was gone as well. "It's time, Sam," her mother said softly.

A blink of an eye, or a week later, they stood surrounding a hole in the earth, looking at the coffin as it was lowered into the ground, hollowed-out and raw. Sam felt kinship with the hole in that regard. Her head was muddled; words made no sense. Everything flowed by her in a mist, like a dream. Her hand closed on a pile of loose dirt and she looked at it, momentarily confused why she was holding it. She let the dirt trickle through her fingers and onto the casket. Onto her husband. Onto Jack. "I'm sorry," her inner voice said, repeating her chant from the night at the hospital, the same fear and guilt coloring the words.

After most of the attendees had dispersed, a face appeared in front of her that she had not noticed before. "I'm very sorry for your loss, Mrs. Nightshade." Officer Webb had removed his hat and held it between two hands. "I know this must be an incredibly difficult time for you and your family." Sam nodded numbly. Webb hesitated for a moment before continuing. "I realize this might not be the best time to ask, but do you know if your husband was doing anything after work on the day of the accident? Anything out of the ordinary?" It took Sam a minute to understand the words, to hear the question and process it.

"Out of the ordinary? No. He was coming home like he always does. Why?"

Again, Webb hesitated. "Mrs. Nightshade, our team that was at the scene of the collision filed their report a few days ago. From their preliminary findings, they are saying that it's more than likely a second person was in the car, in the passenger seat. Whoever was in the car with him was not there when the First Responders arrived."

Sam's breath caught in her throat. Someone else in the car? Her mind was racing, but she could not think of anyone who would be in the car with him. Sam swallowed hard, trying and failing to clear sudden anxiety. "I have no idea, Officer Webb. How can they even tell? He didn't mention anything to me before he left." Sam trailed off as her brow furrowed deeply.

Webb looked at her for a moment before continuing. "I don't work forensics, Mrs. Nightshade, but I'm told they know how to recognize certain pieces of evidence in cases like these, though there is some confusion this time. The passenger side airbag didn't inflate, but there were pieces of trace evidence found suggesting a second person." Webb scratched at his chin absentmindedly. "I checked with your husband's employer and I personally reviewed the security tapes. He left alone that day, and every day dating back in the month of tapes I reviewed. Was your husband the kind of person to pick up hitchhikers?" Webb paused for a moment before adding, "Do you think it is possible your husband may have been keeping any secrets from you, Mrs. Nightshade?"

"Hitchhikers?" she repeated, confused. Then shock filled Sam. "Are you suggesting my husband was having an affair?" she asked angrily.

"No, Mrs. Nightshade, I am not," Webb replied soothingly. "But I find it suspicious that it's likely he left alone but was likely not alone at the time of the collision."

She didn't know how to respond. While running his words through her mind again, Sam suddenly realized Webb had switched from using the word 'accident' to the word 'collision'. "What do you think," Sam began, but her words were lost as her throat tightened painfully.

The police officer did not say anything immediately, and it was clear that he was choosing his words carefully. "I just want to know what really happened that night, Mrs. Nightshade." He stopped for a moment. "Here's my number," he said, pulling out a small card. "If you think of anything, remember anything, please give me a call." She took the card from him, and as he turned to leave, he added, "Again, my deepest sympathies to you and your family." Sam did not respond.

"Not alone," Sam muttered to herself. If Jack hadn't been alone, then who had he been with? And where did that person go after the accident, after the collision?

Chapter 2

Sam found it progressively more difficult to focus on anything as the days passed. She was having trouble sleeping and was haunted by night terrors, from which she would often wake screaming. In most of the nightmares, she would be in the car with Jack as it careened off the road and smashed into a large oak. Oddly, sometimes she would be affected by the collision, her face struck by the inflating of the passenger's airbag, while other times she was a ghostly observer, watching Jack's body as the collision tore his arm free and ripped away half of his face.

Some of the dreams were more focused on the still unknown hypothetical passenger in the car. Sam couldn't imagine Jack having an affair, but asleep, when her mind was at its least vigilant, images tended to appear unbidden. The most recent nightmare was one where Jack and a nondescript woman were gleefully performing sexual acts on each other while he drove. Sam was not there in the car, but floating, bodiless, as if she were watching television. Jack would let out a laugh, nearly a cackle, reveling in his infidelity, and the woman would grin mischievously. The moment of impact would be abrupt, and then time would slow. Jack and the woman's bodies would be ripped apart, frame by frame, as she floated helplessly.

When she would wake up, heart racing, Sam always had to dry her eyes. At least she knew this nightmare for what it was: a foolish nightmare bereft of facts. Then she would think about the woman. No matter how long she thought about it, she could not imagine anyone, man or woman, getting out of the car and running away after the collision. None of this made any sense. Part of her still felt as if she would see Jackson Nightshade standing in the door frame, grinning at her, if only she could turn around quickly enough. Sam felt the tears forming in the corners of her eyes again, then rubbed them away mercilessly.

Two months passed, months of Sam hardly sleeping, of her mother taking trips to the house she and Jack had shared. Sam never returned to that house. It had been put on the market and sold for a loss, rather than Sam losing it in foreclosure. She didn't care either way. Sometimes she spent an entire day staring blankly out the window, or at the wall of her childhood bedroom, still painted pale yellow. In odd moments of clarity, she would notice little details, like the scrap of scotch tape still stuck at a 45-degree angle on the wall, where she had once hung a tear-away poster from a magazine.

Sam's mother worried and fussed, trying and failing to bring Sam out of her near-catatonic state. She had given Sam a variety of over-the-counter sleeping medications, with little to no success. Once it reached the point where Sam would not shower unless reminded, her mother finally suggested seeing a therapist.

"You can't go on living like this, Samantha," she said soothingly. "I can't imagine the pain and sorrow in your heart but try to think about what Jack would have wanted for you. You and I both know he would say you can't mourn him forever, that you need to keep yourself alive and try to be happy. I think it's time for you to talk to a professional, Sam. I only suggest it because I love you and I'm worried about you. You know the importance of therapy. You did go to college to be a psychologist, after all."

Sam did not respond. She had never told her mother what Webb had said, about the second person in the car at the time of the accident, and aside from checking in with her a week or two after the funeral, she had not heard from Webb at all. How could she possibly explain to her mother that not only was her world destroyed at the loss of Jack, but that she had some reason to suspect his fidelity? Even at a miniscule chance, it was a possibility she had never considered before the conversation with Webb, and she had no idea how to deal with that piece of information, as speculative as it was.

Eventually, Sam's mother simply scheduled a therapy appointment for her, then took her to the appointment and sat in on the first few sessions. Sam stared, aware she was in different surroundings but not really comprehending it all. Sam's mother did all the talking, explaining the situation to the therapist, a soft, pleasant woman named Janet. She wore thick-framed glasses, and the way the light fell into the room from the window made the lenses seem to flash, frequently hiding her grey-green eyes below her short brown hair.

Janet and Sam's mother spoke at length about a variety of topics, ranging from Jack's sudden death to Sam's lack of interest in anything and the nightly struggle for sleep. Janet commented that she immediately noticed the deep purple bags under Sam's eyes. Sam stared forward, barely conscious. She found herself absent-mindedly fascinated by the light flashing off of Janet's glasses.

During the third session, Sam began hearing trickles of the conversation. "If this continues, Janet," came her mother's voice, like a distant whisper of wind across a desert, "I don't think I'll have a choice other than to have her hospitalized. She was already so thin, and now that she barely eats, she's almost emaciated. I know she's had an incredibly difficult time with Jack's death, but I'll tell you, I have too. She brought Jack home to meet me when they were still in high school." She paused and sniffled quietly. "He was like a son to me. I can't handle losing my daughter, too."

Sam turned her head toward her mother, her first real movement of the session since sitting on the floral-patterned couch. She opened her mouth to speak, but her lips were so dry, her throat nearly atrophied, that she had to close her mouth and work saliva into her mouth. "Jack," she said in a quiet cracked version of her voice, startling her mother to the point where she put her hand on her heart. "Jack was not alone in the car when it crashed."

Her mother stared, surprise etched on her face. Janet stared at her, too, and Sam felt incredibly self-conscious, feeling guilt roil down her face, as if she had interrupted a conversation of which she was not supposed to be a part, even though they were here because of her. Sam experienced self-realization at that moment, understanding the difficulty she had been causing for her mother for over three months. She noticed – really noticed - Janet for the first time as well, seeing the small mole just above her jawline, the beginnings of crow's feet at the corners of her eyes.

"Where did you hear this?" her mother asked, voice trembling.

"After the funeral, Officer Webb stopped to talk to me," Sam answered, her voice quiet. "He was the same cop who came to our house when – the night of –" Sam cleared her throat and changed direction. "He asked if I knew who may have been in the car with Jack, because there was evidence that he had a passenger. Webb checked the security tapes at Jack's office and he left alone..." she trailed off, unable to talk anymore after so many days of silence. Her throat was burning, mouth dry.

Sam's mother seemed to know exactly what she was thinking. She reached out and put her hand on top of Sam's, squeezing it lightly. "Samantha, you and I both know Jack would never have had an affair."

Now that she had opened her mouth, Sam felt like all she wanted to do was talk, but she physically could not make herself. Instead, Sam nodded, but tears had welled up at the corners of her eyes again.

Janet offered a box of tissues to Sam, which she accepted gratefully. A few minutes of silence passed before Janet asked, "This may be too much too soon, Sam, but do you remember how Jack looked and sounded the last time you talked to him before his accident? Everything I've heard the past three weeks tells me that you and Jack loved each other deeply. If my perception of your relationship is correct, I am certain Jack would want you to remember him the way he was for every day of your relationship."

Sam slowly nodded again. Janet's question had stirred up a ghost of a memory, something small she had forgotten about but couldn't quite remember clearly. Something about the wind, or of someone screaming. Maybe both? The memory swirled in fragmented wisps, but as hard as she tried, Sam could not focus on it. A sudden spark of anger flared up in her. All she ever did was stare and sob and forget things. How useless had she allowed herself to become? How pathetic of her to cause so much worry in her mother. How selfish. Her jaw was still clenched when they left the appointment a few minutes later.

Sleep came a little easier for Sam that night, but her dreams were somehow worse than they had been. She was in some place wholly unfamiliar, standing on an uneven sidewalk. She was there because Jack had told her he would meet her there, but she did not see him, and he should have been there already. Across the street was a small park, the kind in which people exercised their dogs. A dark wind rose, and tendrils of icy fog stretched across the midnight sky, curling frozen fingers around the edges of crumbling buildings before whipping around the corner and sheathing desecrated façades in chilled air. Sam shivered. Everything she could see was bathed in the grey-brown color of decay, the color of dream. The wind swirled, blanketing the city in crystallized mist, coating the shattered shards of glass that used to be windows in thick frost, covering the deteriorating wooden frames in frigid dampness.

The epicenter of this evil wind was in the park. A small pool of blue-white light suddenly appeared there, and it stretched and swirled, growing steadily. Odd, frightening sounds emitted from the light, insectile clicking mixed with deep predatory howls of rage, occasionally interrupted by a noise like the squishy wetness of boots in mud, or blades in bodies. The light expanded, filling the overgrown park with an eerie, haunting glow. The light was suddenly punctuated by an unidentifiable limb, probing into the darkness. It pulled back momentarily before bursting through, and a scream tore itself from Sam's throat.

Sam's eyes shot open as she sat bolt upright in bed, her scream still echoing off the pale-yellow walls. Sweat pooled along her hairline and the thumping of her heart was hard enough to hurt. She pulled a trembling hand down her face and felt slickness. Sam looked down and saw blood, then felt the blood running from her nose. Her legs shook as she stood to go to the bathroom. The light flicked to life, blinding her for a moment. Once Sam's eyes focused, she looked at herself in the mirror: the front of her shirt was covered in blood; her face was pale and wan.

Sam rushed to turn on the shower. Still wearing her bloody shirt, she stepped in and let the hot water rain on her face. The shower water mixed with her blood as it trickled down her body, tainting the pool by her feet. Sam watched as a small pink whirlpool formed and spun down the drain. The panic she felt upon waking faded as the blood continued to flow. Her hands still shook but the warmth was starting to seep in.

A quiet knock at the door was quickly accompanied by her mother's voice. "Sam?" Sam did not answer, did not hear. It felt like everything she ever experienced, every memory, real or dream, was swirling in her head all at once. Everything, and nothing. It was a stupor that came from trying to compress a lifetime into a millisecond.

The door opened slightly, and her mother spoke through the crack. "Sam? Are you ok? It's 3 o'clock in the morning." Her mother stopped for a second, then gasped. "Sam! There's blood everywhere!" Her mother pulled open the curtain. Sam turned her head to stare dully at her mother's face. She knew it was her mother, but her brain would not process more than that. Sam's vision went dark.

Sam flitted in and out of consciousness. In her lucid moments, Sam saw things like her mother replacing a hot compress, pulling the blanket higher on Sam's chest, or pacing in Sam's room. It was still early morning, judging by the tepid light just starting to stream through the window, when her mother's voice roused her from a troubled sleep.

"...three hours ago." Silence. "Resting in bed now. I had to practically drag her there." Silence again, and Sam realized her mother was talking on the phone. "Yes, doctor. Thank you." A moment later, she entered the room and saw Sam looking at her. Sam watched her mother break down and begin to sob. "I've never been more scared in my life," she said, struggling between each word. Before she knew it, Sam was engulfed in a hug. "My little girl collapsing in a bloody bathtub, hitting her head on the way down. What happened, Sam? What happened?"

"I woke up from a nightmare," Sam said slowly, trying to remember. "It was bad, but I can't remember it."

Sam's mother squeezed her hand. "How did you end up bloody and in the shower?" she asked, sniffling. She replaced the damp cloth on Sam's forehead before snatching a tissue from a box and blowing her nose.

As hard as she tried to remember, Sam could not pull all the details to mind. "I think I had the blood on me when I woke up."

Nodding, Sam's mother spoke softly. "I've called Dr. Ferri and he's going to be here within an hour. We're lucky that he was at home and willing to make a house call. He's retiring in a few weeks, you know. I thought about taking you to the hospital but decided it might be better to get you into bed and talk to the doctor first." Sam's mother seemed unsure of whether she had made the right decision. "The way you hit your head, and all that blood. You scared me, Samantha," she finished, squeezing her hand once again.

Dr. Ferri arrived and after an examination, diagnosed Sam as having fainted due to blood loss. "I can see no laceration around your nose, Samantha," the elderly doctor said in his gravelly voice, "but it certainly seems like the sudden blood loss resulted in a drop in pressure. Have you been eating regular meals?" Sam shook her head in response. "Well, there you have it. Blood loss and already lowered blood sugar levels due to lack of food. It is fortunate you didn't end up with a concussion from hitting your head on the tub. Just stay in bed for the morning, at the very least, and you should be feeling better soon. And eat something, Sam. You always were skin and bones, but you need to take care of yourself." He leaned toward her slightly and added in a conspiratorial whisper, "At least do it for your mother. I've known her for over fifty years and I've never seen her like this." He patted her hand in a grandfatherly way as he straightened.

After escorting Dr. Ferri from the house, Sam's mother returned with a tray of food: crackers, cheese, a hard-boiled egg, and a steaming mug of tea. With her mother sitting at her bedside, Sam had no choice but to eat every last crumb of the food, even though her stomach roiled in complaint. The supervised meals continued for weeks, but despite the concerted efforts of her mother to make sure she ate regular meals, Sam still was having difficulty sleeping through the night, or functioning on a day-to-day basis.

A few months after Dr. Ferri visited their house, Sam was surprised by an unexpected topic of conversation from her mother.

"I know I never talk about him, Sam," her mother said one morning in early October, "but I had a terrible time when your father died." Sam could only stare. Her father had died when she was very young, not even old enough to be in grade school, and she only had the faintest memories of him. "I can't say I had as difficult a time as you're having now; that would be unfair to both of us, because only you and I know what we have felt in our own situations. I can tell you, though, that after you went to bed, I cried every single night those first six months."

Sam simply sat and watched her mother. Even as disconnected from life as she had been feeling since Jack died, she recognized how difficult this was for her mother to talk about, despite the number of years that had passed.

"We argued from time to time," her mother continued quietly, "but what couple doesn't? One night, we were arguing about something stupid, I don't even remember what, and he stormed out of the house and drove off." Her mother paused, visibly steeling herself. "Well, he ended up going to this old bar that used to be in town, a hole in the wall he used to go to before we met. After we had you, he rarely drank, but that night..." Sam's mother trailed off, and Sam wondered if it was the memory or the telling that was more difficult. Most likely the combined weight, Sam decided.

When her mother finally resumed the story, her voice held a forced flatness. "Your father became very drunk, and no one at the bar knew him or cared about him, so he left on his own. The best guess the police had was that he forgot he had driven to the bar. He ended up walking out of town and wandering into the woods. They thought maybe he was trying to walk home, but his blood alcohol level was so..." Sam's mother cleared her throat, and Sam could hear the swallowing of deep emotional pain. "He died overnight, of exposure. He passed out in the woods and never woke up again. He died alone in the woods, a few miles from home, because of an argument so ridiculous I can't remember it, Sam."

Sam squeezed her mother's hand, hard. Her mother smiled at her. The tears were flowing easily now, for both of them. "I know this is going to sound ridiculous, Sam, but hear me out," she said in a voice so choked up it hardly sounded like her. "I carried that guilt for a long time, blaming myself for your father's death. Honestly, sometimes I still do. The ridiculous part is what actually helped me start to pick up the pieces again."

To Sam's great surprise, her mother laughed. "One night, I hired a babysitter for you and went to a séance, Sam. I was so desperate to feel different, to feel something other than guilt and sadness. I had seen some psychic on television and I figured I had nothing to lose. I didn't really believe it would help, but like I said, I was desperate."

Sam looked at her mother, eyebrows raised in surprise. She could not imagine her mother sitting at a table trying to talk to dead people. It was absurd, and Sam was about to say so, but thought better of it. Sam's mother laughed at her expression but continued. "The woman who led the séance seemed like the exact opposite of what you'd expect. There were a few things I suppose you might call stereotypical – incense, candles, things like that – but she was not doing a big performance or anything. I'm trying to remember her name. Mrs. Miller, I think it was. The incense helped her focus, she said." Her mother laughed again. It was like the sound of wind chimes in early spring, light and carefree.

Sam studied her mother's face as the story continued. There was so much to take in, from her father's fate to the fact her mother had reached out to a psychic for a séance! Each piece was a shock to the system. Combined, it was almost too much to bear. Sam felt like her head was spinning, but suddenly she was struck with a laser-like focus. "What was that last part? The last thing you said?"

Sam's mother blinked. "Hmm? Oh," she said. "I was saying Mrs. Miller contacted your father and I was able to ask him questions. He would knock on a table. Once for yes, and twice for no." Her mother sighed and brushed greying hair away from her forehead. A teardrop fell from one of the strands and splashed onto her leg, and her smile held sadness once again. "He could hear us, but we couldn't hear him, Mrs. Miller explained to me, but he was able to interact with the world of the living. I was able to talk with him, after a fashion, and I told him I missed him and asked if he was in a better place and..." she trailed off once again. "Look, Sam. The point of this is I went to Mrs. Miller's house as a wreck, and she helped relieve so much of the guilt and sadness I had felt. I know it's not traditional, but maybe something a little different might help you, too."

That night, Sam woke up from a nightmare of a black wind carrying the voices of the dead, and of shadows, and of the souls of shadows. When she looked at the clock, she realized she could not have slept for more than 15 minutes before the nightmare woke her. It took her several hours and a small handful of sleeping pills to calm her nerves to the point of something barely resembling relaxation, and eventually she drifted off again.

The dream returned almost immediately, except this time she could understand some of the voices in the black wind, speaking of their lives and their deaths, their agonies and regrets. When she woke, heart racing, she hadn't even made it 10 minutes this time, despite the medication. Sam abandoned the idea of sleep, and once her hands stopped shaking, she pulled open the drawer of her nightstand and removed a notebook and a black pen.

When she was younger, she had kept dream journals. This one was half-filled with detailed notes on the sleepy wanderings of her mind, and occasionally small doodles or sketches. She flipped through the pages, reading entries at random. When she eventually reached a blank page, she uncapped the pen, intending to write about the black wind and the shadows, but she could not do it. The pen nib touched the page, but she could not force her hand to write words, could not put the thoughts in any kind of order that made sense. Instead, she drew thick, angry lines, sometimes wavy, sometimes sharp and jagged. The lines swirled and swam across the page, dark and menacing. She pushed the pen so fiercely pages tore, and as they did, the wind in her memory grew stronger.

Two weeks later, Sam clutched a shirt that had belonged to Jack and watched absentmindedly out of the passenger window as her mother drove down unfamiliar rural roads. The paved roads were rough with potholes, and narrow. Dust blew upward forming thick clouds in their wake. Autumn was in full bloom, and in a moment of clarity, she found herself thinking the reds and yellows of fall foliage looked like explosions suspended in time, a frozen moment between breaths. The leaves blurred as her mother drove. Sam's eyes burned with the exhaustion that only prolonged sleep deprivation could bring.

"How did you even find this woman way out here?" Sam asked her mother half an hour later.

Sam's mother did not answer right away. Eventually, brow furrowed, she replied, "I think there was a piece about her on the evening news, but I'm actually not sure anymore." Silence filled the car, save for Sam's mother softly repeating, "I'm actually not sure."

When they finally reached Mrs. Miller's house, dusk had already settled in the cool October air. A thick sliver of moon bathed the small white ranch in a soft glow. There was a bare-branched apple tree on one side of the driveway, and an elderly weeping willow on the other. The house looked well-kept, the lawn trimmed and raked. A small wisp of smoke rose from a stone chimney that jutted out of the shingled rooftop. A wind chime dangled above a light maroon door, illuminated by a small porch light. From the driveway, Sam could not tell what the design on the wind chime was, but it jingled quietly as a soft breeze rose, carrying chill and dampness on its fringes.

The woman who answered the door was stocky, with wide shoulders and large hands. An iron-grey bun rested atop a kindly face, with deep wrinkles that reminded Sam of canyons carved by natural erosion from wind and rain. A small brown mole rose from her left cheek. When she smiled at them, Sam saw small dimples form. "You must be Samantha," the woman said in a deep, warm voice. "I'm Irene Miller. Your mother told me about your situation. I'm very sorry for your loss."

Sam gave a small nod of acknowledgement but did not speak. She did not trust herself to speak without a fresh set of tears forming. There was a part of her that hated herself for the constant crying, and although she would never admit it to anyone, sometimes her tears were out of anger toward herself. Mrs. Miller ushered them both into her house, asking them to leave their shoes by the door. "It helps you relax, get more comfortable," she explained. The house had polished hardwood floors and smelled like wood smoke and cinnamon. As Sam removed her shoes, she took the opportunity to take in the decorations that filled Irene Miller's home. Most of the wall hangings were rustic – drawings of Teddy bears framed in solid oak, a painting of a deer drinking from a woodland stream – but one particular bauble caught her eye. It was ceramic, light grey and hanging from a thick black ribbon. Carved into the ceramic face was a quote, attributed to Albert Einstein: "The most beautiful thing we can experience is the mysterious."

"I love that quote," Irene said, noticing Sam. "Whenever anybody thinks about Einstein, it's always the science stuff that comes to mind first, but here he is, talking about beauty and the unknown. I guess that could still be science, but I like to think it's open to interpretation." She smiled broadly, and Sam couldn't help but return a small smile of her own. "Can I get either of you anything before we get to talking? Water? Coffee? Tea? I like to start off with some casual conversation, a little bit of a getting to know you kind of thing, before we sit at the table."

As Irene guided them toward the living room and urged them to sit wherever they liked, Sam assented to a glass of water, while her mother said a mug of tea would be delightful. "Something caffeine free, please" she added as Irene bustled off toward the kitchen. A few minutes later, Irene returned with a polished silver tray, bearing a small porcelain teapot with a matching porcelain cup, a glass of water, and a saucer dish of small, hard cookies.

Once she was certain Sam and her mother were comfortable and didn't need anything else, Irene settled herself into a recliner. "Now, let's start with a quick introduction," she said. She spoke with a steady tempo, with small but noticeable inflections, and Sam got the impression it would take a great deal to upset Irene Miller's world. "My name is Irene, named after my grandmother. I worked at a small insurance company for most of my career, first taking claims and later as an actuary. I retired about 3 years ago. I know it doesn't sound all that exciting, but I enjoyed it."

Irene wore an expression of wistfulness as she continued. "I first noticed there was something a little different about me when I was about 10 or 11 years old. We had moved into a new house – I later found out my parents were able to afford it because it was selling for below market value due to reports it was haunted. Well, to make a long story short, it's true there was a spirit there, and I was able to communicate with it and convince it to leave the house. It was a friendly spirit, but talking to it, I could tell it was unsettled, so I helped it along. Afterward, I told my parents all about it. I didn't really understand at the time that most people can't do that sort of thing. Even as I started in insurance, I kept building up the spirit muscle, as I like to call it, and the rest is history."

Sam's mother went next, talking about her life and her husband and her previous séance experience nearly 20 years prior with Irene. After she finished, Sam took a deep breath. She was still holding on to Jack's shirt, the white logo of the college from which they graduated standing out on the otherwise plain grey. She licked her lips and began to talk about Jack, from their meeting in high school to the day he died. She shared that it would be their one-year wedding anniversary in a few days. It was her first time really expressing everything herself, and it was as if a floodgate opened and stories spilled out.

The order was jumbled as her stream of consciousness took control of her voice. She talked about everything as if she could not stop herself. When it reached the point where she told what Webb had shared with her at Jack's funeral, that he had most likely not been alone in the car, she suddenly felt a part of her brain revolt from the detail-sharing session. Her teeth snapped shut abruptly, making an audible click. Her mother was staring at her, wide-eyed, though Irene seemed placid and unruffled. Nevertheless, Sam could feel a quick flash of warmth in her cheeks as embarrassment reared its ruddy head. It occurred to her that she had not spoken that much in months, probably since before the collision.

"Thank you, Samantha," Irene said when it became clear Sam would not be continuing. "I know how difficult that must have been for you, so thank you for trusting me." Irene let the silence hang for a few moments longer, then smiled, small but warm. "If everyone's ready, let's move to the other room." She ushered Sam and her mother down the hall and into a room that would probably be considered an office. The room was not particularly big, with a single curtained window. The walls were sparse in their decorations. Most notable were a few black and white photographs of nature scenes in bronze frames.

In the middle of the room stood a small, round wooden table. The table's dark stain was offset by a cluster of tall, thin white candles set in the center. Four matching wooden chairs were spaced evenly around the table, mimicking the table's coloring. Sam was surprised; she was still skeptical of the idea of a séance and had expected the room to look different, somehow. More cliché, she supposed was the best way to put it, perhaps with a large, polished crystal ball, and a purple velvet tablecloth, and some kind of elaborate headwear for the host. Instead, it was a simple room without pretense. She wasn't sure if that set her at ease or made her more anxious.

As Sam and her mother sat at the table, Irene lit the candles, along with a stick of incense Sam had not noticed before. A tendril of grey-green smoke rose from it, bringing with it an effusion of jasmine. Irene flicked the light switch off, casting the room into darkness, save for the flickering candlelight. As she took her place at the table, Irene smiled at Sam again. "Let's all close our eyes for a minute and breathe slowly," she said placidly. "Deep, calming breaths. If we can steady ourselves, it makes reaching across the Void more successful."

Sam could hear the capital with the way Irene spoke. To her, it was a proper noun, an actual, tangible place called the Void. Closing her eyes, she did as she was told and tried to calm her nerves, to slow the beating of her heart to a more relaxed tempo. Slow breaths, slow heartbeat. Sam jumped as something suddenly touched her hand, but when she opened her eyes, she saw her mother's hand resting atop hers. Sam's eyes followed the arm up to her mother's face, who gave her a reassuring smile. Her mother squeezed her hand, and Sam squeezed a silent response.

Once Irene was satisfied with the room's stillness, she spoke quietly once again. "Now, we will form a circle." Sam felt Irene's hand clutch her own as soon as the words had left her mouth. "Remember to breathe slowly and deeply as we attempt to cross the Void." Irene's voice was soothing, but her words caused spikes of anxiety in Sam, though she did her best to not let it show. "We will now reach across and attempt to touch the souls of the lost."

Irene began to chant an incantation. Sam's breathing intensified. Without being instructed to do so, Sam and her mother joined the chant, Sam's voice wavering. "We are calling across the Void to Jackson Nightshade. Be guided by the light we offer and join us in this world." After a minute, they had repeated the chant so many times it felt like catechism. Instead of the anxiety she had been feeling, Sam was beginning to be more annoyed than anything. She was about to pull her hands away from the circle when there was a soft rumbling sound from somewhere inside the room. The air took on a sudden chill, cool enough for goosebumps to pop up on Sam's flesh. She shivered as she continued the chant. "Be guided by the light..."

They were still holding hands in a circle when a series of arrhythmic, insistent knocks on the table made them jump. Sam could feel some of the tightness fade from Irene's grip, as if she were relieved at the change in events. "Spirit, are you amongst us?" Irene asked formally. "If you are with us and able to manipulate the world of the living, knock once on the table for yes and twice on the table for no." There was a pause that stretched for what felt like forever, and then a single firm knock rang out. It made Sam's insides squirm. The jasmine scent from the incense was now mixed with something noticeably different. The best way Sam could describe it was that the air tasted stale.

"Spirit, I am asking you to identify yourself," Irene said firmly. "Are you Jackson Nightshade?" There was a long silence. A single knock. Sam released a breath she did not know she had been holding. Tears formed at the corners of her eyes.

"Jack, is that really you?" Sam asked in a quavering voice. After another delay, there was a single knock, and the tears fell freely to the tabletop. "Oh, Jack," she moaned, "I miss you so much." Sam scrubbed the tears from her face and gave a quick little giggle as emotion overcame her. Sam cleared her throat between her sobs.

Now that the opportunity to communicate with Jack was in front of her, Sam's mind seemed to go blank. She had so much she wanted to say and ask, and she wanted to know the truth, but once she was able to speak again she started with, "Are you happy where you are now?" Another knock on the table came as a response. "I'm glad to hear that, Jack." There was a pause, and Sam added, "I wish you were still here with me."

Sam took a deep, steadying breath, and then finally asked one of the big questions she had: "Jack, do you remember what happened on April 11th?" A single knock. "Were you alone when you were driving home the day of the accident?" Heart pounding in her chest, Sam felt like she waited an eternity for the answer, though she knew it was only a few seconds before there was a single knock on the table, indicating yes, Jack had been alone. She could feel the weight of not knowing, the weight of anxiety, lift off her shoulders.

Sam opened her mouth to ask another question, but Irene's grip tightened on her hand abruptly and the older woman gasped. The sharp intake of breath made Sam's eyes pop open. The older woman had her head tipped back, facing the ceiling. Sam felt the bones in her hand shift uncomfortably. She glanced at her mother, but her eyes were still closed and her face was expressionless. The grip tightened further, and a groan of pain escaped Sam's lips. Irene's hand pulled away without warning but the grip did not slacken, forcing the bones in Sam's hand to rub against each other. A moment later, Irene's head thumped heavily onto the table with a sickening crack.

As a feeling of queasiness rolled over Sam, she looked over at her mother. The shock on her mother's face must have been a mirror of her own. Sam opened her mouth to speak, but a groan from Irene cut off the words before they formed. She turned to look at the older woman, who was still face down on the table. "What..." Sam started to ask but did not finish her question; she didn't even know what to say. Irene's head suddenly jerked violently upward, spattering the table with blood from a broken nose. Her eyes were hidden, though by eyelid or shadows, Sam could not distinguish. The older woman was sitting almost unnaturally straight, held erect like a marionette with an invisible puppet master. She groaned again, but the sound was scratchy and pained.

Sam wanted to cry out, to run out of the room, to do something, but everything was happening so quickly. Sam screamed as Irene began banging her head on the table, the thumping noise becoming wetter with each rapid impact. Even in the darkness, Sam could see blood puddling on the table. Irene's head shot up again, battered and dripping blood from her forehead, nose, and mouth. Her nose was swelling. From the corner of her eye, Sam saw what looked like a shattered tooth sitting in the pool of blood on the table. Sam's mouth hung open, dry with shock and terror.

Falling as if the puppet master released the strings, Irene's head smacked into the table one final time and lay still. Sam felt a moment of relief when she noticed the older woman's breathing, as ragged as it was, but the relief truly was momentary. A voice that sounded like dirt and ash scratched in her ears, speaking in a harsh language she could not understand. Sam screamed as she felt something tearing into her shoulders, rough lacerations that became deeper as she was violently shaken. The dirt voice poured its filth into her mind even as she felt the warm blood run down her collarbone and over her breasts. The pressure on her shoulders vanished, and then what felt like large claws or talons raked across her back. She screamed again as agony wracked her entire body. It felt as if those talons were inside of her abdomen, trying to pull them out and claw her to shreds. The light from the room vanished and Sam felt the sensation of being pulled in the blackness.

Chapter 3

Diana Westwood sat at the table, frozen in horror at the events of the last minute. She looked at her hand, the hand that had been holding Sam's until it had been jerked away. "Sam?" she called in a shaky voice. There was a moan of a response, but it came from Irene, the woman who had been leading the séance. Diana rounded on her angrily as Irene slowly lifted her head up from the table. "What happened?! Where is my daughter!?" She surprised herself with her shriek.

Irene turned her face toward Diana, sobbing silently, and in an instant, she regretted yelling at the woman. It had not registered in Diana's mind how badly Irene had been injured. The sight of her blood-covered face, broken nose, and what looked like a missing tooth put Diana in a different mindset. Perhaps it was her mothering instincts kicking in, but she needed to be calm, to help someone who was injured.

She left the room and looked for Sam, intending to grab paper towels or something for Irene. She found no trace of her daughter anywhere in the house except for the half-empty glass of water in the living room from which Sam had been drinking. If she let her emotions take control, she would be in hysterics, and that would not help anything. A deep breath. One step at a time.

While Diana was in the kitchen, she grabbed the phone and called the police. She did her best to not become hysterical, to remain calm while describing the situation to the operator. As she told the story of what happened that night, of her daughter disappearing during a séance, it was obvious the operator did not believe her. As she tried to convince the operator of the truth, she rummaged through the kitchen drawers until she found a few towels and grabbed a bag of vegetables from the freezer. Finally, the operator said they would send out an officer and Diana hung up the phone. With towels and the frozen vegetables in hand, she returned to Irene, who was still crying silently at the bloody table.

Once Irene was cleaned up, Diana asked again about where Sam was, about what had happened. Irene's answer made her tremble with rage. And terror. "I don't know," the older woman said slowly, taking a deep breath. "I have never had an actual spirit come through before, and I think that's what happened." Irene sounded like a defeated woman, someone who knew that not only had she lost, but that she would never recover.

"What? What do you mean by actual spirit?" Diana asked angrily. A sudden lump formed in her stomach, knowing the answer before it came.

Irene groaned as she moved her hand under the table. When it came back into view, she was holding a small piece of rounded wood. "I do the knocking with my knee, using this," Irene confessed in a quiet voice. Even through the injuries and pain, Diana could hear the shame, but that did not blunt her angry response.

"You-you con artist!" Diana spat. "You manipulated us! And how many others? I came here to talk to my dead husband years ago and you tricked me. I brought my daughter here and you tricked her! You should be in prison!"

Irene slumped under the torrent of Diana's rage, but she did muster a response. "Is it really so bad?" Irene asked softly. "When you were here before, I helped you find peace with your life, helped you move on. I was doing the same for your daughter. No, your husband wasn't knocking on the table, but you thought he was, and that made you feel better." Even though she defended herself, Irene's voice was hollow. "When a person is so desperate as to go to a séance to feel better, then they should leave feeling better."

From a certain perspective, Diana could see Irene's point, but it did nothing to quell her anger, or her concern for her daughter. "So where is Sam?" she asked coldly. "SAM!"

Irene put the wooden knocker down on the table and sat silently, for a moment that felt like hours. "I don't know," she admitted in a hoarse whisper. Her voice cracked. "Like I said, I've never had a real spirit appear, and that's my best guess as to what happened." She coughed, bloody spittle foaming at the corner of her mouth. "If that is what happened, then the spirit that came through was definitely not a friendly one." She touched her own face, which was swollen and purple, and winced. "I don't remember most of it, just that it went dark and I heard a terrible voice in my head, but I couldn't understand it. It screamed and laughed and then..." she trailed off. "I opened my eyes and saw my blood all over the table." Those last words were bit off, clipped, and carried a mix of frustration, fear, and shame.

Diana told Irene what she had seen happen, how Irene's head repeatedly pounded onto the table, how her daughter started screaming, but the emotion of the situation finally overwhelmed Diana's forced stoicism and she collapsed onto the floor, weeping openly. Diana heard her own voice echo off the walls of the tiny room as she screamed wordlessly, bellowing out her pain.

When the police officer arrived and found two women crying on the floor, one covered in blood, he immediately radioed for assistance. Neither he nor any of the officers who turned up over the next few hours could do anything to comfort them, or get any explanation about what happened that made any sense at all.

<u>Chapter 4</u>

Something sharp scraped against the palm of Samantha's right hand, bringing her to consciousness. She groaned in agony. It felt like she had gone over a waterfall in a garbage bag. It took a concerted effort to push past the pain and open her eyes. When she did, she felt a jolt as she stared up at a brown-grey sky, with shoddy brick walls on either side of her. A thick grey cloud drifted overhead, bringing with it an echo of thunder. Until that moment, Sam did not realize she was flat on her back. As she sat up, she felt like her shoulders and back were on fire. The movement was enough to send a flare of pain as scabs stretched and ripped open. The sharp something scraped her right hand again. She turned her head slowly to look at what was in her hand, testing her body's aches, careful to not further injure herself. In her hand, she held what looked like the claw of some large predatory cat, though somehow more vicious. It was at least two inches long, and the razor-like tip was stained with blood, a red so deep it was nearly black.

Sam groaned again as she rose shakily to her feet. Her knees buckled and she tried to regain her balance, but ended up slamming hard into the stone wall before hitting the ground. The claw dug into her palm as she landed, making her yelp in pain. Sam was on the verge of throwing the thing when she suddenly realized she was in an alley. Her heart skipped a beat. She wracked her brain, trying to figure out where she was and how she got there. Sam's memories of anything before waking up in the alley were shrouded in fog as impenetrable as the cloud overhead that threatened a downpour.

She took a deep breath and tried to take stock of her situation before attempting to stand again. She was in an alley, which meant she was in a town or a city and not in a more rural area, and it looked like a storm was coming. Sam still had the claw in hand, and she was in a great deal of pain. Not a lot to go on. Slipping the claw into her pocket, Sam looked around for any other clues as to where she was or why she was there, but found nothing. It was just an alley, dim with shadows.

Sam gritted her teeth and forced herself upright, though she did lean against the wall for extra support. Once she was standing, she was able to shamble toward the end of the alley, her balance becoming stronger as she made her way toward the opening. Bits of broken glass and rusted metal littered the pavement and she stumbled over some of the larger pieces but managed to stay on her feet.

When she reached the end of the alleyway, she gasped in shock. A city stretched in front of her, as far as she could see. The buildings were a haphazard mix of steel and wood, the greys and browns blending with the color of the sky so much so that it was nearly impossible to tell where one ended and the other began. Mirrored windows reflected furtive shadows high on gleaming silver skyscrapers. Two buildings down the street stretched toward the clouds, and in between was a wide wooden building Sam guessed was an apartment. It was only a few moments of looking at the buildings, craning her neck to try to find the top of the skyscrapers, before someone bumped into her, causing her to stumble a few steps back into the alley.

Sam lowered her gaze to face whoever had bumped her, to apologize for being in their way, but words failed her as she noticed the people on the street for the first time. There was an unimaginable mixture of ages and ethnicities and styles, ranging from kids with backpacks and jeans to elderly women dressed like 1920's flappers and everything in between. Sam gawked, forgetting manners as she tried to take in everything at once and knowing she caught only the slightest sliver of detail. The chaos of the street was like having the pieces from a thousand jigsaw puzzles mixed together.

Sam noticed something else odd about the people in the street: regardless of their clothing or skin color, they all appeared washed out, like the buildings behind them. They were sallow and faded, like black and white photo negatives. Sam's vision blurred as her head pulsed in pain and she fell to her knees. The sting in her head only lasted a few seconds, but she had to blink rapidly to clear the black spots from her sight. Her stomach heaved and a flash of cold sweat rolled down her forehead, but she did not vomit.

Once her vision cleared and the queasiness subsided, she pushed herself back to her feet. A middle-aged man and an elderly woman across the street were pointing at her. Standing between the man and woman was a third man, tall and straight-backed, unmistakably a police officer. Sam felt a moment of panic as the officer's eyes suddenly turned to meet her own. Had she done something wrong? She had no memory of anything before waking up in the alley. The officer began striding toward her purposefully with an intensity in his eyes that locked her knees.

She wanted to turn away, to run back down the alley and hide, but her legs buckled underneath her again, depositing her unceremoniously on the litter-strewn pavement. She glanced up and saw the cop was already halfway across the street. Sam knew she had no chance to escape. Instead, she simply sat there and waited for him to reach her.

The police officer looked like he was in his late 30s, with close-cropped blond hair and a square jaw and face so hard it looked like it could have broken stone. He looked down at her grimly, though Sam thought she saw a hint of uncertainty in his faded grey eyes. Finally, he spoke. His voice had a thick accent and sounded like chipped gravel. "Who are you and what are you doing here?"

Sam looked up at the officer, who stood straight-backed and hard-eyed. He had a badge, visible on his jacket, which said 4CPD and the name Gunnarsson. Unsure of what else to do, she answered truthfully, "I don't know."

"Are you ill? What is wrong with you?"

Sam stared at him, confused. "Ill? I don't think so," she said, perplexed at his question.

"Your shirt is dirty. Are you injured?" Without waiting for a response, he added, "You're coming with me," and yanked Sam roughly to her feet. His grip could have been made of steel. Sam knew there was no chance she could escape from it even if she didn't feel weak as a newborn kitten. She suddenly processed what Gunnarsson had said: her shirt was dirty? She looked down and saw it was covered in blood splatters, and wondered how she hadn't noticed.

Gunnarsson escorted her out of the alleyway and down the sidewalk. Everyone else on the sidewalk moved out of their way as they approached, even if it meant bumping into someone else. Every one of the people they strode past gawked at her, with expressions ranging from curiosity to horror. *What is going on?* she thought as they sloshed through a puddle. Sam glanced down and caught a quick glimpse of her reflection. Compared to Officer Gunnarsson, she looked vibrant, albeit covered in blood, whereas he had the same washed-out appearance as everyone else.

As they walked, Gunnarsson's hand still clutching her wrist, they occasionally passed smaller side streets. One such street was lined with what looked like vendor stalls. Thin wisps of smoke rose from a handful of them, which she assumed meant they were selling food. The street itself was absolutely packed with people; there was no chance a car could make it through that crowd. With a start, she realized she had not actually seen any cars since she woke up.

Sam noticed other odd things, as well. Sometimes, she would see a person wearing a mask, usually designed to look like an animal. She turned her head toward the statuesque officer to ask about it, but seeing his grim expression, she thought better of it and kept her silence.

A few minutes later, Gunnarsson suddenly pulled her roughly to the left, toward a large brick building. An embossed sign reading 4CPD hung over the double front doors. As Gunnarsson dragged her toward the wide stone steps, the doors burst open and a disheveled man stormed out, yelling at the top of his lungs. "I hate the goddamn cops in this goddamn city! They arrest me every other week for no reason! Damn fools! Harassment! That's all this is! Harassment!" As the loud man pounded down the stairs, he caught sight of Gunnarsson and stopped dead in his tracks. His rage quickly changed into fear, as his dull red cheeks drained to a ghostly white. "You..." he said quietly, his voice shaking. "You are the worst of them!" the man shrieked, and Sam realized his face was not white with fear, but with pure hatred. His eyes flashed over to Sam, then bulged, and his teeth clicked shut in an instant. The man wordlessly ran down the last few remaining steps and disappeared into the chaos of the city.

Sam's unease grew as Gunnarsson pulled open the door and guided her inside. The interior of the police station was mostly made of wood, from the floors to the desks to the paneling on the walls. Gunnarsson pointed at a long bench against the far wall, where a few blank-faced men sat, looking downtrodden. "Sit and wait," he grunted at her. Sam stumbled toward the bench. Was she being arrested? On what charge? What kind of place was this? And most importantly, how did she get here?

Despite the litany of questions roiling in her brain, Sam tried to take in as much detail as possible. There were three men on the bench, two sitting at one end, another by himself as far away from the pair as possible. The lone man had unruly black hair and wore a long coat with a button up vest underneath. The two men on the right were wearing matching dark grey sweaters, matching slacks, and scuffed black shoes. There were about twenty desks to her left in the main room, and most of those had an officer sitting at them, sometimes alone, sometimes interviewing people she assumed were suspects or witnesses. Most of the people in the main room did not notice her, but the few who did stared at her as if her hair was on fire. Sam tried to ignore them, to not let her trepidation show, but that was basically impossible. Glancing at the three men on the waiting bench again, she decided to sit closer to the trench coat man who was by himself rather than the matching pair staring at their own feet. Sam caught the trench coat man looking at her out of the corner of his eye as she sat.

After a minute, the trench coat man spoke quietly, barely moving his mouth. "I bet you have a hell of a story to tell," he whispered in a thick voice like fresh honey. His voice was not deep nor high, but perfectly average, just like his face. "I never imagined I'd actually meet a Bloodwalker. You don't seem to be badly injured, even with your shirt covered in blood, so that makes me think it's not all your blood. There have always been rumors, legends, but to have one sit next to you? That makes getting dragged to the 4CPD worthwhile." Still looking straight ahead, he grinned broadly for a moment. In an even softer whisper, he asked, "Did you come from The Jar?"

Sam's face scrunched up in confusion. Bloodwalker? Jar? 4CPD? She had no idea what this strange man was talking about, and frankly was not sure she wanted to know. There was no doubt he was talking to her, though; the very determined way he stared forward and tried to not be seen talking made that part obvious, at least. "I don't know what you mean," Sam answered quietly, brushing her hair away from her face to try to hide her mouth with her hand as she spoke.

"You don't have to play coy with me," the man said softly. "Name's Gibson. I'm a private investigator. Trust me; I'm not going to tell these clowns anything." Gibson gestured toward the room slightly.

Sam sighed. "I don't know what's going on," she murmured, this time looking at her feet to obscure her moving lips. "I woke up in an alley. The big cop grabbed me, and now I'm here." She scratched a fingernail at the dried blood on her shirt, but there was so much splatter that it was completely pointless to even try to make herself look more presentable.

Gibson shot her a look, his eyes wide with surprise. Just as quickly, he returned to his study of the room. "You just got here?" Sam thought the concern in his voice was genuine, and it made her stomach clench. After a minute's pause, Gibson spoke again. "You need to get out of this place. Now. The last thing you need is to get locked up. I'm going to drop my coat on my seat and make a distraction. Take my coat and leave. Don't run. Walk out like you have every right to. Put the coat on when you get outside, and try to hide your face. My card is in the inside pocket. Meet me at the address." He made as if to rise, stopped himself, and added, "And bring me my coat."

Sam tried to look over at Gibson without being noticed, but she could only see his hand resting on top of his leg, which was bouncing nervously. "Why should I trust you? What's going on?" she asked as quietly as she could. Her throat was scratchy from all the whispering.

Gibson cast a quick, furtive glance at her. "Listen, Bloodwalker. I'll try to explain it later. At my office. And bring my damn coat!" With that, he shrugged out of the long grey coat and strode purposefully up to the police officer at the front desk. Sam noticed Gunnarsson was still there, presumably checking her in to the desk officer. "I've been sitting here for four hours already!" Gibson bellowed at the desk officer. "You have no reason for me to be here, I didn't do anything wrong, and neither did any of these poor people! This is harassment!" he yelled, gesturing to the larger room. Sam remembered the man leaving the station as she arrived, and wondered if Gibson had overheard the shouts from outside.

Gunnarsson took a heavy step toward Gibson, and Sam had to give this supposed private investigator credit for his bravery, as he did not back down from the much larger man. "Sit and wait your turn," Gunnarsson growled in a thick accent, taking another menacing step forward.

Gibson was much quicker than the hulking blond officer and darted toward the larger room, still facing Gunnarsson. "I am not going to sit any longer! These people deserve to be released, and so do I!" Gibson grabbed

43

a ceramic coffee mug from an unoccupied desk and slammed it onto the floor, shattering it into a thousand pieces. Gibson's ploy was working; most of the civilians were turning angry glares toward those in uniform, some of them echoing his words.

As the police officers and those being booked for crimes squared off, Sam saw her opportunity. Slowly, she reached over and grabbed Gibson's coat, but not a single person in the room was looking in her direction. As casually as she could, she folded the coat in half, trying to make it look more like a bundle than a jacket, and quietly, calmly, got to her feet and walked out of the door.

When she was halfway down the wide steps of the precinct, she unfolded the coat and quickly put it on. She popped the collar up as far as it would go and held the front closed with her left hand. Sam turned left, away from the alley where she woke up. Head down, her eyes danced from side to side, looking for a secluded place to stop and figure out what to do next. The sidewalks were just as crowded as they had been before she entered the 4CPD building, but without Gunnarsson's imposing visage to clear the path and draw attention, Sam found the cluster of people almost claustrophobic.

After a few minutes of slow progress down the sidewalk, Sam was finally able to dart down a shadowed alley. It was strikingly similar to the one she had woken up in, though this one had a fire escape ladder halfway down, dangling a few feet out of reach. Sam huddled against the wall of the alleyway, trying to fade into the shadows as much as possible as she rifled through the coat, looking for Gibson's card. In the left inside breast pocket, she felt a sharp paper edge. Embossed on the thick business card in a curling green font were the words, "L. W. Gibson, Investigatory Inquiries and Purveyor of Solutions." Underneath and in smaller, less ornate print, was an address: 1092 North Kainer Heights, Suite 920.

Sam really had no reason to trust Gibson, but she had no reason not to, either, especially since he had helped her escape the precinct. Alone and unsure of what else to do, Sam piled a few waterlogged wooden crates against the wall to use as steps. She climbed up and pulled down the escape ladder, which squealed loudly, no matter how slowly she slid it. She climbed a few flights of the fire escape, idly trying to discern what the original color was supposed to be through the rust. She had learned she was far too easy to pick out in a crowd, the way everyone else here had that odd, faded look to them, so hiding until nightfall seemed like her best bet. Finding North Kainer Heights in the night with no map or even the roughest direction to start seemed daunting, but she shoved the thoughts away, focusing instead on finding a comfortable way to sit, out of sight from the street.

An incessant tugging on her sleeve woke Sam sometime later. She hadn't realized she had fallen asleep, but the exhaustion and confusion of the day had proven too much for her to remain awake and vigilant. The tugging continued, and Sam looked down to see a large rat pulling on Gibson's sleeve cuff with its teeth. Sam bit off a shriek and tried to shoo it away as quietly as she could without getting too close. It ignored her arm flapping and lifted its head to stare at her curiously when she whispered threats. The rat had mottled brown fur, wet from the rain, and its black bead eyes seemed to draw in the scraps of light that pierced the cloud cover. Night had fallen, deep and heavy, while she had slept. Since the rat wouldn't leave, she did her best to pretend it wasn't there. Sam got to her feet and it squeaked an angry protest as it fell from the cuff of the coat. Wide awake and anxious to get away from the creature, she gingerly descended the metal grating of the fire escape.

Moon shadows painted the alleyway, making the wooden crates she had stacked earlier look misshapen and bulbous. Sam's shoes crunched as they touched down on the paving. High above her, she could hear the rat scampering on the steps above. Cautiously, she pulled the coat tight around her and looked at the card in the pocket again: 1092 North Kainer Heights, Suite 920. It did not help to narrow down her search very much, but she could assume the building she was looking for was at least nine stories high, which helped. She found herself remembering the staggering height of some of the skyscrapers near where she awoke and was beginning to think blindly wandering around an unknown city at night was maybe not the best course of action. But she didn't have any better ideas, either.

Sam stepped out of the protection of the shadowed alleyway and onto the sidewalk. She looked around slowly, gathering her bearings, such as they were, and tried not to sigh with frustration and helplessness. The moon broke through the clouds, pooling soft, white light in scattered patches on the concrete, noticeable even with the dull orange streetlights casting their hazy glow. To the left, Sam saw a street sign, swaying from a single bolt in the cool night breeze. Not knowing how else to start, she headed in that direction.

"Bayle Street," Sam said aloud when she was close enough to read the sign, which still wobbled precariously in the night breeze. Sam trudged on until she saw the sign at the next intersection. "Dorian Place," Sam said quietly. Her memories were still shrouded, but Sam made the assumption she had never been so lost in her life, which felt entirely reasonable.

Hours passed as Sam walked down the sidewalk, reading street signs, looking for North Kainer Heights. Most of the signs were written in English, though she did walk past a smattering of Cyrillic and Spanish ones. The architecture was as foreign as the language in those areas, as if roads from Russia and Spain had simply been ripped out of their homelands and dumped haphazardly into this unfamiliar city. The streets were nearly completely deserted, though Sam did not know if that was typical or not. Whenever there was someone in the distance on the same side of the walkway as Sam, she would either cross the street or turn down one of the intersections. On one occasion, Sam saw three or four people walking in a group ahead of her. She had quickly turned down an alley that time and hid herself in the deepest shadows, far beyond the alley mouth. She did not leave her sanctuary of blackness until five minutes after the group of people had passed.

Calves cramping and brain fuzzy from being in a state of constant anxiety, Sam pushed on, trying to suppress the growing feeling of hopelessness that welled up inside her, gnawing away at her will to carry on. Stopping to lean on the railing of a stoop at the corner of McGovern Street, Sam tried to regain her focus, to dig deep and keep going, no matter how bleak the situation seemed. She tried not to cry.

Across the street was a small park, the kind in which people might exercise their city-dwelling dogs. An icy breeze rose suddenly and tore at her clothes, chilling her to the bone. The cold wind came from the direction of the park, and Sam felt a flash of deja vu. Had she been here before? There was a ghost of a memory, like the memory of a dream, that tickled at the corners of her mind. "Where are you, Jack?" she whispered aloud. As soon as she said it, she scrunched her face in consternation. Jack? She knew the name was important, but she could not remember why. She wanted to scream with frustration.

Forcing herself to turn away from the park and the black wind that came from it, Sam trudged forward, reading street signs in the near total darkness. Her legs ached. It felt like hours passed before Sam stopped again, though it could have been ten minutes for all she knew. Standing back from the orange streetlight glow, Sam pulled the card from the coat pocket again, studying the embossed words as if they contained a secret map. Desperate for any kind of clue or sense of progress, she fixed her eyes on the word "North" in North Kainer Heights and decided to head in that direction. *As soon as I know which way is north,* Sam thought with a grimace.

As the first glimmers of faint solar orange began to appear on the distant horizon, people appeared more frequently on the streets. At least the rising sun gave her a direction to head. Sam did her best to hurry without looking like she was hurrying, glancing up in time to read signs, afraid she would never find North Kainer Heights. Sam was also afraid she would be arrested again, though she did not understand why she was arrested in the first place. She knew she stood out, though. Sam's panic rose with the sun, her desperation causing beads of sweat to blossom on the back of her neck. She did not want to waste another day hiding in an alley, especially with no food. Her stomach growled as if to emphasize the point.

Sam pivoted slowly, looking at the tops of the buildings in the distance. She knew the card said Gibson's office was on the ninth floor, so it would be a large building. Sam dared not hope it would be visible from where she stood, but she had nothing but the rising sun and sheer luck to go on. There were two tall buildings in the direction from which she had come, the early morning sunlight glittering off windows on the towering structures. Another colossal building stood to her left, and ahead of her rose a fourth. Sam quickly eliminated the two behind her; she had just come from that way, after all, and had not seen a sign for North Kainer Heights. Should she continue forward, or head toward the building to the left?

Sam decided to go toward the building to the left. It looked taller, perhaps because it was on a hill, and the road was called Heights, after all. She crossed the street, altering the path she had been following for countless hours. Sam walked at a steady pace, careful to keep the cowl of the jacket up as her feet made soft crunching sounds. She always kept the towering structure in sight, though she kept her head down. Sam's neck was starting to ache from being bent at such an uncomfortable angle, but it was better to have a sore neck than to be arrested. It was a stark thought that in other circumstances would have been absurd enough to make her laugh.

After another ten minutes of walking, the surroundings took on a more suburban feel. Trees became commonplace, though the buildings still stretched, large and varied in their architecture. The sidewalk sloped upward, and Sam had a sinking feeling as she wondered if the tower in the distance merely appeared to be a skyscraper due to the changing landscape. She had to continue, though; Sam figured it was getting too bright for her to risk searching too much longer. If she had chosen the wrong direction, she would have to find a place to hide until nightfall and try to ignore the gnawing pit of hollowness that ate away at her middle. She had no idea when she last ate, but the pain in her stomach suggested it was days, not hours.

Another twenty minutes passed before Sam found herself staring in amazement at a rusty green street sign: North Kainer Heights. Her heart raced with anticipation, at the success that seemed to finally be within her grasp. She still had no idea who Gibson was and if he would even be able to help her, but hope buoyed her spirits. Sam turned onto North Kainer Heights and began scanning building addresses. She was in the 600 range, and Gibson's card said 1092. Sam had a strong suspicion that 1092 was the giant structure she had been focused on and only made cursory glances at the numbers as she moved toward the building.

When she got close enough to clearly see the building, Sam gasped audibly. The towering structure she had been searching for all night was the strangest looking building she had ever seen. At the bottom was an odd composite of large, heavy grey stones, the kind she imagined would be used to build a castle in a fairy tale. Three stories up, the building became brick, the reds-and-browns of fired clay chipped by the elements. The next floor appeared to be wooden, with long boards standing cheek by jowl with a few interspersed windows. Above that, steel rose for the remainder of the structure, another ten or more floors up, the modern office building aesthetic comforting in its familiarity yet stark and emotionless, not to mention dangerous looking with the layers below it. Sam shivered as she wondered how the whole thing did not simply collapse.

Sam shot a quick glance in either direction before heading toward the front door, a gigantic wooden thing with iron strapping that looked heavy enough to kill someone if it fell from its hinges. The door opened easier than Sam had imagined, though it let out a prolonged creak as it swung. She pulled it shut as she passed through into a surprisingly modern lobby area, with shaggy orange and green carpeting and a polished wooden front desk. Next to a small glass ashtray, a gaudy lamp shone on the desk, causing light to reflect off the walnut finish. Sam thought it looked like a hotel from the 1970s. The thought gave her pause: what did she know about hotels in the 1970s? Sam grunted and shook her head. Her memory was so spotty, and anything useful was apparently being hidden by details about old hotels.

Luckily, no one sat at the front desk, and she moved quickly to the far wall, looking for an elevator or a stairwell. Sam found both, tucked around the corner behind the front desk, and after a moment's hesitation decided on the stairs. If she passed anyone in the stairwell, it would be so brief that maybe she would go unnoticed. That, and she worried about being in an elevator in such a precarious-looking building.

Pulling open the door to the stairwell, Sam saw that the stairs were covered with rubber tread, which made the air feel stale and harsh. She felt like she was stepping into a hospital. Sam felt a sudden ache in her chest when she thought about being in a hospital, a pain so sharp she closed her eyes. For a moment, she could see a man's face in her mind's eye. He was young, handsome, with shaggy brown hair and warm, loving eyes. The image left her quickly, though the pain in her chest did not.

Sam considered herself lucky to not encounter a single soul while she climbed to the ninth floor. As she pushed the door open, she immediately noticed this floor was like that of a corporation, with eggshell-painted drywall and short, hard-bristled carpeting, which clashed with the hospital styling of the stairwell. A small sign hung on the wall, with an arrow pointing in each direction. Suite 920 would be the final door to the left.

The door to Suite 920 looked like something out of some old detective movie. The polished wood framed a textured glass window, which had black stenciled letters on it proclaiming it the office of one L.W. Gibson. Below his name, she could see the remnants of stenciling, wiped away but still leaving faded smudges. Sam took a deep breath and knocked timidly. From the other side of the door, she heard a voice call "It's open!"

Sam pulled open the door and saw Gibson sitting on a leather couch against the far wall, holding an ice pack over his right eye. "My coat!" he exclaimed, setting down the ice on a small end table. "You brought my coat back. I was getting worried you'd run off with it."

Sam stared, nonplussed.

"I like that coat," Gibson replied matter-of-factly.

She wasn't sure if it was fear, or anger, or exhaustion, or something else altogether that made her snap, but she suddenly had no patience for this strange detective. "You could have told me where to find this place. I slept in an alley with a rat! I don't know who you are or what you are or where I am or what I'm doing here and I want some answers, Mr. Gibson." His name came out as a snarl.

"Well, Bloodwalker," Gibson said. "I can tell you why you're here." Sam glared at him, and he moved his hands in a soothing motion and added, "I don't mean delivering my coat."

"All right then, Mr. Gibson," Sam spat. "Why am I here?"

Gibson grinned widely. "You haven't figured it out? You're here because you're dead," he said brightly.

Chapter 5

Sam blinked at the grinning man on the couch. His words echoed in her head for the space of two breaths before she finally spoke. "What do you mean I'm dead?" Sam asked in a quietly dangerous voice. Gibson shifted uneasily under her glare before pulling a gun out from behind his back and tossing it on the couch beyond his reach.

"I'm not threatening you, Bloodwalker," he said, gesturing with his hands, trying to placate her. Sam's anger, which she had been trying to gain control over, flashed into full, unrelenting fury.

"You're not threatening me?" Sam shrieked. "I wake up in a dirty alley, get arrested, some stranger in the police station tells me to bring him his jacket and, like an idiot, I do! Then, when I finally find where this jackass of a man lives, he tells me I'm dead and takes out a gun! Oh, but don't worry, Sam, he said he's not threatening you!" Sam's face glowed crimson with rage. The tips of her ears felt like fire. Her stare must have been burning a hole in the man because he shifted again. Sam pulled the coat from her shoulders and threw it at him. "Here's your goddamn jacket!" She gave him another hard scowl before turning to leave.

"Wait!" Gibson said urgently. Sam stopped and stared straight in his eyes. "I helped you get out of that arrest, don't forget. Let's start over. My name is Gibson." He stood and held out his hand for a handshake. Sam stared at it as if it were a poisonous snake. After a few moments of awkward stillness, Gibson lowered his hand. "I'm not going to hurt you. It's not every day you meet a Bloodwalker, you know? The gun is a precaution. Because of my line of work, sometimes people don't like me very much."

The anger Sam had felt was starting to abate. "You called me that before, and keep saying that word. Bloodwalker," she said slowly. "What are you talking about?"

"Please, sit," he said, watching her reaction cautiously. Following his own invitation, he plunked back down on the couch. "I'm not sure how to explain this," Gibson mumbled, running his hands through his black hair with the air of someone unsure of himself. "I figured out your name is Sam, from when you screamed it at me a minute ago, but how much do you know about your situation?"

Sam hesitated. She quickly looked around the room, debating between a chair near the door and another closer to the gun, where she could make a lunge for it if she needed to. Gibson must have picked up on her thinking, because he said, "Look, why don't you take the gun and hold it if that would make you feel better?" Gibson stood and took a few steps further away from both Sam and the couch. Sam gave the man a tight-lipped smile, then pulled the gun off the couch and returned to the chair nearest the door. "Do you mind if I sit back down?" Gibson asked, and Sam shook her head no.

"Okay," Gibson said. "I feel like we're making some progress now." He ventured a small, toothy smile toward Sam, which she did not return. The smile vanished in an instant as if it had never been there. "Sam. Short for Samantha, I take it?" Gibson asked, and Sam gave a slight nod. "Great. Nice to formally meet you, Sam." He ran his fingers through his tousled mane of hair again. "So how long have you been here, Sam?"

Sam frowned at the question. "What do you mean? In this city?" Sam asked, idly scratching at her arm. "I don't know. I don't remember anything before waking up in an alley, and I met you right after that."

The investigator nodded to himself. "No memory," Gibson murmured. "That explains a lot, actually." Sam saw his lips moving as the man stared at the floor in front of his feet, but she could not hear him at all. She waited impatiently and was about to start tapping her toe when he looked up at Sam. He had another small smile on his face, but his eyes looked sad, the smile forced. "So, ah, Sam," he began, sounding more unsure than Sam was comfortable with. "Bloodwalker. Yes. That's the best place to start," Gibson said, but then paused, as if uncertain on what to say next. Sam felt her anger growing again, but Gibson continued before she could open her mouth.

"Bloodwalkers are a thing of legend," Gibson said slowly, almost as if he were trying to pull something from memory but wasn't quite sure of all the details. "Imagine, I don't know, imagine going to a farm, okay?" Sam nodded. "What kind of animals would you expect to see there?" Gibson answered his own question. "Cows, pigs, maybe some horses or goats, some chickens, a dog, right? Well, imagine if you saw all those things, but the farm also had a dragon, or a unicorn, or a mermaid. Everything at the farm is exactly how it should be, except for this one gigantic glaring exception. That's a Bloodwalker," Gibson finished, but he looked displeased with his own explanation.

Sam frowned at him. "What are you getting at?" Sam asked, the words tipped with the barest fringe of angry heat. "I'm some kind of a freak?"

Gibson's eyes opened wide and he put up his hands to stall her. "No, no, not a freak," he said quickly. "A myth, or folklore. Something you overhear from a drunken conversation in a bar between two men you've never seen before and will never see again."

"If that's true," Sam said slowly, "then how do you know about it? Is that why I was arrested? You still haven't even said what a Bloodwalker is, either."

Gibson sighed heavily. "Remember how I was talking about legends? Well, what that means, at least in part, is that I never expected to actually see a Bloodwalker, let alone have one in my office." Gibson frowned, looking deep in thought. "There's a lot I don't know, simply because I don't know that this has ever happened. For real, I mean. Let me ask you this: have you noticed any way you're different from everyone and everything else you've seen since you woke up?"

Sam stared at him. "Everything in this city, everyone in this city, looks..." she trailed off, looking for the right word. Gibson nodded encouragingly. "I guess the best word I can come up with is faded. Everyone is grey and looks like they came out of an old photograph." She looked down at her own hands, clutching each other on her lap, and saw how much her skin, her life, stood out even in comparison to the rest of the room.

"Exactly!" Gibson said, grinning again. "So, let's build on that point. You look different from everyone else in the Fourth City. Ah, on that point, local history says this was the fourth settlement in Purgatory, though I've never seen that confirmed anywhere. Anyway, I know you said you don't have any memory before waking up in the alley downtown, but try to think back, to before that time." Sam did as he suggested, trying to force her mind backward, to remember. She even closed her eyes to try to focus, but nothing came to her. Sam's shoulders slumped dejectedly, but Gibson did not let her speak. "Sam, answer this question for me: how did you die?"

Sam's head jerked upward and she stared at the investigator. The doubts she had felt about his sanity doubled. "How did I die?" Sam repeated, confused. She paused, then added, "I'm not dead."

Gibson's grin was wide, showing a full complement of shining teeth. "Now you're getting it, Sam," he said, even going so far as to let out a deep, rich laugh. "Now I, on the other hand, died on the 11th of May, 1932, just outside of Chicago." Gibson lifted the left side of his shirt. "See? Three bullet holes." He prodded at 3 distinct areas of scarred flesh. "Wasn't a great experience, but you learn to deal with things like that here."

Sam's stomach felt like it was doing somersaults. She blinked, trying to clear her mind of what she was hearing. "I'm going insane," Sam said to the air, ending with a shrill note of panic in her voice. She took a deep breath. "No," she amended after a moment, "I've already gone insane. I'm done." She turned back toward Gibson. "You're not really here," she said with certainty. "None of this is actually happening. I must be dreaming. I'm in a coma or something and need to wake up."

"Not quite," Gibson said sarcastically. "I'm very much here, and for better or worse, so are you. The point of all this talk, Sam, is that you are here, in the land of the dead, in Purgatory. You don't belong here, but for some reason, you are here. I'd wager the reason is locked away in that memory of yours."

Sam glanced around the room as if expecting it to fade away, as if she would suddenly find herself in a padded room somewhere, removed from society and put in an institute. Or in a hospital bed, staring up at blinding lights. But the room did not change. Sam's heart felt like it was pounding on her ribcage. "I look different than everyone else because I'm not dead, and everyone else is?"

"I won't promise that's the case, but I can't think of any other explanation," Gibson answered. "And if that is indeed the case, then you truly are a Bloodwalker."

Sam stared at her hands. Dead without dying? And everyone else is alive without living? Whatever she was, whatever this place was, her brain was muddled. Questions formed and vanished quicker than she could make note of them. "Let's assume you're right for a second: is being a

Bloodwalker a crime?" Sam asked. "If it's such a legendary thing, how come I was arrested?"

"Unfortunately for you, that lunk Gunnarsson was the one who picked you up," Gibson said, rolling his eyes. "He's a real piece of work, Old World Viking-type. Probably was a Viking, come to think of it." He paused to rub at his chin. "Hmm. I may have to do some digging on that someday. Regardless, he's a grunt, a soldier, and anything that doesn't fit into his expectations is bad in his eyes."

"Wait," Sam interjected, feeling more confused by the word. "A Viking policeman? What? Why are there even police if everyone is dead anyway?"

Gibson laughed. "Well, think of it this way. First, when people die and come here, they have to make a living, right? Poor choice of words, but you know what I mean." Gibson waited for her uncertain nod of agreement. "So, to make money, most people fall into the line of work they did when they were alive, but there's not exactly a lot of demand for Vikings in Purgatory."

"As for your second question," Gibson continued, "there are police because there are people. Where there are people, there are laws being broken. Since most people want to fall back into their old professions and do what they're comfortable with doing, most policemen stay as policemen, most bankers stay as bankers, and most slumlords stay as dirty, thieving slumlords." Gibson pursed his lips as if to spit on the carpeted floor but thought better of it.

Sam ran these ideas through her head, trying to make sense of everything. Her temples pulsed with stress, with information overload, with confusion, fear, desperation, and pain. Spots of blackness filled her sight, then merged and grew so quickly Sam did not even have the conscious thought that she was about to faint before it happened.

Sam opened her eyes and found herself groggily looking at a white plastered ceiling. Was she even alive? She had been dreaming of a pair of voices, howling in the darkness, one male and one female. Sam tried to remember if there were any words or just screams, but she could not recall.

"Ah. Back among the living. So to speak."

Sitting bolt upright, Sam turned toward the source of the words, hand pressed against her chest. Her shoulders sagged and she let out a sigh of relief when she saw and recognized Gibson, sitting in a wicker chair in the corner of the room. The conversation they had been having, about this place, this world, rushed back into the forefront of her mind like a tidal wave. She was in the land of the dead, but she *was* alive. She was a Bloodwalker. Goosebumps rose on her arms as she remembered, though Sam couldn't say if it was due to excitement, fear, or both.

There was a small round table in front of Gibson, on which sat pieces of his gun. A polishing cloth was clutched in his hand and he smiled at her. "Sorry," he said, turning his attention back to the pieces of his firearm. "I didn't mean to upset you. I know it's a lot to take in."

Brushing a strand of hair away from her left eye, Sam studied the investigator. He moved with a practiced grace as he cleaned and reassembled his gun. "What's the point of having a gun?" she asked. "I mean, you can't kill someone if they're already dead, right?"

Gibson did not look up from his task. "It's like this," he said, with a hint of caution in his voice. "When most people see a gun, they panic. It's a great tool for forcing a physical response. Take it from me," Gibson said, looking up to grin at her, "it's no fun getting shot, so most people will do what you tell them to do if there's a gun in your hand."

Sam considered his words, but also listened to what Gibson omitted. "You didn't say whether or not you can actually kill someone with a gun here," Sam said quietly, watching for any change in the man across the room. "Have you ever shot someone with that gun, Gibson?"

The cloth moved over the same part of the gun, cleaning an area that had already been polished. Gibson kept his head down, staring at his own hands. "Yes," he said finally, exhaling the word on a breath that conveyed reluctance. Once the word was in the air, Gibson's resolve seemed to strengthen, and he continued. "Guns here are just as deadly as guns in the living world, though the ammunition is different. Don't ask me to explain; I don't know the technical differences. I also don't know what happens when someone dies here. No one does. Or maybe someone does, but no one I've ever met. Maybe they stop existing anywhere. Maybe there's another hell like this. Maybe they get Unborn again."

"Unborn?" Sam asked, blinking.

"Ah, sorry," Gibson said, masking the heavy topic behind another small smile. "When people in the living world die and appear here, sometimes they're referred to as Unborns. Seems fitting, wouldn't you say? People are born to the world of the living, and unborn to the world of the dead."

So many questions raced through Sam's mind. This was completely unbelievable, and yet she could see, hear, and feel the world of the dead all around her. Sam's stomach growled noisily. She realized she hadn't eaten a single thing since waking up in the alley. "So," Sam began awkwardly, "what about food here?"

Gibson dropped the gun with a thud. "I'm so sorry!" he blurted out, looking sheepish. "Not much of a host, am I? People here, us Unborns," he bowed his head self-mockingly, "we eat, of course, but we don't really need to, if you catch my meaning. It's more of something we do because it's something that we used to do." Gibson grimaced. "I haven't gotten paid lately. The problem with taking jobs for deadbeats is tracking down the money after the job is done." Gibson left the room and returned a few minutes later with a mug of black coffee and a chipped porcelain plate with half a dozen water crackers and a few chunks of a red-and-green-flecked white cheese. "It's not much, but it's what I've got at the moment."

Sam accepted the plate gratefully, but she hesitated a moment before eating. She noticed Gibson watching her. "It's not poisoned," he said, clearly trying to be reassuring.

Sam looked at it, trying to mask her apprehension. "I've never eaten dead people's food, that's all," she said, looking at him. They stared at each other for a few seconds before both burst into fierce laughter. Sam rolled the first chunk of cheese between her fingers before placing it atop the cracker and eating it. Her eyes popped open as the cracker touched her tongue. It was delicious! In the back of her mind, Sam knew that part of it was likely due to how long it had been since she had eaten anything, but the cheese was firm and savory. The red flecks, she learned, were some variety of spicy pepper. Sam had never been one for spicy food, but she would make an exception for this.

As she took the fourth cracker from the plate, Sam made a conscious effort to slow down, to chew her food deliberately. With the way the past day had gone, she did not know when she would be able to eat again. "I still don't know why you're helping me," Sam said before grabbing another cracker, "but I do appreciate it. What comes next? You said you didn't get paid for your last job. Maybe I can help you collect?"

Gibson shook his head immediately. "Even people who don't know about Bloodwalkers would see you and immediately know you're different," Gibson said. "Some of the religious types might think you're an angel and start following you around, thinking you'll lead them out of here and up to Heaven. Others might see you and wonder if you look the way you do because of some sickness and wonder if you're contagious. It's too risky."

Sam frowned. "So I'm stuck inside, except when it's night and I can travel unseen?" she asked. She scowled at herself for letting her frustration be so obvious in her tone. Memory or no memory, Sam knew she would not be happy becoming a shut-in, but she hated when she sounded whiny.

"Burn victims," Gibson said, as if that was an answer that made any sense at all.

She stared at the dead investigator as if he had gone mad. Maybe he was mad; maybe she was mad and imagining everything. This was a dangerous train of thought to board again, but Gibson derailed it when he spoke.

"Burn victims," he repeated. Gibson wore a considering expression, which was only accentuated by his index finger tapping on his chin. "There may be a way, but it wouldn't be particularly comfortable," Gibson continued after a moment. Sam said nothing, waiting for the man to gather his thoughts. "Some Unborns are a bit," he trailed off, searching for the right word, "self-conscious, let's say." Sam quirked an eyebrow at him, silently prompting him to elaborate.

"Well, it's like this," Gibson explained. "People here usually show up in the same way they died." He lifted his shirt again to show the bullet wounds. "I didn't survive these. When I woke up here," he gestured vaguely around to indicate the world at large, "my bullet wounds were already scarred. If I weren't faded, I imagine they would have been pink and raw. We Unborns don't have blood, in case you haven't figured that out. At least not in the way you'd imagine it. Not a lot of red in this world. That's my best guess as to why we look the way we do. But you? You are something different altogether, Bloodwalker."

58

Sam was mulling this new information over while Gibson continued. "So as I said, people are Unborn in the same way that they died. For me, no big deal. I got a couple of holes in me, but how often do I have my shirt off on the street? I wear a shirt and it's fine. You, on the other hand, look like you're alive, and a shirt isn't going to be enough to hide that. What would work, though, is a mask."

"A mask?" Sam asked, confused. "Do you guys celebrate Halloween or something? Wouldn't that only work once a year?" Sam tried to blink away the mental image of dead people trick or treating in the afterlife. There was something charming about it, but she needed to focus.

"Burn victims," Gibson said for a third time. "When they are Unborn, they aren't exactly the prettiest people to look at, and they know it. Same with some gunshot Unborns, if they get it in the face. Hell, even car accidents. Most people want to have as normal of an afterlife as they can and looking like, well, *that*, isn't great for self-confidence," Gibson said. His tone was flippant but it seemed like he was doing it for show. "The mask business is pretty big-time in the afterlife."

"A mask," Sam said flatly. "Are they people masks, or animals or something? I don't know how I feel about walking around with some cheap plastic mask scratching my face and a rubber band digging into my ears."

"Some upscale mask shops will do a custom mold, if you're rich enough, but then we'd have to bring you out into the open, so not a good idea," Gibson replied. "Plus, neither of us is rich. I'll go down to a few markets and see what I can find."

"Human mask?" Sam asked, trying to hide her reservations about this plan. She scratched at her cheek, as if the plastic mask she had imagined was already digging into her flesh.

"Gloves, too," Gibson said, noting her hands. "You need to cover any part of your skin, or else you'll draw too much attention. I don't know what kind of masks the markets will have in stock about your size, but I'll get what I can get."

"Please don't get anything stupid," she said quietly. "And thank you, Gibson. You know, for helping me. You really have no reason to, but I appreciate it."

The grin reappeared on his face. "Don't worry, Sam. I'm keeping track of my hours and expenses," Gibson responded, and with that, he opened the door and was gone.

Chapter 6

Sam sat in a hard chair and stared at the wooden door, tracing the letters visible through the embedded pane of glass with her eyes. She twisted her body, putting her legs over the arm of the chair, but she couldn't get comfortable. A small round clock, mounted on the wall, clicked noisily with each second. Emotionally, she flitted between boredom, frustration, anger, and fear. After twenty minutes of uncomfortable shifting on the chair, literally listening to each second pass by, Sam gave up and decided to explore the office apartment.

The bedroom held all the typical items she would expect, such as a dresser and an end table with a lamp on it. There was a grimy window on the wall to the right. She was very relieved to see there was a bathroom; Sam had felt too self-conscious to ask whether dead people needed a toilet. The office area had two windows, a desk, the sofa where Gibson had been sitting when she had knocked on the door a few hours ago, and a pair of chairs with wheels. Sam assumed these were for when Gibson had clients. There was a large wooden bookcase on the wall near the door to the outside hallway.

A fourth window centered the far wall of the kitchen, which provided a stunning view of a dirty brick wall and nothing else. The kitchen was small but functional, and surprisingly clean. A metal tea kettle sat on the stovetop. As tempted as she was to look for more to eat, Sam simply walked around the room before returning to the chair in the office.

The wait for Gibson stretched, an endless pull toward an expiration of time, toward oblivion. Sam glanced at the clock. Only an hour had passed since the investigator had left the apartment. She let out a disgusted groan and flung her head back with irritation, staring at the ceiling. Sam started counting to one thousand. Then two thousand. Six thousand.

With a dramatic sigh, Sam pulled herself out of the chair and went over to the bookcase she had noticed earlier. Sam's eyes opened wide with surprise as she studied the titles on the shelf. She hadn't expected Gibson to be so well-read, or even make a pretense at it. Pulling a paperback copy of Jane Austen's "Pride and Prejudice" out of its slot on the case, Sam riffled through the pages, feeling the cool wind that came from the rapidly fluttering paper. When she reached the inside of the front cover, she gasped and nearly dropped the book. Inscribed on the title page were the words, "Dear Lawrence, I can never thank you enough! – Jane Austen". Slowly, Sam put the book back on the shelf. She had intended to read it, but seeing that it was signed by Jane Austen! That was too much to process.

It suddenly struck her as odd that she had no memory of her own life before waking up in the alleyway but knew about plastic Halloween masks and Jane Austen. Sam pushed against the mental block in her head that kept her memories separated from her awareness, closing her eyes to focus on remembering. Images of books and toys from her childhood appeared, misty and insubstantial enough that if she tried to focus on any one object, it would fade away like morning dew in a sunbeam. Sam could see figures, some small, some large, and she could see colors, but faces were blurred and shadowed. It was as if everything important was hidden in plain sight. Eyes still closed, Sam heard a voice. "Everything they whispered is coming true." Her eyes shot open and it took her a few moments to realize the voice she had heard was her own. Why had she said that? She really had gone mad.

An impulse to shower seized Sam, as if the water would wash away the confusion, give her back her memories, or even wake her up from this nightmare. Sam watched her reflection in the mirror as she undressed, removing her shirt, which was filthy from her time in the alleyway. Sam gasped as her arms went above her head, feeling a tearing at her shoulders, like her skin was ripping open. Dropping the shirt on the floor, she stared in horror at scabbed furrows in her flesh. Blood began to ooze through the cracked scabs, funneling toward her breasts. Sam noticed they followed along a dark trail of dried blood on her skin. Her eyes quivered as Sam had a sudden flash of memory, of invisible talons ripping into her, of blood flowing freely, of flashing lights and screams and black winds.

Sam held herself upright with her hands on the vanity, trying to force her breathing to be slow and deep. She inhaled, sucking wind through pursed lips, and lowered her head to exhale – and that's when she saw it. On her left hand, encircling the second finger from the left, was a ring. A gold ring, unmistakable as anything except for a wedding band. She rubbed her temples, wondering if she had seen it but not truly noticed it before.

Sam's right hand shook as she reached across to touch the ring, her mind filled with disbelief, even as she spun the ring slowly around her finger, feeling the metal slide over her skin. She was married! That conscious thought echoed in her mind, acting like a trigger, and Sam experienced a rapid succession of disconnected flashbacks, of trying on her wedding gown, of a sunlit patch of grass where reception photographs were being shot, of walking past the rear windshield of a car that had been painted with the words "Just Married". She could not see the face of her husband, but she knew he was real.

Sam tensed her muscles and watched the blood drip from her shoulders, falling into the porcelain sink with audible plunks, like a leaking faucet. That memory of talons and screams was real, too, she knew, and it filled her with overwhelming terror. What had happened to her? She pressed trembling hands onto the wounds, trying to stem the bleeding, to hold together the scabs that looked ready to burst like dams. Blood pushed up between her fingers, slowly painting her hands red. Letting go of one of the twin wounds, Sam pulled open the vanity drawer and found a few rags and medical tape. She gave the supplies a dark look, anticipating the pain of applying them after her shower.

Sam stripped out of the rest of her clothes and stepped into the cramped shower. The hot water smelled odd, as if it had been carbonated and went flat, and it stung as it pounded on her wounds. Sam yelped with pain at the first drops, but seeing the layers of dirt pool and swirl down the drain was deeply satisfying, so she forced herself to continue, at least in brief moments. Steam had filled the tiny bathroom by the time Sam twisted the shower handle to the off position.

Looking at herself in the mirror, Sam realized the fresh water had done her a lot of good. Her short-clipped blonde hair had regained some of its natural perkiness, and though her cheeks looked a little sunken, they also had some renewed color. Ruefully she remembered how much of a disadvantage that color would give her in this cursed place.

Her shoulder wounds looked better, somehow. Carefully, she dried them as much as possible and bandaged them with the rags she had found earlier, pulling the tape taut enough that it hurt. She worked quickly but efficiently, gritting her teeth and forcing herself to stay focused on one problem at a time. She looked at herself in the mirror, and even though she looked frightened, Sam also thought she looked alive, which was something no one else in this world could say. She felt ready to take action, to accomplish something. She smiled at herself in the mirror.

As she stepped back into the bedroom and felt her skin pebble at the temperature change in the air, Sam suddenly realized she had no clothing to wear other than her dirty things she had left in a crumpled pile on the floor. Sam sighed as she grabbed the stained jeans and shirt and pulled them on. They were stiff with dirt and blood, and itched against her bare skin, but it was all she had. Sam hung up the towel in the bathroom and returned to the office, flopping on the couch, awaiting Gibson's return. She fell asleep almost immediately.

Sam slept like the dead, her breathing soft, slow, and shallow. She dreamed of sitting in the passenger seat of a car, driving down a quiet two-lane highway through rural pasturelands. A pristine white car, shining with a fresh coat of wax, drove slightly faster next to her. Sam watched the car as it slowly passed by, like a lily blooming horizontally from the earth, its tires spinning faster than she could track, pulling rock and oil off the pavement and adding it into the stream of exhaust that poisoned the world. Sam made eye contact with the young woman driving the white car, and they smiled quietly at each other, the way decent total strangers do when they make awkward eye contact. The white car sped on, and Sam watched the trees and bushes and slat-sided farmhouses rush by in the world outside of the car.

The sky burned a vivid blue, bright and reflective, with wisps of white painting tiny lines too insignificant to be called clouds. The car she was in followed the road to the left while Sam stared out. Straight ahead, a thick black and grey cloud hung like foreboding winter, a threat and a promise of retribution, though she wasn't sure if it was retribution for the exhaust or the audacity of contentment.

With a jolt, the car jerked to the right, its tires skidding as it went into a sudden slide. Sam screamed and turned her head toward the driver, then screamed again. A man sat in the seat, his face blurred like television snow, crackling and popping and fading in and out. In an instant the man dematerialized completely, leaving the seat vacant, the wheel spinning as if flaunting its independence.

In a panic, Sam reached toward the steering wheel, trying to get control of the speeding car. It didn't matter that there was no driver; the car sped along as if someone were depressing the accelerator. A thin sheen of sweat burst out of her palms and instead of getting a grip on the wheel, it spun out of her control and veered hard to the right, directly toward a large oak. In the moment before the car collided with the gigantic tree, her eyes sprung open.

Sam was afraid she might crack a rib with how forcefully her heart was pounding. Slowly, Sam was able to catch her breath, to wipe the moisture from her forehead with the back of her hand. The dream re-lived itself, in the way dreams do upon waking, a replay of the horrors of the mind's eye. Sam knew in her heart that the man in her dream was her husband, but there was still some block on her memories keeping her from seeing his face or remembering his name. Was the dream a dream, or was it a memory, a glimpse into the past that had somehow led her to this place. Maybe she wasn't dead, but in a coma somewhere, stuck between the living and dead worlds? The thought chilled her to the bone.

She twisted the ring on her finger, spinning it around in place, trying to distract herself from the dream, from the fear. Sam wanted to scream, to let out all her frustration and rage, but more than anything, she wanted to remember.

It was another half an hour before Gibson returned, carrying a pair of large burlap bags. He saw she was awake but distracted. "Hey," Gibson said quietly, making Sam jump. "Didn't mean to startle you," he added, setting the bags down on the desk. "I wasn't sure you knew I was back. You were staring into space. How are you feeling?"

"I-" Sam stopped, unsure of what to say. So many thoughts raced through her head it was hard to grasp onto any one thing and bring it to the forefront. Gibson stood waiting, patiently giving her time to gather herself, which made Sam feel a bit foolish. She noticed then she was gripping the ring on her finger tightly, and blurted out, "I'm married."

Gibson nodded and said, "I wouldn't be much of a detective if I missed that one. I noticed your ring at the police station. I didn't say anything when you said you were having problems remembering because I was afraid it might be too much of a shock. Besides, I've heard of some women wearing their mother's rings, or continuing to wear a ring after their husband has died, things like that. Do you remember anything about him?"

Sam debated against herself, trying to decide whether to share the dream with the investigator. Finally, she simply shook her head no. "I used your shower while you were gone," Sam said. "I have cuts on my shoulders. When I saw them in the mirror, I had a bunch of memories crash into my head at once. It made me dizzy. I remembered getting married, but not his name, or what he looked like. I remembered-" Sam stopped suddenly, closing her mouth with a small click of teeth. She had been about to tell him about the memory of the screams and the black wind, but she decided against it. "What's in the bags?" Sam asked instead, changing the subject.

Gibson smiled broadly. "Ah, well this one," he said, lifting the bag further to the left, "is a little bit of food I was able to pick up for you. Nothing extravagant, mind you, but better than cheese and crackers." Sam's stomach growled with enthusiasm, and she had to swallow the sudden rush of saliva that filled her mouth. "And this one," Gibson continued, lifting the other bag slightly, "is your disguise." Sam felt a nervous anticipation. He handed her the bag. "Go ahead. Take it out."

Sam opened the bag apprehensively, afraid to look down. She took a deep breath, then reached inside. Her fingers brushed against what felt like feathers as she felt around for an edge to lift what was in the bag. Sam found a grip and hoisted out...a bird? She looked up at Gibson with a puzzled expression.

"It's a firebird, a phoenix," Gibson said with a grin, responding to her unanswered question. "Mythical bird of prey, reborn from the ashes, that whole thing." He scratched worriedly at his chin at her expression. "I saw it down at the market and it seemed too perfect to pass up. The Phoenix is all about a fresh start, and with you not remembering much, it seemed appropriate. What do you think?"

Sam studied the mask, picking out small details. The feathers were individually secured to it, dyed in gradient shades of red. The beak was some kind of black, lightweight material. It felt hard and cool like metal. Sam traced her finger along the mask, then pulled away abruptly, nearly dropping the mask on the floor. The tip of the beak was razor sharp! The phoenix mask would completely cover her head so that not even the back of her neck would be visible. She was a little worried about having to wear something that would engulf her entire head. How would she breathe? Also inside the bag was a full-length black cloak with red trim, and a pair of snug black velvet gloves.

"I'm very impressed with the craftsmanship," Sam said, pulling on the gloves. "I was a little bit worried you'd buy a goat mask or something." She laughed a nervous titter of a laugh. "Thank you, Gibson," Sam added sincerely.

The man echoed her amusement. "Well, I can't have you staying here forever," Gibson answered, wearing his usual smirk. "Imagine the scandal! Married woman moves in with local roguish detective! It would be the headline in all the papers!"

Despite everything that had happened in the last few days, Sam laughed. She laughed so hard she struggled to breathe, and for so long that Gibson wondered to himself if she was on the cusp of having a complete breakdown, though he said nothing. Sam had the same thought, and it only made her laugh harder.

*　*　*　*　*

Officer Robert Webb was sitting at his desk when a piece of paper skimmed into his sight. He looked up to see Bill Zidiba's round face looking down at him. Zidiba looked out of place with his boyish looks and plump cheeks, but he was a 20-year veteran. "Thought you'd be interested to see this," Zidiba said in a gruff voice that didn't match his appearance. "It came through Missing Persons an hour ago."

Webb picked up the paper and his eyes immediately widened in surprise. "Samantha Nightshade?" he said aloud. "Disappeared during a séance, mother and another woman present, blood everywhere..." Webb trailed off. "They said she was abducted by a ghost!?" he exclaimed as he continued to read the report. Webb looked up from the paper. "Zidiba, has anything else come out of Forensics about her husband's car crash?" The other officer shook his head.

"I figured you'd ask that when I gave you this report, so I made a few calls before coming over here," Zidiba answered. "Forensics still thinks there was a second person in the car, and maybe that second person is the reason the car hit the tree. Johnson is the lead from Forensics, and she told me the splatter pattern in the car looked like it happened from the inside. They're waiting for tests to come back from the lab before they confirm anything, but Johnson said, off the record, is the passenger somehow tore Nightshade's arm off. She said it was a guess, but there was enough evidence to make her say it. Again, off the record. Maybe he picked up a hitchhiker looking for a thrill kill. Johnson told me the coroner on that case said she had never seen anything like it. Looked like the arm was torn off with a giant claw hammer."

Webb nodded slowly. He remembered seeing the body after the accident, missing the right arm and part of his face. Webb had been a member of the police force for longer than he cared to admit, but that was one of the grisliest scenes he had the misfortune of seeing. And now the wife was missing. Webb clenched his fist. There were too many questions on this case, and in the back of his mind, Webb knew this would be the case that he would fixate on long after his retirement. "Thanks, Zidiba," Webb said in a voice cracking with strain. "I need to make some calls."

Chapter 7

Night fell, heavy and deep, and grey-blue steam rose from a manhole cover in a brick-paved alleyway. Mixed in with the garbage and broken glass, Sam was hidden deep within the shadows, crouching motionless in the full phoenix disguise. In the distance, she saw a discarded jacket, torn and dirty, hanging limply over a rusty metal barrel. Beyond that, a few steps inside the mouth of the alley, she saw Gibson handing an envelope to a man she did not recognize. The man nodded, his wide-brimmed hat bobbing quickly downward. Transaction complete, he and Gibson turned away from each other simultaneously. Gibson made his way toward Sam in the darkness.

"Are you sure you're up for this, Sam?" Gibson asked tentatively. She must have hidden better than he expected, because he was looking about eight feet to her left. Sam rose from her crouch, which obviously startled Gibson, though he tried to hide his surprise.

"You've been letting me stay rent free for a week," Sam said flatly. "We've gone over this. You need to get paid, and I want to help if I can." Sam did not remind Gibson he had promised to help her do some digging into her memory block, nor did she need to. Gibson had told her that he had an old contact who might be useful, but information was not cheap to acquire. "Did you get anything useful out of that guy?"

Gibson adjusted the collar of his trench coat. "Yep. My client," he stopped to spit angrily on the ground, "has been holed up in a flophouse a few blocks from here. It might get dangerous, Sam. I'd feel better if you stayed here, or went back to the apartment."

Sam shook her head. "I'm coming with you, end of discussion."

Gibson shrugged, sighed, but did not argue. "Come on, then. Stay ten steps behind me. I won't tell you to try to blend in, because you won't be able to with the phoenix getup. Act like you have every right to be going where you're going and don't let anyone stop you. Own the space you move through." Sam nodded impatiently. They had gone over all this at least a dozen times before.

Luckily, there were not very many people on the sidewalk this late at night. Sam trod silently behind Gibson, feeling the moisture of her breath on her cheeks as she exhaled, the warmth quickly chilling once exposed to the outside air. She felt oddly at ease wearing the cloak and mask, as if she and the firebird had some sort of kinship. The cloak enveloped her, hiding her skin, her gender, everything. She moved like a phantom, blending into the darkness as if it were part of her. Sam grinned behind the sharp beak on the mask, imagining herself as some sort of superhero, an Angel of Wrath.

Gibson stopped and made a quick hand signal behind his back. He had taught Sam three basic signals: come, wait, and run like hell. This time, Gibson indicated she should wait. Unsure of what to do, Sam crouched and pretended to tie her shoe. Behind the phoenix mask, her face glowed crimson with embarrassment at her inability to think of something less cliché. Gibson simply waited a few moments, casually looking down both sides of the street, then up at the heavily-windowed building across the way. To Sam, it looked like a replica of Gibson's apartment building, but smaller and more run down. A similar mismatch of building materials marked the structure's age, with moldy grey-green rock at street level. Gibson had taught her it was kind of like counting the rings on a tree. "If a building has stones like castle walls at the base, it's probably 800 years old, if not older. Steel is in the past 100 years. In some parts of the world, there are houses made entirely of clay. You can even see the handprints on the walls from where those early Unborn builders packed the wet clay."

After ensuring he had not been followed, Sam watched Gibson cross the street and pull open the wooden door that nestled into the stonework. It resisted opening at first and creaked loudly when it finally did move, the sound echoing off the buildings clustered along the almost deserted street. Sam counted to twenty before crossing the road to stand next to the door. Gibson's plan was that he would go upstairs and confront his delinquent client, and Sam would be waiting outside. "In case the filthy reprobate hightails it," Gibson had said. She had fought to accompany him into the building, but could understand his perspective. Sam felt a little silly, like extra baggage, or a child told to wait in the corner while the grown-ups took care of things, but she did as they agreed. She had told the investigator that she wanted to help, and he set her on guard duty. Sam sighed behind her mask and settled her back against the rough stone wall, preparing to wait.

In her mind, Sam knew it had only been about ten minutes since Gibson had entered the building, but it still felt like forever. Noises echoed strangely in the night, which lay across the city deep as a snow drift. Once, Sam heard footsteps reverberating off the stone walls toward her left. Every muscle in her body tensed in anticipation. Glancing in that direction, she saw a tall, slender figure wavering drunkenly. Sam could not make out their face, but she slumped with relief when the figure wobbled and turned back in the direction from which they had come.

Time stretched toward infinity, a giant hourglass holding enough sand to fill a dozen beaches. Her anxiety only exacerbated the feeling that she had been standing outside, exposed despite her disguise. Gibson's instructions had been for her to stay outside and wait for him to return. If he was gone for twenty minutes, she was to go inside and move as quietly as possible up to the eleventh floor and evaluate. Gibson's delinquent client was in room 1105, but she had no way of knowing when twenty minutes had passed.

Sam decided she had waited long enough and was about to open the front door when she heard shouting from inside the building, accompanied by the pounding of shoes on stairs. She took a quick step away from the door a split second before it burst open with enough force that it would have knocked her to the pavement. Exploding through the doorway was a wide-eyed man. He looked young, maybe in his mid-20s, and had stringy hair that swung wildly as he turned toward her. He wore a light black jacket, which flapped behind him like giant bat wings as he dashed forward.

"Move!" the man shouted at her. He reached out a hand to shove Sam out of his way, and his palm pressed up against the beak of her phoenix mask. The man shrieked in agony as the beak split his palm in two, with a splash of silver-white liquid splattered across her mask. Sam wanted to shriek, too, but her mouth had gone dry with horror. The man fell to the ground, clutching his hand, screaming wordlessly. Even though the man was covering his hand, Sam could see his fingers and tendons dangling uselessly. Eyes still wide with shock, Sam wiped the viscous Unborn blood from her mask, flinging droplets from the tips of her gloved fingers. Bile rose, burning her throat.

Gibson burst through the door a second later, his gun glimmering silver in his hand. The detective took in the scene quickly. "I told you it would be better to pay me what you owe me, Davis," Gibson sneered at the man lying screaming on the pavement. Gibson shot a quick, questioning glance at Sam, silently letting her know he would want to hear the full story later. "I don't enjoy doing this kind of thing, but when you hire someone to do a job, you have to pay them at the end of it. I'm sure you wouldn't want me to let your former employer know what you've been up to."

The man, Davis, looked up at Gibson, clearly terrified. Sam saw the man's face pale, despite the already faded appearance, and she realized she had never actually asked Gibson what work he had done for Davis. "I've got your money," Davis said in a quavering voice. "Don't shoot me, man. I'm just getting your money." He let go of his mangled hand for a moment and reached inside his black jacket, pulling out a crumpled envelope the sickly yellow-brown color of cigarette smoke stains. Davis tossed the envelope toward Gibson's feet.

Sam watched this exchange, grateful once again for the mask that hid her face. For the first time, Gibson truly frightened her. His posture was rigid, his jaw clenched hard, his gun arm unwavering. Gibson glared down at Davis, who had resumed his feeble attempt to hold his hand together. Sam shivered.

Gibson tore open the envelope and riffled through its contents. "This is only 400," Gibson said in a dangerous voice. "You gave me three up front, and now another four. The job was for fifteen. I may be a dumb Chicago kid, but I can count well enough to know three plus four doesn't make fifteen, Davis."

Davis was still sitting on the ground, knees up protectively near his face, his hands between his knees and chest. The silver-white blood from his hand was pooling on the concrete below him. He whimpered at Gibson's unspoken threat, then spoke in a trembling voice. "That-that's why I didn't come see y-you yet, man. I-I can get you the rest by Friday."

Gibson sighed and shook his head. "I already gave you three extra weeks, Davis." Gibson turned his head and spat on the ground. "Why is it that you don't have my money?" Gibson's voice was cold, the sound of someone preparing themselves for violence.

Tears fell freely from Davis, splashing into the growing circle of blood. "You-you know what kind of man Old Man Ladi is, the things he-he does to people," he stammered. Somehow Davis seemed even more afraid to talk about whoever Old Man Ladi was than he did of Gibson standing over him with a gun pointed at his head. "It-it's better for everyone if Ladi loses everything, b-b-but I don't want to lose everything t-too."

Sam's confusion grew. Gibson had told her the less she knew about this debt collection, the better, but she had a feeling none of this was going the way Gibson had hoped. Old Man Ladi? He sounded like a mobster, and the way Davis's eyes kept darting around as he spoke made her stomach clench. "I did my part, Davis," Gibson said, the coldness hardening to steel. "It's not my fault you weren't able to hold up your end on this deal."

Davis's eyes went wide. "My end of the deal!" he blurted, voice strengthened by indignation. "I hired you to help me get out of Ladi's operation, and to make as big of a dent in it as possible! I was the one who got you samples of the stuff he sells, and I was the one who nearly got caught doing it! What have you done, Mister Detective?" Davis's anger was reaching fever pitch. Sam was unsure of what to do, so she simply stood and listened, silent as a specter. "You said it wouldn't be easy, but you'd get me out, and instead you come to my home and threaten me, then have your ghoul slice my damn hand in half!"

Sam took great offense at this creative retelling of events and opened her mouth to call Davis out on his lie, but Gibson spoke first. "I took those 'samples' of yours to a man I know and trust. Do you know what he said, Davis?" Gibson asked, his own anger rising. "He said, 'This is the worst imitation of Synthosyn I've ever seen.'" Gibson shot a hard look at the man on the ground. "He also said, 'There's no way to trace this back to Old Man Ladi. This could come from anywhere.' Now you tell me, what kind of stunt were you trying to pull, dragging me into this and giving me this dreck? If this is the stuff Ladi is peddling, he'll put himself out of business when word spreads he's pushing a knockoff of a knockoff of 'Syn."

"A drug?" Sam wondered. She couldn't imagine what else this mysterious Synthosyn could be. And why would Gibson need a sample? Sam's bewilderment grew.

Using his good hand to push himself off the ground, Davis stood. His knees wobbled for a moment, but he was able to keep his balance. "Look," he said, obviously trying to inject some calm into the conversation. "Old Man Ladi is a bad dude, and everyone knows it. I didn't want to become part of his organization, but they forced me to."

"I know that," Gibson said with a sigh. "We've gone over this all before. You hired me to get you out." Davis opened his mouth but Gibson did not let him continue. "We both thought the 'Syn would have some kind of marker that would point right at Old Man Ladi like a neon sign, but it didn't happen. Like I said upstairs," Gibson concluded, "we've hit a dead end. You've got two options: keep working for Ladi, or grab whatever you need and run. Either way, I did what I could on your job and need to get paid. I told you at the beginning I couldn't make any promises."

Davis shook his head. "I can't go back there, man," he said, his voice quivering slightly. "Don't you have any cop friends who aren't on his payroll that will take the samples seriously?" Sam saw Gibson's expression change for a moment, as if he had a sour taste in his mouth, but the investigator quickly masked it. "Do you know someone, Gibson?" Davis asked excitedly. "If you do, if you can really get me out of this," Davis hesitated. "I can pay you more than the fifteen hundred we agreed on." Davis paused and glanced in Sam's direction. He shuddered, though Sam wasn't sure if it was because of her or another bout of weakness in his knees. "If you can get me out of this and take down Ladi," Davis said barely above a whisper, "I can get you ten times as much. A hundred times."

Gibson rubbed a hand down his face. "You're offering me six figures now?" he asked flatly. "You can't even pay what you already owe me."

"No, no," Davis said, waving his uninjured hand frantically. "Hear me out, man. If you can get inside his organization, you can get more stuff to bring to the cops, right? I saw that look on your face, man. You know someone who can help, but you said the 'Syn I got you wasn't good enough. You become part of Old Man Ladi's family, you see the inside of things, you'll know what is good enough," Davis pleaded.

Gibson did not move. The gun was still pointed directly at Davis's head. His eyes flicked over to Sam momentarily, then slowly, reluctantly, he lowered the gun. "We shouldn't be talking about this outside," Gibson murmured. "Why don't you invite us in?" he added, gesturing toward Sam. "I'm sure my..." Gibson trailed off, throwing a quick smirk in her direction, "ghoul would enjoy a change of scenery."

Sam followed Gibson and Davis through the heavy front door of the apartment building. The lobby layout was similar to Gibson's, but with a stone and wood motif that looked old and worn. An old-fashioned lift-gate elevator clanked down from somewhere high above, and the three of them stood silently, lost in their own thoughts and not meeting each other's eyes. Davis opened the lift-gate awkwardly with his uninjured hand and stepped aside, allowing Gibson to enter first. Sam stared blankly when Davis gestured her inside; he must have thought her an idiot. There was no way she was going to let the squirrely man create any kind of distance between herself and Gibson to attempt another escape. Davis sighed and stepped into the lift, at which point Sam wordlessly followed. The ride up felt longer than it should have, in part due to the oppressive silence.

Once Davis opened his apartment door and gestured them inside, he visibly relaxed. "I'll be back in a few minutes," he said, raising his split hand as an explanation. "We have a lot to talk about."

The differences between this apartment and Gibson's were immediately apparent. For one, Gibson kept things relatively neat, but Davis was a slob. Sam could not think of any other word for it. Stacks of ratty-looking newspapers were piled on the couch, the floor, and a small table by the window. Dirty clothes were draped over the back of the couch and in a pile in the corner of the main room. There was a musty smell of small rodents hanging heavy in the air, but Sam didn't see any cages to indicate he kept a pet mouse or anything of that nature. The odor made her want to gag.

"I think you make him nervous," Gibson murmured under his breath. "Stay quiet and keep him off-balance. I don't trust him." Gibson went over to the couch and grunted as he lifted a stack of newspapers and dropped them unceremoniously on the floor. A puff of dust exploded into the air as they hit the filthy carpet. Sam decided she would stand silently in front of the door instead of making space to sit. Besides, she didn't want to think about what kind of creatures could be living in this mess, and the last thing she wanted was a rat to nip her on the hip during the interrogation.

Davis returned to the room, his hand heavily bandaged, and flicked his eyes toward the door. He froze for a split second when he saw her standing there, regaled in her phoenix mask and cloak, then stumbled as he started moving again. He took his place in a chair in the far corner of the room, which was covered in a heap of clothing; Davis simply dropped on top of the pile as if it were a cushion. "How's the hand?" Gibson asked snidely.

"Hurts like hell, thanks to your ghoul," Davis replied, angrily gesturing toward her with his bandaged hand. He took a deep breath, obviously calming his nerves. "Look, I know it's a bigger job than we talked about, but here's my thought: if you can take down Old Man Ladi from the inside, you can take a chunk of cash as big as you want on your way out."

Gibson stared at the man for a moment, then burst into a full fit of laughter that lasted nearly a full minute. "Let me get this straight," he began, wiping a tear from the corner of his eye. "First, you hire me to have some of Ladi's drug samples analyzed to turn in to the cops. When that didn't work, you try to run away. You get caught, then pay me less than half of what we agreed on in the first place. Now, you suggest I take a massive risk by working my way into Ladi's organization, then ripping him off right before the cops bring him down?" Gibson turned toward Sam and spoke with a voice that immediately lost its joviality. "This was a waste of time. Let's get out of here." As he stood to leave, Gibson looked back at Davis. "You've got 24 hours to get me the rest of my money. Don't even think about running."

"Wait! Wait!" Davis said, his voice cracking with urgency as he rose from the chair. "I'm sure there's a way to make this work!" Gibson did not acknowledge him as he walked to the door. Sam turned and reached for the handle. "Wait!" Davis cried urgently once more. "What about your old partner? What about Billy?"

Gibson froze. A heavy, uncomfortable silence fell, punctuated only by panting gasps coming from Davis. The silence could have been chipped like ice. Finally, without moving, Gibson said coldly, "What do you know about Billy?" Sam shivered inside the cloak. As menacing as Gibson was before, it paled in comparison to the way he spoke now. Davis evidently felt the threat as well because he took an involuntary step away from

Gibson's back. "What do you know about Billy?" Gibson asked a second time, and Davis stepped back again, but stumbled over the pile of newspapers Gibson had removed from the couch earlier and fell onto the chair.

"Ah," Davis said in a quavering voice, "ah, I mean, ah-"

"SPIT IT OUT!" Gibson roared as he spun on his heel to face Davis. Gibson's hand flashed into his trench coat so quickly Sam barely noticed. Pointing the gun at Davis once again, Gibson bellowed, "TALK, DAVIS! NOW!"

Even from a distance, Sam could see Davis's hands shaking as he put them up in front of himself protectively. Sam took a step toward Gibson and gently put her gloved hand on his shoulder. He glanced at her out of the corner of his eye. "Put the gun away," she whispered. She felt the muscles in Gibson's shoulder tense for a moment before relaxing. Gibson took a deep breath, let it out slowly, and then lowered the gun, but he did not return it to the holster inside his coat. Davis's hands were still shaking.

Gibson inhaled deeply again. "What do you know about Billy?" he asked, clearly moderating his tone. Standing at Gibson's side and looking at his profile, Sam watched him form a grin, though it was more rigid than friendly, and the sudden change was unsettling. "Let's talk about our problem." Davis kept his eyes fixed on the investigator's face. "You mentioned Billy. My old partner," Gibson said, plainly steeling his voice. "The way you said it, you made it seem like this somehow ties into your situation. Explain." Sam touched him on the shoulder again, and he looked over at her and sighed. She felt some of the tension fade from him as he let out the breath. Gibson leaned against the wall, though Sam was unsure if he was preparing for a long conversation, or trying to keep himself from getting angry again by altering his posture to something more casual. Sam remembered what Gibson had said about keeping her Bloodwalker status a secret, so she stood silently in her cloak, doing her best impression of a looming specter.

Gibson's change of tact worked wonders on Davis, who soon shared his theories on why he thought Ladi was involved with Billy's murder. "I know it doesn't make a lot of sense for a mobster," Davis said confidently, "but he keeps records of everything he does, or orders done. It's all locked up in a secret panel in his office. I overheard Ladi one day when he was out in the main warehouse. I was just moving some boxes of 'Syn, you know, but Ladi came through to do a "spot inspection," he called it. He walked around for a few minutes like he had nowhere important to be, until he sees Kenny." Gibson looked at him blankly. "Kenny's the warehouse manager," Davis answered quickly. "Probably the fourth or fifth highest guy in Ladi's organization. Big guy, blond hair, dumb as a rock."

"So anyway," Davis continued, "Ladi spots Kenny and rounds on him like a damn Doberman on a hunk of meat. I'm sure Ladi didn't want anyone to hear, but he couldn't help himself. Starts shouting at Kenny, stuff like, 'I told you to get rid of both of them, not just one!' Nobody saw Kenny after that day, and I don't think he skipped town." Gibson looked at him with a mixture of frustration and disbelief. Davis spoke up quickly. "There's more, man. The next day, I was one of a handful of guys to get shifted from the warehouse to Old Man Ladi's mansion. Working security, odds and ends when people asked for stuff, you know? Well, one day, I'm just standing at the door to Ladi's office, standing guard, right? This guy I've never seen before or since gets escorted into Ladi's office. He's carrying one of those file folder things, and it said Dorsett and Gibson on the label." Gibson grunted.

"Let's assume everything you said is on the level," Gibson said slowly. "You've built a nice story for me here to go after Ladi for revenge, but revenge won't bring Billy back. You said I'd get paid for this job." Davis nodded enthusiastically.

"If you get into Old Man Ladi's office and get the files from behind the secret panel, you'll see he has stacks of cash in there, too," Davis said quickly. "Emergency funds, I heard one of the other guards call it. From what that guy told me, the panel is behind this ugly painting of a boat. It's on the wall, right behind Ladi's chair. So, what do you think? Get yourself in tight with the Family, get on guard duty, and wait for your chance to break into his office. Take the files to the cops and walk out with a briefcase full of cash."

"If it is so easy," asked Gibson flatly, "why not do it yourself?"

"It's a two-man operation," Davis answered, giving a toothy smile that he clearly thought was charming. "If we get on guard duty together, you can slip in while I keep watch for you. Then you stash the briefcase somewhere else for a bit, and grab it after the next pair of guards arrives for their shift."

Gibson was silent for a moment as he rubbed his chin thoughtfully. Finally, he shook his head. "You're forgetting something important. According to your story, Old Man Ladi already planned to have me killed when he had Billy murdered." Gibson sighed deeply and looked toward the window. "We were investigating a case in Southtown, a breaking and entering, a burglary. This woman, pretty young thing, came into our office and reported it. She seemed scared, telling a story about how she was in a terrible relationship when she was alive, how her boyfriend used to hit her and choke her. She couldn't get away, because he threatened her family, and she was trying to protect them. One night, she has enough, pops a bunch of pills and never wakes up again. Her abusive boyfriend gets sent to prison and takes a shiv in the gut the first week. The boyfriend finds out where she lives in Purgatory and starts threatening her all over again. Poor girl can't even get peace when she's dead."

Sam listened to this story, captivated and horrified. Even the idea of being in such a relationship made her heart ache for the woman, but as she tried to put herself into the mystery woman's shoes, she felt an icy fear creep up her spine. To be hunted beyond the grave, to have not one but two lifetimes of abuse.... Sam gratefully let that train of thought die when Gibson continued.

"Long story short, almost everything she said was true, but she was paid off by someone to lure Billy and me to this house. Billy was at the house and I was with the girl, so he went inside to look around before I got there. We get halfway to the house and she suddenly turns toward me and buries her face in my chest. I can feel her sobbing right away. She tells me she met some guy who said he could protect her, but he lied to her. She didn't know his name, but said he was big and blond." Gibson shot a pointed look at Davis. "Sounds like he could have been your Kenny." Davis nodded.

"The girl tells me the blond guy who said he could help her ended up threatening her," Gibson continued, "saying he would tell her boyfriend she was dating someone else and give him her address, garbage like that, unless she got Billy and me to go to this house. I don't know if she took a liking to me or had a sudden change of heart or what, but she wouldn't let me go to the house. She told me the whole story. By the time I got to the house, Billy was already dead. Whoever killed him had left, probably when they realized I wasn't there too. I never saw the girl after that day, either."

Sam felt a heaviness in the air when Gibson finished his story. Looking at Davis, Sam could tell he felt it, too. Sam had no idea Gibson used to have a partner, but she was not sure if she would ask him any questions later. This was obviously something with which he was still struggling. After a prolonged silence, Gibson broke it by saying, "So the thing you've forgotten, Davis, is that Ladi probably already knows my face. If your story and my story are tied together like they seem to be, or the way you hope they are, then Ladi already wanted me dead, though I can't say I know why. It's going to be impossible for me to become a member of his organization if he knows who I am and what I look like."

Davis shook his head immediately. "See, the thing with Ladi is that he usually just gets reports, then decides what to do," he explained. "What probably happened is one of the guys near the top told him you and your partner were sniffing around or getting to be a problem. Ladi would have listened, asked some questions, and then told that guy to take care of you both. Since I saw Ladi and Kenny in the warehouse, I'm guessing Kenny was the guy who brought you to Ladi's attention."

"I don't like how you used words like 'usually' and 'probably' here, Davis," Gibson said dryly. "Not fostering a lot of faith in this hypothetical. That being said, what you're saying is what I've heard about other organizations as well. The man at the top is typically hands off while he calls the shots." Once again, Gibson rubbed his chin, and he stared at the wall. His eyes were glassy, unfocused. Finally, he turned and looked at Sam, who gave a miniscule nod. Gibson shrugged his shoulders before turning back to Davis.

"All right," Gibson said. "You get to work finding a way for me to get assigned to guard duty, and I'll talk to a man I know who might be able to get me some information I need. It won't come cheap, though, Davis," Gibson added, casting a dark look at the man. "Don't forget you still owe me 800 from before. Hell, I might need that much for expenses on this job. And if you so much as think of running..." There was no need to finish the sentence.

Gibson opened the door and let Sam out of the apartment first. Sam had no idea what time it was, but she was glad her phoenix mask protected her face from the damp night. "That meeting didn't go exactly the way I expected," Gibson admitted with a rueful smirk. "Thanks for your patience. Tomorrow, I'll reach out to a guy I know. Name's Harold. Used to be a cop. Not a very friendly guy, but well-connected."

The walk back to Gibson's apartment was quiet and contemplative. "What's with this Synthosyn stuff?" Sam asked, breaking the silence as they turned onto North Kainer.

"Hmm?" Gibson looked confused for a moment before clearing his throat abashedly. "Sorry; I was lost in my head. I was wondering how far I can trust Davis. He was talking about a lot of cash. More than enough cash to sell someone out." His eyes became distant again, unfocused; maybe he was imagining what his life would be like if he had a sudden cash windfall. "Synthosyn is the drug of choice for Unborns. There are a bunch of slang terms for it, but the most common is 'Syn. Probably the closest thing to heroin we have here, at least in terms of its effect on people. It's synthetic, as you probably guessed from the name. I have seen it but would never touch the stuff. It glows bright orange, believe it or not. Really catches your eye."

Sam considered the idea of a bright orange designer drug. In one respect, she could see how that might be appealing to some people; in a world that looked washed out and faded, it probably felt like consuming life itself. "Do people inject it?"

"Not exclusively," Gibson answered. "There are all sorts of ways to use it. Injection gets to the rush the fastest, but also rots people the fastest, from what I've seen."

"What do you mean, rots people?"

Gibson was quiet for a moment. "Think of a person as an ear of corn. I know this is a weird analogy, but it's the best I can come up with right now. Do you have any idea how late it is?" He chuckled. "So, you've got your corn, tough thick husk wrapping up the juicy bits. If a swarm of flies landed on the husk, they'd move around it, shit on it, whatever else flies do. But the corn on the inside is unaffected, right?" Sam nodded. "But, if instead of flies, a swarm of corn borers somehow found themselves on the husk, they'd burrow through it and get inside. They would dig in and eat the insides, but the husk itself would be more or less unaffected, unless you looked closely. There you are, shucking an ear of corn, but when you pull down the husk, it's soft, black, and rotten. Covered in bugs and larvae. 'Syn is like those corn borers. People who use it too much, their guts liquefy. Whole body collapses in a puddle."

Sam shivered. That seemed like a terrible way to die, even if you were already dead. "That's horrible. Why would anyone ever use it if they knew that's what could happen?"

Gibson surprised her by laughing. "Why do people smoke cigarettes, or drink booze? They know they could get cancer, or poison themselves. It's an escape. Some people just think they need to escape a little harder than others." There was a brief pause before he brought up the other subject Sam was curious about. "I don't know if Davis's story was true, about my old partner. In a way, that doesn't even matter. Like I said before, revenge won't bring Billy back." The silence fell again, heavier than before. The weight of the night blanketed the air. Their footsteps felt magnified in the dead silence.

Gibson spoke a few minutes later as he began climbing the small set of steps that led to the entrance of the apartment building. "Some people push 'Syn and get rich, never caring about the people who get addicted to it, never caring if they end their Unborn life, their second chance, as a bag of skin full of fluid. Ladislav Milovanović, better known as Old Man Ladi, is one of those people." His voice grew harder as his monologue continued. "That's why I'm going to take him down."

Sam had a couple of thoughts on that, but couldn't get them organized in her head. It felt like trying to snatch an eel out of a flowing river; she badly needed to sleep. Stumbling over the hem of her cloak and catching herself on the building's door frame, she mumbled, "Let's see what we can do. Tomorrow."

Chapter 8

In the days that followed, Gibson made preparations for the job, including contacting Harold, the ex-cop acquaintance. Gibson made it very clear to Sam that Harold was not a friend. "He was a good cop," Gibson told her on the third night, "but he became a dirty cop, and then an ex-cop. He's the worst kind of low-life: too caught up in his own self-interests to give a damn about anything beyond his own lust and greed." Gibson paused, smirked, and finished by saying, "Harold's basically a walking Deadly Sin."

While the time was busy for Gibson and he spent most of every day outside of the apartment, the days were increasingly dull for Sam. She found herself wandering around the apartment, thumbing through books, staring out the window, and feeling generally malcontent. She found Gibson's lockpicking tools, complete with a trio of locks that were clearly designed for practice. Fiddling with the locks quickly became a habit, and she had something of a natural skill at it. As the nub of the hook rubbed against a tumbler, Sam could visualize the inner mechanisms of the lock. It took her a number of hours to actually unlock the first one, but she felt a rush of satisfaction and accomplishment nevertheless.

Eventually Sam wandered around outside the apartment, exploring the building itself. The architecture changed dramatically every few floors, changing from straight narrow stone hallways on the lower levels to wide, modern drywall with close-cropped carpeting. Sam was surprised at how invigorated she was by her explorations, and even more surprised when she found a doorway to the roof. Curious, she pushed the door and propped it open with a broken chunk of stone that sat nearby.

Sam spent much of the next few days on the rooftop, staring out at the Fourth City, marveling at the scope of everything. Even as she looked over the city, she would be unconsciously fumbling with the tools from the lockpicking set. It had become somewhat of a nervous habit, a pastime to keep her hands doing something, but the time invested was helping her become acclimatized to the process, which made her only want to practice more. Staring out at the city, atop the hillock that was Kainer Heights, the view was simply spectacular.

An odd, uncomfortable thought occurred to her a few days after she had first discovered the rooftop retreat: what if she jumped? She had no inclination toward suicide, but the gaping maw of the Fourth City pulled at her from atop her watchtower, offering her weightlessness and discovery. Sam approached the ledge and peered down into the distant street below. Empty and calm, like a still pond on a late autumn day, the only sound coming from her hands where metal rubbed against metal, seeking yet another tumbler. She sat on the ledge, feet dangling into the void, and stared into the heart of the city. Hours passed, the faded sun of the world of the dead disappearing behind the towering skyscrapers of mankind's hubris, existing even in death, and still the question bubbled in the deepest recesses of her mind: what if she jumped? Sam had no answer. In the end, it was thoughts of her unknown husband and the life that she somehow left behind that veered her away from that line of thinking. She did not return to the rooftop the next day, or any day thereafter.

A week or so later, there was a knock on the door that startled both Sam, who was laying on the couch twirling a lock on her finger, and Gibson, who stood behind his desk, leaning imperiously over a scattered pile of documents. Sam moved quickly and quietly into the bedroom and closed the door almost all the way, leaving it cracked open enough to be able to hear without being seen. Gibson waited a few extra seconds, then opened the door and ushered Davis in, exclaiming in surprise when Davis handed over an envelope with another 400 dollars.

"I told you I just needed a few days," Davis said, a sense of pride in his voice. "And I have started telling some of the guys about my friend Chuck, who would be an excellent addition to the Family." Davis gave Gibson a little wink. "DiRazzo is Ladi's right-hand man. I am going to be one of the guards for him tomorrow night. Ladi's opening a new club, with DiRazzo as the manager. I'll try to put in a good word for you, Chuck."

"Don't seem too eager, Davis," Gibson warned. "I'm just an old friend, reliable and loyal, who needs to make a few bucks. Keep it simple."

Davis nodded impatiently. "Where's your ghoul?" he asked, rubbing at his bandaged hand and grimacing. Sam looked behind her, to the corner of the bedroom, where her phoenix mask and cloak were folded neatly on the dresser. Should she don the outfit and appear like an apparition? Although she grinned at the idea, she discarded it immediately.

"Don't worry about my business," Gibson snapped irritably. "Do your part and let me worry about mine. I need time to get ready." Davis gave Gibson a sorrowful look and left the apartment without another word. Sam waited until she finished a silent count to 10 before re-entering the main room. Gibson's face still held the lines of irritation on it when he looked at her, but it softened quickly.

"I still don't like this plan," Sam muttered. "It's an awfully big risk just for a little bit of money." She fidgeted with her fingers as she talked, wringing her hands and tapping her fingertips against each other.

The investigator didn't answer, and instead opened a small, flat bag that was on the table in front of him and pulled out two thin metal bars, one of which was curved at the end. "I noticed you've been using my lockpick set," he said with a knowing grin, "so I dug up this one from storage. You can keep mine. Have you made progress with it?"

Sam felt a little sheepish as she answered. She had tried to be careful, to put things back the way she found them, but hiding things from a private eye was challenging. "I've popped open all three of your locks a handful of times. I'm working on getting faster." Abruptly, she realized what he was doing, and fixed him with a stern gaze. "You're changing the subject. I still think what you're planning is too risky."

"I know you haven't been here long, Bloodwalker," he chided, "but a hundred thousand is more than just a little bit of money. I don't trust Davis any more than you do - less, I'm sure - but if he's even half-right, that's more money than I would make in five years." Gibson must have noticed the expression on her face because he paused and changed his approach. "It's a risk," he added in a placating voice, "but if I'm able to get revenge for my partner, take down a crime boss, and get paid very handsomely at the same time, it's a risk I have to take."

"I understand all of that," Sam said, anger creeping into her voice, "but that doesn't mean I have to like it or think it's a good idea." She paced the room irritably, and Gibson's silence set her on edge, her displeasure growing by the minute. Eventually she sighed and flopped dramatically onto the couch. "If you're going to insist on doing this incredibly STUPID thing, then at least let me help you. There are probably some places I can go more easily than you can, with my disguise. Or I can be a lookout or something. No one would know who I am. Hell, no one would probably even look in my direction." Gibson opened his mouth but Sam cut him off before he started. "And don't you say it's too dangerous for me, Mister Gibson."

"I would never," he replied, though his tone was one that said that was exactly what he was about to say. "The truth of the matter, Sam, is that I don't know the best way to approach this yet, so I don't have anything you can help me with." Her eyes flared with anger and he added a belated, "Yet."

Sam let out an irritated growl and stalked into the bedroom, emerging a few moments later wearing the phoenix cloak and mask. "I'm going out for a walk," she said, the words clipped. "I need some air." Gibson did not respond. Sam slammed the door as she left the apartment.

The earliest hints of dusk were settling into the dust-colored sky as Sam stepped out onto the sidewalk. Through her mask, she inhaled deeply. She could smell rain in the air. Small groups of people cluttered the sidewalk, but not enough to be considered crowded. Unsure of which direction to walk, Sam closed her eyes and spun on her heel. When she opened her eyes again, she was facing the apartment building she had just exited. Sam let out a small, sardonic laugh, and went left.

A few minutes' walk took her to a part of the city that was rundown and partially vacant, but not entirely unpleasant. A copse of sickly-looking trees grew here and there, creaking loudly with the gentlest breeze. Sam looked up as she passed underneath the branches of the first clump of trees, thinking their dry brown leaves looked like mud puddles on the dirt-road sky. She strode on.

A bell chimed in the distance behind her, coming from deeper into the city proper. It sounded again, and again, echoing off the buildings as if it were hunting. Sam hadn't considered churches in the afterlife and the thought of people who had already ended up in this dead purgatory trying to pray their way out of it made her immensely sad.

After half a mile or so, the road forked, and Sam went right, which took her up a steady incline. The buildings in this part of the city were more rustic and unkempt, spaced further apart. She noticed that every building had at least a few broken windows, and only sometimes was there a tarp or blanket hung up in the opening. Goosebumps popped up on her arms as Sam suddenly realized she was alone on the sidewalk, unsure of when she had left the other people behind. A deep, low rumble of thunder sounded from further up the hill. Sam craned her neck to look up in the sky and saw a dark, massive cloud emerging over the crown of the hill, billowing in the high-altitude winds. If she had any hope of not getting caught in the storm, she had to head back to the apartment right away, even if her anger at Gibson had not fully subsided.

Sam turned around and shrieked. Standing a few feet from her was a motionless figure, swathed in a stained brown cloak and fox mask. The figure did not react to her scream. Sam's memory flashed back to the story Gibson had told her about cloaks and masks, about people who were disfigured in their deaths often wore them out of shame or fear. Catching her breath, she stuttered out an apology. "I'm-I'm sorry I screamed," Sam began, "but I didn't know you were behind me. You startled me."

There was no response. The figure was short, no more than four feet tall. Her heart sank as she had the thought that this person maybe died as a child and was possibly alone in this world of the dead. She considered the fear she would have felt had that been her fate, and her heart ached for the poor child. Sam crouched, bringing her phoenix-covered face level with the fox-faced figure. "There's a storm coming," Sam said gently. "Do you have a place to go, some kind of shelter?"

The figure silently cocked its head to the right, like a dog trying to understand its master. Sam repeated herself but with more basic words. "Big storm," she told the figure, pointing at the black cloud. "Do you have a house?" Sam asked, pointing at the surrounding buildings. The fox figure straightened its head and lifted a gloved hand. It crooked an index finger, signaling Sam to follow. "Oh, um," Sam said awkwardly. "I have a place to stay already."

The figure bent its finger again, then turned toward one particularly battered-looking house. "That's your home?" Sam asked slowly. "Okay, go inside. I need to go back to my home now." As soon as Sam started to move down the sidewalk, the fox-faced figure stepped in front of her, blocking the path. It raised its hand and crooked its finger again. Sam looked around, and back up the hill at the encroaching clouds. "You want to show me your home?" The figure nodded. "Okay, just for a second," Sam said with a sigh, "then I need to go home."

The fox figure bounded up the dry, crackling patch of grass and around the back of the small house. Sam had to hurry to keep up. The child stood at the back door, waiting for Sam, crooking its finger rapidly before pulling the door open, moving aside to let her go in first. Sam took two steps inside and felt her stomach clench. The air was musty and smelled like rotting flesh. Flies buzzed angrily, creating a ceaseless insectile drone. A dirty table stood in the same room, but there were no other pieces of furniture Sam could see. Standing inside a broken, dust-covered door frame in front of her were four other cloaked figures, all exactly the same height, all wearing identical fox masks. Sam jumped when the door closed behind her as the first fox figure entered the house. The one behind her gave her a little push in the small of the back. Sam stumbled forward, barely keeping her balance from the unexpected shove. Apprehension growing, she tried to turn her body so she could see all five of the fox children at the same time.

"This is a very nice house you have," Sam said, trying to hide the tremor in her voice as she edged closer toward the door. "I'm glad you are all together as a family. I have to go now. Stay inside. Please. Big storm." A loud peal of thunder shook the fragile house as if to punctuate her words.

In eerie unison, the four foxes took a step closer to her. Sam couldn't see their legs move beneath their cloaks; it was as if they floated toward her. Sam took another step backward, jumping in surprise when she bumped into the fox figure she had met outside. "T-time for me to go," Sam stuttered, reaching behind herself with one hand as she tried to find the door handle.

Sam howled as she felt something sharp dig into her arm just above the wrist. She whipped her head around and gasped when she saw the fox mask grinning up at her, with warm, sticky blood trailing down the jawline. The eyes on the mask narrowed hungrily, and Sam realized it was not a fox mask, but the creature's actual face! Careful to avoid the fox's mouth, Sam pushed the tiny creature aside and tried to create separation. She needed to get out, and the four other foxes were quickly closing the gap. The fox that bit her lunged again. Sam moved out of the way and it smashed head first into the dilapidated wall. The other four snarled as its fellow pushed itself off the trash-strewn floor, effectively blocking her way for a moment.

Sam grabbed the door handle and twisted. As the door opened, all five of the foxes raced toward her, yipping loudly. She felt a tug at her cloak and searing pain a moment later as fangs sank deep into her calf. Sam kicked her foot wildly and sent the monster into two of the others, then dashed out the door as fast as she could.

Rain was pounding down now, soaking her cloak immediately, mixing with the blood from the pair of bite wounds. The crimson stream stood out like a neon sign in the faded world of the dead. Sam did not look back to see if the foxes followed, but had no doubts that if they wanted to, they could easily follow her trail. She ran down the hill, nearly losing her balance, until she reached the corner of North Kainer Heights. She pushed herself even as black spots appeared in her vision, running with adrenaline-fueled desperation. Panting and sweating, she finally looked back to make sure she hadn't been followed. Nothing moved up the winding roadway. Sam did what she could to stem the bleeding on her arm, but there was nothing she could do about her calf at the moment. She made her way back to Gibson's apartment building, thankful for the rain that would wash away her trail. She slammed her body into the wall next to the front door of the building, trying again to catch her breath. Sam took another look behind her: still no foxes, or anyone else on the street, but even in the blackness of the storm, she could see red droplets splashing onto the concrete beneath her feet.

Sam was grateful that both the lobby and the elevator were empty as she made her way up to the ninth floor and Gibson's apartment. She breathed deeply, trying to steady herself as she leaned against the cool metal wall, but she could feel the life draining out of her from the wounds, could feel herself becoming simultaneously dizzy and distant, even as she continued to apply pressure. The elevator shook to a stop, staggering her. After the elevator door opened with a muted chime, Sam took a handful of tottering steps toward the glass paneled door labeled L.W. Gibson. She took her left hand from her right wrist, which had been applying pressure to the wound, and fumbled for the doorknob. The black spots had multiplied, swimming through her vision, and Sam started to see double. Or maybe triple. The world spun, but she tried one last desperate time to open the door. Her hand met the glass, stuck for the briefest moment, then uselessly slid down as Sam dropped to the floor.

Night had fallen in Sam's mind, deep and heavy, black as gunpowder and as inescapable as midnight fog. Rain slammed into the windows, but Sam was unaware of any reality outside of her own head. In her mind, she wore a white dress in a dim, candlelit room. She was riding in the eyes of a ghost of a memory, the way a silhouette portrait can be drawn from a person's outline without capturing any of the details.

She sat on the edge of a bed and stared at a man facing away from her. He wore a black suit, and his shaggy brown hair swayed a little as he struggled with something she couldn't see. The man grunted with satisfaction as a cork popped free of its bottle. Sam heard the clink of glasses as he turned around, the champagne bottle in one hand and two elaborately worked wine glasses in the other. "Champagne, Samantha Nightshade?" he asked with a broad smile.

"Absolutely, Jackson Nightshade," she answered, returning his smile with one equally warm. The conscious part of her felt a rush of emotion at the words of the memory ghost but was powerless to do anything other than watch. Jackson came over to where she sat and bent down to hand her one of the glasses before kissing her deeply. She could faintly taste strawberries as her tongue swirled around his playfully. He gently pulled away and she sighed, relishing the kiss as he poured champagne, then half-filled his own glass before setting the bottle on a nearby table. They clinked glasses, kissed each other again, and made love for the first time as husband and wife. Both the Sam watching the memory and the Sam in the memory were content. When the memory fell asleep, the watcher awoke.

Sam opened her eyes and found herself flat on her back, staring at the ceiling of Gibson's apartment. She felt the tears rolling down her cheeks, the tightness in her throat, and she remembered her dream. Sam knew it was not just a dream, but a memory of her life before everything changed. She tried to push herself up and cried out, barely making a sound. She opened and closed her mouth several times, desperate to generate moisture. Lifting her right arm, she saw the tightly-wound bandages and watched as they slowly turned red. The blood acted like a trigger, and she remembered the foxes, and the painful, awkward running through the thunderstorm as her arm and calf left a crimson trail in her wake. She felt drained, physically and emotionally. Her husband, Jackson. Jack. She had dreamed of their wedding night. Sam's heart felt like it had shattered into a million pieces. Would she ever see Jack again? The tears sliding down her cheeks were like a mirror of the outside storm, which raged with a ferocity that made her wonder if there were tornados in this dead world.

Gibson must have heard Sam's gasping sobs because he rushed into the room moments later. She could tell by the look on his face that he had been worried about her, though he masked it well. Without saying a word, he helped her into a somewhat upright position before handing her a glass of water that was sitting on the end table. When he was sure she had the glass under control, he asked what had happened.

Sam tried to answer. She really did. She opened her mouth to tell him about the fox masks that were actually faces, about the house where she had been attacked. Instead, Sam sputtered. "It sh-shouldn't be like t-this." A dry cough, raw and angry, forced its way out of her, ripping at her throat. "Jack," Sam wheezed. "My hus-husband is Jack. I sh—shouldn't be here. I shouldn't be here!" Her vision blurred as the tears formed again. Angry and ashamed, she closed her eyes and turned her body away from the detective. But when Gibson's hand closed over her own, she cried harder.

"You're starting to remember, Bloodwalker," he said quietly. "I can't imagine how much that hurts, but it's a good thing. The more you remember about what happened before, the better chance you can get back to where you belong." Sam nodded without looking at him; she did not dare hope to return to her life, as badly as she wanted it. Caught in the clutches of lamentation, all the worst possibilities floated through her mind. She would never see Jack again, and he would never know what happened to her. There were still gigantic chasms in her memory. Did she have a child? That question, and her inability to answer it, doubled her misery.

Sam awoke sometime later, after the storm had finally quieted down. She had not realized she had cried herself to sleep, but the thin pillow was damp. Gibson was no longer in the room, for which she was grateful. The sadness in her heart still sat heavy, threatening to overwhelm her at any moment, but Sam was able to angrily push it down and force herself to focus on what needed to be done. She needed to live this Unborn life one moment at a time if she had any hope of returning to the world of the living, to Jack. She couldn't look toward the end; whatever needed doing, it was going to be a step by step process, and lying around sobbing wasn't going to get her anywhere.

Cognizant of the wounds on her wrist and leg, Sam carefully rose from the bed and hobbled toward the main room of the apartment. Gibson was sitting on the couch, fidgeting with his lockpick set again. He put down the bent metal pick when he saw her standing there in the doorframe. He smiled cautiously. "How are you feeling?"

She stumbled slightly, and Gibson was there in an instant to help her to a chair. Sam nodded her thanks. "I feel miserable," she answered, trying not to sound glum, "but there are things that need to be done, and I'm ready to get to work." Sam hesitated before adding, "I appreciate all the help you've given me, Gibson, but I don't belong here. I need to find a way to get back home."

Gibson nodded. "Of course you do, Sam. But first, tell me how it came to be that you ended up dripping blood in the hall." He reached down to the floor next to the couch and pulled up her phoenix cloak, which was torn in several places and had numerous dark, almost black stains. "Not only is this a mess, but the custodial staff are not going to be happy when they see that elevator." He waited for Sam's startled look before shooting her a wink and a grin. "I cleaned it up already. Wouldn't want them finding the blood of the living."

Sam let out a breath she hadn't realized she had been holding. Looking at the torn cloak, Sam started to explain. "I was angry at you for not letting me help you and wanted some fresh air, so I went for a walk. You saw me leave, wearing that." She gestured toward the cloak. "After a little while, I started going up this road. It went up the side of a hill, or a small mountain." Abruptly Gibson leaned forward, his eyes narrowed. His intensity caught Sam off guard.

"You went toward the peak?" Gibson asked in a clipped tone, his voice anxious.

Sam swallowed the lump that suddenly rose in her throat, then nodded. "You and I never went up the hill before, and I wanted to get away from you, so I went that way." The anxiety on Gibson's face was clear as day, but as much as she didn't want to tell him what happened, she knew she had to, so she pressed on. "There was no one around. The street was deserted, lots of boarded up houses and garbage. Broken windows. I made it part way up the hill before the storm clouds came across the peak, heading in my direction." Sam hesitated. "When I turned around, there was someone behind me. I thought it was a kid, wearing a mask. A fox mask."

Gibson sprung to his feet with a choked yelp. "Heaven above, Bloodwalker!" he exclaimed. "Your story is getting worse by the second. Why didn't you run?"

Sam gave him a flat look. "Why should I have run, Gibson? You told me sometimes people who have bad deformities from their deaths wore cloaks, which is why I would be able to wear one without attracting notice. When I saw what I thought was a little kid wearing a cloak and a fox mask, it made my heart hurt. Not only dying as a child, but having to hide forever? I felt so sorry for the little fox."

"What happened after that?" Gibson asked softly. "Did it attack you?"

"No. At least, not yet," Sam answered with a sigh. "I tried talking to it. It didn't speak to me, but it wanted me to follow it, so I did, thinking that..." Sam trailed off. "Looking back on it, I don't know what I was thinking. But I followed it into its house, and there were four other foxes in there. That's when I was attacked, and when I ran. Those fox masks weren't masks, Gibson. Those were their actual faces." Sam shivered at the memory.

Gibson shook his head, then rubbed at his eyes, but gave Sam a comforting smile. "You have no idea how lucky you are, Bloodwalker," he said. He shook his head again.

"What were those foxes?"

The smile evaporated from his face as if it had never been there. Gibson stood and paced the room. It was only five steps in either direction before he had to turn, and she watched him repeat his little loop half a dozen times before he spoke. "Have you ever heard of Dybbuks, Sam?"

"I don't think so, no," she answered, brows furrowed.

"Okay," Gibson began, taking on a professorial air even as he continued his laps. "A Dybbuk is an old Jewish concept. It's an evil ghost, like a mean trickster, that possesses people. You ever hear criminals say, 'The Devil made me do it'?" Sam nodded, still confused but starting to see where this was going. There was a hard pit forming in her stomach as Gibson continued. "Same idea. If someone is possessed by a Dybbuk, they act very strangely, sometimes speak in tongues or have a completely different personality, hallucinate and things like that. There are different beliefs about the origins – some people from the living world think Dybbuks are the souls of the dead that didn't move to the 'other side'," Gibson scoffed with amusement, "but at its core, it's a malicious spirit."

"You think the fox-faced kid was a Dybbuk?"

"It's hard to say without seeing it myself," Gibson answered carefully, "but I have heard from a number of sources about bad things happening in that part of the city, Sam. Plus, think about it. We're in the Land of the Dead here, the World of Spirits. Where else would a Dybbuk end up? Add in the stereotype of a trickster fox and maybe you see where I'm coming from. People much smarter than me have referred to Dybbuks on the peak, but I always figured they were being poetic or something."

Sam silently mulled it over. Jewish folklore was not something she knew anything about. "They didn't try to possess me, though," she said finally. "They attacked me. They bit me and clawed at me!" She held up her right wrist as evidence.

"You're in Dead World, remember?" Gibson answered quickly. "Even a Dybbuk would assume you're already dead. A spirit can't possess a spirit. Instead, they take a more direct approach. They devour the body, blood and all. When they tasted your red blood, filled with life and warmth, they would have known right away you were something new in this world."

"Could they have possessed me once they knew?" Sam asked, unable to keep the tremble from her voice. That thought horrified her more than she cared to admit. She scratched uneasily at her arm, thinking of the fox spirits living under her skin.

"My guess – and this is just a guess – is they were as surprised to find a Bloodwalker as you were to be attacked by Dybbuks. By the time they figured out what you are, you were long gone. They're supposedly manipulative and vicious, but not particularly smart. You're very lucky to be here, Sam." Gibson paused and cracked his knuckles. "Maybe it would be best for you to not go out alone anymore."

Sam grunted. She knew that was coming. "Absolutely not. You're in here fidgeting with that damn lock for hours on end and I have to sit here and wonder if I'm ever going to see my husband again?" Sam knew that was not exactly a fair thing to include, since Gibson had nothing to do with that, not to mention she herself enjoyed working with lockpicks, but she couldn't help it. "I can't sit here and wait forever. I need to find a way out." She emphasized the final word with a growl.

"Believe me, Sam," Gibson responded, gesturing in a calming manner, "I know you're frustrated. I can't even imagine how scared you must be. But I can't have you bleeding all over the city for everyone to see. If the wrong person finds you, you'll never get back; the cops will throw you in The Jar and throw away the key."

Sam blinked. The Jar. When she had first met Gibson, he had said something about The Jar, and she had forgotten all about it. "What's The Jar?" she asked. Idly, Sam wondered if Gibson had mentioned it to try to deflect away from the topic of her going out by herself.

Gibson laughed. "You know, sometimes I forget just how little you know about this place." Sam's expression made him laugh again. "Nothing personal," he added. "The Jar is a prison, basically. It's a giant, round tower, and there's only one way in or out. Because of the shape and the single exit point, it got the nickname The Jar. There are some people who think it's part prison, part research laboratory, but no one really knows for sure. The guards are," Gibson hesitated, searching for the right word, "abnormal. Unique, let's say. At least, according to rumors."

"Abnormal?" Sam raised a questioning eyebrow.

"Think of it this way, Sam," Gibson continued, "you live a full life, work as a prison guard, maybe have a family and a white picket fence and a dog, and then you die and show up here as an Unborn. You probably fall back into what you've always done, so back to guarding a prison. One thing about this Unborn life," Gibson put a healthy dose of scorn into the last word, "is that not everyone can handle it. There are a lot of people out there who expected that when they died, they'd finally have some peace. Gates made of pearl and all that. Instead, they're dropped into a world that for most everyone is an eternal slum. Some people crack, lose their minds. Some people lost them while they were still alive. Every serial killer, every rapist, every child predator, they all end up here, and that prison guard is locked inside The Jar with them every single day. Makes you wonder if the system is set up so the guards guard the prisoners, and vice versa. Keep everyone involved in that sordid side of life locked away. That's enough to change almost anyone in the best circumstances, and The Jar is far from the best circumstances, according to rumor." Gibson paused, letting Sam process what he had said, and perhaps to add a touch of drama, before finishing. "You see, Sam, the guards, they don't ever come out."

Sam scrunched her face in confusion. "What do you mean they never come out? That doesn't make any sense. How are there rumors about a place when no one comes out?"

"Good question," Gibson said with a smile. "Some people have been here for centuries. Millennia. To hear some of those people tell it, The Jar wasn't like that at first. Guards would work shifts, leave, and go home. I've even heard stories about the prisoners being let out to exercise in the fenced-in yard. As time passed, though, The Jar filled up with the worst mankind had to offer. As The Jar filled, the prisoners began to change. And the guards. About 200 years ago, a handful of guards released some prisoners back into the city. They went on a rampage, killing indiscriminately, until the prisoners and guards were all killed. Obviously, I wasn't here at the time, but I've heard more than a few times that they were insane with rage. The stories say some of the guards attacked innocents with their teeth, taking bites out of people. Don't know that I believe that part; just sharing the rumors."

Sam shuddered, thinking about a sudden onslaught of maniacs ravaging a city. "That's horrible," Sam murmured softly. "It hasn't happened again, though, right? Did anything change to keep it from happening again?"

"There were some announcements and laws passed down from the Fourth City regional government to try to regain control over The Jar. They also increased the size of the police force – you remember Gunnarsson, the cop who snatched you, I'm sure," Gibson said with a wink. "He was one of the ones who were brought in after that incident. Nothing quite like hiring a handful of Vikings to restore law and order," Gibson finished sarcastically.

"Enough of that, though," Gibson continued. "Davis told me about a building he thinks is part of Old Man Ladi's organization, and it's not too far from here. I am going to go check it out myself tomorrow. Do a little bit of daylight recon. And you, Miss Invincible High and Mighty

Bloodwalker, are staying here, in the apartment, and resting. Your encounter with the Dybbuks was more than enough excitement for the both of us."

Just under 24 hours later, concealed in her cloak and mask, Sam sat on a stoop and waited. She was in a place called Midway, an aptly named district in the city as it was roughly halfway between the outskirts where she had encountered the Dybbuk clan and the enormous skyscrapers that towered over the rest of the city like a spike. The concrete was warm beneath her, and the sunlight, tepid though it was, added to the heat. Beneath the mask, she was already dripping sweat, and she had only been on the stoop for a few minutes. Still, she got what she asked for.

"You keep telling me how much I'll stand out as a ghoul," Sam had said to Gibson, unable to keep a tinge of satisfaction from her voice as she closed in on what she knew would be the checkmate of her argument, "but everyone averts their eyes from ghouls. In the disguise, I might as well not even exist in this world. Let me help you, at least as your lookout!" Gibson grimaced. It had taken a bit more convincing before Gibson finally relented, but in that moment, she knew that she had won.

Now she sat in broad daylight, a pair of empty glass bottles hidden under her cloak, waiting for Gibson to make his arrival. She agreed with his assessment that their plan would work much better if she got to the lookout first. Even just sitting on the stoop was enough to make the entire building vanish, for all intents and purposes. It was remarkably handy to be able to make people so profoundly uncomfortable with no real effort, especially when one was performing actions that were of rather questionable legal authority. Which was to say, illegal by any definition of the word.

Another few minutes passed before Gibson made his arrival, sauntering down the sidewalk on the opposite side of the road in a way that made Sam think of a particularly proud peacock. He walked like he owned the place, which was exactly the point; much like how Sam's cloak made her practically invisible, Gibson's swagger was enough to make most people not question his presence. Still, a reconnaissance mission such as this required a lookout, and that's where Sam and the glass bottles came in.

As she watched, sweat from her palms making the glass slick in her grip, Gibson moved confidently up to a double door at the front of a squat building and tried the handle. Sam was unsurprised when the door failed to open. She saw the private eye reach into an inside pocket of his coat and pull a familiar case free: his lockpick set. Keeping himself upright, he began working the metal probes into the lock. Even from a distance, he looked like a man fiddling with a key that wouldn't quite turn; certainly not someone to draw a second glance. Despite herself, Sam had to give the detective some silent praise for his convincing acting. If she hadn't known what he was doing, she wouldn't have paid him any attention either.

With a start, Sam realized she had stopped paying attention to the sidewalks and the people on them. She had scant descriptions of "people to watch out for" as Gibson had put it, but neither the "narrow blond man with a scar on his right cheek" nor the "dark-haired refrigerator on legs" were in sight. She let out a sigh of relief. Gibson straightened slightly and nimbly tucked the case back into his overcoat. With a little hop of delight, Gibson twisted the handle and pulled the door open just enough to poke his head through for a moment. He threw up two fingers on his left hand, signaling he was going inside, and slipped into the darkness beyond the door.

Gibson hadn't been clear on what he expected to find in the building, other than a few rumors he had shared with Sam that indicated that the building was somehow tied to Old Man Ladi's illicit dealings, possibly acting as storage. Sam took the lack of sudden gunfire to indicate Gibson was still undetected within the building. Now that he had gone inside, however, she found the pair of glass bottles to be profoundly worthless. Their plan had been that if she spotted someone suspicious approaching the building while Gibson was at the door, she was going to throw one of the bottles against the brick wall. The noise would signal to Gibson that he should expect company. For his part, Gibson would then pretend to be completely intoxicated and simply confused about what door he was trying to enter. It was a risky plan, especially with his concurrent scheming to become one of Old Man Ladi's employees, but he insisted they needed reliable intelligence and not to simply take Davis's word for it.

A few silent minutes passed in the balmy sunlight, though it was warm enough to make Sam feel as if she were being slowly boiled in her own juices. Abruptly there was movement at a second-floor window, and Sam spotted Gibson's face, a jaunty smirk plastered upon it, as he gave a cheery wave before disappearing into the darkness. She shook her head ruefully. Whatever ill luck had cursed her to be dragged to this dead world had also stuck her with a well-meaning, highly-intelligent, and downright silly clown of a detective. Despite herself, she smiled behind the phoenix mask.

A few seconds later, a different face peered out the window, and Sam's blood went cold. It was impossible to pick up many details from across the street, but the thin-jawed face definitely had blond hair coming down the sides of it. The "narrow man", as Gibson had described him, was not only in the building, but he was plainly trailing Gibson, and she had no way of letting the detective know of the imminent danger he was in. Her mind raced, trying to formulate a plan. Her first thought was to run across the street and try to get in the front door herself. She had snuck her lockpick case on this mission, despite Gibson's insistence that it was not necessary. Once inside, though, would she be able to find her way upstairs in time without getting caught herself? Unlikely.

Her next idea was shaky, but there was no time to waste. Sam looked down the road in both directions, making sure the walking refrigerator of a man was nowhere to be seen, then scurried across the street, trying to make mental calculations as she moved. Stopping half a dozen paces from the building, she looked up at the window where first Gibson and then the narrow man appeared, cocked her arm back, and hurled the first of the glass bottles up at it as hard as she could. The end result was pathetic, as the sweat from her hand caused the bottle to slip free prematurely, shattering against a rafter beam only a few feet in front of her.

Sam cursed under her breath and frantically wiped her hand on her pant leg. She only had one more shot at this. Taking quick but careful aim, she flung the second bottle skyward and smiled with satisfaction as she scored a direct hit, causing not only the bottle, but also the window, to shatter in an explosion of noise. Even as the glass rained down from above, Sam began scanning the sidewalk for anything else she could throw at the building, or possibly defend herself with if it came to it. A small chunk of rock, clearly broken off of the wall, caught her eye. It wouldn't work well as a blunt instrument, but it was jagged enough that she would be able to puncture flesh with enough force. She clutched it in her left hand, hiding it inside the copious sleeve of the phoenix cloak.

Makeshift weapon in hand, Sam then rushed toward the door where Gibson had slipped through and tried the handle. Locked, as expected. Her heart was racing but she needed to clear her head and think. Would it make sense to beat on the door, dressed as she was, the cloak sticking uncomfortably to her skin in multiple places due to her sweat, and try to cause further distraction? She took a deep breath, lifted her head toward the perpetually grey sky, and shrieked. Sam was a ghoul, at least by disguise, and therefore eyes would slide away from her like eggs on a greased skillet. But if she intentionally drew attention toward herself, what would be the end result? As for the smattering of people on the street, she didn't care; but as for the blond man in the building, if she could distract him from his pursuit of Gibson...

Sam shrieked again and again, trying to make as much of a racket as possible. She slipped the stone into her back pocket and repeatedly kicked at a metal railing until she knocked it loose from the concrete in which it had been set, all the while screaming, shredding her throat.

The door to the building opened and a dark-haired man emerged from the shadows. Sam saw him out of the corner of her eye as she continued to kick at the railing. In the back of her mind, she had the rather insane thought that if she broke the railing completely free, she could wield it as a club. What she really wanted was Gibson to get his ass outside and away from this place before he got hurt.

The dark-haired man moved closer, clearly apprehensive about approaching what he undoubtedly suspected was a deranged ghoul. The door to the building, she noticed, was still ajar. When the man moved one step closer, Sam acted on pure impulse. She suddenly shifted her body weight, turning toward the dark-haired man. He gasped in surprise, then grunted in pain as her kick connected with his knee cap. With him hobbled and bent over, she pushed him hard in the back, sending him sprawling toward the ground, his forehead cracking noisily against the railing. Her legs carried her toward the open door even as she processed the violence she had committed on the man, a sense of dread billowing in her midsection. She hoped she hadn't killed him with her impulsivity. Sam glanced at the heap of a man and let out a relieved sigh as she saw his back rise and fall with the rhythm of breathing.

Now that she was in the doorway to the building, however, Sam wasn't sure what to do. She didn't want to enter and get lost, or possibly stumble into the blond man she was sure was hunting Gibson. The room on the other side of the doorway was large and carpeted, but the carpet was stained in several spots with what looked like oil, or perhaps blood. A wooden shelf of small cubbies half-filled the wall to the right, each cubby had a tag underneath it that made Sam think of mail slots. To the left was a set of stairs that led up, and on the opposite wall was a large double door. Perhaps this building held offices for Old Man Ladi's high-ranking gang members? The idea of a gang giving its officers private spaces in a single building seemed odd to her, but so much of this world was odd. Sam checked the door knob from the inside and found that it turned easily: a one-way lock. She was concerned about the heap of a man she had left outside waking up and taking her by surprise, but there was no time to waste. Sam stepped into the room and closed the door behind her with a loud click.

Sam was very curious about what was beyond the huge door in front of her, but she shoved the thought away as ruthlessly as she had shoved the man to the ground. Mind racing, she moved toward the cubbies and felt a small spark of satisfaction when she saw she was correct in assuming they acted as mail slots. Her eyes scanned the names and she tried to memorize as much as she could, thinking every piece of information could be useful in Gibson's mad operation. She also swiped every piece of paper she could get her hands on, stuffing them into the waistband of her blue jeans. This was not what she was here for, she reminded herself.

Even in her frantic mental state, Sam knew going upstairs was a bad idea. So was opening the door and seeing what was beyond. If there were more guards or employees on the other side of that door, she would be in a lot of trouble. She suddenly wished she had followed through and kicked the handrail free of the cement; at least then, she could have shoved it through the handles of the double doors and prevented them from opening. Sam felt the time slipping away, so with no other feasible options coming to mind, she took a deep breath and shrieked again. There was a chance Gibson hadn't heard it from outside, but being able to face the stairs and scream directly at them might make the sound waves carry differently, might help him hear. There was a sense of logic to the thought, regardless of scientific truth. It felt like the right thing to do, so she screamed a second time, a third, a fourth, felt the tearing at her throat and larynx. After the fourth scream, she heard what could only be footsteps above her head. She scraped out a fifth shriek, just to be sure, and bolted out the front door, slamming it hard behind her.

The dark-haired man she had kicked was just now rising up, unsteady on his damaged leg. Sam pulled the rock out of her pocket and used the blunt side to crack him in the back of the head, sending him sprawling back to the concrete. She really needed to get out of here before it got completely out of control, if it wasn't already.

Just as she was contemplating what to do next, the door burst open and Gibson came stumbling out, a panicked look in his eyes. "Run!" he barked before leaping from the landing down to the sidewalk. Sam didn't hesitate, though Gibson's longer legs kept her from catching up. Half a block away from the building, he turned right down a side street, then quickly crossed the road and down an alley. Sam was a few seconds behind him, and as she reached the alley, she saw Gibson leap and grab the bottom rung of a fire escape ladder.

Sam ran forward and climbed the ladder the best she could with her sweaty palms and sweatier cloak. Gibson followed as soon as she was clear of the ladder. "Keep going!" he rasped, and she did without hesitation. When she reached the third floor of the fire escape, Gibson finally said, "Okay, okay, stop." He was doubled over, sucking wind, leaning on the railing. A few moments passed before he lowered himself to the landing, sitting with his feet on the step below. Sam glanced around to make sure no one was around before pulling her mask free, exposing her face to the world as she began wiping the sweat off her forehead with the sleeve of the cloak.

"That –" Gibson began, still breathing heavily, "that did not go the way I had planned." Sam stared at the investigator, waiting for him to say more, but he didn't. She let the silence stretch as she tried to cool down, going so far as to remove her cloak, an action that surprisingly did not get a response from Gibson. Leaning on the cool metal railing of the fire escape, looking down the alley toward the street, Sam could almost pretend she wasn't trapped in Purgatory. It all seemed so peaceful and downright ordinary. She realized with a start that she was deliberately distracting herself from reflecting on her violent actions outside of the building Gibson had infiltrated, the way she pummeled the man who had come to confront her without thought. She didn't know if he had been a threat, but she treated him as one, surprising herself with her ferocity.

"Was it worth it?" Sam surprised herself by speaking the thought aloud. She was wondering if her violence had been necessary or appropriate, and with a rising feeling of bile in her chest, was coming to the conclusion that it had not been. Gibson took the question as one directed toward him.

"It was pretty dicey in there, but yeah, I'd say it was worth it."

She turned to look at him and caught his eye, which had regained some of its customary twinkle as he reached into his coat pocket and pulled out several carefully folded papers, now crumpled from the frantic escape. "Shipping manifests, Sam," he said, handing her one of the pages. "Documents that confirm that not only is that building part of Ladi's operation, but that they're prepping to transfer a massive shipment of Synthosyn from their warehouse to a nightclub downtown. Makes perfect sense, right? Couldn't be an easier way to sell that poison than to offer it up next to a cocktail."

Sam looked over the manifest and was surprised by how brazen it was; everything was labelled in plain language. No code words, no need for interpretation. It was as straightforward as shipping crates of carrots to a restaurant. "I don't know what any of this stuff is," Sam said, pulling out the papers she had swiped from the mailbox cubbies, "but I figured I might as well take what I could."

Gibson's eyebrows rose as the double-handful of paperwork came out into the open. "Where did you get all of this?" he asked as he smoothed out the top sheet. Sam explained as he read through page after page. He was so engrossed in his reading that he didn't admonish her for straying from their plan when she decided to enter the building herself.

"Oh!" Gibson exclaimed. "This is interesting." He handed one of the papers back to her and she looked down at it, forehead wrinkling as she read.

"What's this? Looks like a Human Resources form or something. Used for potential new hires?"

"That's exactly what it is, Sam," Gibson replied. "It's for me, for the job Davis and I are working on."

With a start, Sam looked at the top of the page where, next to the rather ominous wording "Potential Asset" was the name Frank Peters. It was a name she remembered from a conversation between the two men, a pseudonym for Gibson's attempt to infiltrate Ladi's organization. She read over the notes, which indicated that "Frank Peters" was recommended for employment by Byron Davis, a member of the "Product Security Team" and that Mr. Peters had something of a criminal record, though mild compared to the things Old Man Ladi had been accused of. Written at an angle on the side was "Davis is reliable" with a signature Sam couldn't decipher.

"Looks like my odds of getting hired are pretty decent, Sam," Gibson said with a grin, which quickly faded as his jaw tightened. "I will bring that bastard down." The quiet determination in his voice sent a chill running up Sam's arms.

"Did the blond guy see your face?" Sam asked. She had been more concerned with their immediate safety, but now that the threat had passed, she realized just how much of a risk Gibson had taken. "Is he going to be a problem? I saw you in the window, but then he looked out the window a few seconds after you left, as if trying to see who or what you were looking at. Even from a distance, that man looks like trouble."

Gibson shook his head. "It was pretty dark inside. Lots of weird shadows and turns. If he saw me, it was only the back of my head. I heard him coming when I was waving to you from the window and moved away. I was able to get down a hallway and hide behind a desk. After he went by, I heard the window break – I assume that was you? – and he went rushing by me again. Then he thumped down the stairs and I heard some heavy door slam shut."

"I saw that door," Sam said weakly, thinking about how close she had come to trying to open it. It was all too easy to picture herself opening the door and coming face to face with the blond man. She had no doubts that the tiny chunk of rock she had been prepared to use for self-defense would have proved wholly ineffective. Not for the first time, Sam wondered what would happen to her if she died in this place.

Gibson must have noticed something in her expression because he gently placed his hand on top of hers. Looking up at her, he gave Sam a small smile. "I think we've had enough adventure for today," he said. "Let's head back to the apartment. We need to get ready for the meeting with Harold tomorrow. If you still feel up for going, that is."

Sam nodded and started pulling her cloak back on. "I'm going with you to meet him. After the Dybbuks on the hill, a little thing like today's chase isn't going to stop me."

They waited on the fire escape for another twenty minutes, just to be sure there weren't people searching for them, but no one so much as walked by the alley. Gibson descended first, poking his head around the corner as a final precaution. A moment later, he motioned for Sam to climb down the stairs and join him.

Their return to Gibson's apartment building was largely silent, with each of them lost in their own thoughts, replaying the events of the day. The night was at its deepest, most desolate hour by the time as the entrance came into sight. Gibson broke the silence. "I assume there's no way to talk you out of going to meet Harold, Bloodwalker?" Sam shook her head immediately, instinctively and unnecessarily pulling her sleeves longer to cover up the bite wound from the Dybbuk. Gibson sighed. "He wants to meet at a club called Alley Cats." Sam raised a questioning eyebrow, and Gibson sighed again. "It's a burlesque kind of joint." Belatedly, he added, "Harold's a bit of a sleaze."

After a shower and a chance to unenthusiastically pick at a bit of dinner, Sam crashed on her bed and fell into a deep sleep. She slept late, awakening to the sound of Gibson tooling around with his lockpick set. As the afternoon fell into dusk, Sam donned the phoenix mask and cloak once again. Having already repaired her cloak from the encounter with the Dybbuks, she begrudgingly had stitched up new rips from the adventure the day before and had carefully scraped the dried blood and dirt from the cloak as best she could. Between the Dybbuks and the building linked to Old Man Ladi's operation, her phoenix garb had been through a lot lately.

Gibson waited for her in the living room, leaning against the wall and wearing the same trench coat he had on when they first met at the police station. His black hair was mostly hidden by a large, flat-brimmed hat, and what wasn't hidden was bristling out from beneath the hat like two-day old stubble. As they stepped into the hallway, Gibson shut the door behind them. "We'll need to take the subway downtown. Stay close."

Chapter 9

The metal-grated steps that led down to the subway reverberated with each of Sam's footfalls despite her efforts to move as softly as possible. When she wore this disguise, she liked to think of herself as a phantom, no more than a human-shaped wisp in the night, but the metal stairs broke the illusion with each step. A bank of fluorescent lights flickered at the bottom of the stairwell, casting the walls in a sickly yellow light that made Sam think about abandoned mental hospitals in horror movies. The walls were covered in graffiti: sometimes words, sometimes images, but none of it pleasant. Sam shivered beneath her cloak. "I had been wondering why there were no cars or buses here," she said softly, trying to distract herself from images of asylums. "I've only seen people walking."

Gibson grunted. "There are cars, but only for the super-rich, and that type almost all live downtown. Only a few live outside the Fourth City limits. Where you got picked up by Gunnarsson is miles from downtown. My apartment is even further. Sometimes it helps to be more remote, even if it's not exactly convenient for business trips like this. Out of sight, out of mind can be a useful thing for a private detective."

As they descended, Sam nearly gagged at the unmistakable smell of wet rodents. Her nose itched with the desire to sneeze, and she longed to squeeze her nostrils shut between her fingers, but it was impossible while wearing the phoenix mask, and removing the mask was not an option. It was disgusting, but breathing through her mouth helped cut the stench, at least a little, though the air on her tongue made her want to vomit. "Does it smell better on the subway?" Sam asked in a whisper.

"Eventually. But enough of that. We need to focus. There are worse things down here than the smell." He squeezed Sam's gloved hand reassuringly. "Just stay close."

They reached the bottom of the stairs and followed the path to the left, toward the subway platform. Many of the tiles were missing from the decrepit walls, and those that remained were covered in mold and grime so thick Sam couldn't see the original color. Sam heard the faint echoing machinations of a subway car in the distance, the telltale click-clack of the wheels on the rails making her think of bones in a divination bag, rattling before being cast and analyzed by macabre fortune tellers. *Clearly the subway station is doing wonders for my imagination,* she thought with more than a touch of chagrin.

Sam's eyes swept over the subway landing from left to right. The walls were tattered at best, the vacant spots colored with ancient black adhesive. Pushed against the walls were a handful of mismatched benches, all of them missing at least a few wooden slats, and one missing so many it could hardly classify as a bench. Sitting on the bench was a dark, unmoving shape: a man with long, flowing black hair, wearing a long, flowing black coat, which trailed onto the floor. She could not see his face. The coat matched his hair perfectly, so much so it was hard to tell where hair ended and coat began. Between Sam and the man was a rusted trash can, and in front of him were a few tiled pillars in as much disrepair as the walls.

Further to the right sat an oblong metal box, its body a reflective silver. A short, skittish-looking woman wearing a brown skirt smudged with grease leaned against it. A few feet away from her stood a dark, unmoving shape: a man with long, flowing black hair, wearing a long, flowing black coat, which trailed onto the floor. She could not see his face. Next to him were the tracks, with a faded yellow paint strip marking the edge of the safe zone for people to stand while waiting for the subway to arrive.

Sam's eyes shot back toward the man in black and a cold shiver gripped her spine. She had an intense feeling of déjà vu. Had she seen this man before? For some reason her eyes moved quickly toward the benches, which stood empty, then back at the man by the tracks. What man? There was no one there. Sam gave her head a little shake. She was seeing things.

Sam realized Gibson had stopped next to her and was looking at her with a puzzled expression on his face. "You all right, Sam?" he murmured. "You stopped walking."

Sam was about to nod her head when she saw a dark, unmoving shape: a man with long, flowing black hair, wearing a long, flowing black coat, which trailed onto the floor. He stood with his back to her, between two support beams. There was something about him that made her stomach clench in fear. He looked familiar, but she had no idea where she had seen him before. Sam stared at the black figure as she answered Gibson. "There's a man over there, near the pillar," she whispered. "Long black coat, can't see his face." Sam hesitated, then added uncertainly, "I-I think he keeps moving every time I look away. Do you see him?"

"Yes, I see him." Gibson answered quietly. There was uneasiness in his voice, which made goosebumps pop out all over Sam's body. "How sure are you that he's moving when you look elsewhere?"

"Almost certain," she answered breathlessly. "What is he?" The subway rattles were closing in quickly. It was hard to tell with the echoing in the tunnel, but Sam thought it should be at their platform in less than a minute.

Taking her hand, Gibson said, "Just keep your eyes on him and let me guide you. He won't get on the train. Stay close to me and keep your eyes on him."

"Wh-what is he?" Sam repeated, her voice unsteady. The man in the black coat stood stock-still. Before Gibson could answer, Sam gasped and looked right. There had been a woman on the platform, short and squirrelly. Sam remembered her clearly and wanted to warn her, somehow. The woman was gone. Where had she gone? Wait. Warn her of what? Sam's brain hurt. Why was Gibson holding her hand? She pulled her hand free, which made him look over his shoulder at her.

"Sam!" he hissed. "You were supposed to..." Gibson trailed off. Why was he angry at her? Where had the short woman gone? Sam would have seen her walk past, and the subway still had not pulled up to the platform. The place the woman had been standing was now empty, save for a man with long, flowing black hair, wearing a long, flowing black coat, which trailed onto the floor. She could not see his face.

"Gibson," Sam said uneasily. Something was very, very wrong. Sam fumbled blindly for the investigator's hand but couldn't find it. She shot a quick look in his direction to find his hand, then looked back up. A pale, eyeless face was practically pressed up against her own. Sam shrieked like a banshee, the sound echoing off the subway terminal walls. Its mouth was a gaping maw full of teeth, protruding like needles. A repulsive stench emanated from the creature's mouth, making Sam gag. A thick clear liquid streamed slowly between those teeth, and its greasy black hair did nothing to hide the horrible features of this monster. Its claw-like hands were mere inches from the sides of her head. Each hand only had four fingers, but the nails on them were like talons, and they shone in the flickering fluorescent lights. She screamed again, and again, and again; her heart felt ready to burst out of her chest. Sam opened her mouth to shriek again, but stopped herself as she realized the creature was not moving and had not since she saw it in front of her face. Experimentally, she took a step backward, making sure to keep her eyes locked onto where this monster's eyes should have been. It did not move.

"DON'T LOOK AWAY!" Gibson bellowed over her screams. Everything happened so quickly. "I'm going to put my hand on your shoulder, Sam," Gibson said, forcing calm into his voice. "We are both going to stare at it and get on the train. Do not look away, not even for a second." The subway car came to a squealing halt to their right. "Keep looking at it, Sam. I know it's horrible, but force yourself to remember every detail. I'll guide us to the subway."

Sam stumbled sideways awkwardly, but she never broke eye contact with the shrouded figure. She felt her cloak swirl slightly as the air from underneath the subway car pushed up through the narrow gap between itself and the platform as she crossed the threshold. The figure had not moved, thankfully. Sam kept staring at it as the doors of the subway closed in front of her face, the soft whisking sound a sharp counterpoint to her pulse, which battered a rapid drum beat in her ears. Her eyes followed the figure as the train slowly clattered into the poorly-lit tunnel that stretched out in front of them.

When the black-shrouded monster finally disappeared from sight, Sam let out a breath that felt like she had been holding for days. "You okay?" Gibson asked, his voice tinged with surprise. "You look worn out. Too much exercise for you?" His tone carried a playful teasing, but Sam picked up on a hint of concern, as well.

"What was that thing?" Sam asked angrily, voice quivering. "How can you sound so relaxed? Whatever it was, it almost..." She trailed off when she noticed the confusion on his face. "You don't remember it, do you?" Sam said wonderingly. "It's like it makes you forget it's there." If Gibson didn't look washed out already, Sam would have said he looked suddenly sick to his stomach. "A man in a black coat," Sam said wearily, "not moving whenever you look at him, but the second you look away you begin to forget about him."

"Him," she added with a scowl. "I keep calling it him. I don't know if it was a man, or a monster, or something else." Gibson's complexion twisted to a color even more obviously ill. "You told me to remember every detail. I do. I remember how I looked away from it for a split second, and when I looked back, it was an inch from my face. My face!" Sam realized she was shouting and looked around the subway car self-consciously. Thankfully, it was empty, but she took a deep breath to regain control of herself before continuing anyway. "What was it, Gibson?"

The color, such as it was, was slowly returning to Gibson's face. "On my bookshelf at home," Gibson began slowly, "there is a book. A sort of encyclopedia, you might say. It's rather unorganized, basically a list of strange things people have seen and experienced in this world." Gibson made a sweeping gesture with his right hand. "Most of it is unsubstantiated, but in a lot of ways, this entire existence is unsubstantiated." He essayed a smile and a chuckle, but when Sam continued to give him a hard stare through the eyeholes of the mask, he let both die.

"As for the thing you say you saw, and what I probably saw as well, it has been given many names, but the most common is Void Hunter," Gibson continued, dropping the levity completely. "It's a very rare creature. Well, maybe. Probably. It's hard to say for sure since it forces you to forget it if it doesn't kill you. The story in the book in my apartment, if you think it's reliable, is that three curious scientists – biologists, I suppose – decided to travel the world of the dead and catalog all of the rare or unique beings they encountered."

The subway car churned around a corner in the dimly-lit tunnel, the rocking of the floor beating an uneven counterpoint to Gibson's words. Sam felt tight with nervous energy. She did not regret going on this trip to meet Harold, but she was anxious to get it over with and to get back to the relative safety of Gibson's rundown apartment building. That realization surprised her, but it reinforced the level of terror she still felt at facing that horrifying monster.

"Why do they call it that?" Sam asked hesitantly, trying to regain her composure. "Will it still be there when we get back?" She forced herself not to start massaging the skin between her thumb and index finger on her left hand with her right – an old nervous habit.

Gibson looked side to side, as if to reassure himself they were alone in the subway car. "The thing to remember, Sam, is these are all just stories," he said. "Void Hunter is just a name some scientist made up. Hell, it might have been some kid who made it up, or the whole story could be made up." Sam nodded, anxious for him to get to the point.

"So the story," he continued carefully, "is that these three scientists were wandering around, talking to each other and they encountered something like what you saw. What we saw. It wasn't until the first scientist..." Gibson trailed off for a moment as he searched for the right word, "disappeared, let's say, that the other two were able to fix the Void Hunter in their mind and kept it in constant eye contact. The two remaining scientists thought it was not really a part of this world, but something in between this and the living world, or maybe this world and whatever happens if you die in this world. They said it existed between worlds, which is how it moves so quickly and why it's so easy to forget about it."

Sam tried to digest all this information. Her pulse beat rapidly, red hot at her temple as the last vestiges of fear and adrenaline gripped her heart in an icy chill, her body at war with itself as to how to physiologically react. She pulled her hands apart with a frustrated sound and wondered at what point in Gibson's story she had begun massaging the soft flesh of her left hand. "Will it still be at the subway station?" Sam asked again.

There was a long moment of silence, broken only by the screeching of subway brakes as it slowed down at another platform, preparing to pick up any passengers heading toward the downtown district. Three wild-haired youths boarded, the obnoxiousness of their appearance bested only by the obnoxiousness of their attitudes. They went to the far end of the subway car and began making loud, rude noises, then guffawing in a way that reminded Sam of braying donkeys. Gibson stared into her eyes; Sam felt like he was seeing through her phoenix mask and knew he was wondering what to say, wondering if he should have forced her to stay at the apartment. She did not give him a chance to voice that opinion.

"So, what other options do we have to get back if there's a chance the Void Hunter will be at the platform?" Sam asked brusquely, infusing her tone with as much solid confidence as she could muster. "I'd really prefer not to walk," she added, smiling slightly behind her mask. The smile faded as she heard another round of abrasive cackling from the three youths at the far end of the car.

"My subway stop should be safe," Gibson answered quietly, "but we'll get off the car one stop early, to be sure. It's not too far to walk." The conversation lulled as both of them fell into their own thoughts. Sam became lost in the rhythm of the subway car, the way the dim blue lights on the tunnel walls refracted in a steady tempo off the scratched metallic walls inside of it. She found herself thinking about her husband, wondering what he was doing at that moment, and she felt any remainder of positivity sink out from under her. Sam's memory of Jack was so dim and spotty; it felt like she was trying to read a book that had almost all of the pages torn out of the binding, but she pored obsessively over the pages that remained.

The subway squealed to another stop, but no one got on at this station. Reflexively, Sam stared out onto the platform landing to be sure that no featureless man in a long black coat stood there, waiting for her. This platform was in markedly better condition than the one from which she and Gibson had boarded; there was only one burned out bulb in the banks of lights and the walls were noticeable for their lack of mildew or graffiti. The floor looked freshly waxed, reflecting the soft glow from the fixtures above, bathing the station in placid whiteness.

The three young men exited at the next stop, making lewd comments and shoving each other playfully as they pushed their way through a small crowd waiting to get inside the subway car. Sam and Gibson silently moved deeper into the car as if magnetically repulsed by the new arrivals. The newcomers filled most of the seats in the car, but none moved too close to them. Sam overheard someone mutter the word "ghoul".

"We get off at the next stop," Gibson said as the train moved again. He stared out the window, not looking in her direction.

Sam didn't respond. She heard him, heard his voice, but did not really process what he had said. At her lack of response, Gibson resumed his silent reverie. She was thinking about how even in the world of the dead, people ostracized each other. If someone had been horribly disfigured in life, why should they suffer for it in death, as well? Idly, Sam wondered what people assumed she looked like beneath the phoenix cloak and mask.

Not for the first time, she wondered how many people would recognize her as a Bloodwalker on sight, or if they would assume she were diseased, as the first people who had seen her had. When she had woken up in the alley, the first person who had spoken to her was Gunnarsson, the mountain of a police officer, who had asked her if she was ill. Their trek to the police station had been one of people fleeing from the mere sight of her.

The train clattered through the next tunnel, but Sam was oblivious to her surroundings. Time passed mellifluously, sliding from second to second in interconnected bubbles like drops of water forming an ocean. Beneath the phoenix mask, Sam's face was hard, the muscles tense. She squeezed her eyes tightly shut. Her brows furrowed and teeth clenched, Sam tried to conjure up more memories of her husband, of her life before awakening to death.

"This is our stop," Gibson murmured softly some time later, jerking his head in the direction of the platform. Most of the crowd from the previous station was filing out, a disorganized gaggle of voices and bodies jumbled at the double doors that led out into the subway terminal. Sam took a few unsteady steps toward the crowd but stopped at Gibson's voice. "Wait until most of them are through." He inhaled slowly, causing air to whistle between his front teeth. "I should mention," Gibson continued, "there are not a lot of masked people here, and the ones who are around usually aren't very popular." There was another pause, and Gibson added, "Just don't want you to be caught off guard."

When most of the passengers had disembarked, Gibson nodded to her and moved to join the remainder of those exiting. The few people who noticed her wore uneasy expressions on their faces and edged away as much as they could manage. Inwardly, Sam sighed; she was getting pretty sick of being treated like a pariah. She tried to catch a glimpse of the subway station while waiting her turn to pass onto the platform. Her heart skipped a beat when she saw a motionless man with long black hair, crouching with his back to her. He was wearing a black coat that trailed onto the floor. She must have gasped, because Gibson turned toward her, alarm painting his face. "What is it?" he asked urgently.

As she watched, the man on the platform stood straight and turned around. He held a battered saxophone, but it gleamed in the fluorescent lights. He pressed his lips together a few times in rapid succession, then began to play. Sam let out a breath she had not known she was holding. "Nothing," she lied, embarrassed to tell him the truth, even as her heart was still racing. A few people in the crowd stopped to watch the man's performance, but most ignored him completely and headed toward the stairwell to street level. Sam pointedly did not look in the direction of the saxophone player as she and Gibson made their way to the stairs.

Sam's first glimpse of the Fourth City downtown district knocked the wind out of her. She had tried to prepare herself for what it might look like, based on what she had seen when she first woke up in the alleyway all those weeks ago, but preparing for this was impossible. Every building towered beyond perception, piercing the brown-grey clouds with no sign of slowing their ascension toward the heavens, as if the people who built these monstrous structures thought they might be able to literally climb out of the city and reach Heaven itself. She had seen images of the great cities of the world on TV, of course, but it was a very different experience seeing overhead helicopter shots of a city on a screen compared to standing at street level. Being surrounded by a city as massive as this one was enough to make Sam speechless.

Cars raced through the city streets, ignoring pedestrians and traffic laws alike. None of the models or designs were familiar to her, and she found herself wondering if they ran on gasoline, or if some brilliant engineer had developed a different fuel system in Purgatory. The sidewalks were overflowing with people, a helter-skelter dance of the wealthy and those who wished to be seen with the wealthy. Enormous electric lights hung from reinforced cables along the roadway, bathing the proceedings in an ethereal blue-white glow. Even the air smelled like money.

Gibson nudged her gently on the arm. "C'mon," he urged in a voice pitched low enough not to be overheard a foot away, "Alley Cats is a few blocks from here. Don't get lost." With that, Gibson took a purposeful step onto the sidewalk and joined the rushing rapids that were the wealthy citizens of the Fourth City, leaving the sanctuary that was the doorway to the subway station.

*   *   *   *   *

Webb sat in a worn plush recliner in his living room, rubbing his eyes in the pale lamp light. A storm churned outside, hurling rain and lightning with equal fervor. The tube-style television was on, but grey and white dots danced across the screen, accompanied by a soft static hum which filled the air. Reception was always poor during storms, and this was one hell of a storm. Webb had never been much of a television watcher and found the static background noise just as useful for relaxing as any show he managed to pick up over the air. On a small wooden table to his left was a stack of papers he had nearly memorized. It was every document he could get his hands on relating to the death of Jackson Nightshade and the disappearance of his wife, Samantha. He had reached out to friends in different departments to get their reports, compiled and cross-referenced everything, but he was still just as befuddled as he had been two months ago. Maybe more.

It felt like every piece of information added more questions than it answered. He had been told by one of his training officers in his younger days that almost every cop had a case they could never solve, a case that would eat away at them until the day they died. Webb's mind always returned to this case in idle moments. He supposed he should be grateful that if this was his unsolvable case, at least it came at the end of his career and not in the beginning. He lifted himself out of the chair with a groan and a predictable creaking of bones that had not been a part of him a few short years ago.

Robert had spoken with Diana Westwood, the girl's mother, about a month ago. Well, he had tried to speak to her. Shortly after the night Samantha had disappeared, Diana was found wandering a rural road six miles from her home, completely unresponsive. She had been admitted to psychiatric care and had been borderline catatonic for the first few months, though she had recovered somewhat the last he heard. The hospital director said that she had begun expressing herself through art. The doctors reported that she drew monsters or demons or something, and that she didn't draw so much as scratch with a pen. The director expressed his concerns about her psychological condition, and added she might not be fit to leave the hospital anytime soon, if ever. Robert slowly paced around his living room, trying to get the blood flowing in his legs. He hated feeling old.

Then there was Irene Miller, the woman who had conducted the sham séance. She had confessed without prompting that she tricked people into believing that they were talking with spirits, but insisted that it was only a way for her to help her clients cope with their losses. There was no evidence of a clever kidnapping. Aside from the missing Nightshade woman, of course. Miller spoke of demons, which made Webb order a drug test of both the psychic and the mother. Two eyewitnesses and neither of them could provide actual answers, and he refused to believe there was any supernatural involvement in the woman's disappearance.

He skipped a step with surprise when the telephone rang out. Lightning flashed, illuminating the room and casting odd, flickering shadows. "Webb," he said as a means of greeting. He never received phone calls from anywhere other than work. His throat, dry and cracked, now felt constricted with the tightening of his vocal cords. He never received good news from work.

"Detective Webb?" came the voice from the other end of the line. A young man's voice, eager but afraid of making mistakes. He envied the voice. "This is Tyler Powell? From Forensics? I was told you were looking into a case and asked to be informed of similar situations?" Powell went silent for a moment. Webb grunted acknowledgement, wondering if the boy always ended every sentence with a question, or if he was simply nervous to be calling Webb's home well after hours. "We got a call a few hours ago, an old lady was taking out her garbage at the Somerset Apartment complex and found a body?"

Powell cleared his throat. "Are you asking me or telling me, Powell? Not everything has to be a question."

"S-sorry, sir." Powell stammered. There was a hesitation, and Powell felt a surge of guilt for snapping at the kid. Powell picked up the recap a moment later. "So, uh, the old lady at Somerset found a body. At least, part of a body. Seems like someone went after a homeless guy, but there's a lot of pieces missing. The medical team said it looked like he had been hacked apart. Maybe with a hatchet, maybe with a crowbar. They didn't want to say for sure, but they found some bite marks near his neck, too." Webb grunted again as he felt his stomach tighten. He had been with the department for a long time, and while you never really got used to the details, you could block out a lot of them.

Powell cleared his throat again, plainly uncomfortable. Thunder rumbled outside. "CSI turned in the report about half an hour ago," Powell added. "I'll have a copy of it waiting for you tomorrow."

Webb rubbed his eyes with his free hand, then stifled a yawn. "Thanks, Powell."

A static silence filled the receiver for a moment, before the younger man spoke again. "I hope you don't mind me saying so, Detective, but you sound like shit. Get some rest. The report will be at the front desk." Powell did not wait for a response before hanging up. Despite himself, Webb chuckled; the kid had more guts than he thought. Lightning flashed outside, illuminating the world for the briefest of moments. The storm was getting worse.

Chapter 10

By the time they reached Alley Cats, Sam felt incredibly grateful for her phoenix garb. While it had garnered a lot of frightened or disgusted looks from people out to enjoy the Fourth City nightlife, it also allowed her ample space to practically stroll down the sidewalk at leisure. Apparently even the idea of being within arm's length of a ghoul was abhorrent. Meanwhile, Gibson had to practically scratch and claw his way through the horde of pedestrians, at least until he started sticking right in front of her instead of to the side.

Alley Cats stood out like a broken and bloody thumb in comparison to most of the establishments they passed, and not only because both of the letter "A"s in the club's sign had cat ears crudely drawn on them. Across the street were enormous towers that appeared to be completely built out of glass, the mirrored façade flashing between every imaginable color as it reflected the neon-lit advertisements that lined the street. While almost every building on the street was cheek-by-jowl with its neighbor, there were gaps on either side of Alley Cats, as if the structures themselves shied away from such a disreputable establishment. Sam giggled to herself when she realized she had a kinship with the club in that regard. The street-facing windows were darkly tinted and smudged, and one was covered with a large, ill-fitting piece of sheet metal. It was the kind of building that would fit perfectly in the outskirts of the city, but in this bustling high-rent commercial area, it felt incredibly out of place. Even from across the street, she could feel the thumping bass hammering its way through the concrete walls. There was no line waiting to get into the club, just a surly-looking barrel of a man wearing a cheap, frayed suit, standing with his arms crossed in front of a wooden door coated with a thin layer of chipped red paint.

Gibson glanced over his shoulder at Sam and flashed her a quick, reassuring smile, then waited for an opportunity to cross the street. Sam followed, hurrying but not running, even as she heard revving engines in the distance. The bouncer grinned a wide slice of a smile that looked like it had been made with a hatchet as Gibson approached. "Lawrence," he laughed with a deep, heavily-accented voice, clapping the investigator jovially on the shoulder hard enough to make the smaller man's knees buckle slightly. "The manager pontificated his belief you had made yourself scarce, permanently, as it were, after the events following your most recent patronage of our fine, upstanding establishment," the bouncer continued happily. "I, however, postulated that Mister Lawrence Gibson was indeed too sly of a fox to capitulate to the denizens of the City Fourth without word of it spreading to the highest of the low, such as those of us who participate in improving the ability of our clientele to patronize this fine, upstanding establishment." The bouncer broke into a raucous guffaw of a laugh. Sam stared at him; if she had ever seen a human embodiment of the phrase "don't judge a book by its cover", then this man was it.

"Nice to see you again, Morris," Gibson answered, shaking the larger man's hand. "I appreciate your faith in my reputation, my friend," Gibson added. Sam watched this exchange, perplexed at the subject of the conversation. She wondered if she would ever have the nerve to ask Gibson about it, and quickly decided that she didn't want to know the details even if she had the nerve.

The bouncer shot a quick look over toward her, then lowered his voice conspiratorially. "The ghoul, Gibson," he asked quietly, "with you?" Gibson nodded. "Not your normal company, but I'm sure you have your reasons. Never let it be said Morris Grinwell judges another man's company, or even recalls whether or not another man even had company."

Gibson quickly reached into his pocket, then shook the man's hand again. Sam noticed a small wad of paper bills pass between them on the shake. "Have a great night, Morris. We'll try not to make too much of a mess." The bouncer laughed loudly as Gibson led the way inside.

The first thing Sam noticed in the stiflingly warm hallway was the smell. If the perfume counter from every department store she had ever visited were dumped into a cramped, poorly lit corridor, it might be close to as strong as this odor. Maybe. As long as it was mixed with the scent of stale sweat and spilled beer. Sam's throat felt coated with the smell, and she gagged behind her mask. The volume of the music made her insides hurt, and she felt her temples begin to pound a steady counter beat to the pulsating rhythm.

Sam saw colors flashing on the wall ahead as Gibson turned a corner in front of her. She followed and found herself staring into a large, open room, with multitudinous lights of seemingly every hue beating in coordination with the music. Four raised platforms dotted the room like tiny islands, each with a scantily-dressed performer dancing atop, three women and one man. In the middle of the far wall was a large stage, presumably where main acts would perform. Tables were set up haphazardly around the room. Most of the tables were occupied by at least one person, almost always a man, unsurprisingly. Gibson barely scanned the room before heading off to the leftmost wall, where a rotund, red-cheeked man grinned up at the nearest performer. A collection of empty glasses lined the perimeter of two sides of his table. Sam wondered if this Harold character would be of any use if he was completely drunk.

"There's our boy!" Gibson exclaimed delightedly as he approached the drunken man's table. He made a quick gesture to Sam as he pulled a chair out at the table, motioning her to sit. "How have you been, Harold?"

Harold looked up at Gibson, drink and confusion clear on his face. His eyes widened suddenly as recognition dawned. "You," he slurred, "you're the reason I'm drink." Harold coughed fitfully before correcting himself. "The reason I'm drunk," he said, a hard emphasis on the last word.

"Come now," Gibson chided. "You knew we were meeting tonight. No need to be all dramatic." He grabbed one of the empty glasses and peered into it before setting it back down. "You've been hitting it pretty hard, Harold. That nervous to see me again?" Abruptly, all playfulness dropped from Gibson's voice, which was now deep and sounded edged with frost. "Or does something else have you worked up?"

Harold's eyes were half-closed while Gibson spoke, but the change in tone made them pop back open. "Last time we met, Lawrence, you didn't fight fair." Harold's words dripped like honey, slow and liquid. Even wearing her mask, Sam could smell the liquor every time the ex-cop opened his mouth.

"Fight fair?" Gibson asked, his eyebrow raising quizzically. "I hadn't realized we were fighting. You know I consider you one of my closest friends in this wretched half-life, Harold." His sarcasm was obvious to Sam, but Harold didn't seem to pick up on it. The song changed, or at least the melody did; the pounding bass drum never stopped beating in time from one tune to the next.

"Closest friends," Harold laughed, coughing again. "You scammed me out of, how much money?" He fumbled at his fingers as he tried to count them, but he had difficulty getting the fingers on one hand to touch those on the other. "At least two thousand. Then you say you want to meet me again? Why should I want to help you, unless you're paying me back? Detective," Harold scoffed. "You're a thief."

Sam watched as the two men bantered back and forth, Gibson alternating between bombastic charm and sarcasm while Harold responded with drunken accusations. Most of which were probably true, she realized abruptly, as Gibson never denied even the slightest of them. Between this accusation and the job he was running with Davis, Sam suddenly wondered just how much of Gibson's income came from investigating, and how much came from scamming.

Much of the conversation was about events that took place years before, as far as she could tell. Eventually, however, Gibson brought up the business at hand. "Look Harold, I know you're not a cop anymore, but Synthosyn is destroying this city. Maybe the whole world. I have a chance to make a big dent in that." He stabbed his finger onto the table. "Here, in the Fourth City. Doesn't that appeal to your sense of righteousness, at the very least?" Gibson gave the man a pleading look. When Harold did not respond, the investigator sighed before adding, "Look, if this job goes off the way I'm planning, I can appeal to your wallet, as well."

Suddenly, Harold glanced over toward her and his eyes widened, as if he had not noticed her there before that moment. "Lawrence," he blurted, his words bubbling between his lips, "there's a ghoul at the table."

"The ghoul is with me," Gibson answered dismissively, waving his hand in the air as if brushing the statement away. "What matters –"

"Why do you have a ghoul, Lawrence?" Harold interrupted. "If you ask me, all the ghouls should be sent out to Old Town. Get those creepy masks out of our city and let them be cared for by the wise and powerful Sages." The final few words were positively dripping with derision. Harold even laughed darkly to himself. "Sages," he repeated. "Bunch of old fuddy-duddies who can't appreciate the finer things death has to offer." He turned to watch the undulating dancer atop the nearest pedestal. Her breasts were exposed now, the skimpy top sitting in a crumpled pile at the edge of the rounded platform. Her torso glistened with sweat. She noticed Harold's

122

gaze and gave him a smoky smile. Sam interpreted the dancer's expression, and it was clear she could spot an easy mark as quickly as anyone else in this dead world.

Gibson watched the former policeman, waiting to continue the conversation. A few minutes passed before Harold turned his attention back to the table. His eyes widened in apparent surprise at seeing he was not alone. "What matters," Gibson began again, "is whether or not you can get me the documents I need. Almost everything I need is already done, but I need your help or else Old Man Ladi–" Gibson hissed, realizing he said something he should have kept to himself.

"Old Man Ladi," Harold growled. He made the name sound like a curse. "I was almost ready to help you, Lawrence, for old time's sake, but Old Man Ladi... What is wrong with you? Are you trying to get yourself killed? Again?" Suddenly, Harold's eyes looked sharp and focused, as if the name had sobered him immediately. He darted a look toward Sam, so quickly she thought maybe she was imagining things, before reaching for a glass, the only one of the dozen on the table that had any liquid in it at all. Uneasily, Sam watched as his face took on a look of drunken stupor again. She realized Harold's drunkenness was an act, but it was too late to say anything. His fingers clumsily fumbled at the glass, causing it to tip and spill on her gloved hand. Uttering a drunken curse, Harold dabbed at her glove with a napkin. With speed and precision, he suddenly pulled the glove off.

"Bloodwalker!" Harold spat as soon as he saw her exposed skin. Sam's heart skipped a beat and she tried to hide her hand in the folds of the phoenix cloak, but the damage had been done. Gibson stood, knocking over his chair. The woman dancing on the nearest island had turned to face them again, though this time she wore a puzzled expression. "There have been rumors about you moving around Fourth City with a ghoul, Lawrence," Harold sneered, sounding as if he had not had a single drink all evening. "You're not a bleeding heart, so I wondered what was in it for you." He shook the black and red glove at the pair of them in a clenched fist. "You have a lot of enemies, and now I can make some money from your dirty secret. It's the least you owe me."

A shriek and two loud bangs from somewhere behind her made Sam turn around instinctively. Three men carrying firearms of some sort had stormed into the club. As she saw them, they flipped over a pair of tables to stand behind, and fired into the scattering crowd. Harold shot Gibson a smirk and yelled, "See you in Hell, Lawrence!" before scampering to the nearest raised dais.

The dancing woman had already huddled behind her platform, but Harold wasted no time shoving her out into the open to make room for himself. Her scream was cut off in a flash as two bullets struck her, one in the left shoulder and a second in the forehead, causing her head to snap violently backward. The same clear fluid that had leaked out of Davis's hand when he had sliced it open on Sam's phoenix mask burst out of her shattered skull like a ripe melon being crushed by a sledgehammer. Sam retched even as Gibson grabbed her exposed hand and pulled her roughly toward the main stage at the rear of the building.

"Keep your head down!" Gibson bellowed as he darted from table to table, looking for cover from the hail of bullets that streaked across the club. In a less chaotic moment, Sam would have laughed at the obviousness of the instruction. A bullet skimmed past Gibson's head and he jerked away instinctively, wide-eyed. At some point during his scramble across the room, Gibson had managed to pull his pistol free from the holster under his jacket. "When I shoot, you run," he barked from halfway across the club.

Sam had so many thoughts rushing through her head but the clamor was too much to let her grab onto any one of them. Partly out of frustration, partly out of fear, Sam shrieked, "Who are you people?!"

Gibson looked at her and gave a silent countdown on one hand as he flexed his fingers around the grip of the pistol with the other. Sam nodded, breathing heavily, trying to regain control over herself. When Gibson put down his last finger in the countdown, he reached over the shelter of the overturned table and blindly fired twice in the general direction of the shooters.

Sam darted toward the main stage, furthest away from the attackers, keeping her head as low as she could manage. She heard the crack of gunfire as she ran and felt something pull at her right shoulder. Reflexively, Sam screamed, though she did not feel any pain. She dove head-first toward the wall of the stage, desperate to reach safety, however temporary it may be. Skidding the final few feet, Sam twisted to slam her back into the raised side of the stage, knocking the wind out of herself. Her heart was thumping hard enough she thought it might burst free of her chest. Sweat poured down her face inside the mask. She wished there was a way she could wipe it off of her forehead before it got into her eyes, but she would have to remove the phoenix mask. With a laugh that felt like the beginnings of a psychotic break from reality, Sam pulled the mask upward and used her one remaining glove to absorb the sweat. *Anyone in here right now is trying to kill me already anyway,* Sam thought ruefully.

Gibson fired two more rounds before following her pathway and leaping into the coverage of the stage, pressing his back into the raised wood next to her. "Well," he panted, "this did not go as planned." He gave her a quick grin, but Sam saw how forced it was. She watched sweat roll down his forehead like raindrops on a window, and the skin around his eyes was white with tightness. Gibson reached into his pocket and pulled out eight bullets. He let out a sigh as he began to chamber the rounds. "Once I start shooting, you get up on stage and get through the curtain as fast as you can. There's a door to the left that leads to the alley. Get out and get to the subway station. I'll meet you there. They're after me, but they won't hesitate to fire at you, either. I don't know if they're Ladi's guys, but even amateur hit squads don't like to leave witnesses."

Sam opened her mouth to protest, but Gibson stopped her with a raised finger. "You need to run, but don't go back to the apartment. Wait at the subway, and if I'm not there in an hour..." Gibson trailed off. Sam imagined that for him, having died once already, the prospect of dying again, maybe permanently, was not one he liked to contemplate. "Go to Davis," Gibson said after another burst of gunfire from the attackers. "Keep your disguise on. Write a note that says Gibson wants his money. Take the money and run. Get a new cloak and mask and run. No arguments." A chunk of wood whirled in the air above their heads, broken free by the hail of bullets. He looked at Sam, and she saw determination in his eyes. "Get ready."

Gibson closed his eyes and inhaled deeply before springing into action. He fired twice around the corner of the stage, then darted back toward the center of the room, shooting once more before diving behind yet another overturned table. Sam wasted no time in leaping onto the stage and rushing through the glittering maroon curtain, instinctively keeping low and holding her arm up to protect her head. She heard a pained yell from the main room, a scream that was definitely not Gibson, and she smiled grimly. Hopefully, the man struck by Gibson's shot would be unable to continue the fight. Sam turned left, passing a few rickety wooden tables lined with makeup and other assorted cosmetics, then followed the corridor as it turned right. Directly in front of her was a thick steel door with the word EXIT painted on it with rough red strokes.

Slamming through the door, Sam heard another barrage of gunfire from inside the club. She gulped down the chill night air and rubbed her hand down her face, pulling away rivulets of sweat before lowering the phoenix mask once again and tucking her exposed hand into the furrows of her cloak. The mouth of the alley was teeming with pedestrians, apparently oblivious to the death and chaos occurring inside the building. Gibson had told her to go to the subway station, but she hesitated.

When the idea struck her, it was hard not to run into the crowd on the sidewalk. Remembering her experience being the lookout for Gibson's exploration of Old Man Ladi's building, she scavenged around the alley for a few moments, trying to find something useful, something that could be used as a weapon, if necessary. A large, empty glass liquor bottle caught her eye and her lips curled darkly as she pulled it into her cloak. Stepping onto the sidewalk, Sam shoved her way through the crowd, buffeted in all directions but always striving forward. Within a few moments, the pedestrians realized a ghoul was in their midst and did their best to give her space, but there were so many people in motion that it was nearly impossible. She wondered if they could smell her sweat, her fear, as she shambled her way toward the front door of Alley Cats. Sam hoped she wasn't making a huge mistake.

It took nearly two minutes for her to make her way to where Morris, the bouncer, should have been standing, but she could not see him anywhere. She had found the man rather charming, in an archaic way, and despite the pit of ice in her stomach, hoped he was simply on the other side of the door, acting as a gatekeeper from the sanctity of the burlesque bar instead of pretending to be a boulder in a river, attempting to maintain his place despite the incessant flood.

When Sam was finally able to pull open the tinted glass door, her stomach clenched as her worst fears were realized. Lying on the floor just inside the hallway was Morris, his skull a shattered explosion of bone

126

fragments covered in silvery blood. She hoped Morris was at peace, whether in another afterlife or whatever other metaphysical state of existence or nonexistence he may be in now that he had been murdered. Sam felt something twist inside of her and was unsurprised when she recognized it as the cold desire for revenge. Morris did not deserve this fate. She gritted her teeth.

The music still pounded in the air, beating an eerie rhythm for the scene of violence and death. Gunshots snapped irregular intervals, but there were considerably fewer than when she had escaped through the back exit. *Gunshots are a good sign,* Sam thought, because it meant Gibson was still holding his own. Grey smoke churned at the end of the hallway, frequently highlighted by flickering colors from the stage lights. Sam strode down the hall toward the central room, purposefully adjusting the glass bottle in her grip. She took a deep breath before carefully edging her eyes around the corner.

There was so much to take in that Sam felt overwhelmed. A man, presumably one of the attackers, was crawling with agonizing slowness toward the bar that took up the majority of the wall on the right. He was only a few feet from being able to get his head behind the bar. A second man was crouched behind a splintered wooden table, fumbling bullets into his revolver. A third lay motionless on his back, a few feet away from the second. A flare of red-orange light far to the left, accompanied by a loud pop, gave her a rough idea of where Gibson was hiding. She pulled back into the hallway. Now that she was so close to acting, sweat greased her palm and the bottle threatened to slip from her grasp. Hastily, she swapped the bottle to her left hand and wiped her right surreptitiously on her cloak before taking another deep breath to steady her nerves and finalize her plan.

Sam moved toward the crawling man as quickly as she could, staying low to the ground and as quiet as possible. The cloak trailed through broken glass, splintered wood, and splatters of silvery blood. The man had been able to pull himself almost entirely behind the bar, with only his shins and feet still exposed. With as much haste as she dared, she curled around the edge of his outstretched legs and smashed the glass bottle over the back of his head. Despite the force she used in bringing the glass down on his head, she doubted the last attacker had heard it over the whip-like cracks of the firefight he was having with Gibson.

Sam crouched behind the bar and dragged the man the final few inches that was needed to completely conceal him, then searched around frantically for another bottle, planning an encore on the final gunman. Clutching a three-quarters empty bottle of bourbon, Sam took another steadying breath before peering around the end of the bar. The shooter was still distracted by Gibson's occasional return fire. Sam was impressed Gibson had been able to stretch such a small number of bullets so far, but she knew he had to be almost out. Crouched on tiptoes, Sam emerged, holding the bourbon in her ungloved hand, and quickly closed the distance between herself and the attacker.

About a yard from him, the man happened to glance over his shoulder and see her coming at him, bottle raised. Sam's furiously pounding heart skipped a beat, but the sight of her apparently did not immediately process in the man's head, as he returned his attention toward deeper in the room, where his prey hid. A split second passed before he whipped his head back around and let out a surprised shout.

The momentary delay was all Sam needed. The bottle crashed onto his forehead and face, shattering into infinitesimal shards. The grunt that passed through his lips, and the subsequent thud as his head hit the floor, left Sam feeling grimly satisfied.

There was a throaty cough, immediately followed by Gibson's shocked voice. "Sam? Is that you?" She watched as he emerged from behind an Arabesque column deep in the shadows of the room. "What the hell are you doing here? I told you to run, not to swing around for some barroom brawling!" Sam bristled with indignation. She had quite possibly saved his life, or whatever he wanted to refer to his existence as, and he had the nerve to berate her? Gibson's shoes crunched over glass as he approached. His left arm hung limply at his side, but he appeared otherwise uninjured. His steps were unsteady. The firefight lasted only a few minutes, but it felt like hours, and Gibson's lack of balance reflected the natural adrenaline crash.

Gibson peered down at the unconscious man that lay sprawled at her feet, studying a face that oozed silver-white blood. "Not one of Old Man Ladi's," he muttered before kicking the man hard in the ribs. A groggy groan passed the man's lips. "At least not that I recognize. Just coincidence I was asking around about Old Man Ladi. Harold was right when he said I

128

make a lot of enemies." Sam thought his voice lacked conviction, as if he were saying the words to try to force himself to believe them. "We need to get out of here," he added. "We're lucky the cops haven't burst in yet and made a mess of things."

Sam coughed, choking back a laugh that bordered on hysteria. Made a mess of things? The club looked like a tornado had ripped through it. They stumbled across the strewn rubble with the haste of people who knew their lives depended on getting clear of suspicion at a crime scene. Once they were on the stage, they practically ran to the back exit before bursting into the alleyway. Before reaching the still-bustling sidewalk, Gibson brushed himself off with his right hand, carefully not moving his left arm at all. "Without being sure who those goons were, we can't go back to the apartment," he said between the muffled thumps of his hand forcefully brushing away debris. "I have a safe house south of the city. We'll take the subway. Stay close. I need to think."

Aside from being jostled in every direction by the crowd, the walk back to the subway terminal was largely uneventful. About a block away from Alley Cats, Sam could see the flashing blue-and-red lights of emergency vehicles approaching. She wondered when she should tell Gibson about Morris's fate, but a look at his face through the eyeholes of her phoenix mask showed her a man gritting his teeth, full of grim determination. Sam wondered if he was wearing a mask of his own, and if it was for his sake, or hers.

The subway station was packed with people trying to see and be seen in the most expensive part of town, the terminal acting as a vein filled to bursting with the lifeblood of the downtown district. The outfits worn by those exiting the subway were as varied as it was possible to be, but regardless of dress, all were immaculate in their apparel. Sam recalled Morris's outfit, and then, unbidden, the memory of his battered corpse. Wearing the phoenix cloak and mask, she truly was separate from everyone in this world of the dead. She supposed she should be thankful, but her disguise created an impassable chasm both physically and emotionally. She normally did not care what other people thought of her, but Sam was fixated on the concept of isolation in the world of the dead. Even with Gibson, a man who knew all her secrets and took her in when he had no real reason to, she felt the distance. Everyone in this world had experienced death, had passed from one world to the next in the most natural way. What should be the only way. Yet here she was, seeing the end credits before the movie even reached the second act. She didn't realize it at the time that her melancholic introspection offered her a much-needed distraction from the carnage inside Alley Cats.

Unsurprisingly, the subway was nearly empty when Sam and Gibson boarded, as the night was still young enough for significantly more arrivals than departures to the Fourth City's nightlife. Gibson maintained a forced stoicism, his back unnaturally stiff, as he moved to the far corner of the subway car. When he reached the last row of seats, however, Gibson threw himself into one with the self-control of a bushel of apples being dumped from the roof of a skyscraper. Sam took the seat next to him, self-conscious about her posture compared to the deep sagging slouch that had Gibson in its clutches.

The train departed. Gibson stared blankly forward, eyes unfocused, and Sam was unsure if she should break his reverie; perhaps he just needed time to think, as he had said on the streets above. Without warning, he turned to her in between the first and second stops on the line. "We have a lot to discuss, Sam," Gibson growled in a throaty whisper, pitching his voice low even though the only other passengers sat at the other end of the car. It was an odd comment, one that made her vaguely uneasy. "Later. Five more stops."

Sam lost herself in the clacking of the subway car, the hydraulic swoosh of the doors opening and closing for the few scattered passengers, the flickering of the fluorescent lights in irregular intervals. Some time passed before Gibson tapped her on the shoulder. "It's our stop in a moment, Bloodwalker" he said dully. They were the only ones left in the car.

The platform at their stop was somehow more derelict than the one near Gibson's apartment. There was more graffiti visible than there was wall, most of it illegible. What could be read was obscene. Patches of mold grew on the floor, emboldened by the steady dripping of water from the roof of the cavernous terminal station. Sam tried to convince herself it was moss instead of mold, but the smell was far too foul for the prevarication. An old man slept on the floor against the wall, a balled-up coat for a pillow and a blanket that was more holes than cloth over his body. Sam wondered if the man had been homeless before he died. *Or maybe he hasn't even realized he's dead,* Sam thought, sadness filling her. It was hard for Sam to tear her eyes away from the sleeping man.

Gibson led the way up the stairs and out into the cool night. The road was patchwork and worn down, with bits of brick occasionally popping through cobblestone, interspersed with plain pea stone gravel that looked like it had been dumped in lumpy piles and spread over time by foot traffic. There were streetlights, but spaced so far apart that the patches of darkness outweighed the small pools of light they cast. Sam moved her head and neck in a small circle, stretching out the crick that had developed during the subway ride, and found herself looking upward with her mouth open. She had never noticed stars in Purgatory before; all of the other places she had been in the Fourth City had been too well-lit. Myriad possibilities and theories popped into her overtired brain, ranging from the implausible to the outlandishly fantastic. Were these the same stars that she would see in the living world, as if the two worlds overlapped the same space? Or was this dead world its own planet, somewhere off in the distant universe? Sam forced her brain to relative stillness, to focus on the immediate, but she could not help but wonder if, were he to look up in that moment, Jack might be able to see the same stars in the world of the living.

Chapter 11

Gibson's safe house was as derelict as the rest of the general environment in this area of the city. It was small, with a combined kitchenette and living room, a tiny bedroom, and a bathroom in which Sam could touch opposite walls without straightening her arms. Aside from the dust and dirt of disuse, there was occasional scrabbling of what Sam hoped were mice in the walls and not something worse. "I pay the rent yearly," Gibson explained in a flat voice, "under a fake name. Management never bothers me, as long as the rent comes in, and I pay early. It helps to have a place to hide when things get too hot." He looked around, banged his fist twice on the wall where the unknown creature was moving behind the drywall, and added, "It's not my favorite place to be."

A small cot stood in the corner of the main room, which Gibson offered to her. "I haven't been here in almost a year, and who knows what might have taken up residence in the mattress." He went to the bedroom a moment later, face carved from rock cast in melancholy curves.

Sam doffed her cloak and swept her hand across the cot a few times to clear away some thick chunks of dust. A minute later she was laying on the cot, staring at the ceiling, listening to the tiny claws of the mice as they alternated between tentative steps and scratchy sprints. Her mind felt like it was bursting, overwhelmed by musings and observations and the events of the night. Sam struggled to organize her thoughts as they flitted from one thing to the next. It felt like watching a slideshow with a thousand pictures that had been shuffled into random order. She had no idea how long she stared at the ceiling, struggling to keep up with the haphazard crashing like white water rapids in her mind.

When she finally fell asleep, she dreamed she was sitting at a table with Gibson, his face a static carving. He did not speak, despite her promptings and proddings. It was like trying to crack open an oyster with an autumn leaf. The longer the dream went on, the more unnerved she was by his silence, and the way his eyes stared forward as if refusing to acknowledge her presence.

Sam woke but the dream continued, in the way the mind sometimes clings to the edges of dreams as they ebb away with the rubbing of eyes and stretching of limbs. Exhaustion had settled onto her during the night, wrapping her tightly with an invisible blanket that felt like it weighed 200 pounds. When Sam opened her eyes, she saw the room in daylight for the first time, noticed the water stains on the ceiling, the cracks in the plaster, the metal frame on the apartment's only window, held together with rust. Gibson was not in the room with her, and both the bedroom and bathroom doors were open, their rooms vacant. She stumbled to her feet, putting a hand on the wall to steady herself, and heard the scampering of mice in response.

It took some time for her to feel fully awake and alert. Her body ached with the exertion and adrenaline crash from the events at the club. Sam pulled open the tiny cabinet drawers but found them empty of anything edible. An open, dust-covered bag of what might have once been pretzels sat limply in a cabinet of its own. They looked like nothing so much as a fuzzy grey-green clump of moss.

Letting out a sigh, Sam gave up on her search for food and instead examined her phoenix cloak. It was stiff with grime and the silver blood of those who had been wounded or killed at Alley Cats. At some point it must have snagged on something, because it had a three-foot-long rip on the left side. The mask was in little better shape, wearing the scars of the night before. Her one remaining glove had a hole in it almost the size of her palm. Sam tossed the glove onto the ruined bundle that was the cloak and went to add the mask before thinking better of it and setting it reverently on the cot. The cloak she rolled into as compact of a ball as she could and plunked it down in the corner of the room.

Gibson came back about an hour after Sam had woken up, carrying a rolled newspaper and a cloth bag in his right hand. Sam could tell his left arm was heavily bandaged underneath his coat, though it seemed to have more range of motion than it had the night before. "Morning, Bloodwalker," he said with a joviality Sam immediately recognized as forced. She made no comment. "I brought a little food, and look, we made the front page!" He dropped the newspaper on the counter and it unfurled. In large, bold-faced print across the top of the page read the words "Chaos at Club Leaves Multiple Fatalities". The subtitle pronounced the number of victims as 11.

Sam felt her stomach tighten as she read the article. Absent-mindedly, she noticed reading about it was somehow more upsetting than living through it. Every action she and Gibson had taken the night before had seemed so necessary and obvious at the time, but each one took them further down a path that led to this story in the newspaper. All the blame was placed at the hands of two men, both of whom were found unconscious at the scene, and now both in the custody of the Fourth City Police Department. The FCPD was investigating whether a third man, found behind the bar, was working with the other two, but no conclusions had been made as of press time. The list of victims made up the entire third paragraph. The dancer's name had been Olivia Armelo; she had been hired by Alley Cats a week prior. Seeing Morris Grinwell's name in print brought a pang of sorrow.

Gibson slid a loaf of freshly baked bread across the countertop toward her. Sam was oblivious as she read. It was surreal to read about her exploits in the newspaper, the article startling in both the accuracy and inaccuracy of its claims. The newspaper said two or three men killed the bouncer, stormed the club, and opened fire, but suggested the bartender had hid until there was an opportunity to stop the gunmen by smashing liquor bottles over their heads. Sam had to give them partial credit, as it made logical sense, but that theory completely ignored the fact that the bartender was one of those killed. If he had been the one to stop the gunmen, who would have killed him?

When she finished reading, Sam was tempted to start it over again, feeling a compulsion to pore over the words for clarity into the why of the thing. The violence, Harold's hiring of the gunmen over some slight from Gibson, the recognition of a Bloodwalker from her exposed hand. Individual pieces made sense, but when combined into the memories of the events at the club, she was overwhelmed. Gibson interrupted her ruminations. "Have some breakfast, Sam," he said softly. "We need to talk."

Sam slowly lowered the newspaper, unsettled by his words, and the tone with which he delivered them. She noticed the bread, but her uneasiness thrust her hunger to the backburner. "Talk about what?" Sam asked, carefully keeping her own tone level and calm. He met her gaze but did not speak. As time stretched, Sam felt herself become fidgety, anxious for him to talk. "The thing I can't figure out is why last night happened," she blurted, unwilling to bear the heavy silence any longer.

Gibson brushed off a worn wicker chair with his good hand before sitting down. His face tightened, contorted with the effort of choosing his words carefully. "In general, I'm left alone, but I'm not the most popular guy in the Fourth City, Sam," he began. Sam heard the tension in his voice. He reached across the table to slide the bread an inch closer to her, almost absentmindedly. "When I was alive, if my actions led to someone getting arrested, then great, I did my job. The problem is most of the time, they get out of prison, and when they do, it's pretty rare they've signed up for the church choir." The sardonic twist of his mouth was bitter. "It's no different here, except for the fact you get to have all of your enemies from your entire life after you." Seeing Sam's puzzled look, Gibson continued.

"I testified against a street thug back in '28," Gibson explained, rising from the chair and beginning to pace the room. "He died in prison later that year. When I got here, he was waiting for me, and he had made a few new friends, other guys I had helped put an end to in the living world, one way or other. At best, I'd call it a complete disaster." Gibson stopped pacing and turned his back to her, staring at the cracked wall. "Unfortunately, most of the cops here couldn't care less about the squabbles between some convicts and a gumshoe, especially one that predates their time in the afterlife, so it was up to me to find a solution." He turned, his eyes looking haunted.

"I've been thinking about what Harold said last night, Sam." Gibson's voice was barely above a whisper. Sam opened her mouth angrily, but he held up a hand to forestall her. "Yes, he is a double-crossing rat bastard, but something he said actually made some sense, though not in the way he said it. Maybe. The Sages." Sam's eyebrow curled quizzically. "There's a place far outside the city, usually called Old Town. No electricity, no running water, stone buildings. Think Old Testament, hence the name. The Sages are what the people of Old Town are called. I've never seen it myself, but the rumor is Old Town is kind of like a monastery, filled with all of the great philosophers of all time, making some sort of new Library of Alexandria."

Gibson grunted, suddenly giving off an air of frustration and impatience. "Look, the point is, you might be able to get some answers there, Sam. You're a Bloodwalker, maybe the first of your kind. You're like a myth come to life, like Zeus himself knocking on the door asking to borrow a cup of sugar. The odds of meeting you in that police station are probably the same as me meeting Dracula at a speakeasy. But Old Town, full of philosophers and scientists and who knows who else, they might be able to get you back home. That's something I don't think I could ever figure out, even with an eternity in front of me."

Sam felt her heart racing at the possibility of finding a way clear of the madness of the Fourth City and back to the living world, back to Jack. "Why didn't you say anything about this before?" Sam asked, trying not to sound demanding. She stood, leaving the bread untouched. "When can we leave?"

Gibson made a soothing motion with his hands. "First of all, I'm a private detective, and I don't ever have any reason to deal with Sages. A lot of the work I do is remembering people's stories and comparing them to other people's stories, but interacting with the Sages? That's like me asking you what you drew on your first day of school when you were six years old. It's a fun bit of trivia but completely irrelevant to everything else, so you never think about it."

Sam nodded grudgingly, forcing her brow to smoothness to mask her irritation. What he said made sense, but she wished this news had come out months ago. She had nightmares, sometimes, of Jack grieving her, of him getting on with his life and marrying again, of him having an affair and driving around town with a mysterious woman in his car. That last one made her brain itch, as if the memory scraped on something real, but despite her nightmares, she knew in her heart Jack would never cheat on her. *But if he thinks you're dead?* The thought came unbidden and unwanted, the questioning voice inside her head punctuated its taunt with a dark, sadistic cackle.

"You really think these Sages would be able to help me?" Sam asked, trying to mask her lack of temerity. Gibson nodded, his jaw set. "Okay," Sam responded, trying to pull in his confidence and make it her own, "where are they, and when do we go?"

Gibson stared at her, motionless. "Old Town is west of the city," he said finally. His voice sounded odd, monotone. "Subway will go part of the way, then it's a walk out of town. Not sure how far the road will go. Might be some trudging through the wastelands. Desert."

Gibson's clipped sentences made Sam's stomach queasy, filling her with uneasiness. Trying to ignore it, she repeated, "When do we go?"

"You're going alone."

Sam felt her stomach drop out from underneath her. "Alone?" she cried, unsuccessfully keeping the sudden panic out of her voice. "I can't go al-"

"I've got people trying to kill me, Sam!" Gibson interrupted, slamming his fist down on the counter. "I've got no money, hit squads coming after me, and you're a liability! All I've done for almost six months is take care of you, babysit you, spend every last dime on getting you food and a disguise and everything else under this cursed sun! I don't have time to wander out in the desert and talk to the Sages! I'm already dead!" Gibson panted, his face contorted with rage. "Take this," he bellowed, shoving the bag of food across the counter in her direction, "and get out!"

Sam cowered under his anger, hands shaking near her face. "Wh-why are you yelling at me?" she squeaked in a voice she barely recognized as her own.

"I thought I told you to get out!" Gibson roared. He grabbed a glass from the countertop and threw it against the wall, shattering it into a million fragments. "Take your food and get out!" He stalked to the bedroom and slammed the door, causing the window to rattle in the metal-and-rust frame.

Sam grabbed the bag from the counter, hurried to pick the balled-up cloak up from the floor, and left the apartment as quickly and as quietly as she was able. Her heart was pounding and tears pooled at the corners of her eyes. What had gotten into him? She had never been yelled at like that before, and she was ashamed by her cowering reaction. Her mind was racing and blank at the same time. Sam stumbled down the dilapidated hallway, eyes scanning everything and recognizing nothing through clouded vision. Her legs were unsteady, knees quaking at every step, causing her to bump into the walls. Her shoulder banged heavily against a door and she fell into the room as it opened unexpectedly. The door slowly slid closed again. Laying on her side on the floor, clutching her bloodied cloak, the tears finally began to fall. She sobbed, howled, and cried. Sam knew it was more than Gibson's sudden outburst that was tearing her world to shreds; it was a massive amalgamation of things finally catching up to her. Gibson's anger had been the breaking point that had finally let all the emotion come crashing out at once, the explosive end to a makeshift dam that had held back her despair. An hour passed, or maybe half a day, before Sam was completely exhausted and cried herself to sleep on the floor, still clutching the tattered cloak.

*   *   *   *   *

Lawrence Gibson stared at the spot on the wall where the glass had struck and shattered. A small dent pocked the drywall, and even had this been his own home as opposed to a low-rent safe house, he knew he would never have repaired the mark. He replayed the scene in his own mind, his decades of investigative work forcing him to notice every detail. Most of all, he remembered the shock and hurt on Sam's face. No. Not hurt. Betrayal. She had trusted him to help her, and those innocent, doll-like eyes had gone wide with fear. Of him.

Even lost in his self-loathing contemplation, Gibson could hear her, somewhere nearby, sobbing loud enough to wake the dead. He tried to filter it out, but it was impossible. He had not cared about another person in so many years that he had forgotten what it was like to have someone important in his life. It was when he realized he loved her that he had decided he needed to send her away, for both of their sakes. It was not a romantic love, but one like a sister, like a family member, and that was a complication he was simply unable to deal with at the moment.

Part of it was that he was unwilling to risk losing someone close to him, especially the first person he had cared about in the years since his partner was murdered. A big part, probably bigger than he would ever admit even to himself. She would be safer away from him, and it would be easier for her to try to get back to where she belonged if she were on her own. Once he had decided she was safer on her own and more likely to

138

succeed, to get her life back instead of keeping her around for his own selfish reasons, he bought her all the supplies he could afford. He could never explain his actions to her in person. Gibson knew that if he tried to make her understand the danger that she would argue, and he would relent. She was very good about getting her way, and he begrudgingly admitted she was frequently right.

An image coalesced in his mind of Sam, bloody and dying on the street, looking up at him with fear and resentment. His heart ached at the thought. At least out in the world, heading toward the Sages in the west, at least out there she would have a chance. He was prepared to die and knew that Davis's plan was a fool's errand. He couldn't risk having Sam as a target for Old Man Ladi. Especially since word got out he was traveling with a ghoul.

Gibson swore, then walked to the smudged window to look out over the street. Hours passed as he stared a hole into the street, eyes fixed on the landing just outside of the building. He would not leave the safe house until she was long gone. In his mind's eye, he saw her wide, tear-filled eyes again, looking at him with such pain. Such pain. Unconsciously, he dug his fingernails into the palms of his hand, not even noticing when thick, silver liquid began to drip onto the floor.

*   *   *   *   *

Webb sat at his desk, a thick stack of large, glossy photographs in front of him. He had flipped through each one more times than he cared to think about, studying every detail of each photo. If he closed his eyes, he could pull the images to mind with no effort. Not intentionally. Drumming his fingers on his desk, he stared out the precinct window. A robin sat on a branch, slurping down the final bit of worm it had dug out of the ground.

His desk phone rang, pulling his attention. "Yeah? This is Webb."

"Detective Webb, it's Tyler Powell."

"How are things in Forensics, Tyler?" Webb suddenly felt wide awake and alert, as if someone had put smelling salts under his nose.

"A lot of one-way conversations," Powell answered with a laugh. When Webb did not respond, he cleared his throat awkwardly. "Sorry; just a bit of forensic humor."

"Did you have something for me, Tyler?" Webb barked, then took a deep, calming breath. Webb hadn't realized how on edge he was, but he had no right to be rude to Powell for trying to inject some levity into his job. The kid spent all day studying corpses and the places where they became corpses. Webb forced a smile to his face, hoping the younger man would be able to hear it through the phone. "Or did you call to test out pick-up lines? I'm flattered but not interested."

"Uh-yes," Powell stammered. Webb dropped the smile. "I know you've been keeping an eye on this potential serial we've been tracking. Damnedest thing, almost impossible to find a connection. If it weren't for the similarity in the corpses, we'd never have considered the possibility. Not one body in a few months, then three turn up in a day, then another three days later, and another two weeks before we have anything else. Lot of variety in attack, areas of the body with wounds, but all of them have at least a few chunks of flesh simply gone, like they were ripped away with a claw hammer or a crowbar."

"I've seen the pictures."

"Oh, of course." Powell sounded anxious. Webb was angry at himself for snapping at the kid, but not much he could do about it now. Maybe he would take him out for a beer some time to make up for it. "Anyway, two nights ago, Roberts gets a call about a body all ripped up, but this time, there's a witness."

Webb sat up straight, eyes wide. "Witness? What did they say?"

"Keep in mind I'm hearing this from Roberts, who heard it from someone else, so it's already passed through a few hands." The anxiety in Powell's voice had turned to caution, and maybe reluctance.

"What was it, Powell?"

There was a pause, during which Webb heard the younger man take a breath as if steadying himself. "The witness said he heard a scream from outside, so he got up to look outside. Natural enough, right? He said it was dark, but in the moonlight, he saw what looked like two people wrestling before one of them kicked the other. Maybe between the legs, maybe the knee, he said he couldn't tell. The suspect then leapt on top of the other man and started biting him. Biting, Detective. Witness hears a scream, horrible thing. Told Roberts that scream will haunt him for the rest of his life. He ran to the phone and called 9-1-1."

Webb listened to this story with his eyes shut, trying to picture the scene. "Where?"

"He lives over in the Oakridge Apartment complex," Powell answered. "Our witness was on the phone with dispatch but said he knew there was no way we'd make it in time and instead of watching from the window, he went outside and tried to scare away the attacker."

Webb scoffed but made no comment.

"Witness said he went outside yelling something about having a gun and the attacker got up and ran." Powell paused again. Webb felt a sense of foreboding in the silence. "Witness said the attacker ran, but after a few steps, dropped down and ran away on all fours. Disappeared into the night."

Incredulity filled Webb. "What? Like a dog or something?"

"More like a werewolf." Webb grunted. "I'm telling you what he told Roberts, Detective," Powell continued quickly. "I know. I don't believe it either. It was dark, the witness is elderly and was near hysterics, but I figured I should pass along the latest. There was a trail of blood that the First Responders followed into the tree line, but there were no tracks of any kind, and the blood trail ended suddenly in the woods." Webb could hear Powell shuffle through papers on his desk before he added, "Keep your silver bullets handy, Detective." The phone went dead.

Webb hung up the receiver and stared at it as it sat in its cradle. A werewolf? That was complete bull. It had to be. Right? A few minutes later, Webb grabbed his car keys and walked out of the building. The Oakridge Apartment complex was only about 20 minutes away, and it was time to do a little digging himself.

*   *   *   *   *

"What's with this guy?"

The voice outside the thick metal door was young, a forced gruffness clear as day around the edges. The Unborn lamb, fresh and innocent, led unwittingly to the slaughter. This one opened his mouth before the Shearer, though he would fall in line all the same, or he would be crushed beneath the boots of the world.

A second voice laughed darkly before answering. "This is our friend Symon."

The man inside the locked metal room grinned broadly. He was tall and slender, with curly blond hair that fell in waves, sometimes partially covering his eyes. Symon wasn't his real name, of course. His real name had long been forgotten, lost to the sands of time as they fell like the stars from the heavens. Symon moved closer to the metal door and whispered through the paper-thin crack that served as the only source of light. "You'll know everything about me soon enough, Little Lamb."

The yelp from outside the door was deeply satisfying.

Feeling emboldened, Symon dropped the whisper in favor of the voice of command. It was sonorous, like a chant in church. "From the foundation of this cursed world of the damned, it was His will to wage war on those He saw fit, and He commanded an army of every nation, every creed, every tongue. They wore no uniforms, had no battle hymns, but they were His, and they worshipped Him the way a drowning man worshipped the shoreline." The men outside the door shouted at him to stop, but Symon ignored them. The intensity of his words grew. "With each new land He conquered, His army of dedicated soldiers would grow! Each new man would worship Him more than the man before! His will was limitless! His power insurmountable! He is then! He is Forever! He is me and I am HIM!"

At his final word, the sound of thousands of simultaneous clicks echoed outside of the thick metal door. The door where Symon stood made an identical click before swinging open. Symon watched as the eyes of the two guards widened in surprise, then in fear as he sprang into action. His fist crunched against the throat of the first guard, causing the man to splutter as he asphyxiated. Symon grabbed the second guard's wrists, forcing the barrel of the guard's firearm upward, under the man's chin.

"He that leads into captivity shall go into captivity: he that kills with the sword must be killed with the sword. Here is the patience and the faith of the saints, Little Lamb."

A single blast of gunfire joined the thunderous roar that filled The Jar.

Chapter 12

Sam awoke on the floor of a maintenance closet, confused by her surroundings. She yawned and felt her face, stiff from dried tears, and the memories came crashing back into her head like a tidal wave. Gibson, furious, raging at her to leave, to get away from him and out of the city. Sam did not feel sadness, no desire to cry. That time had passed, and alone as she was, she was not going to be some sobbing damsel, even if she was trapped in the world of the dead. She set her jaw and stood, teeth grinding with fierce determination and anger. Sam hesitated for a moment before grabbing the bag of food and her cloak, but she did take them. There was no telling how difficult it might prove to find her own supplies, but this final reliance on Gibson's generosity grated on her. She told herself she was simply being practical, not dependent.

After pulling on her mask and one remaining glove, she threw the tattered remains of the cloak around her shoulders before carefully arranging her exposed hand deep in the curled folds of cloth. With any luck, anyone who bothered to look at her for more than a second would assume she had lost the arm, whether in life or in death, and would move on with their day. The bag of supplies hung heavily inside of her cloak. The last thing she needed was to get mugged, and from what she had seen of the Fourth City, ghouls very rarely had possessions beyond their disguises.

Her back was stiff from sleeping awkwardly in the closet, but she forced herself to stand at her full height as she stepped out of the building and into the street. It was late morning, as far as she could tell, which meant she hadn't slept for too long, at least. The sky was grey and overcast, the way it was on most days, which only added to the feeling of everything in this world being faded and almost translucent. In the chaos of the night before, Sam had not really seen the neighborhood. It was remarkably run down, even for the outskirts of the city. Most windows were gone, and only a handful even had rough coverings, usually in the form of strips of cloth. Wooden boards were probably too expensive for the people who lived in this area. It was easily the most impoverished area of the Fourth City she had seen since arriving.

Sam strode purposefully down the sidewalk toward the subway terminal. As much as she hated to admit it, she really had no idea of what to do other than to follow Gibson's advice and try to reach Old Town, to seek aid from the mysterious Sages. With a name like that, she imagined they were probably her best hope of escape from this horrible place. She saw only a handful of people on the street on her way to the station, and all but one of them sat on the ground, despondent and too lethargic to even lift their heads as she strode passed. They had the appearance of people who had nowhere else to go, people who could grab all their possessions in mere seconds if necessary. For the first time, she really wondered about the government of the Fourth City. If there was one, it appeared the mayor or whoever was in charge did not care much about the residents. There were a lot of seemingly abandoned buildings in this district, and in several of the others she had visited with Gibson. People should not be homeless when there are abandoned buildings that could be turned into apartments if they weren't already. Even buildings as decrepit as the ones on this block had to be better than sleeping on the streets. The fact that these people hadn't taken it upon themselves to set up in any of the buildings, though, made her question her understanding of this place. Grimly, Sam reminded herself she did not have time to get involved with social causes in a city in Purgatory.

The stairwell that descended toward the subway platform was reminiscent of the ones near Gibson's office, with flickering and burnt out fluorescent bulbs serving as sporadic light sources, just as many coruscating fitfully as completely dead. Sam's eyes slowly scanned the entire platform, consciously watching for anything that could possibly be a Void Hunter. Apparently her nearly fatal encounter with it, and the subsequent conversation, had been enough to permanently cement the horrible creature in her mind. This far away from the downtown district, and in such an impoverished area, she was not surprised to find the station completely deserted.

While she waited for the train to arrive, Sam studied the subway map. Although it was difficult to read beneath the dirt and scratches on the Plexiglas casing, it was obvious she would have to change trains in the main downtown hub, the same stop she and Gibson had used the night before. Her mind flashed rapidly through the memories of the previous night, of the chaos at Alley Cats, of Gibson's despondent attitude after they had escaped. Sam's eyes narrowed and she ruthlessly shoved the memories away. She had to move forward, physically and mentally, or else she would never get out of the Fourth City, let alone back to her rightful life.

The train arrived empty, coasting along automatically, and Sam boarded. Unbidden, she found herself imagining a single body in a massive metal casket. The thought made her shiver. The next two stops were silent. Perhaps it was the time of day that was keeping people away from the subway stations, but it still made her feel nervous. The last time she had traversed the Fourth City on her own was fraught with traumatic memories. That experience had ended with her passed out in the hallway outside of Gibson's office apartment after running from bloodthirsty fox-faced Dybbuks. Once again Sam pushed away memories she was not ready to face.

Passengers finally boarded the subway at the next stop, the last one before the central hub. Having had nearly half an hour on the train by herself had dulled Sam's wits. A stupor, born out of something resembling boredom, as astonishing as that was, had settled itself into her brain. The light fixtures were all functioning this deep into the heart of the city, and the floors were swept and polished. Men and women in suits were milling about, many clutching briefcases and newspapers in their hands. Sam wondered about the mental health of people who live their lives working in big business, then find themselves living their deaths working in big business. She had always thought she would be uncomfortable in a stuffy corporate job, and having one that you could never leave felt insurmountably daunting.

The central terminal was busy, but not so crowded that it was challenging to navigate. She found the platform where her next train would eventually whisk her into the western outreaches of the Fourth City, into the unknown. The line had seven stops on it, and at the seventh, she would have to get out and start walking outside of the city limits. Sam clenched her jaw to remind herself she needed to be tough in her independence, but she hated feeling like she was stumbling around blindly. Always forward, she told herself fiercely, clenching her jaw.

Sam leaned against a bannister while she waited for the subway to arrive, conscientious of her phoenix mask and torn cloak as she was so close to the scene of last night's crimes. Her hands were sweaty and her fingers were getting numb from clutching the bag of food underneath her cloak. Her stomach growled, but she did not dare eat anything in front of anyone. Along with her hunger, her apprehension was spiking. If anyone asked her any questions, or worse, recognized her from the vague descriptions in the newspaper, her day would get a lot worse. Fast.

The train arrived in a cacophony of squealing brakes and electrical surges. Sam let out a sigh of relief as she stepped onto the train and spotted a quiet corner at the far end, practically right behind where the conductor would sit, if the trains had conductors. The window embedded in the top half of the locked door showed a handful of manual controls and dials. Sam wondered how long ago the switch was made to automatic subway trains. If the automation technology had only recently reached Purgatory, what other changes might be in the Fourth City's – and the dead world's – future?

She found herself thinking again about the process of dying, and what it must be like to wake up and face the reality that, as a recently-deceased person, it was time to get back to work. For someone, that meant designing these pre-programmed subway routes for dead people to get to their jobs every morning of their dead lives. Surprisingly, Sam had to stifle a giggle at the thought of them working dead-end jobs.

With her back to the wall, Sam felt a little safer. Thankfully, she was in a nearly empty car. Three men, all in suits, sat by themselves in rows near the sliding door that led to the next car. Each one was reading the newspaper and paid no attention to anything beyond the printed words on the page, for which she was grateful. The train clicked along, and Sam lost herself in the rhythm. All three of the suited men left the train at the first stop, determinedly focused on ignoring everything outside of their own little worlds, and Sam was alone once more.

Tentatively, and with repeated furtive glances at the connective door, Sam opened the bag of food that sat on her lap and peered inside. There was a large loaf of bread, a good size wedge of a salty cheese she had grown to enjoy but could never remember the name of, a container of peanut butter, and a handful of tin cans filled with beans or fruit. Sam tore a small chunk of bread free from the loaf and slid it under her mask. The train car remained empty for the next two stops.

At the fourth station, Sam was beginning to feel more at ease. She had passed through a large swath of the city unnoticed, had eaten, and had a destination firmly in mind. Even if she was unsure of its exact location, her plan was to simply follow the road out of the city and look for a sign to direct her to Old Town.

When the door between the subway cars slid open with a blast of hydraulics, Sam bit back a curse. A hard pit formed in her stomach as she saw the man who passed through the tiny metallic vestibule. He was average height and build, with faded brown hair, and he wore what was unmistakably the uniform of a police officer. Whether this was some kind of transit officer or a city cop, Sam was not sure. He glanced down at a paper clutched in his hand, then slowly scanned the subway car. There was no one else in the car and nowhere for her to hide. The officer stared at her, his face creasing visibly even at a distance, then looked down at the paper again.

"You," he said in a voice with a clipped accent, loud enough to be heard over the clattering subway, "Ghoul. Stand up. Slowly."

Sam's heart raced. Beads of sweat formed and streaked down from her hairline, threatening to sting her eyes. She did not move. His gruff demeanor reminded her of Gunnarsson, the huge blonde police officer who had dragged her to the police station shortly after she had awakened in the alley. He took a few firm steps toward her before repeating himself. Sam's mind was blank from panic. She needed to get out of this situation before she got arrested. Or worse. The subway car clicked forward, ignorant of the standoff happening inside its bowels.

Crazed thoughts flashed in her mind, including trying to attack the cop with the bag of groceries she still held, concealed beneath her cloak, but she dismissed them quickly. Unsure of what else to do, Sam got to her feet as quickly as she was able and pulled hard at the door to the conductor cab, but it resisted her attempt to open it. The officer was startled for a split second at her sudden movement but recovered quickly and raced toward her. The door gave way, opening with surprising weight, and Sam darted into the cockpit, slamming the door shut behind her. The cop was only a few steps behind, screaming at her, his face purple and furious through the thick window embedded in the door. Scanning the dials and buttons on the dash, Sam tugged a lever labeled Warning: Emergency Brake.

The subway screeched, showering the outside tunnel with sparks, and causing a jostle like an earthquake inside the train. The officer yelped as he was thrown into the air, and Sam turned just in time to see his head smack into the window hard enough to cause a crack to spider web on the Plexiglas. A smear of silvery blood filmed on the other side as his face slid down the window before his body fell heavily to the floor. Sam was panting, her warm, moist exhalations making it hard to breathe inside her mask. She forced open a door that led to the train tunnel and whispered a quick hope the officer was not too badly injured - he was only doing his job, after all – then leaped from the train onto the gravel-covered tunnel floor below. Sam sprinted as fast as she could down the tunnel, terrified of being caught if the cop had a partner elsewhere on the subway train.

Her mind raced faster than her sneakers as they crunched on the stone, the bag of food thumping against her leg with every other step. She was positive that had she not taken action, she would have been arrested and questioned, and if anyone placed her at Alley Cats the night before, or recognized her as a Bloodwalker, she may have ended up in The Jar. Sam didn't know why, but the nickname for the prison sent waves of fear up her spine.

Should she keep running down the dimly-lit tunnel, leaving footprints in the gravel? That seemed like a foolish way to try to escape, leaving a clear trail for anyone to follow. Would she be safe if she left the tunnel at the next subway station? Probably not. If the transit cop had a description or photograph of her phoenix mask and cloak, going to street level was a terrible idea. The thought crossed her mind of trying to hide in a maintenance tunnel, but if there was a search for her, it would only be a matter of time before she was caught.

Sam slowed to a jog, then took a few dozen walking steps before stopping altogether. Blood pounded in her ears. She took a few deep breaths, counting to five in her head before releasing each one, trying to steady her heart rate. As the drumming of her pulse quieted, Sam strained, listening for anyone in pursuit. She heard nothing except her breath and heartbeat. The subway train was long out of sight, with several curves and nearly ten minutes of running between her and it. If the cop had only been knocked unconscious by her pulling of the emergency brake, he would almost certainly be awake by now. Sam hoped he had survived the force of the impact. She knew sometimes people were confused after being concussed. Maybe he would forget he had seen her. Sam didn't think she was that lucky. She just needed enough time to get out of the city.

Trying to rein in her thoughts and decide on a plan, Sam closed her eyes. The lights in the tunnel flickered behind her eyelids, but she ignored them. There were no flawless plans, she realized immediately, but after a few moments, she knew what she would do. First, she needed to conserve her energy, in case she needed to run later.

To Sam's surprise, two sets of concrete stairs and elevated walkways appeared on either wall of the tunnel a few minutes later. She did not hesitate in climbing the stairs and walking on the underground sidewalk, which must be there for maintenance personnel. The next terminal platform came into sight shortly thereafter. It was completely empty. She had counted on that, being so far outside of the bustling heart of the city's downtown district.

Sam crossed the platform, the thud of her footfalls amplified by the stillness in the cavernous tunnel, and continued down the maintenance sidewalk on the other side of the landing, walking along the yellow line that marked the edge of where people could safely wait for the next subway arrival. As she descended the stairs back onto the gravel tunnel floor, Sam tried to ignore the itchy feeling of being watched. A few uncomfortable minutes later, she found a maintenance tunnel.

Sam tucked her bag of food behind a large box of unused fluorescent light tubes just inside the tunnel. Judging by the number of burned out lights, she couldn't imagine anyone finding the bag. She hesitated for a moment, rummaging around in the bag before removing a bottle of water. She drank slowly, conscious of the need to ration her supplies. It tasted like morning breath. Gritting her teeth, she dropped the bottle back into the bag before pulling her cloak off her shoulders. Sam wrapped it carefully around the food bag. She hoped that would be good enough to keep rodents away from her supplies. She knew she was taking a big risk, but if the police had a description of her disguise, was it any more of a risk than keeping it on? Her hands shook as they reached up and removed the phoenix mask. She set it carefully at the top of the stack, the sharp-beaked avian visage glaring accusingly. She felt vulnerable and exposed, wearing her jeans and a long sleeve shirt with no phoenix protecting her.

Sam knew this was an incredibly dangerous decision, but she had made it based on two thoughts. First, the city streets would probably be less crowded due to the time of day and location. The Fourth City, for all its size and scope, seemed to be very densely populated in the central district, thinning rapidly outside the center. She had not been to this part of the city before, but she had lived in the northern part of the city for a few months and had been in the southern part last night, and neither place had been something she would describe as busy. She was making a reasonable, if risky, guess.

Second, and the part Sam felt less confident about, was the idea that most people would not recognize a Bloodwalker on sight. She remembered the confused people on the sidewalk when she had first stumbled out of the alley, and Gunnarsson's ignorance of her situation as well. They were all alarmed and avoided her as if she had the Black Plague, but she had not heard the word Bloodwalker until after she had sat next to Gibson in the processing line at the precinct. Harold had recognized her as a Bloodwalker as soon as he had seen her exposed hand, but he was well-connected and a former cop, so maybe it was a story he had picked up somewhere. One police officer knew her for what she was, and one did not. It was thin evidence and a pitifully small sample size to base her future on, she knew, but she also didn't feel like she had any other better option. The phoenix mask was almost certainly too widely known at this point.

For the first few steps, Sam's legs betrayed her façade of confidence, feeling like lead as she left the sanctuary of the maintenance tunnel and returned to the platform she had passed a few minutes prior. Thankfully, the terminal had remained deserted, though the itch on her neck returned. Her knees shook. In a state of hyperawareness, Sam noticed that one of her sneakers clicked with each step on the concrete platform. As quickly as she could, Sam spun around mid-step. If there was anyone watching her, she wanted to catch them before they had a chance to hide. She stared hard, taking in every detail, but nothing moved. After waiting for a few breaths, she bent to dig out the chunk of gravel that had embedded itself in the tread of her sneaker, then scratched at her neck. Sam whipped her head up, simultaneously hoping to see no one and whoever or whatever was watching her. The terminal was still completely empty. She wished she felt relieved.

Sam pressed on, telling herself she was imagining things, that her nerves were getting the better of her. She watched the grey sky creep ever closer as she climbed the decrepit staircase toward street level before cautiously peeking out at the sidewalks from the protection of the stairwell. A man with lank grey hair and a tattered tan coat shambled away from her, presumably another of the Fourth City's homeless citizens. Garbage littered the sidewalk. Somehow this part of the city looked even more disheveled than she expected. A few signs hung over door frames, marking the corpses of abandoned storefronts. The wind whistled sharply in Sam's ear as she took the final few steps to ground level. So far, her plan was working. So far. She shook her head with embarrassment. She had been out of the subway tunnel for less than a minute.

Sam's feet crunched on broken glass as she walked to the first of the vacant shops. The shelves inside the murky depths were almost completely empty, though it was impossible to tell how long ago the store had been looted. Glancing quickly in each direction, Sam clambered through the gaping window. She needed two things, and what better place to start than here?

The arrangement of the shelves reminded Sam of a pharmacy. A broken cash register sat open and overturned on the counter. Sam traversed the snaking aisles quickly, taking in everything, or more specifically, the lack of everything. She had not expected to find everything she needed immediately and felt no frustration, only determination. It was past time to fend for herself. In the back of the shop was a wooden door, hanging uselessly from busted hinges. Beyond that door was a small room, perhaps a manager's office or break room. Countless sheets of paper littered the floor. An old wooden desk leaned against the far wall, one of its spindly legs snapped. The drawers were all pulled open, and empty. Sam turned a slow, full circle on her heel, making sure she had not missed anything. Once she was positive she had no better option, Sam crouched by the side of the desk and unscrewed the leg on the opposite side of the broken one. The eight-inch piece of wood wasn't much, but in a pinch, she could use it as a cudgel to defend herself. She slid it up her right sleeve and left the store through the same gaping hole that had been the front window.

The door of the next shop was simply gone, and the inside looked as if it had been firebombed. Sam gave a cursory look inside before passing it by. An alleyway abutted the shop, filthy and pungent, and devoid of anything useful.

The next doorway she passed through turned out to be the lobby of an apartment building. It had the look of something well-cared for in the past but had become neglected and fallen into disrepair. The internal architecture was vastly different from Gibson's office apartment. This space looked more like a flophouse in which a street hustler would rent a room in an old black and white movie. Dust was thick on the tattered, carpeted floor and Sam felt a sense of relief when she noticed there were no footprints in the dust other than her own. There were three stories to this building. Sam decided to start at the top and work her way down.

Sam felt her buoyed optimism sag slightly as she entered abandoned rooms with impunity. Unfortunately, she found most of them were as picked over as the shops had been. Rusted metal bed frames took up most of the space in any given room. She briefly considered trying to remove one of the legs from a bed frame to replace the length of wood hidden up her sleeve, but abandoned the idea, wondering if tetanus existed in Purgatory. Occasionally the rooms held a small dresser, wood warped and rotting more often than not.

At the end of the hallway, Sam pulled open a door leading to the stairwell. The third-floor search had been entirely worthless. As expected, the layout of the second floor was identical. There was considerably more rubble on this level, with chunks of wall lying shattered on the carpet, which looked like it had been set on fire in several places, marked with inky dark char. Room after room held the same rusted bed frame, never with a mattress. Sam wondered if there had been mattresses in the past, or if the previous renters had simply slept on the metal. She cringed at the thought.

Halfway down the hall, Sam opened a door and stared. This room was considerably more comfortable, with several worn but thick blankets crumpled on the bed frame, though the air was musty from lack of circulation. There were two dressers, both of which were in better condition than anything else she had found before. In the corner of the room was a heaping pile of - stuff. Sam struggled to come up with a better description for it. Clothing was predominant, but she saw little bits of things sticking out, ranging from wood slats to a cook pot to what looked like a metal lunchbox. Sam was still in the door frame, straining her ears for any sound of movement. She did not want to steal from anyone, but the person who acquired all these items could be long dead. "For the second time," Sam reminded herself. The internal struggle was palpable, her scruples battling - but eventually losing to - her sense of self-preservation.

Stepping into the room, Sam shut the door behind her as quietly as she could and started digging through the unsorted pile of randomness in the corner. She tried to memorize the rough pattern of colors and shapes before taking it apart, so she could reassemble it after she had dug through the pile and hopefully the owner, if he or she was still around, would never notice anything was missing. A fork and a cook pot were wrapped up around a mildewed blanket. A little lower in the pile, Sam found a half-eaten bag of round, salted crackers, which she left alone.

Just as she was beginning to consider giving up on the enormous pile of miscellany, she pulled on a thick piece of black cloth. Like a snake uncoiling or a magician pulling dozens of handkerchiefs from some unseen location, the cloth stretched and grew, eventually revealing itself to be a thick, black pullover hooded sweatshirt. Sam held it up reverently by the shoulders. It would be enormous on her, which would be advantageous. Sam saw it had a pocket across the front that was joined in the middle, so she could keep her hands hidden, and keep her cudgel in her hands without anyone noticing.

Sam pulled the sweatshirt over her head. With grim satisfaction she noticed the hood covered most of her face, casting her in shadow from the cowl. It was certainly not as concealing as the phoenix mask, but it also would pass any but the closest scrutiny. Hopefully anyone who saw part of her face would dismiss her lively appearance as a trick of the light. After reaching the floor and finding nothing else of use, Sam hastily reassembled the pile as best she could.

Next, Sam rummaged through the dressers. The first two were filled with books, spines facing upward to display faded titles. As much as she loved to read, Sam did not think weighing herself down with books was a particularly smart idea. The rest of the first dresser housed neatly folded men's clothing, which she left undisturbed with a further sense of guilt.

The second dresser held assorted pieces of metal and electronics, mostly circuit boards. In the bottom drawer, shoved to the side, was a small metal tin. A thick white piece of tape with the word 'Syn' on it was stuck to the silver cover. Sam tried to remember all the details of Gibson's lecture on the substance. Synthosyn, it was called. Some kind of a synthetic drug, though its effects remained hazy to her, unsure if she had ever learned what it did. Something about bugs and corn? Sam shoved the tin into the front pocket of her jeans. She had no intention of using it herself, but she may be able to barter with it at some point, and it was light enough to not slow her down.

Sam was building a mental image of the occupant of this room when the door swung open behind her. She had been picturing a squat, obese man with glasses, a stationary homebody grown plump with inactivity. The tall, wiry man who stepped into the room was the exact opposite, aside from the glasses. He was a pale man, even for Purgatory, with deep reddish hair, and Sam watched his face darken as understanding and rage filled him. Still crouched in front of the dresser, Sam froze, her mind blank.

"What-what-what-" the man spluttered in apoplexy with a voice like rocks on a chalkboard. "What are you doing here?" he screeched. His body was tensed but he had not moved from the door frame. Sam's thoughts spun like pictograms on a slot machine. The only thing she knew was that she had trespassed and it was a coin flip's difference on which of them was more surprised by the other. Suddenly, he seemed to realize she was wearing his hooded sweatshirt. "Thief!" he bellowed angrily, face further coloring. The man took a forceful step in Sam's direction.

Sam reacted without thought as something instinctual and primal took hold of her. She darted toward him and slid the wooden cudgel out of her sleeve. Her sudden movement caused the man to cry out in surprise, but Sam was already swinging the cudgel at his shin. The man grunted with pain as the wood slammed against the bone, causing him to tumble forward. In one fluid motion, Sam stood and swung the cudgel downward, cracking him in the back of the skull as he was falling. There was an unpleasant sound of something being crunched as his face smacked into the floor. He did not move.

Sam exhaled as understanding dawned on her. She had just attacked a man, a man who had done nothing wrong. Where that violent confidence had come from, Sam had no idea. She was the criminal, the one who had broken into his apartment and stolen from him. Sam's hands shook. She closed her eyes to try to steady her nerves, telling herself she had to defend herself, that he would have hit her, or worse, and her only crime was trying to survive. Sam knew she was lying.

She looked down at the desk leg-turned-weapon she held in a white-knuckled grip and saw silver-white fluid dripping from the end of it. She shook it, trying to get the blood off of it, then squeezed her eyes tight, intent on erasing the visual from her memory. It only cemented itself further. This was very different than when Davis's hand was sliced in two by her phoenix mask all those months ago. She had been in the wrong place at the wrong time with Davis, and he had been trying to push her roughly out of the way. When she had helped Gibson escape from the warehouse, she felt justified in fighting back against criminals. This was different, and it made her feel sick to her stomach. Taking slow breaths did not help her arms and legs from quivering as the adrenaline dissipated. As quickly as she could, Sam left the building, leaving all the other rooms untouched. Her hand still squeezed around her makeshift club as if the two were glued together as she shoved it into the pocket across the front of the sweatshirt.

Stumbling along the sidewalk, Sam could not get the image of the man she had injured out of her head. Unconsciously, she traced the curve of her cudgel with her index finger. Deep in her brain, Sam knew she needed to focus, to get what she needed and get off the street. Time flowed, steady and silent, as Sam wandered blindly. She stumbled over a cardboard box, scattering the contents across the chipped and dirty sidewalk, not hearing the angry shouts of the homeless man who had painstakingly collected the odds and ends. Sam trudged onward, a slave to the shambling rhythm of her sneakers as she put distance between herself and the man she had attacked.

Sam's dark reverie was finally broken when a figure stepped out of an alleyway a few feet in front of her. A figure wearing a filthy brown cloak, and a mask that looked like the face of a fox. Sam's scream tore at her throat, stretching the delicate muscles to the brink of shredding. The Dybbuk grinned widely.

Chapter 13

Sam staggered backward, arms windmilling, before thudding hard to the ground. The Dybbuk stepped closer, slowly, as if it were savoring the opportunity to torture her. The grin widened. Sam scuffed her sneakers against the ground, trying to back away, but she knew she would never be able to escape from the monster while she was sitting on the sidewalk.

The Dybbuk kept its approach steady, its red-stained cloak rustling slightly with each unseen step. The desk leg bounced in Sam's sweatshirt pocket, completely forgotten in panic. As diminutive as the Dybbuk was, it seemed to tower over Sam, its menace casting a visage ten times its physical height. Fear filled Sam, though it was not a fear of dying. She knew now that when she died, she would find herself in this Unborn city, or another like it, free to live her death however she chose. Instead, the fear that coursed through her veins was at the idea of never making it back to the living world, to Jack, the fear that no one would ever know what had happened to her. Sam's arms trembled under the strain of trying to skitter away from the Dybbuk before giving out, elbow smacking the pavement. On the verge of hysteria, Sam pushed out through frustrated tears, "W-what are y-you going to d-d-do to me?"

The Dybbuk stopped its methodical approach, the mask-like face taking on a quizzical look. The corners of its mouth twitched. "W-what are y-you going to d-d-do to me?" the Dybbuk echoed. It appeared confused that the words had come out, confused at the meaning, but no more confused than Sam.

"You can talk?" Sam blinked at the creature in front of her.

The Dybbuk's expression mirrored Sam's. "You can talk?" Its voice was a strange mix of a growl and a gasp, like biting cold wind reverberating in a cave. Its echoing of her words was unnerving, though Sam was somewhat mollified it had not attacked her. Yet.

Sam pushed herself upright, staring at the odd little fox demon. It cocked its head slightly to the side in a distinctly canine fashion, then plunked down on the sidewalk across from her. Sam saw what looked like long-dried blood on its chin, and an unsettling thought popped into her head.

"You're the same one that bit me!" she blurted out, forgetting the Dybbuk would simply repeat her, which it did without delay. Staring at the demon, who watched her curiously, it seemed she was not in any immediate danger. She wracked her brain, searching for any memory of the Dybbuks talking during her last encounter with them, but her memories said they were silent, communicating through gestures.

Sam stood cautiously, keeping her gaze on the fox. It rose as she did, watching her raptly. Sam thought of a puppy looking adoringly at its master. "Well," Sam began, searching for a way to leave the Dybbuk behind without triggering its anger, "I hope you find your way back to your house. I'm going now." She took a tentative step backward as the Dybbuk parroted her in its raspy voice. As soon as her foot touched the ground again, the Dybbuk took a single stride closer, maintaining an identical distance. Thankfully, it still did not appear poised to attack, but Sam was not about to let her guard down. Her previous encounter with the Dybbuk had not felt particularly threatening, at least at first.

"Stay?" Sam felt foolish talking to the vulpine spirit as if it were a dog, but she had no idea what to do. Once again, the Dybbuk echoed her, but continued to keep an even distance from her as she backed away. "Gestures," Sam reminded herself, "they communicate through gestures." Feeling rather silly, she pointed at her chest, then pointed further down the sidewalk. "I'm going that way." Sam enunciated her words slowly, hoping the Dybbuk would understand, "you stay here." She then pointed at the Dybbuk, then at the sidewalk in front of it. Once again, the fox turned its unnerving, blood-stained face at an angle, as if trying to comprehend. It repeated her and stayed in lockstep as she took another step backward. This was getting her nowhere. Sam glanced around at the vacant street, wondering if she could count on it remaining vacant. Sam was afraid she was drawing far too much attention to herself.

A sigh escaped Sam's lips as she realized what she would have to do to get out of this predicament. Slowly, so as not to be threatening, Sam moved toward the Dybbuk. It cocked its head to the side once more as it watched her approach. When she was only a few feet away, Sam crouched in front of it and whispered. "Look, I know you're just going to repeat me anyway, but I need to say this so I don't feel like I'm going crazy." She closed her eyes as it started to repeat her words back to her. This was getting annoying. "You can come with me, but so help me God if you try to bite me, I will find a way to destroy you." Remembering the man she had left on the floor with a cracked skull, Sam shivered. Hopefully it wouldn't come to that. "I'm going to hold your hand, and I'm going to pretend you're my daughter." Once again, Sam waited for the fox ghost to repeat her. Under her breath, she added, "I can't believe my life has come to this."

Cautiously, Sam reached out her hand, making sure the Dybbuk saw what she was doing, and touched the creature. The tiny gloved hand clenched in Sam's was cold and frail, its chill permeating the red-brown cloth in radiating waves, but it did not pull away, instead looking up at her with the same rapt expression on its face. Sam shook her head in disbelief.

The Dybbuk kept pace with Sam, its short legs needing twice as many strides to maintain her speed. She watched the top of the Dybbuk's head from the corner of her eye, wary of the potential for a sudden attack, though that was becoming less and less likely by the second, she realized. As the minutes passed with the Dybbuk trotting at her side, Sam was surprised to realize she felt something akin to sympathy for the demon. Oblivious to her changing emotions, the Dybbuk began to skip contentedly, its joy at the situation obvious. Despite the history she had with Dybbuks, and this one in particular, Sam felt her attitude toward the tiny beast soften, at least a little. *Just a mother and daughter out for a walk,* Sam thought with a faint smile. "Out for a walk in the world of the dead." Her smile vanished, but the Dybbuk softly purred with pleasure.

Once the initial awkwardness faded, Sam began to wonder what had led to this dramatic change of behavior. She tried not to let her mind wander too much, however, as the Fourth City held many dangers, even if there was nothing obvious in sight. Sudden breezes whistling through her hair could simply be the wind, or the icy breath of some foreboding creature. Life in the world of the dead required constant vigilance.

Sam and her ghastly companion reached the stairs that descended into the depths of the subway station without incident. At the top of the stairs, Sam hesitated. She looked down into the shadow-shrouded stairwell, then at the tiny fox by her side. Sam fought the urge to sigh; she noticed she had been doing an awful lot of sighing lately. How was she going to explain to the Dybbuk she needed it to stay here while she went back into the tunnel and wandered off into the unknown in search of knowledge in Old Town?

"No."

Sam jumped in surprise. The word was spoken softly, in a vacuous voice that recalled images of black holes. The Dybbuk was staring at her with that unnerving face, still clutching her hand. It repeated itself, more forcefully, "No." She had only been walking with the fox demon for a handful of minutes, but hearing it speak outside of parroting was unbelievably unnerving. Sam had not realized how presumptuous she had been by assuming the Dybbuk was incapable of anything beyond echolalia.

Mind racing, Sam crouched before the tiny creature, putting herself on eye level. "No? What do you mean no?"

The Dybbuk's porcelain-esque mouth cracked open to speak, but no sounds came out. As the raised eyebrow ridges of its rigid face curled furiously downward, Sam had the impression it was searching for the right words but couldn't find them. The Dybbuk howled in frustration. Abruptly, an expression of joy burst onto its face. Using its free gloved hand, the Dybbuk pointed at itself, then at Sam, then down the stairwell. It looked at Sam expectantly.

Sam had a feeling this was coming. "You're going to follow me no matter what I say, aren't you." It wasn't a question. In a way, the Dybbuk's attachment to her was sort of endearing, even if the creature was a demon that had bitten her. Bitten her! That fact brought a cascade of interesting thoughts and horrifying memories, but Sam couldn't focus on any one of them and they splashed into the recesses of her brain to be dredged through later. The Dybbuk once again pointed at itself, then Sam. This time it also crossed its fingers, which Sam interpreted to mean they were inseparable. Fingers still intertwined, the Dybbuk pointed into the darkness of the subway terminal.

Sam stood and squeezed the tiny frigid hand gently. "Okay then," she said, acquiescing, "come on." Sam's sneakers echoed off the battered concrete walls as they descended into the depths. Could she really trust this creature? She would need to sleep eventually. Did Dybbuks need sleep? It had bitten her before; would it attack her when she was at her most vulnerable? The torrent of thoughts about the demon battered at her once again, but one thing stuck out: this Dybbuk had bitten her, a Bloodwalker, and then it was drawn to her like metal shavings to a lodestone. Gibson had not been able to tell her much about Dybbuks, but she was certain she would have remembered anything about Dybbuks becoming relentless in pursuit of their prey. Besides, she had managed to escape them, to outrun them, before she had collapsed in the hallway outside of his office door. That was months ago, far from a relentless pursuit. Perhaps this Dybbuk had changed in some way, from consuming the blood of a living person. That could explain its rudimentary development of language, of its echoing. The more she considered it, the more childlike and dependent the fox demon became in her mind, and the more she wanted to protect it.

Sam led the creature down the stairs and onto the gravel of the subway tunnel, retracing her steps back to where she had stashed her few belongings. The trip aboveground had not been as fruitful as she had hoped, but it would have to do. Her goal had been to find a new mask, cloak, and something with which to defend herself. What she ended up with was a tin of a drug she didn't want, a hooded sweatshirt that was gigantic enough to fit three of her in it, and a chunk of wood. Along with the sweatshirt and club, she had acquired a companion of sorts, though Sam wasn't sure if that was a positive. It was a far cry from the visions of a dagger or a brand-new cloak.

The Dybbuk shuffled along the rocks, kicking up small puffs of dimly-lit dust. It was holding Sam's hand a little bit tighter now, as if it were uncertain and afraid. She had been considering ways of making the Dybbuk feel more at ease, scolding herself for how quickly she was going soft on the ghastly creature. Sam's internal struggle about how to behave toward the fox demon continued long after she had gathered up her bundle of belongings from the service tunnel and continued her trudge toward Old Town and the Sages. The icy, clawed hand of the Dybbuk was clutched in her own at every step, a constant reminder of her perplexing relationship with the spirit, and with the dead world as a whole.

*   *   *   *   *

The eerie, unnerving silence that permeated the general vicinity of the Oakridge Apartment complex was broken by the slamming of the door of Webb's car. He looked around. A dumpster surrounded by a wooden fence stood at the far end of the lot, a strand of yellow police tape dangling like a diseased tongue from the closed lid. Just beyond that rose a moderately-sized forest, which stretched about 30 acres. The apartments themselves had off-white vinyl siding, with black shutters around the windows. It was a simple property, originally designed for people in their later years but not quite ready for a nursing home. Now it was something of a hybridization, with some younger folks using it as transitional housing while they established themselves in the careers of their choice. Webb turned slowly, taking in the full scene. The silence was oppressive.

Turning back toward the dumpster, Webb tried to build a mental picture of the attack, based on Powell's description over the phone. A middle-aged man, alone in the parking lot, or at least thinking he was alone. A younger man bursts out of the darkness and strikes, a whirling dervish of fists and feet. The killer eventually pounces on top of the older man, hitting him with...something. Webb opened his eyes, banishing the re-creation in his head. He refused to believe the attacker killed a man by biting him, and the part about bounding off into the woods on all fours was simply more than he could handle.

"Excuse me."

Webb tensed in surprise at the sonorous voice that came from behind him. He was not used to being caught off guard. Spinning on his heel, Webb found himself not quite eye to eye with the speaker. The man was standing uncomfortably close, and Webb took an involuntary step backward. He was shorter than Webb by about an inch, with striking jade green eyes peering out from under a wave of well-maintained brown hair. The man was in his early 30s, his close shave showing unblemished skin.

"Can I help you with something? Who are you?" Webb asked, putting as much authority into the words as he could muster. Webb knew he was overcompensating for being surprised, but he didn't care.

"Just a tenant here," the man answered smoothly, not the least bit intimidated. "Who might you be?" The man's piercing gaze was steady and hard, though his words were like liquid silver. "Forgive my rudeness, but we did have a murder here two nights ago, after all." Webb thought he saw the ghost of a grin cross the man's face. Detective Webb showed the man his badge. His tone was unwavering. "A pleasure to meet you, Detective. I'm Michael Brown. You'll forgive me if I don't shake your hand." The man nodded his head downward, indicating a pair of bulging black trash bags.

Webb watched as the man threw the garbage bags into the dumpster before walking back into the apartment building, smiling unctuously. It was entirely possible that Webb was looking for any excuse to not be looking for a werewolf and was projecting onto the rather smarmy tenant, but Michael Brown made him uncomfortable. Webb sighed. There was something about the Oakridge complex that was unnerving. He felt like there were eyes on his back, no matter which direction he turned. He hadn't felt that sensation since he was a rookie.

After moving a few strides closer to the woods, Webb stopped and watched as a wind ruffled the polychromatic treetops, whipping through the branches before swirling across the ground toward him. He shivered as the biting cold gust reached him, and shivered again a moment after it passed. It was an unseasonably warm day. The frigid wind felt out of place, though Webb chided himself for being foolish. Another few steps toward the forest and a second frozen blast of ill wind shoved him roughly backward. His brow furrowed with confusion and anger. Taking a deep breath, Webb lifted his right foot, preparing to step toward the woods again. As if on cue, an icy curl of wind twirled itself around him, causing him to stumble. Was his pebbled skin simply reacting to the frozen gusts, or was there something else in the air that was disquieting?

He took a few steps backward, off the grass and back onto the paved parking lot of the apartment complex. It felt as if he had just stepped out of an industrial chiller. Experimentally, Webb stepped back onto the grass. He was immediately greeted by a glacial gale, powerful enough to knock him off his feet. Webb went back to his car and leaned against the side, staring at the small field and forest in front of him. His mind reeled over what had happened, too many thoughts to process at once, like dozens of trains all vying for the same slot at a terminal. Finally, one of those thoughts solidified. Detective Webb got in his car and drove away as quickly as he could.

Four days later, Webb was finally able to convince himself it had all been coincidence, or imagination, or a bad dream, and returned to the Oakridge complex. The day was cool but not unpleasant. A crow squawked in the distance as Webb stood in the parking lot once again, staring toward the woods. A diesel-powered truck roared quietly somewhere out of sight. No slimy tenants snuck up on him to hide laughter about the dead. It was a very ordinary day, with very ordinary sights and sounds. Steadying his nerves, the Detective stepped onto the grass. Nothing happened. He laughed, feeling foolish. Of course. It had all been a bad dream, or an aging man's faltering memory. Almost callously, Webb crossed the field and entered the woods, as if to assert his dominance over it.

An hour later, Detective Robert Webb fumbled blindly for the radio on his hip, staring at something that convinced him it had not been a bad dream after all.

Chapter 14

The first night of sleeping with the Dybbuk as a companion could generously be described as fitful. The slightest movement or noise made Sam's eyes pop open, immediately seeking out the fox demon. Without fail, the Dybbuk would be in the same spot, two feet away from her, crouched and turning its head from one end of the service tunnel to the other, watching over her like a mother with a mewling newborn. Apparently the Dybbuk did not require sleep.

Sam eventually gave up on the idea of any kind of efficient rest. Brushing away the gravel that had embedded itself in her side, she stretched awkwardly and rubbed at her eyes with the palms of her hands. The Dybbuk rose from its haunches and watched her rapturously. "Good morning," Sam groaned as she stretched again. The Dybbuk echoed her greeting in its deep, gasping voice. It was startling to realize how quickly her relationship with the Dybbuk was becoming one of companionship. Idly, Sam wondered how odd it was that one's perceptions could change literally overnight, but she assumed that not being viciously mauled by a bloodthirsty fox demon when it had every opportunity to do so probably would change a lot of people's perceptions. Sam grinned sardonically at the creature.

They crept past three stations during their excursion in the subway tunnel before physical and emotional exhaustion overwhelmed Sam. No trains had traveled past her and the fox; perhaps the subway maintenance crews in the world of the dead were not very efficient and the train she had stopped was still being repaired. She forced herself to keep moving until she found another service tunnel. She had no idea how much sleep she had the prior night, but it didn't matter. She had to keep moving. Looking at the cylindrical hunk of wood she had taken from the desk, Sam briefly debated attempting another foray to the city above for supplies, but dismissed it as being too risky. Besides, judging by the Dybbuk's attachment to her, she might already have a surprisingly vicious defender at her side.

A thought occurred to her suddenly as the crunching of stone underfoot droned on. Grabbing a small, tart apple from her bag, Sam turned toward the fox demon. "Do you need to eat actual food, or do you only eat people?" she asked, proffering the wizened fruit. The Dybbuk sniffed at it curiously before turning away. *Well, that answers that,* Sam thought as she stepped out into the tunnel proper, a grim smile on her face.

Sam and the Dybbuk trudged their way down the subway tunnel for a short while before the tiny demon whimpered with a voice like a distant roll of thunder. Sam crouched down to look into the creature's eyes and was unnerved to see them wide with panic. The mouth on its mask-like face opened, revealing rows of tiny pointed teeth, but it made no move to attack her. Instead, it struggled and pushed out a single word. "Hide." The Dybbuk was trembling with fear. As Sam stood back up, she heard what the Dybbuk's sharp ears had picked up: the howling whistle of a subway train as it roared down the tunnel in the distance. The tunnel was wide enough that the train would be able to pass without them being struck, but it did seem the tunnels grew narrower the further out from the city's heart she traveled. There was also the problem of being seen. It was almost certain the police would be looking for the person who resisted arrest and shut down a subway line for half a day, and even without the damning cloak, how many people would be wandering around in the subway tunnels?

Grabbing the taloned hand of the fox demon, Sam ran as fast as the Dybbuk could manage. They needed to find a service tunnel, maintenance closet, anything. They needed to be out of sight as soon as possible. Clouds of dust marked their trek, and there were the inevitable footprints, but that simply couldn't be avoided. Sam tried to pull the subway schedule to mind as their feet crunched on the dirty gravel. If the train were to stop at the closest terminal, it would be leaving the station and heading toward them within four minutes. The subway would be traveling a lot faster than they were, so it would be on top of them probably three or four minutes after that. Seven minutes total, at best.

Sam remembered the map that was hung from the wall of every station: the further from the Fourth City's central district, the further apart the stations were spaced. So far, it held true that the more distant stations also rarely had people waiting for the subway to whisk them away into the metropolis's heart, but it wasn't only people she needed to be wary of. Her experience with the Void Hunter left her immune to its memory

166

manipulation, or so she hoped, but Sam still did not want to encounter another one. Caution was her best friend, her only defense. Running blindly terrified her. There was still so much she didn't know about the world of the dead. Panting from exertion, Sam glanced down at the Dybbuk as it scuttled beside her. So much she didn't know.

Counting down in her head as they ran, a mental clock connected to a proverbial time bomb, Sam's eyes flickered off the tunnel walls in search of anything that could hide them. The sound of the train leaving the subway terminal echoed behind them, and then all around them. She glanced back, instinctively looking for lights from the subway, but nothing yet. There were too many curves to be able to see it right away, but the noise was growing steadily. By the time she would see lights, it would be too late. Grunting, Sam lifted the Dybbuk into her arms before lengthening her gait. The Dybbuk's frame was tiny, cold, and frail, much like its hand, and it was light as a toddler, for which she was grateful. Sam certainly was not used to running while holding a toddler, but the terrified repetition coming from the creature spurred her on. "Hide. Hide. Hide." It clutched her tighter.

The Dybbuk's ribs jutted out like rocks in the shallows of the sea as it bounced in her grip with each footfall. Her leg muscles throbbed, refusing to relax after their contractions. The bag of food clanked against her leg as she ran, but Sam was afraid to drop it. She estimated they had fewer than two minutes to find sanctuary. Heart racing, Sam tried to exhale upward in hopes of blowing some of the sweat from her forehead, away from her already stinging eyes. The clatter of the subway was louder with each heartbeat, echoing off the narrowing stone walls. They rounded another bend in the tunnel. The train sped closer.

Breathe.
"Hide."
Clatter.
Run.
"Hide."
Breathe.
Pain.
"Hide."
Breathe.

Sam skidded to a halt, kicking up a thick cloud of dust. The pain in her legs was only exceeded by the searing burn of her lungs as she gasped for breath. Blinking away sweat, she moved closer to the wall and crouched, setting the Dybbuk and the food bag down on the gravel. The subway train roared with inevitability as it raced toward them. Sam pulled at a small metal grate she had seen as she was running, but it barely budged. She planted her feet on the wall on either side of the grate and put her entire body weight into it. Her fingers tore open and dripped hot blood onto the stone below, but the metal barely groaned. Desperation filled her as she sprang back to her feet and kicked at the grate. The headlights on the subway train were a shimmering reflection on the wall of the bend behind them. She kicked again, denting the cross-hatched metal. Pivoting sideways, she slammed the bottom of her foot against it as forcefully as she could, stumbling as the metal flew from its hinges.

Wind curled around the tunnel as the subway sped toward them. Sam grabbed the Dybbuk roughly by the wrist and shoved it head-first into the newly-opened ventilation shaft. "GET IN!" Sam bellowed, following the fox demon head-first. "MOVE!" The train roared in an eardrum-shattering cacophony as Sam scampered into the shaft. Sam buried her fingertips in her ears, desperate to shut out as much of the noise as she could from the train as it screamed passed. The Dybbuk was screaming as well, a tiny but terrified squeal of fear, at odds with the vacuous sound Sam had heard come from the creature before. The subway seemed to stretch forever, the electric buzz and boom of heavy machinery torturing Sam, who had buried her head in her arms. The Dybbuk's feet scratched on the metal as it crawled deeper into the vent. Sam debated if she should stay where she was but decided to follow the panicked creature. The vent was narrow enough that she hit her head on the top of it with almost every movement and the train's roar echoed with overwhelming intensity, but Sam forced herself to follow the Dybbuk.

The Dybbuk's feet disappeared around a corner. When Sam rounded the corner, she saw the fox demon curled up in itself, face bowed downward, tiny arms covering its head. The thundering of the subway cars was noticeably dampened around the bend, but the Dybbuk was clearly terrified. Sam wrapped her arms around the creature as much as she could in the confines of the ventilation shaft, trying to comfort it. At the first touch, its face reflexively shot upward to stare at her, wearing a menacing look, but it softened in an instant to the pained expression of a wounded animal. The frigid beast snuggled into the curls of her arms, shivering in terror, even after the train had completely passed. Sam was slightly unnerved to realize how much she had not only adjusted to having the Dybbuk by her side, but how much her attitude toward it had changed as well. Not that long ago, the creature had been instrumental in one of her most horrifying experiences since she arrived in the world of the dead, and now she was pulling it closer toward her chest in an attempt to comfort it and assuage its fears.

Sam was almost positive there were two more stations in this tunnel before it reached the end, which meant as soon as the reverberations of the subway car faded, she loosened her grip on the Dybbuk and shimmied backward out of the ventilation shaft. "Come on," she whispered, encouraging the fox demon to follow. Sam's eyes fell on the overturned food bag as she exited, and she hoped there were no particularly keen-eyed police officers on the subway train that had blared passed. Shoving the contents back in the bag, Sam noticed a small, folded piece of paper jutting out from underneath a tin can. Her brows furrowed as she pulled the paper free. Unfolding the paper, Sam read the scrawled words, then shut her eyes, holding back tears of anger, frustration, and sorrow. She crushed the paper in her hand, shoved it deep into the recesses of the bag, and then opened her eyes. There was too much to deal with at that moment to worry about other things.

"We need to get to the next terminal before the train heads back toward the city," Sam told the Dybbuk, which was no longer quivering with terror now that it was out of the ventilation shaft. She hoped the platform would be empty, so she and the tiny fox demon could pass by unseen.

A ten-minute walk brought them to the beginning of the now-familiar upward ramp signaling the impending subway terminal. There was a distant squeal of train brakes as they walked along the narrow sidewalk. The Dybbuk clutched Sam's hand tighter. A minute later they reached the station, empty save for a sleeping homeless woman covered with a black-stained cardboard box. All but two of the fluorescent bulbs were burned out, casting shadows upon shadows. The terminal smelled like mildew and animal excrement. The tartness in the air tickled Sam's nose, but she pinched her nostrils together, forcing away a sneeze. The Dybbuk chittered softly as a metallic clunk of the subway reverberated down the tube, a precursor to the train's return trip.

Stepping softly to not wake the sleeping woman, Sam led the Dybbuk toward the ticket booth. It was potentially safer than heading to the surface, unless there were police officers on the subway car ready to search the area. It seemed unlikely the police would have skipped searching here on the way down the track, so Sam felt reasonably confident in her decision to remain in the terminal and simply let the subway pass her by on its way back toward the city proper.

The train was getting louder, though it was still distant enough that Sam felt calm enough to not feel the need to rush. She located the entrance to the ticket booth, tucked away in the corner of the station. It was padlocked and Sam felt a flare of panic. The thick plastic window at the front of the booth was immobile, designed to keep a distance between the non-existent employee and the customer. The Fourth City truly was a place of haves and have-nots. She could almost hear the angry uproar that would have occurred had there been no one working at the ticket booth in the heart of the city, yet only a few stations away there was almost nothing separating the terminal from a mausoleum. The echoing of clanking metal grew ever closer. The Dybbuk's frigid claw squeezed her hand tighter as it began to shiver in anticipation of its return.

Sam pulled the Dybbuk further away from the subway tracks, searching on the far side of the ticket booth. There was only a solid wall, with no way into the safety of the ticket enclosure. That left either hiding in a dark corner, hoping no police searched the area, or heading to the city streets. Sam glanced down at the trembling fox demon. Its face still gave her a sense of pause, but at the same time, she wondered how she could ever think of this pathetic little creature as fierce or frightening again. Sam took one more furtive look around the subway terminal before ascending the shadowed stairwell.

The air above ground was thick as a dense fog rolled over the outskirts of the Fourth City. Though it was late morning, the small slivers of sky Sam could see through the fog reminded her of the dusky grey of late October. Sam wondered if Purgatory had different seasons. She had never thought to ask, and hadn't noticed much of a difference in the weather since waking up in the dead world.

A sporadic cool breeze toyed with her hair, an odd sensation after walking in the stagnant subway tunnel for so long. The buildings could generously be described as decrepit, a stark reminder of the level of poverty in most of the city. More than one structure had clearly burned in the past and had been simply abandoned instead of repaired. Occasionally, the cool breeze brought with it the smell of ash and char. Windows like bruised, empty eye sockets stared down at Sam, causing an itch between her shoulder blades. The Dybbuk skipped merrily by her side again. It did not seem to notice the feeling of being watched, or it did not care, or it was simply happy to be out of the subway tunnel.

The wind swirled around Sam's ankles before darting further up the street, cleaving a momentary path through the fog. Sam looked around the silent street. It was hard to see very far through the haze, but it looked like almost every building had been damaged by fire at one time or another. How bad must the inside of the buildings be that the homeless woman would choose to sleep in the subway terminal instead of at street level? As much as Sam wanted to have a more useful weapon than the wooden desk leg, she was afraid the buildings would not be safe to enter due to the potential for collapse. Not to mention whoever or whatever might be lurking inside. Through gaps in the fog, Sam could imagine flames dancing from rooftop to rooftop, sometimes spreading down the sides, sometimes leaving buildings relatively unscathed, sometimes burning them down to nothing but ash. It was difficult to imagine what this place would have looked like before it had burned.

The streets were empty, save themselves.

A few minutes later, the fog dissipated, and Sam gasped at the sheer level of devastation that revealed itself. This part of the city was completely ruined. The destruction was so widespread that areas free from scorch marks were noteworthy. Heaping piles of ash dotted the surroundings in regular intervals and the air smelled like a bonfire. It made Sam feel like an insect in a child's sand castle. The Dybbuk was still skipping, blissfully unaware of the sense of foreboding rising inside of her. Sam had still not seen or heard a single person since the subway terminal. It was remarkable how exposed she felt, walking down the sidewalk with nothing but hills of char on either side of her. A chill ran up her spine, but it had nothing to do with the wind.

It was easy to lose track of time with no change in the environment. Sam's mind wandered before fixating on the folded piece of paper she found in the overturned supply bag. How dare that man manipulate her, abandon her, throw her to the wolves - or the foxes, she amended, a flash of ruefulness briefly supplanting her rage. The rage returned, however, increasing in intensity as if making up for the momentary lapse. The flame inside her wanted to dump the supply bag on the ground and set it ablaze, a miniscule sacrifice in memoriam to the fire that had devastated this part of the city in the past.

Abruptly, Sam realized the ashen mounds of burned buildings had become irregular, interspaced with large swathes of crumbling concrete. She doubted her previous supposition that one large fire had burned the district. Sam cast a glance behind them to mentally calculate if a single blaze would have been able to cover the distance. She didn't think so. An image of warfare burst to mind, of rebellion or gangs or any number of things, all with the same result: devastation. Sam shivered at the thought of block after block of the impoverished battling each other tooth and nail for control of limited resources. Looking at her surroundings, it was all too easy to imagine. For the first time, Sam wondered what she would be like if she managed to make it back to the living world, to Jack. Would she be the same person she was when she left, or would her experiences here forever taint her, twisting her core into something darker, perhaps more bitter and gnarled. A second, contrary thought sprang to mind out of the closing folds of the first: would she remember anything at all?

Chapter 15

The sidewalk had disappeared, fading imperceptibly into the road. Before long, the paved road disappeared as well, dwindling into a dirt path. Sam and her fox demon companion crossed beyond the Fourth City border hours ago. Her legs ached from the exertion, but she was too afraid to stop. The landscape was sparse and flat. Distant trees, dead and decaying, were the only things that broke up the monotony. Night had fallen, but it was impossible to say exactly when that had happened. Sam's gait had morphed as well, from a steady, determined stride to the shambling stutter of weariness. She felt like she was constantly on the verge of falling flat on her face, but forced herself to stay upright. Her eyes stung, her lungs burned. The Dybbuk was no longer skipping, and hadn't in some time, but showed no other sign of fatigue.

Hours later, their surroundings were entirely in the clutches of night. Stars sparkled high above, but Sam couldn't stop to appreciate them, or look at them as she walked, out of fear of falling. She needed to keep going. The Dybbuk looked at her, its plastic-like face showing concern. "I'm fine," Sam mumbled. Or tried to mumble. She wasn't sure if the words came out. There was a buzzing in her head, disorienting and constant. It made her brain itch.

Wandering down the night-shrouded dirt road, it was remarkably easy to lose track of time. As she stumbled around a turn in the path, a flickering light appeared in the distance. "There are stars in front of me," Sam muttered. "Am I lying down? Why are my feet still moving?" She closed her eyes, squeezing them tightly. Oh, how her eyes hurt. When she opened them again, the flickering light was still there. "It's a campfire!" she gasped, stopping in her tracks. She tried to stop, at least. The signal from her brain was delayed in its transmission, and she took a few more faltering steps before the message was received and her feet stopped shambling.

The campfire looked like a beacon, a flare from a sinking boat in a murky sea, but Sam didn't dare risk approaching. It was impossible to see anything around the fire, but she didn't think the Sages of Old Town would be huddled around a fire in the middle of the night. Her brain was muddy with exhaustion, but she still had enough presence of mind to know she needed to find somewhere to hide for the night. She needed sleep. Badly. The problem was there was very little variety in the landscape; she had essentially been wandering across a barren prairie the last few hours.

Sam looked left, opposite of the campfire. There was a shape rising out of the gloom. A tree? Sam crouched low, to put her face next to the Dybbuk's. She had to put a hand on the ground to maintain her balance. "I need sleep," she murmured as softly as she could. Gesturing toward the tree, Sam added, "Can we hide over there?"

The fox demon cocked its head at her, then in the direction she had gestured. Its eyes shone softly in the darkness, like a stalking cat. Sam struggled to stay in a crouch instead of sitting on the path. She thought if she sat, it would be nearly impossible to get back up again. Sam's legs had cramped up hours earlier. She adjusted her stance with a wince and a quiet groan. Finally, the Dybbuk turned back to her and nodded.

"Yes. Hide." That black hole of a voice cut into the night's silence like a miniature subsonic boom. Sam wobbled upright and shambled into the wilderness. She wasn't sure if her legs or eyes hurt more, but she knew she would be sore for days to come. At least it would be easy to find the path once the dull sun of the world of the dead broke the horizon.

The tree was further away than it seemed from the main road, though part of that was likely because of their sluggish pace. It was the best Sam could muster. As the minutes passed, Sam had to fight down the urge to dry heave. She would eat something once they were safely hidden, not before. When they finally drew close enough to the tree to see it clearly, Sam stopped reflexively. The tree was dead, unsurprisingly, but it was much larger than she had expected from the road. Huge, gnarled roots broke through the cracked ground like colossal worms. Greyish bark peeled in curled strips on the massive trunk. High above, spindly branches hung like twisted marionette strings. Bats fluttered overhead as she walked around the gigantic tree.

Sam encircled the tree three times before finding the spot she thought would be both most comfortable and most sheltered. Sitting on the ground, Sam slowly slid herself under a particularly thick clump of roots that had lifted off the ground, as if the tree had come close to falling in its younger years, but hung on and later thrived. The Dybbuk followed her, waited for her to get settled, then curled up protectively between her and the opening, eyes fixed on the world above. Sam grabbed a can of fruit in sugary syrup out of the bag and ate greedily, slopping the thick liquid down her chin as she devoured the contents. The bag made a functional if uncomfortable pillow, and the moment her head rested on it, Samantha Nightshade fell into a deep, motionless sleep. She was too exhausted to dream.

*   *   *   *   *

Robert Webb paced on the outside of a police cordon set up in the woods just past the Oakridge apartment complex. The findings had so far escaped the attention of local reporters, thankfully, but he absentmindedly wondered how long that would last. Strands of yellow tape, flapping in a steady breeze, separated him from the grisly finding he had made the last time he was in this forest. He remembered the odd shapes, which tickled the back of his brain, reminding him of letters for which he never knew the names, of hieroglyphs or runes. Or, more likely, they were simply unlikely blood splatter patterns. Scattered around the site were body parts. Some had been full limbs, others simply chunks of indeterminate flesh. Despite his years on the job, that discovery had unnerved him in a way that he hadn't thought possible. The memories crashed back, unbidden, curdling his stomach. He forced himself to focus on his steps instead of... Focus. Left. Right. Left. Right.

A decaying stump of a maple marked the arbitrary end of his pacing. Webb turned, keeping his back to the forensics team that was scouring the area behind the police tape. He tried to ignore the sounds of heavy things slopping into evidence bags.

Left.

Right.

"Webb." The man who stepped suddenly in front of him, breaking his stride, was Captain Walter Bixby. Bixby was short, with close-cropped black hair, gone mostly grey in the past few years. Like Webb, he was only a few years from retirement, though Webb thought the Captain looked his age, while Webb could pass for a man 15 years younger. At least in his own opinion. "Walk with me."

Webb did as he was ordered, trailing a half-step behind and to the left of his superior officer. The sounds from the crime scene faded quickly. Bixby did not speak until they were well out of earshot of the cordon. "Robert," he began. Bixby paused, sounding surprisingly unsure of himself, and cleared his throat. "Listen, Robert: we've known each other for years. You're an exceptional officer, and a good friend. You know that we are friends; Hell, you were at my daughter's wedding!" Bixby went silent for a moment. "But this case, this discovery – well, it's got a lot of people talking. You haven't been yourself in a while, not talking to anybody at work, and then you call in about a pile of corpses in the woods?" Bixby stopped and turned to face Webb. "I say this as your friend. I've heard some rumblings from people wondering if Internal Affairs should be notified about this. There's a serial on the loose, no one seems to know anything or be getting anywhere in this investigation, and then suddenly a cop not assigned to the case has a breakthrough? I'll vouch for you, Robert, and I will do my best to keep I.A. from getting involved, but I'm sure you can see why there's rumors floating around."

Bixby seemed to run out of steam. Webb wasn't sure what to say in response to all of that. He had known Walter for over 30 years, and 'excitable' was not a word that would ever come to mind to describe the Captain. Internal Affairs? Webb had no idea he had drawn that kind of attention. "Are you serious about I.A., Walter? That's crazy."

"I haven't heard anything from above." Bixby sighed. "But if two flatfoots are talking about it, you can't help but wonder how many others are thinking about it." There was a pause, and his face contorted, though Webb wasn't sure if it was anger or frustration. "Go home. Pack some clothes and take a trip. You need to step away from this investigation, and from the office."

"Are you suspending me, Walter?" Webb unconsciously clenched his fists by his sides.

Bixby met his gaze levelly. "Enjoy some time off, Detective. I'll call you in a few weeks." With that, the Captain turned back in the direction of the crime scene.

Webb stared back along the path for so long he lost track of time. Thoughts churned inside his head, the words of the Captain echoing in a never-ending spiral, intertwined with the sounds of the crime scene. He needed to get out of these woods. His mind felt numb. Webb's fingers twitched for a cigarette, even though he had quit nearly 20 years ago. Eventually, he slowly began to make his way out of the forest. The sun barely broke through the canopy of trees, casting uneven spears of light into the earth below.

"Hello again, Officer." The sonorous voice that shattered the silence came from Webb's right. He turned, startled, and stared at the man. Slightly shorter than himself, with brown hair and bright eyes the color of jade. Webb must have had a look of confusion on his face. "You don't remember me?" the man asked with a tone of mock outrage. "Perhaps this helps?" He pantomimed carrying two heavy loads, one in each hand, followed by a small laugh.

"Brown," Webb said. "Michael, right?"

The man smiled, obviously pleased. "You remembered! I'm delighted." The smile faded quickly as Michael Brown looked around. "I would like to speak with you about what you found in these woods, Officer Webb. Do you have a few free moments?" The grin returned and he gave Webb a conspiratorial wink.

"Say what you're going to say, Mr. Brown." Webb had found the man unnerving and suspicious the first time they had met in the parking lot at the apartment complex. This encounter doubled down on his initial impressions. A cold wind shook the trees, injecting the air with a frigid edge.

"But Officer Webb," Brown protested slyly, "we wouldn't want others to overhear our conversation! Besides, I was not entirely true with what I said. There's someone else who would like to speak with you about this investigation." He tapped the side of his nose and grinned again. "Please, Officer. It will only take a moment." Brown pivoted and shambled off deeper into the trees as Webb watched, nonplussed. Brown looked back over his shoulder, grinned at Webb, and gestured for him to follow.

He knew he was disobeying the Captain's orders by remaining involved in this case in the slightest, but he had learned over the years to trust his gut instincts. Right now, his gut was saying he needed to find out more. Maybe Brown was going to confess to the murders and Webb's suspension would be lifted, though that seemed far too much to hope for. Maybe Brown was just a creepy eccentric who got off on wasting cops' time. Webb sighed and followed, crunching his way through the dry undergrowth, following about ten paces behind. Uneasiness filled him with every step, but he followed. This was far from the first time he felt uneasy when working on a case.

Brown stopped near a particularly tight clump of trees. "This man has some information for you, Officer."

From behind the brush stepped a tall man, with wavy blond hair that hung over one eye. He plucked a small twig off the shoulder of his white suit and smiled unctuously. A bright red tie was tucked neatly into the folds of the jacket. "Greetings, Officer," the unknown man trailed off and looked at Brown for a moment. He had a vaguely British accent, though it came and went, as if the man had worked on getting rid of it but hadn't been entirely successful. The unknown man continued. "Webb, is it? A pleasure, I'm sure. My associate tells me you're investigating those ritual slayings," he gestured vaguely in the direction of the crime scene.

Webb nodded tersely. "And who are you?" A mystery man wearing a suit and hiding in the woods? He had a very bad feeling about this.

"My, my, where are my manners?" The man bowed, his hand moving behind his back formally. When he lifted his face back toward Webb, he wore a wide grin, like the Cheshire Cat in a suit. "I've gone by many names, Mr. Webb, but you can call me Symon. I'm the man you've been looking for."

Webb was suddenly grabbed from behind, his arms trapped behind his back. Brown had moved around him while Symon had his attention. "Let go of me!" Webb growled. He struggled to free himself, but Brown was surprisingly strong and held him fast. "This is assault on a police officer!"

Symon took another step closer and began unbuttoning his coat. "You see, Mr. Webb, I find myself in a very unique predicament." The coat dropped to the ground and Symon loosened his tie. "I have something of a history of convincing people to do what I want, but subservience isn't always enough." The shirt was half unbuttoned now and going over his head as he steadily approached the still-struggling police officer. "This body," Symon slowly dragged a fingertip down his own muscular chest, "is much more preferential to the other, but one must do what one must do."

Webb watched with confusion as Symon arched backward, then forward, head toward the forest floor. Webb's horror grew as Symon's skin split in large chunks, with thick soot-brown tendrils jutting out of his back. His flesh molted from his body, replaced with an exoskeleton of bister-brown bones, sharp-edged and thick as armor plating. Symon's hair fell to the ground in clumps as a crown of ashen spikes burst out of his skull. Webb fought and tore at the hands that held him as best as he could, but Brown kicked him in the back of the knee, buckling his legs, sending him face-first into the ground. He felt his nose shatter as it smashed into a rock before Brown pulled him roughly upward. There was nothing left that was recognizable as Symon. A thick, serrated, blade-like tail stretched into the air, covered in the same bone plating as the rest of his - its - body. Kneeling on the ground in front of this monstrous nightmare, all the years of training couldn't prevent Webb's mind from shattering.

When it raised its head to stare eye to eye with Webb, a gaping maw of razor teeth roared at him, propelling a misty spray of acidic saliva onto his face. Webb screamed as it burned his skin. The tail flicked upward, then forward, slicing effortlessly across Webb's exposed throat. Time slowed down for Webb as the wound spilled a torrent of blackish blood onto the ground. Webb watched, detached from the reality of his imminent death, as the creature grinned at him.

As Webb began to lose consciousness, he felt a sensation of floating. He wondered if he was dreaming, or flying, or dreaming of flying, but the very last thing to go through his mind was the nightmarish serrated blade of a tail as it punctured his skull.

* * * * *

Sam awoke at the sound of a shout; it took her a moment to realize it had been her own. She had been having a horrible dream, though she could remember no details, only emotions, with terror at the forefront.

Beneath the roots, the Dybbuk sprang to its feet in a tight crouch, looking her up and down as if to check for injury. "I'm okay," she breathed, trying to slow her heart rate. It was one of those dreams where it was so frightening she never wanted to think about it again, but because she couldn't remember, her mind naturally gravitated toward sifting for details. Deep in the hollow of the decaying tree, Sam shivered. It was a cold morning. She reached into the food bag, which still retained the shape of the back of her head from its use as a pillow. Sam's fingertips brushed against the crumpled note from Gibson. She closed her eyes. Angrily, Sam flicked it deeper into the bag. She dug out a hard end of bread and gnawed on it, focusing her annoyance on the stale crust.

As the bread slowly dissolved in her mouth, Sam's thoughts returned to the note. She wondered if she would ever see the investigator again, if he was still alive. Or Unborn, she supposed. It was easy to forget the people she saw walking the streets weren't alive, at least not in the traditional sense. Days had blended together to the point where it was hard to remember how long she had been stuck in the afterlife, and little details, like the fact that the people who inhabited this world were dead, tended to be forgotten. Sam grimaced at her own callousness.

The stark morning sunlight barely produced any warmth in the chill morning air. The fox demon watched Sam stretch once she had escaped the confines of the root system and mimicked her motions. Despite her dark mood, Sam giggled. "Right," said Sam assuredly. "Today, we find Old Town." She had no way of knowing whether that was true, but she needed confidence from somewhere.

"The Sages will know of some way for me to get back home," Sam told herself. Pain coursed through her heart as she thought of Jack. She wondered what he was doing at that very moment, if he was thinking of her from the world of the living, if he was still holding out hope his wife would return to him. Sam felt her spirits sliding and forced herself away from that line of thought. One thing at a time.

Carefully, she peered around the edge of the hulking tree in the direction of the fire she had seen during the night. Nothing moved, save for some stray ash dancing on the wind. She supposed someone could be sleeping on the ground, hidden from sight, but that was unlikely. The sun was high above the horizon already. Anyone sleeping outside would have been woken hours ago, unless they had been as physically exhausted as she had been. Still, Sam moved slowly and methodically as she stepped out from behind the tree, Dybbuk at her heels.

The grass, such as it was, crunched under Sam's feet as she cautiously approached the abandoned campsite. The fire had been larger than she imagined from a distance, but well-contained within a stone ring. Whoever made the fire obviously had no qualms about someone finding it, as there was no effort made to disguise it. Sam walked around the ashes a few times, trying and failing to determine how many people had been there, or slept there, the night before. She quickly gave up; she was not the type of person to enjoy camping trips and had no tracking skills.

Just as Sam had decided there was nothing she could gather from the abandoned site, a voice broke the silence. "Ah, there you are." It was a withered voice, cracked and dry. Ancient. Despite that, Sam jumped, awkwardly turning on her heel to face the source. A hunched man, white-haired and leaning heavily on a thick walking stick smiled at her. He wore a dark brown cloak, the color an almost perfect match to his walking stick.

"Who are you?" Sam asked, unable to keep a tremor of anxiety out of her words.

He raised an eyebrow quizzically. "I'm sure you could guess," the man said calmly, giving her another thin smile. "Come with me, and I will show you. I assure you I mean you no harm." He gestured for her to move closer, and when Sam did not move, he smiled again. This time, he was clearly amused. "You've been looking for us, Bloodwalker," the man added.

"You're one of the Sages?" Sam gasped. He bowed his head slightly in acknowledgement.

"Come with me, Bloodwalker," he said, gesturing her to follow. The man began to turn away from the campsite but stopped halfway and spoke over his shoulder. "I noticed you have a rather unusual traveling companion. It can come as well, as long as it behaves itself." The man took several faltering steps away from her, trudging carefully as the ground inclined slightly. Sam followed, quickly closing the distance. She studied the man as she approached, trying to pick out as many details as possible. He moved so slowly, walking with that makeshift cane, and yet he managed to appear out of nowhere when she was studying the remains of the camp. Where had he come from?

"Is Old Town nearby?" Sam asked loudly, assuming the old man's hearing was not very sharp. Without turning around, he motioned again for her to follow him. Dust kicked up around Sam's feet as she followed in his wake. The incline was subtle but stretched far enough that by the time she caught up to the man, she was several feet above the camp. When they reached the top of the hillock, Sam gasped in shock. The ground fell away, forming a rocky cliff face below her. A dirt path along the inside edge of the windswept precipice sloped steeply downward into the roughly square valley. It was there, deep in the earthen canyon, where a small group of structures rose from the ground like stone roots. Unlike the buildings in the Fourth City, these were all the same style and material, white stonework glittering faintly in the dull sunlight.

"Welcome to Old Town, Bloodwalker," the old man intoned formally. He led the way down the sloping path and chatted amiably, though Sam only half-listened. Along with a brief history lesson, the man formally introduced himself as Elder Yanish. He was part of the Assembly of Elders. It was the Assembly that had the premonition someone was seeking them. Someone with a dire need. Someone unique to the world. "Even discounting your being a Bloodwalker," Elder Yanish quipped, "the fact you travel with a Dybbuk makes you quite the unique individual." Sam didn't speak during the descent. Listening to Elder Yanish was enough to overwhelm her.

"What happens next?" Sam asked when she was finally able to break the spell of Elder Yanish's chatter.

"Next?" Elder Yanish responded, seemingly startled by her interruption. "Well, I expect you're hungry, so I will take you to a place where you can get some food. While you're eating, I'll inform the Assembly of your arrival. We expected you yesterday. We had the campfire burning to help you find your way." There was a slight hesitation before he added, "I, at least, certainly didn't expect a Dybbuk, though." There was a second pause. "Being dead is such a strange life," Elder Yanish mused quietly to himself. The hard-packed dirt on the path made for a jarring walk. Sam clenched her teeth against the impact of every footfall, impressed that Elder Yanish was able to maintain his balance with apparent ease.

When they reached the bottom, Elder Yanish led Sam to a one-story slate-roofed building. Sam squinted. Up close, the glimmering buildings were almost blinding. She followed Elder Yanish gratefully through a heavy wooden door into a room that was warm and smelled of flowers and baking. Of comfort. The interior had the feel of a tavern, a common room for the locals to gather and talk or play cards. Polished tables made of dark wood stood in orderly rows, with matching benches spaced evenly apart on each side. "This is our town inn," Elder Yanish explained dutifully. "We don't get many visitors out here, but occasionally someone ventures out into the wastes, seeking some bit of knowledge, and finds themselves here. Please, sit. You're welcome to stay here as long as you'd like."

Sam did as she was told and sat on the bench closest to the door, while the Dybbuk sat cross-legged on the floor next to her. Maybe it was the radical change of environment of Old Town compared to the Fourth City, but this room made her antsy. She felt unnerved and vaguely in danger. The hairs on the nape of her neck stood on end and quivered.

A few minutes passed in silence before a slender, middle-aged woman came bustling into the room through an opening in the back Sam hadn't noticed. "Ah!" the woman exclaimed. "Look atchu!" She had a thick accent and slurred her words together, but her manner was affable. "Talka th' town, you are! Heard you 'as comin' a few days ago, and here you are." The woman beamed at Sam, a dazzling smile that encouraged relaxation. "Name's Telli Cross, and I keep Th' Cupboard nice an' clean." There was definite pride in Telli's voice.

"The Cupboard?" Sam asked, then immediately felt foolish. It was obviously the name of the inn, but Telli's way of talking was making Sam feel out of sorts. To try to cover for herself, Sam said, "It's very nice in here. How long have you run this place, Telli?"

Telli leaned on the table with her fists and looked at the ceiling. "Lessee," she began, still staring upward, "I'd say 'is been a good, ah, hund'd an' thir'y years now." She looked back down at Sam and grinned. "Th' Cupboard's been good to me, an' I do my bes' to be good to it. Now, down ta bus'ness." Telli suddenly wore a very stern expression. Sam felt a brief stab of fear before the innkeeper said, "Whatcha wan'ta eat, dearie?

I've got bread tha's just abou' ready ta come outta th' oven, and a big kettle a' soup, pipin' hot. If ya wan' sum'thin' else, y'll have ta wait."

"Bread and soup sounds wonderful!" Sam answered quickly. Then, realizing she had no money whatsoever, she quietly asked, "How much will it cost?"

Telli threw her head back and laughed. "How much will it cost? Ta feed a Bloodwalker? Dearie, it's ma honor ta give ya sum'thin' to eat." With that, Telli went to the back of the room and passed through the door into the kitchens.

Sam looked down at the Dybbuk and wondered once again if it needed to eat, or enjoyed eating. Actual food, as opposed to the silvery blood of the dead. Telli returned a few moments later carrying a beautiful wooden tray with a wooden plate piled high with steaming bread, and a matching bowl of soup. The soup consisted mainly of a golden-red broth, with tiny slices of shallot and some kind of green herb Sam didn't recognize floating on the surface. The aroma was heady and made her think of autumn. She offered the Dybbuk a chunk of bread, which it sniffed curiously before turning away. "Suit yourself," Sam said casually before picking up her spoon. She ate greedily, using the bread to sop up the final remnants of soup.

Telli had disappeared into the kitchens while Sam ate and only returned once she had finished. "More, Dearie?" she asked. Sam was tempted to say yes but decided against it. One thing she had learned since waking in the Fourth City was that it was best to always be prepared to run, and having an overstuffed belly would make running a very difficult task. The memories of times she had to run to save her life played through her mind. Sam sincerely hoped she was safe in Old Town. If the Sages refused to help her, or lacked the knowledge on how she could return to the living world... Sam let the thought trail off, unwilling to finish the sentence in her head. The Sages were her best chance of escape, of survival, of returning to the life she unwillingly left behind.

Sitting at the table with the Dybbuk at her side, Sam wondered what was going to happen next. Was she supposed to head somewhere else after she ate? She didn't remember Elder Yanish indicating anything to that effect. Telli popped out a third time, bringing with her a small plate with a couple of small pastries that had dollops of a purple jam atop them, but she

184

just set the plate on the table in front of Sam, gave her a warm smile, and retreated back to the kitchens.

A few minutes later, the door to The Cupboard opened, drawing Sam's attention. A man walked in moving with a limp, as if his leg were too stiff to move at the knee. He wore an outfit of greys and browns, and on top of that a black coat, almost a duster, that nearly reached the floor. He gave Sam a wry grin, nodding his head in her direction, which made his hair, which was silver and below his shoulders, bounce slightly in front of a full, well-kept beard. He moved toward a fireplace along the far wall, the pronounced limp making his rhythm uneven. Sam watched the man curiously, wondering if he was there for her, or if it was just a coincidence.

Sam was surprised to see the man suddenly lift a guitar from beyond the fireplace. She was no musician, but she could tell this guitar was not the work of a master craftsman. Still, the man began to play, plucking out a few quick melodies to warm up. He gave her another grin, twin to the first when he had entered The Cupboard, and began to thump his way in her direction, holding the guitar by its neck. Sam took a bite of the pastry and waited. The purple jam was sour at first, but had a sweet aftertaste that she found very satisfying.

"Do you mind if I sit?" the man asked once she reached her table. His voice was gruff but not unkind, more like the deep scratchiness of age after a lifetime of cigarette smoking.

"Not at all," Sam answered. She slid the pastry plate in his direction as he fell to the bench across the table from her. He smiled appreciatively and snatched up a pastry, popping the whole thing into his mouth in a comical way. Sam didn't know what to make of this man, but he had a roguish charisma that put Sam at ease. She could imagine him as a boy, getting into all sorts of mischief but never getting the full punishment for his actions because of his charm.

"The name's Glen," he said after finishing the pastry. "Glad you finally made it here. I'm something of a local celebrity, or I was until you arrived, at least." Somehow he made his voice even gruffer, but he was clearly feigning anger, which he then spoiled with a wink.

"Celebrity?" Sam asked. "You seem more like a boy who is notorious for stealing pies from window sills." Glen held his free hand up to his chest in mock outrage, which made Sam laugh.

"I'm more like the town bard," he said, lifting the guitar in front of him and strumming a few chords. "In fact, when we had an idea you were coming, I almost started writing a new song in your honor, but I wanted to meet you first to see if you deserved it." His fingers flew across the strings as if the notes themselves were punctuation.

"I don't know if I deserve much of anything," Sam said somberly. "I came out here to Old Town to beg for help."

Glen didn't stop his playing while she talked, but he did play softer. "Everyone deserves a song, Bloodwalker," he answered. "Not everyone gets a chance to hear it from a bard as skilled - no, *talented* as yours truly."

Despite her melancholy, Sam laughed. "Well aren't you humble? Fine, then, play my song for me."

Glen's eyes went wide in feigned shock. "I haven't written it yet!" Sam laughed and shook her head. "Songs about a person are best written after you get to know the person. How am I supposed to write a song about a mysterious stranger coming to Old Town if I don't even know their name or what they're after?"

Sam blushed slightly at the not-so-subtle comment about her lack of introducing herself. "I'm Samantha, but I go by Sam, at least to my friends." She reached across the table and offered a handshake to the older man. He smiled and shook it.

"Well, I'm going to assume we're friends, Sam, since you shared Telli's pastry with me. She doesn't make those for just anyone. But you'll have to be patient with the song. Real art, even from geniuses like me, sometimes takes time." With that, Glen rose from the bench, gave her a respectful nod, and made his way out of the inn, still carrying the guitar and strumming away as he left.

Alone in The Cupboard once more, Sam rubbed at her temples. She still had so many holes in her memory, so many unanswered questions. When she met people like Glen, it was sometimes easy to forget they were dead. She had never learned if it was considered rude to ask people about how they died, or how long ago. Anyone she met could be a new arrival or hundreds of years old – well, that wasn't quite right, since people didn't age here, but the point still stood. She realized she was distracting herself with unimportant details instead of focusing on something that had been bothering her for some time, specifically putting her faith in a group of people who had no reason to help her. The concept struck her as extremely foolish, but she had forced the thought down. Now that she was in Old Town, it was impossible to ignore.

As if her shameful dependence on the kindness of others were a summons, Elder Yanish entered The Cupboard. "The Assembly will see you now, Bloodwalker." Sam joined him by the door, the Dybbuk trailing at her heels. Yanish led the way out of the tavern and toward a large, round building in what Sam imagined was the dead center of Old Town. He held the door, allowing Sam and the Dybbuk passage before he followed. The inside was dimly lit, with interspersed torch sconces the only source of light. "The Assembly will join you in the Adjudiary," Yanish said quietly. Sam's shoes made muted noises on the dark stonework floor with every step. A pit was forming in her stomach. This was leading to the moment of truth, so to speak, and she had no idea what to expect. Her confidence and conviction were frazzled, hanging on by the barest of threads.

The Adjudiary was behind a pair of large doors, like a miniature throne room in a palace. They swung open easily when Yanish pushed on them, well-balanced despite their size. "Please," he said softly, "wait here. There's a chair in the center of the room for you." Yanish glanced down at the Dybbuk. Meeting Sam's eyes, he wore an apologetic smile. "Your companion can enter, but will have to wait along the outside wall."

Sam nodded mutely and entered. Her stomach roiled, an emphatic exclamation to her thudding pulse. As soon as she and the Dybbuk entered, the doors were shut behind her, and they were alone in the Adjudiary. The subtle smell of incense rose from the handful of torches that lit the room. Sam walked slowly along the curved wall of the room. The wall was all one piece, constantly curving to create a perfect circle, and aside from the torches and the single chair, it was completely empty. With no idea of what was going to happen, she crouched next to the fox demon. "I need you to stay here and stay quiet, okay?" she said. It stared at her, brows furrowed. "Please, just stay against the wall." Thinking about how the creature often acted as her protector, Sam pointed to the chair and added, "I'll be safe. I'm going to sit over there. Nothing to be worried about." On a whim, she reached over and stroked her hand behind the fox's ear. It leaned into the gesture, clearly enjoying it, but did not protest when she rose back to her full height.

Sam moved slowly toward the center of the room, keeping an eye on the Dybbuk. It wore a look of sadness, but it did not move. By the time she sat, having turned the chair slightly so she could keep an eye on the fox demon, it had dropped into a crouch, as if ready to leap forward to be by her side in an instant. In a strange way, it warmed her heart and gave her some comfort. Having to console the anxious Dybbuk had been a welcome distraction from her own nervousness, and now it was returning the favor.

Although Sam's eyes adjusted to the relative lack of light in the Adjudiary, her sense of time became muddled and confused. The room was like a sensory deprivation chamber. The fox demon still crouched, a static detail in a static room. Sam forced back a yawn. The Assembly sure was making her wait; maybe being dead removed any sense of urgency.

Sam was about to start pounding on the wall and demand to be let out when thin bars of light shot into the room as a dozen or more doorways opened in unison. In each doorway stood a figure, cloaked in shadow. The sound of boots on the floor echoed as they simultaneously stepped forward before being punctuated by the doors slamming shut. The momentary flash of light had been enough to ruin her adjusted vision, and the torches seemed foggy and dim once again.

"Are you what you are?" The words came from everywhere and nowhere, echoing and reverberating around the room. Sam couldn't tell if it was one speaker or several, or everyone. She was cut off before she had a chance to answer, or to even formulate a response.

"Is she one? Is she one?" A shiver rode up Sam's spine. It was difficult to perceive distance in this room, but she thought the figures were moving closer. The echoing voice, or voices, loud enough to mask any footsteps. Somewhere in the room, the Dybbuk growled and let out an eerily high-pitched yip, a sound Sam didn't think the demon capable of making.

"Does her heart still bleed?" Something unseen crawled up the back of her leg. Sam tried to swat a sweaty hand at it but her arms were frozen in place, fingers clutching the wooden arms of the chair. Panic shot through her as the something slithered and curled past the back of her knee. Sam tried to push away the sensation of the unseen something as it crept toward her navel. There was a sensation of legs as it moved up her body and the image of a giant millipede came to mind unbidden. She wanted to scream but her throat was paralyzed with fear. She turned her head, attempting to keep an eye on all of the encircling figures. It was impossible. They were definitely moving closer now, their bodies blocking off the faltering torchlight and casting themselves in silhouette.

Without warning, a blast of white lit the room, blinding her. The shadowy figures disappeared like phantoms, vanishing without a trace. The sensation that a creature had been crawling up her body was gone as well, though Sam rubbed a palm down her front to be certain. The Dybbuk appeared by her side so quickly it was as if it were an apparition. It clawed its way onto her lap and nuzzled against her like a terrified dog. The sudden arrival and frightened affection of the fox demon was surprising and almost overwhelming. The final vestiges of icy fear Sam had felt toward the Dybbuk melted away as she gave the terrified creature a quick, comforting squeeze.

Sam's eyes readjusted to the brightness of the Adjudiary. Vague shapes appeared first, tall, dark, and rectangular. There was a low murmur coming from every direction. The fox demon shivered on her lap, its bony arms clutched around her shoulders in a scared embrace. Sam made a soft shushing noise. There were words in the murmur that slowly filled the room, words she could almost pick out. The shapes resolved themselves into a large wooden structure, like a judge's bench, with smaller turret-like spires cropping up to provide a second row of seating. Close to two dozen faces stared down at her and the Dybbuk from their perch. She recognized Elder Yanish in the back-right corner, and Glen, the self-proclaimed town bard, on the opposite side, but both men's faces were as blank and rigid as everyone else in the group. At the head of the bench sat a woman wearing crimson robes and a matching hat. She also wore a stern, almost angry expression. For several long moments, Sam and the unknown woman met each other's gaze in silence. Then the murmuring started again. Sam recognized some words as English, but she heard other languages mixed in, a muddied mess of dialects and accents. Without any noticeable alteration or transition, every person sitting at the bench spoke in unison.

"She is one."

Sam felt a cold shiver race up her spine, setting off waves of goosebumps down her arms. She is one? One what? Frightened and frustrated by the low, incessant chant, she opened her mouth to ask that very question. Before she could utter a word, however, the woman in crimson spoke, the other voices falling immediately silent.

"We, The Assembly, recognize you formally as Bloodwalker."

Craning her neck to look up at the imposing woman, Sam didn't know how to respond. The crimson woman said it as if it were a title, declaring her not as a Bloodwalker, but as *The* Bloodwalker. Should she say thank you? Was she the only Bloodwalker in the world of the dead? Had there ever been one before? For the first time in a very long time, Sam wondered who she was. She could identify herself as a woman, a wife, a survivor, as cunning or cautious or a hundred other things. But could she, should she, now also identify herself as a Bloodwalker? *The* Bloodwalker? She had a thousand questions to ask.

Lost in her own thoughts, Sam was jolted back to reality when the judicial bench disappeared in another flash of white light. The people who had been towering above her were now standing on the floor. All wore the same robes as Elder Yanish, save for the woman in crimson, who stood at the front of the clustered Assembly. She must have noticed the expression on Sam's face because she said, "You look to have many questions, Bloodwalker. Ask, and we shall answer."

The questions in Sam's head swirled as if they were in a whirlwind, flying by too quickly for her to grasp. Eventually, she caught one and asked, "How did you do that?"

"The Adjudiary is built to very particular specifications, Bloodwalker," the crimson woman said. Sam still couldn't figure out what her accent was; she was thinking South African but wasn't positive. "The Assembly can do things here we cannot do in other places."

Sam puzzled over that response. It was remarkably vague. Perhaps she should start with simpler and more direct questions. Looking at the crimson woman, Sam realized she didn't know her name.

"I am Assemblist Kratha." The answer came before Sam could even open her mouth. Sam wondered if Kratha was able to read her mind or was simply perceptive.

"Both," Kratha answered with a smile that made the harsh angles of her face look strangely smooth. It didn't soften her overall stern demeanor, but it did make her look almost cherubic. The image of a cranky and overtired baby angel popped to mind. Sam blushed as she immediately remembered Kratha could read her mind, though the other woman's expression did not change. Sam was overwhelmed by the events from the last few minutes. She had gone from bored to terrified to threatened, and now they reached what amounted to a casual chat. It was more than enough to upset her equilibrium.

"My apologies," Kratha said smoothly. "It is surprisingly easy to forget how people feel the first time their thoughts are explored." Sam shrugged, trying to express that it was nothing to apologize for, though she couldn't help but feel somewhat violated. Kratha smiled ruefully before continuing her explanation. "It's a skill that has become part of The Assembly over the years. Not everyone here in Old Town can do it, of course; it requires much study to achieve, and we certainly do not welcome new members to our group frequently." Sam noticed some nervous shifting of feet at that comment, but no one else spoke up.

Sam sat silent, staring up at the mysterious woman in crimson. She wanted to ask about Jack, about how to get home, about everything, but what came out was, "Why is it people here have jobs? If they are spirits, why don't they fly around or something?" As the words left her mouth, Sam felt her cheeks flush with embarrassment for a second time. Here she was sitting in front of people who had ascended beyond at least one constraint of the human species, and she asked about afterlife labor policies and why the people inhabiting the world of the dead were not flying. Sam was mortified.

Assemblist Kratha did not answer the question; undoubtedly Sam's mental state played heavily into that decision. Instead, she said, "This world of the dead you see here, this Purgatory, is essentially a shared collective hallucination. When a new soul arrives, they subconsciously begin to believe in that hallucination, stemming from those who have been here for eons. That is my understanding, at least, and our collective theory of this world." She gestured vaguely to the members of The Assembly gathered behind her.

"There are other theories as well. Some people in this world will quote The Book of Revelation to explain this existence." Sam stared blankly. Kratha smiled ingratiatingly then began to recite in a sonorous voice. "And I looked, and, lo, a Lamb stood on the mount Sion, and with him a hundred forty and four thousand, having his Father's name written in their foreheads. And I heard a voice from heaven, as the voice of many waters, and as the voice of a great thunder, and I heard the voice of harpers harping with their harps, and they sung as it were a new song before the throne, and before the four beasts, and the elders, and no man could learn that song but the hundred and forty and four thousand, which were redeemed from the earth."

"Do you understand what that is saying?" Kratha continued. "Those verses from Revelation suggest Heaven has space limitations. Likely not in terms of physical space, but that only so many people are allowed in before they shut the gates, so to speak." Sam nodded. Kratha smiled approvingly. "So, let's assume Heaven is already full, and Hell is the negative of Heaven, an unmalleable mirror image dichotomy that has the same limitations on population. Now, consider the billions of people who have lived and died in the history of mankind. Both sides, Heaven and Hell, good and evil, would have undoubtedly already filled their quota by this point. Therefore, everyone else for the rest of time would end up here, in this faded world of the dead."

Kratha sighed, sounding resigned. "Perhaps this place will be the battleground between the forces of Heaven and Hell." There was a pause that stretched for several moments before the woman in crimson said, "Not the official theory of The Assembly, but a popular one, and it does explain some things. I find it requires a bit too much reliance on faith for my comfort, however."

Sam mulled over the metaphysical monologue, curiosity tickling her brain. What she needed to know though, was how to get home. "I," Sam began, but her throat clenched tight with nerves, and she had to start over. "I'm not supposed to be here. I'm still alive. I miss my life, and my husband. I want to go home." The Dybbuk slightly tightened its claw-like hands on her shoulders.

Assemblist Kratha's eyes widened ever-so-slightly, then her brows furrowed. She studied Sam so intensely that Sam felt like an insect under a microscope. "You have a block," she said eventually. "I should have expected this."

"A block?"

Kratha looked concerned. "Your memories are incomplete, Bloodwalker. Perhaps it's a result of your arrival in Purgatory."

Sam squeezed her eyes closed. "When I first woke up here, I was bloodied and bruised, and had no idea what was going on." Her voice was quiet, almost timid. Reflecting on those first days in this world was difficult. "My memories have come back slowly, but there are holes." Sam took a deep breath before continuing, afraid to ask her question, and afraid of the answer. She opened her eyes and met Kratha's gaze and tried to keep her desperation from showing. "Can you remove the block?"

Wordlessly, the rest of The Assembly moved closer to where Sam was sitting. The feeling of being under a microscope returned tenfold. Eyes of every shade stared down at her, cold and calculating. She felt like she was a cow being weighed for market. She met Glen's eyes. He stared as disconnectedly as everyone else. Kratha's eyes were closed; she was the only member of The Assembly not trying to bore a hole into her. With unnerving synchronicity, Kratha's eyes opened at the same moment everyone else's closed, as if Kratha and the others were on opposite sides of the same coin. "It is done, Samantha Nightshade," the leader said. "Sleep, and when next you wake, the block will be gone." At Kratha's words, the torches in the room glowed brighter than what would seem possible. A door swung open, adding its own sliver of light to the room.

"Please," Kratha said, gesturing to the open door. "Elder Yanish will return you to The Cupboard where you may eat and rest." Sam rose from the chair and waited, setting the Dybbuk on the floor next to her. She could see that Kratha had more to say. "We will speak further after you wake." She paused, a pronounced hesitation. "There will be much to discuss." Sam thought she saw a look of soft sympathy cross the woman's face, but it was gone so quickly that it was just as likely it had never been there at all.

Chapter 16

Nightmares chased Sam, an endless loop of every horrible thing she had ever imagined or dreamed of in her life. Red-eyed bats with razor-sharp fangs swooped down from cathedral ceilings as she ran through an endless hallway, trying to escape from something just beyond the range of her vision. The shadows swirled and amalgamated and reformed into things even more terrifying. From somewhere unseen, a row of thorns cut deeply into her arm as she ran. She cried out in pain but did not slow.

In the recesses of her mind, Sam knew it was all a dream. She could feel the cold sweat erupt on her forehead from within the dream, but could not stop it, could not awaken. In the nightmare, she ran and screamed and hid and bled and cried. Doors lined the endless hallway at evenly-spaced intervals, like a hotel that stretched toward infinity. As soon as she imagined it, the hallway became carpeted in a tacky orange and blue pattern. Cheap brass candelabra-style lamps appeared out of nowhere between the doors, adding a soft white glow to the hallway that still stretched ahead.

She knew that behind every door was a choice she had made in her life that had set her on a different path. Sam also knew she could not run forever, and although she still couldn't see what was chasing her, it was getting closer and would not stop. She needed to choose a door. She needed to make a choice. Sam skidded to a halt, hunched over and panting. She cast a glance at the darkness behind her and saw it closing in faster than she had expected. As it reached the lamps affixed to the walls, the bulbs crackled and burst. Sam grabbed the nearest door handle and turned. Locked. She wanted to scream, but instead spun as quickly as she could and grabbed the handle on the other side of the hall. Locked. The darkness was only a few doors away now. She could hear voices in the black, taunting and threatening her, promising to do horrible things to her for all of eternity. Panic set in. Uncertain of what else to do, she raised her fist to pound loudly on the door.

Sam sat bolt upright in bed as a loud knock on the door startled her out of the nightmare. She immediately felt the awkward dizziness of being lightheaded, but with an excruciating pain that made her scream. The fox demon bounded onto her bed with a look of concern stretched across its molded face.

Memories of her life before being dragged into the world of the dead crashed into her brain like a freight train into a brick wall. Her honeymoon. Garlic bread, then police at the door. Identifying Jack's body. Her husband, dead. Not knowing why his car crashed. The possibility of an affair, and the queasy feeling of some other woman mourning him the way she did. The nightmares, and the uncontrollable shivers in the shower after she awoke with a bloody nose. The séance. The screaming, flesh-ripping demon that crossed through the portal that night and dragged her mind and body into this living nightmare. The memory of its talons passing through flesh and bone, piercing her brain, locking into the grey matter like a hook into a fish mouth before being reeled back into the world in which it belonged, and dragging her along with it. It was a thing of the world of the dead and could not exist outside of it for long. It was hungry, and it had feasted upon her memories while they passed through the void. Her eyes were squeezed tight against the tumultuous crash of the wave of memories as they returned to her, the invisible venomous block extracted by the will of The Assembly.

The Dybbuk's vacuous growl forced her eyes open, forcing Sam back into the present instead of the endless corridors of the past. Towering above her was Assemblist Kratha, her expression a mix of concern and sympathy. "I saw them all when we removed the block," she said softly. "I would tell you something comforting, like 'I've seen worse', but I don't want to lie to you."

At some point during Kratha's words, Sam's pain broke down and transformed into pure numbness. Her head still ached, suddenly overfull. Kratha's arms went around Sam's shoulders and pulled her into a comforting embrace. Sam remained stiff and numb. She had cried over her old life more times than she could count. Crying again wouldn't help. It was time to be cold, calculating. It was a time for determination.

Pulling her head away from Kratha's torso, Sam tried to speak. "I-" Sam started, but her voice was tight. She cleared her throat.

195

"Take your time, Bloodwalker," Kratha comforted. "You are handling this well. Considering what you went through, much better than I had expected."

"I don't want to go back anymore." As the words passed her lips, Sam realized that she wasn't sure if she meant back in her memories, or back to the world of the living. Reliving the pain of Jack's death and the subsequent uncertainty of what had happened was horrible enough, but now she could remember the feeling of finding out the first time. It was like it had happened twice. The cuts on her soul were deep and jagged, having to experience everything again. Those cuts would never heal, never scar over. Tears threatened to well in her eyes again, but she reminded herself that the time for crying had passed.

"Is he here?" No answer. Sam's resolve strengthened, and she asked again, surprising herself with her ferocity. "Is he here? I need to know!"

Kratha looked down at Sam imperiously, studying her carefully. "Yes."

Sam felt all the air rush out of her as if she had been punched in the stomach. Jack was alive. No, Jack was dead, but here, in the world of the dead, he was alive. Sam struggled to keep her thoughts focused. She wanted to see him again, the way he was, before the car crash. She wanted to hug him, to feel his cheek press against her forehead in their embrace. She wanted to talk to him, to ask him what happened that night.

"We, the Sages, can see the world in different ways," Kratha explained, obviously choosing her words carefully. "Whether we stumbled upon some mystical technique, or our centuries of study provided us with insight, or some other quirk of fate, we are able to peek through the veil of shadows that encompasses the world of the dead. Our individual power with this ability varies, but anything outside of the crater in which we have built our village is available to the mind's eye."

Sam studied Kratha, analyzing her every word. Deep in her heart, she knew her grasp on sanity was tenuous at best. The flood of memories threatened to drag her down, like an undertow of emotional pain. Adding Kratha's explanation of psychic ability and soothsaying to her thoughts was like strapping a lead weight to her chest while trying to stay afloat. She had been trapped for months in this world - Purgatory, whatever it was - and at that moment, she felt more lost and overwhelmed than she could remember.

"Where is Jack now?" Sam was impressed at how steady her voice sounded.

Kratha took a deep breath and stared into Sam's eyes before answering. "East."

"East?" Sam demanded. "That's all you can tell me? East?!"

"I will excuse your rudeness once, Bloodwalker, as you are going through a great deal of emotional turmoil," Kratha said flatly. She took a steadying breath before resuming in a calmer tone. "I have a tale for you." Sam opened her mouth angrily but Kratha cut her off. "Please. Listen."

When she was certain Sam would not interrupt, Kratha continued. "This is a dead world, full of Unborns, with no hope of salvation. When we were alive, like you, we did not know what would happen when we died. Now that we are dead, we do not know what happens when we die again. In many ways, we are more powerful, more closely connected to the currents of the universe in death than we were in life. Existing here is much like being alive, except we do not age, and therefore do not die of old age. There is a natural fear of dying here, just as in the living world, but death here comes from violence, or accidents. Because of that, some Unborns have dedicated their lives, such as they are, to wisdom during our comparative immortality."

Sam nodded impatiently. She had heard most of this from Gibson months ago. "The Fountain of Youth," Kratha continued, "was sought after by those afraid to die in the living world. Here, there have been individuals who have sought a similar boon. To them, a timeless body was not enough; they wanted more. Invulnerability. Power." For the first time, Kratha appeared unsettled, and although Sam was baffled as to where this was going, she kept quiet. "The Sages are not omniscient. We never have been, and I doubt we ever could be. We can see things others cannot, but only when we look for them. Your husband, Jackson Nightshade, is here in Purgatory, but at the moment, his mind is not his own. There is a taint inside him, something I have felt before..." Kratha's expression hardened. "He's back."

"Back?" Sam asked. She was struggling to follow Kratha's stream of consciousness. "Who's back?"

Kratha ignored the question. "Have you ever watched a fire, Bloodwalker?" Sam nodded, confused at yet another shift in conversation. "Imagine solid, hardwood logs, firm and dry, placed atop a small flame, sacrifices upon a tiny altar. They sit there, balanced carefully so as to not roll away from the flame. They are giants, staring down at the tiny curls of fire." Kratha paused and waved her hands in a complicated pattern. The illusion of a fire sprang to life out of thin air, dancing merrily four feet above the floor. Sam's eyes went wide at the display of what could only be described as magic. The illusion gave off no warmth, but it was flawless in its appearance.

"Imperceptibly, the wood is being worn down from underneath by the tenacity of the flames." The ghostly fire lifted higher into the air, enabling Sam to see the tendrils of flame lick the blackened underside of the wood. "In time," Kratha continued, "those logs, so solid and stoic, become worn down and splintered inside as the fire grows and consumes them. The first cracks on the sides of the logs appear long after the fire has broken through the outer bark. Before then, it's impossible to see the change. By the time you do see the change, it's too late to repair the damage. The fire finds the weaknesses you cannot see and eventually breaks through. All that remains is ash." The illusory fire winked out of existence as Kratha returned her hands to her lap.

"I don't understand what that has to do with me or my husband, or frankly anything else," Sam said. She wished her words didn't sound so sullen, but she couldn't help it. "I want to know where my husband is. I want to know what you mean: his mind isn't his own." All of the frustration and anger she held onto so tightly boiled over. "I want to wake up from this nightmare! I want to go home and have my husband alive with me! I WANT TO GO HOME!"

Tears splattered on the floor as the scream still reverberated in the small bedroom in The Cupboard. Sam sobbed and coughed, her throat clenched under the stress of the deluge of memories. A second shriek tore itself free and burst out. The feeling of Kratha's fingertips pressing against her forehead made Sam open her eyes in surprise. An instant later, her eyes slid shut and Sam was fast asleep.

"Sleep, Bloodwalker," Kratha murmured, stroking the top of Sam's head gently. "Much will be asked of you soon enough."

Dusk had fallen by the time Sam woke. There was no Thanatosian pull toward unending sleep, no drowsiness. She remembered shrieking and crying, remembered Kratha touching her forehead and the rapidly diminishing buzz in her head as she fell backward onto the bed. She had not dreamed. All the memories and thoughts that had howled and raged earlier in the day had settled in her brain; it was the difference between an active blizzard and the relative peacefulness in the hours after it ends. Sam felt no urge to scream or complain. The past was the past, and it was time to deal with making things as right as they could be.

Sam rose from the bed. The first thing she noticed was a neatly-folded pile of clothes atop the dresser. The Sages had provided her with a new outfit, made from a strange material she didn't recognize, the color of an old penny. The pants were loose and flexible, with several pockets on either hip. Underneath the folded pants was a hooded tunic of the same color. Set carefully atop the outfit was her small tin of Synthosyn, along with three knives in matching sheaths, two of them with thick, studded bands of metal that curved around the outside of her knuckles, forming a thick bellguard. The curved metal offered little protection, but could be used like brass knuckles.

She slid the tin into one of the tunic's pockets, but her fingers hesitated momentarily above the knives before she determinedly freed one of them from the brown leather. The blade shone like a moonlit pond, showing a reflection of her face along its length. Sam slipped it back into the sheath and set it aside, pulling on the pants first, followed by the tunic. The fit was perfect, each hem contoured to her figure while leaving ample flexibility. Forcing reluctance aside, Sam strapped the blade that lacked the bellguard to her right calf and the others around each of her upper thighs. She had felt a little silly while looping the first sheath around her thigh, but now, looking into the lone mirror, she felt confident. She felt dangerous.

Kratha was waiting for her downstairs. "I don't know what you did to me," Sam said evenly, "but thank you." She plucked at the tunic momentarily. "Thank you for these, as well," she added. She was never one to look for charity, but it seemed all she had done since arriving in Purgatory was benefit from the generosity of others. Sam sat on the bench opposite the Assemblist, who had changed out of her crimson robes into a simple brown and tan dress that looked to be made of the same material as her new outfit. "I remember everything, at least I think I do," Sam continued, accepting a glass of water from Telli, the inn's proprietor, with a grateful smile. "One thing I don't understand, though: why did you tell me about the fire?"

Kratha smiled. "I did nothing except encourage you to rest. All of the changes came from inside yourself." She waited for Sam to finish chewing on a chunk of flatbread Telli had set on the table before continuing. "You asked what I meant by your husband's mind not being his own. There is one great shame The Assembly bears." It was plain to see how difficult it was for her to say what she was saying. "It is very rare we have new people come to Old Town to live amongst us. Our typical visitors are drifters, disenchanted with the Unborn life, trudging through the wasteland outside of the Fourth City who stumble upon us purely by chance. The Assembly adds someone new maybe once every hundred years. Sometimes more, sometimes less, but it is an exceedingly rare occurrence."

"The last time we did, we welcomed a man into our midst. He arrived in the dead of night. I'll never forget the first time I saw him. He was wearing a long black coat, the kind that flared at the bottom seam, with a black waistcoat over the top, cinched with a lapel clip. He had a mischievous grin, almost boyish, and the dark ruffled hair of a boy as well. This man projected charisma like the sun projects warmth, and it took less than a week for him to become part of The Assembly." Kratha stopped to sip from a steaming mug of tea that gave off a faint scent of peppermint. "He introduced himself as Symon, a doctor by trade, from London. He was vague on how he had died, but there is certainly no law requiring the revelation of how one died. As I said, Symon was confident and charismatic, a man of science who loved to learn. No. That's not quite right," Kratha corrected herself. "Symon was a man of science who had an unquenchable thirst to learn."

Sam was transfixed by the tale, though she had no idea how it was at all relevant. The flatbread and her own clay mug of water sat forgotten. The thoughts that had ricocheted around her brain a few hours ago were a whisper in a windstorm; Kratha's story was captivating. "A few years passed, with Symon's influence growing exponentially. He wanted to know everything. One thing he had discovered was that many of the members of

The Assembly had developed their own tricks and kept them secret from the others. He ferreted nearly all of them out, but kept the knowledge for himself. Everyone wanted to get closer to Symon. We were iron filings to a magnet. I was not Assemblist at that time, but it was very easy to see how quickly he was climbing the ranks, all but guaranteed to lead The Assembly in the future."

"The darkness within him didn't break through his façade until he had been here for a few years, and when it finally did, most dismissed it as a misunderstanding, or denied it outright. His temperament began to shift, from welcoming to exclusionary, from grateful to condescending. When news spread of his research..." Kratha closed her eyes and shook her head, as if trying to dispel the ghosts of the past.

"Symon had gathered tricks to make himself more powerful, but also to use as blackmail. Some of the Sages had developed techniques that were strictly forbidden. A few of those being blackmailed turned on him in the end, but most were more loyal to him than our organization. Old Town was split in twain by the conflict, with both sides unleashing things that should not exist on their former colleagues and fellow residents. Dark spirits acted as proxies in the battle, summoned from planes beyond our own. One such spirit was used for assassinations but broke free of its constraints. It hunted in the flickers between the blink of your eyes, always on the edge of vision, waiting to devour its prey. Imagine my horror when I saw one in your memories." Sam shivered, remembering her encounter with the Void Hunter. Kratha dry-washed her hands with a disgusted look on her face. "Unnatural things. Eventually they scattered, as did Symon and a few of his adherents, though most were captured and executed. These were the darkest of days."

"You never said what Symon was researching," Sam said, filling the silence that hung heavy in the air.

"No," Kratha sighed, "I did not. One of the Elders Symon had been blackmailing finally admitted to Assemblist Rikard, who was the leader then, what he had been doing on Symon's orders, namely searching for a way to return to the living world. Symon's theory was that as Unborn, he would be invincible in the living world. He wanted eternal life, not eternal death. It was only as the pieces fell around him that the extent of his scheme was revealed. Symon had developed the ability, no doubt built from his own natural charisma, to control others. Small shifts, usually, but enough to set others down a path they would not have otherwise chosen were they of sound mind. At least at first. He honed the skill like a muscle, and very quickly had half of Old Town as his personal playthings."

Kratha shook her head in disgust. "According to testimony after the fact, after surpassing a certain number of people under his control, the bonds he held over them weakened, and some individuals could exercise free will, with enough concerted effort. One Elder who had been captured during the battle confessed to teaching Symon about an experiment he had conducted in object manipulation in the living world. Elder Brannon had never shared how he had come to one day lose the function in his right arm, why it had suddenly withered, dead beyond dying, until that testimony. The Unborn flesh was not meant to pass into the world of the living. Although his experiments were successful, the part of him that passed through the portal was irreparably damaged."

"What happened after that?"

"After that," Kratha said, "we began to keep a very close watch on Symon from a distance. We struggled to accurately pinpoint his location in the world, but we tried. His attempts to reach the living world intensified after the battle, but we were powerless to stop him."

"So you just watched him get stronger?" Sam asked, gasping. In Sam's way of thinking, if the Sages, specifically The Assembly, had given Symon the tools and training to become so dangerous, it was their responsibility to stop him somehow.

"As I said, it is a shame we bear," Kratha said sadly. "After some time of monitoring him, we were surprised when one day he disappeared from our insight. A few thought perhaps he had been killed, but without proof, most were unwilling to entertain that possibility. The next day, he reappeared, but he had been changed. At some point he had learned how to change his own shape into something wholly unnatural and not of this world, or the living world. He became a true monster, a creature out of nightmares, or perhaps from the same place the Void Hunter called home before being pulled here. We hypothesize that by changing into this creature, he has been able to step back into the living world, then revert to his human form. Further, we believe there must be some complication, or else it is unlikely he would have returned."

Sam mulled this over. Finally, she asked, "Is Symon here now?" Kratha nodded, and Sam took a deep breath. She feared she already knew the answer to her next question. "You said he had been able to control others. You also said Jack's mind is not his own. Does Symon have control over my husband?" Sam bolted to her feet and fought back the tears that formed when Kratha nodded again. She would not cry. She would not. "How do I get him back?" The determination in her voice startled her.

"There is much for you to learn and discover, Bloodwalker." Kratha clasped her hands together around Sam's own. "So much, and so little time."

"Please don't take this the wrong way, but can you give me the short version?" Sam asked. She was moving toward the stairs now, with Kratha gracefully following. "My husband is in the grip of a madman. Keep talking while I pack. It's not that I don't appreciate your hospitality, but I need to leave here. I need to find Jack. How do I free him from Symon?"

"The short version," Kratha said flatly. "How can I condense hundreds of years of information into minutes? I will try, for the sake of us all." Telli returned, setting a fresh pot of tea on the table they had just vacated. Kratha smiled warmly at the inn's proprietor before she retreated into the kitchen once again. The Assemblist opened her mouth to speak, but hesitated as she noticed the fox demon sitting on the floor behind Sam. "Do you know how unusual it is that you have a Dybbuk as your traveling companion? At the risk of sounding egotistical, I believe The Assembly collectively holds the greatest store of knowledge in this dead world. Having said that, I have never heard of a Dybbuk attaching itself to anyone or anything outside of its pack. Tell me: was it always so amiable?"

Sam shook her head. "No. The first time I met it, I didn't know what it was. I thought it was a kid wearing a mask. It tricked me, led me into a house, and there were a bunch of them inside. When I tried to leave, it bit me." She shuddered at the memory of the stark terror that had filled her in that room.

"I expected as much," Kratha said. "My theory is this creature is attached to you because it consumed some of your blood. From what I have observed, I would also say not only was it drawn to you, but that it has begun to change into something else. I'm not sure if I would call it evolution, but your Dybbuk displays far more intelligence than we have seen in their kind before."

Sam let out a frustrated grunt. "What does that have to do with getting Jack away from Symon?"

"Who are you?"

Kratha's question caught Sam off guard. She stopped gathering her few belongings from the room. "Samantha. Samantha Nightshade," she answered, confused.

"What are you, Samantha Nightshade?"

"What am I?" If Kratha's first question caught her off guard, this one made her feel like she was balancing on the edge of a precipice. "I don't understand," Sam said slowly. The Assemblist stared at her, unblinking and expressionless. "I'm a woman. A human. I'm stuck in a world of dead people and I want my husband back."

Kratha shook her head. "Not good enough. That will never be enough to kill Symon."

"Kill?" Sam gasped. In the back of her mind, she knew it would probably come to that, but the memory of the shattered skull of the man in the apartment building appeared unbidden in her mind's eye, accompanied by the same panic and queasiness.

"Symon is a threat to this world and the world of the living, Samantha," Kratha answered pragmatically. "What you are, what you failed to state as your identity, is a Bloodwalker. Perhaps *The* Bloodwalker." The emphasis was obvious. "You will need every ounce of your blood if you are going to succeed."

Sam resumed putting her old clothing into her bag, as much to avoid making eye contact with Kratha as because it needed to be done. "This whole thing is ridiculous," she said softly, "How would I even recognize him?" The fox demon was stalking the room, sensing her agitation.

Kratha slammed her palm down atop the dresser. "Samantha Nightshade, you must eliminate your self-doubt. I failed. The Assembly failed. You will succeed, because you must succeed. You have the tools for success, but your mind is getting in the way of your heart. Trust your heart, Bloodwalker. Let your heart guide you, let your blood sing, and trust your instincts."

Sam clenched her jaw and nodded. Kratha was right. She was being childish and rude. "I need to leave, Assemblist Kratha," Sam said, forcing her tone to be respectful, and headed toward the door of her bedroom. "If there is one thing that is most important for me to know, tell me now. Please."

"While you were sleeping," Kratha said in a softer, but still determined tone as they descended the stairs into the main room of The Cupboard, "I viewed Symon. He has overthrown The Jar and is leading a massive group of prisoners into the Fourth City. He has extended his control over the entire prison population. This leaves me no doubt that his power, his control over the reality of this world, has multiplied exponentially. I doubt Symon is interested in subverting the citizens. He has his army already. Now he will want to test his power. If the city burns, he will have made his first real mark on this world, and I fear news of his conquest will spread, his army will grow, and we will enter an eternity of darkness. If he finds a way to bring his army through the portal, the living world will not be able to stop him. Even if Symon alone passes through and finds a way to remain, he might be powerful enough to reshape the living world into his own image. He would become a tyrant in two worlds." Kratha clenched her eyes shut tightly as if imagining that outcome. "You must succeed."

As Sam pulled open the door of The Cupboard, the Dybbuk heeling her closely, she was surprised to see The Assembly waiting for her outside. Elder Yanish stood at the front of the group. "A token of our gratitude, Bloodwalker," he said, proffering a large, rectangular black and gold colored box in his outstretched hands.

Sam took it, unsure of what to expect, before grunting in surprise. It was heavier than she had anticipated. When she removed the lid, she found herself looking into the empty eye sockets of the most complex mask she had ever seen. A snout for a nose, and long, upright black ears with gold enameled pinna stared up at her. Gold paint acted as eyeliner, swirling in an intricate design. "Anubis is an Egyptian God," Yanish explained with a smile. "He watched over the dead."

"No pressure," Sam said, trying to hide her anxiety behind a grin.

Several members of Old Town wished to say slightly longer goodbyes to her. First was Telli, who handed her a bundle of food and told her in no uncertain terms that she needed more meat on her bones. Despite everything, Sam laughed. She had known the innkeeper for less than a day and already Telli felt like family.

After Kratha and Yanish said their final goodbyes, Glen appeared from the back of the mass of Old Town denizens. He limped toward her with a purpose, still holding onto the guitar he had picked up inside The Cupboard. "I am honored to call you a friend, Sam," he said in his gravelly voice. Sam smiled up at him, meeting his eyes through his grey locks. He lowered his voice and spoke quickly. "If I know anything about anything, it's that Kratha is too cryptic for her own good. I don't know exactly what she told you, but the one thing you need to do is trust yourself. Your blood rebels against this world, and you only need listen to it." He took a step back, a guilty expression suddenly appearing on his face. In her peripheral vision, Sam saw a frown on Assemblist Kratha's face.

In a louder voice, Glen said, "You'll have to come back when you're done in the city." He strummed a few chords and gave her a wink. "Should have the song done by then."

On impulse, Sam took a step forward and hugged the old man. "Thank you," she whispered into his chest. "I will remember your advice. And that song better be ready when I get back."

*   *   *   *   *

Fourth City Police Officer Magnus Gunnarsson sat at the reception desk of his precinct. A dozen tiny pieces of wood were strewn across it, the remnants of a pencil he had been breaking, trying to see how many times he could snap a single pencil. His record was fifteen. Irritated, Gunnarsson swept the shattered bones of the pencil to the floor with a grunt and grabbed another new one from a drawer. He hated being on desk duty.

People entered the precinct sporadically. Most were twitchy and nervous, afraid of their own shadows. The braver ones would approach the desk and try to get information from Gunnarsson, and he would stare at them until they went away. On rare occasions, a civilian would not leave him alone and would try to make a scene. Gunnarsson did not like people, and he could not be intimidated.

A thousand years ago, he had dedicated his axe and his life to Odin, had died in service to Odin, and woke up in this cursed world. The wish for all was to awaken in Valhöll, legendary Valhalla, to continue to serve Odin and prepare for the doomed battle of Ragnarök. Many would undoubtedly be claimed by Freya and forever dwell in Fólkvangr, the Warrior's Field. He had never seen any of the others he had fought and killed and died with in this hell, and he knew that between The Allfather and Freya, loyal servants would not be abandoned, yet here he was. Long ago, Gunnarsson had decided that Loki the Trickster must have snapped up his soul and dumped him here. Mischievous wretch.

When the door to the precinct opened again, Gunnarsson lifted his gaze with a scowl. A dark-skinned man with greying hair entered. His steps were firm and confident, his back straight, and his eyes flickered around the room as he gathered information. A scar wrapped around his neck, announcing how he had died. The man stepped up to the desk and met Gunnarsson's gaze without hesitation or fear.

"My name is Robert Webb," the man said in a firm, even voice. "Are you hiring?"

*   *   *   *   *

Wearing her new clothes and with the Anubis mask resting at the top of her bag, Sam felt invigorated as she stalked from shadow to shadow, a wraith in the night. The Dybbuk followed behind her, its face grinning widely in pleasure at returning to the city. They had passed the decrepit sign announcing their passage into the city limits an hour earlier and were making their way back toward the heart of the city, toward Jack. Toward Symon. She clenched her jaw, grinding her teeth determinedly. The fox demon appeared to sense her mood and took it to heart, growling softly whenever it sprinted through the occasional pools of light formed by moonlight as it broke through the thick clouds.

The final parting words of Assemblist Kratha echoed in her mind, as the leader of Old Town shared some last-minute advice. "Your blood sings, Samantha Nightshade, because it is alive when everything around it is dead," Kratha had told her as they both stood at the top of the crater in which sat Old Town. "I am certain Glen shared this with you, despite my instruction that you find your own way, so it won't change anything for me to echo his words. Your blood rebels against this world because it does not belong here. There is wisdom in your blood; learn to trust it. Learn to believe in yourself." Then and now, Sam found herself thinking about the man who had caught her in his apartment, the man she had attacked with the makeshift club, thinking about how she had moved like a predator, her movements guided by instinct alone. Or perhaps by blood alone. She wondered if that was what Kratha had meant.

The entrance to the subway terminal came into view. They had seen no one in these barren streets, but they would soon enough. Sam pulled the Anubis mask free from the bag. The hood on her tunic had two slits in it, perfectly spaced apart to allow the stiff ears to burst through the top while securing the hood in place. Pulling it down over her face, she found its weight distributed in such a way that it was not an encumbrance, and the long snout made an easy handhold for small adjustments. This was the first time she had donned the mask. Sam was surprised at how comfortable it was to be enclosed within its shell. She twisted her neck in every direction, familiarizing herself with the weight and preparing to make a mental note of any limitations in her mobility, but there were none. There were no issues of heat or breathability, despite having the mask on her face and the hood over the back and top of her head. It was as if the mask had always been a part of her.

"How do I look?" she asked the Dybbuk, grinning behind the ebony snout.

The fox demon regarded the mask of the Jackal God before letting out a howl of anticipation. Sam interpreted that howl: Finally, it was time to hunt.

*   *   *   *   *

Charles Mayes hummed tunelessly to himself as he walked around the small apartment he rented in the eastern quadrant of the Fourth City. He bustled about with a watering can in hand, pouring water for exactly four seconds into each of the planters that filled the apartment. The morning ritual would take the better part of an hour. He loved gardening, but the afterlife wasn't exactly a green-thumb's dream, so he made do with a plethora of clay pots. There were small ferns, flowers, and even a few vegetables. The vegetables were always his favorite.

Thunder rumbled quietly outside his window as the dirt soaked up the water, the shade changing from light brown to the deep, rich color of devil's food cake. He missed devil's food cake almost as much as he missed having a full garden. Charles went back to the kitchen to refill his watering can, still humming, as the thunder rolled again. What he had heard finally processed in his brain and he set the watering can down on the counter. He hadn't seen very many thunderstorms since coming to this world. It always looked grey and faded outside, but a good thunderstorm was great for a garden.

When Charles looked out the window, however, the sky didn't look particularly threatening. In fact, it looked less overcast than normal. He craned his neck around as much as he could to look for the dark clouds he expected but couldn't see them. Maybe they were overhead. He unlocked the window and slid up the sash. The noise burst through the open window. When Charles stuck his head out the window, he immediately identified the source. The street to his right was teeming with people. There were hundreds of people, almost all men, perhaps even several thousand. They were bellowing as they progressed up the blacktop, breaking windows as they walked. This was no thunderstorm: it was a street riot!

As he watched, he saw a small explosion burst to life in a storefront a block away from his building. The rioters were throwing Molotov cocktails through windows, causing as much damage and chaos as they could as they marched toward the heart of the city. In the distance behind the crowd, Charles could see flames licking out of lower level windows, the fronts of some buildings already turning black from the fires. He did a quick count of how many floors up the fires had reached. His apartment was on the 15th floor of a 52-story building, and it looked like the fires had only spread up to the 6th or 7th on the buildings the riot had already passed.

Charles was faced with a few options. He immediately dismissed the first that popped to mind, namely racing downstairs to try to get out of the building before the rioters reached it and set it on fire. There was no way he would make it in time. There was a back exit to the building, but there was no way of telling if the riot was contained to one street or not. The second option was he could stay where he was and hope that either they wouldn't set his building on fire, or that the fire wouldn't reach as high as his apartment before being extinguished. This also seemed like a poor decision. He looked around his apartment and mentally said goodbye to the plants he cherished so much, hoping that he would see them again, unharmed.

By the time Charles climbed to the 18th floor, the stairwell had become clogged with people pushing in either direction. He had seen panic like that only once before, in the moments before the derailed, overturned train in which he had been a passenger had burst into flames. The suffocating closeness of so many people, the smell of their sweat and frenzy filled his nostrils, then and now. When he was alive, stuck on that train, he felt helpless. His thoughts had gone blank. Like many of his fellow passengers, he stood there and accepted his impending fate. He was not going to give up this time, though. He would never give up again. Thinking of his pepper plants and how they needed his care to survive, Charles continued to ascend toward the roof and his only chance of making it through whatever storm was brewing below. An explosion from the street, loud enough to be heard over the cries of the people in the stairwell acted like an exclamation point on his internal dialogue. He would never give up.

*   *   *   *   *

Holding onto a strap as he stood on a subway car, Lawrence Gibson mentally ran through a final check on his equipment. In his front inside pocket were his wallet and several pieces of fake identification. A shoulder holster rested beside that pocket, holding a revolver. This was the one Old

Man Ladi's goons were supposed to find when they searched him. It was obvious enough even one of those idiots should be able to find it without him drawing attention to it. On the inside of his right thigh was a smaller pistol which, if everything went according to his plan, would eventually be snuck into the shoulder holster once the first gun was confiscated. A sheathed knife was dangling between his shoulder blades, held up by a rather clever re-stitching of his coat. Finally, tucked into his right boot, was a spare pistol. That was for emergencies; it held but a single shot.

He knew he was running through his equipment and his plan in his head as much because it was the right thing to do before attempting to execute such a painfully stupid thing as ripping off a drug lord mobster as it was a way to not think about Sam. Gibson knew he had done the right thing by sending her away, but he had regretted his method since the moment the door closed behind her in his apartment. He hoped she had found what she needed in Old Town. Maybe the Sages had been able to send her back to the living world.

Enough about her. He needed to focus. Today was a day for stealing from the mob, for taking a large percentage of Synthosyn out of circulation before it hit the streets. It was a day for hitting Old Man Ladi where it really hurt: his bank account.

The train would be reaching the central terminal soon, where Davis had arranged for Gibson to meet some of Ladi's thugs. Assuming he passed their initial screening, he would be escorted onto a second train, into a private car, where he would be blindfolded and taken to where Old Man Ladi was hiding. Gibson smirked. Blindfolding him. Cute. As if his career as a private investigator didn't require him to know every street, every back alley, every fire escape in the Fourth City.

As the brakes began to shriek, Gibson felt the itch of anticipation. It was a day for action.

*   *   *   *   *

Symon's band of angry, coerced convicts tore through the eastern blocks of the Fourth City with ease. The local police, dispatched to quell what they believed a riot, were quickly overrun. This was the test run, the sandbox in which to build his castles of strategy and cunning. Each granule would be shaped and molded to his specifications, at the whim of his mercy and ruthlessness. He grinned widely, thinking on what he had seen in the past few hours as the horde of puppets at his command decimated everything, their reign of terror stretching through the night and into the first splashes of morning. News would spread quickly about his conquest in the east, and would spread even faster once the Fourth City fell. As he marched at the head of a river of criminals that stretched farther than the eye could see, Symon cackled. There would be no quarter. Not on this day, nor any other.

Chapter 17

Sam and the Dybbuk stepped from the subway car in the Fourth City central terminal. She was as awake and alert as she could ever remember being in her life. Determination fueled her. Determination, and the pull of a reunion with Jack. In the back of her mind, she knew she would have to go through Symon one way or another to get to Jack, but she hoped she would see her husband first. The thought of seeing his face again gave her goosebumps.

Sam had expected an early morning bustle, but the terminal was largely empty, so much so that she could see beams of faded sunlight cascade down the stone stairs, her view unobstructed by those using the underground rail system. It made her uneasy. Something was wrong.

The street above, the central artery of the city, was similarly abandoned. Sam raised a hand to shield her masked eyes from the sun reflecting from the towering spires that made up the financial district. She turned her head slowly, sweeping the street with a steady gaze. Compared to what she expected, this was a ghost town, with only a small group of people hurriedly moving up the sidewalk in a tight cluster. They moved like a frightened school of fish, turning in unison up the steps of a towering office building and disappearing behind a glass key-coded door. Behind the face of Anubis, Sam's brows furrowed.

The sound of an explosion to her right drew her focus. Sam moved toward the smoke that rose in the distance, wondering what was happening. The final growlings of the explosion faded, but behind that came a low rumbling, like the churning of gigantic cogs in an enormous machine. Sam increased her speed to a trot, the fox demon keeping a steady pace by her side.

*   *   *   *   *

"Hey, rookie!"

213

Robert Webb sighed. With 30 years of experience on the force, he was not used to being called rookie anymore. He spun in his chair and faced the man who spoke. "What is it, Cartwright?"

Jacob Cartwright grinned. He was a young man, brash and excitable. "There's a riot coming downtown from the eastern part of the city. Word is there was a mass breakout from The Jar." Cartwright noticed the confused look on Webb's face. "Huge prison in the outskirts of the city. Hundreds of convicts, the worst of the worst. Maybe thousands. All the precincts out that way are being overrun, so it's up to us to provide backup."

"I'm confused why you're smiling, Cartwright," Webb said.

The younger man tossed a bulletproof vest at Webb. "This is a once in a lifetime experience, rookie. Hundreds of convicts broke out of the highest security prison I've ever heard of. Today we get some real action."

Jacob Cartwright's smile never faded, even seeing the grim look on Webb's face. If anything, the grin grew larger. Webb opened the drawer of his desk and pulled out the pistol that had been issued to him. It almost looked like a Sig Sauer P226, but there were a few small details that were different enough to make it distinct. Most notable was the wider butt and the duplexed row of fat-tipped slugs that filled the clip. It felt awkward in Webb's grip, but he had been told these bullets would permanently end the Unborn. He hoped he wouldn't have to use it, this day or any other, but there was a bad feeling in the air, and men like Cartwright always made him uneasy.

Sliding the pistol into the holster on his left hip, Webb nodded at the enthusiastic young officer and grabbed the vest. "All right. Let's go."

*　　*　　*　　*　　*

Gibson stepped from the subway car, preparing his most ingratiating smile. He was confident it would be enough to lower the guard of Old Man Ladi's thugs. If Davis was right and Ladi was the one who ordered his men to murder Gibson's partner, then he would have his revenge soon enough. If Davis was wrong, at least Gibson was still going to hit a drug pusher right where it hurt, and hit him hard. All the intelligence he had gathered suggested Ladi was a discriminating employer, only welcoming people who displayed a particular skill or set of personality traits into his "Family". Ruthlessness, loyalty, and a lack of ambition were highly valued. Old Man Ladi certainly wouldn't want anyone thinking they could take over his operation.

He was still mentally reviewing his notes as he glanced around the terminal. His eyebrows rose in surprise. The station was surprisingly empty, bordering on deserted. A woman and a child ascended a stairway in the distance, the child staying close to the woman's side. An elderly man stumbled out from the ticket booth and went to the restroom. That was it; three people in the terminal, aside from himself, and clearly no one from Ladi's racket.

Gibson checked the time on the huge clock mounted to the wall above the stairs where the woman had disappeared. They were late. Or maybe Davis had ratted him out and they had set an ambush. His muscles tensed, preparing to dive behind a nearby garbage can if he was suddenly attacked, but no attack came. Perplexed, Gibson cautiously made his way across the cavernous platform and up the steps to street level.

The woman and child caught his eye immediately, striding purposefully up the sidewalk. Thick plumes of smoke curled in the distance. Gibson looked around, searching for Old Man Ladi's lackeys, or an impending attack, and found nothing. The streets were unsettlingly empty. As he looked back to his left, Gibson watched as a newspaper fluttered across the vacant street. He had heard stories of nuclear weapons from some of the Unborns who had arrived in this hell after he had. Were it not for the buildings still towering all around him, Gibson may have expected a bomb had gone off. Instead, it was like a bomb that only targeted the Unborn. Except for the woman and the child.

He looked back in their direction and nearly choked. That was no child. He hadn't noticed it at first with the entire street so unexpectedly empty, but the child in a mahogany tunic was not human. A stray breeze lifted the hem slightly as it walked and Gibson saw the padded underside of a paw with three curved talon-like nails arching toward the sidewalk. Dybbuk! What was a Dybbuk doing in the heart of the city, walking alongside a woman who treated it so casually it may as well not even be there. No normal woman would mistake a Dybbuk for a child. The memory of a bloodied and unconscious Sam, a crumpled mess in the hallway of his apartment, burst through like a beam of sunlight through winter clouds. She was not a normal woman, at least not for this world, but that couldn't possibly be her walking side-by-side with a fox demon. Could it? Maybe he was just so desperate to see her again that he was imagining things. Whoever this woman was, she moved with a determined, graceful stride, confident and dangerous. As circumspectly as he could, considering the lack of people on the street, Gibson followed the unusual pair.

* * * * *

Sam stopped a few feet shy of rounding the corner and took a deep breath. The mob of convicts would be in sight when she turned. Was she really going to step out in front of a riot, armed with a few knives, and confront Symon? Would she even be able to find him in the crowd? She glanced down at the Dybbuk and saw the fox demon looking up at her, the mask-like face curved into an expression of anticipation, a small fang jutting out between hard lips. Inhaling deeply a second time, Sam stepped out to face the crowd.

The closest rioters were about a block away from her. It was impossible to pick out any single detail in the rolling wave of humanity. Sam had the impression the mob was a huge snarling face, painted with hatred and uncontrollable rage. Assemblist Kratha's words echoed in her mind. "Let your heart guide you, let your blood sing, and trust your instincts."

Behind the mask of the ancient Egyptian God, Sam closed her eyes. "Protector of the Dead," she muttered under her breath. "If you've got anything for me, Anubis, now's your chance."

* * * * *

Gibson watched as the woman with the Dybbuk stepped around the corner of the towering steel building. He had no idea why it was happening, but judging by the smoke, explosions, and screaming voices, it seemed a riot had taken shape in the Fourth City. He had never heard of the like, but he had always been told there was a first time for everything. Why would she be putting herself in the path of the disturbance?

He hurried to get her back in sight. By the time he reached the spot where she had disappeared from his vision, his mouth fell open. She stood motionless, hands at her sides, in the middle of the street. He wanted to shout at her to run, to hide, to get away from the hundreds of violent rioters destroying everything in their path, but his throat had clenched tight. The Dybbuk crouched next to her and despite its brown cloak, Gibson could tell it was bristling with anticipation, like a cat watching a squirrel. There were no doubts as to its species now. As the crazed rioters spotted the woman and the Dybbuk, they reacted like a swarm of bees, with every one of them focused solely on rushing toward them with single-minded rage. For the first time since he had died, Gibson was truly terrified.

And then the woman began to dance.

*　　*　　*　　*　　*

Sam moved like a ballerina, twirling around them with grace, her twin blades darting and slashing with every step. She disassociated and moved without thought, allowing her instincts, her blood, to direct her every movement. She kicked the side of someone's knee, buckling him to the ground, and with one fluid motion drove the knife in her right hand into his chest, hilt deep. She rolled to her left, causing one man to stumble into two others, and slashed at the first man's hamstring with the knife in her left hand. He howled in pain as he fell to the ground. Springing to her feet, Sam removed the knife she had buried into the other man's chest, just in time to perform an upward stroke with it, thrusting through the jaw of yet another of Symon's followers. The silvery blood of the Unborns dripped from the snout of the jackal god's mask and both blades as she twirled in her deadly dance, filling her nose with the smell of faint copper. *Trust your instincts,* Sam thought. *Trust your blood.*

Occasionally she would catch a glimpse of the Dybbuk as it snarled and leapt from one of its victims to another, clawing and biting as it moved, leaving a trail of fallen bodies in its wake. It was a fearsome companion, and she was grateful for its aid.

Sam shouted in surprise as a 2x4 smacked across the nose of the Anubis mask. The blow was hard enough to stagger her to a knee, the mask hanging crookedly. Pushing herself upright with a hand that still clutched a blade, she growled in frustration. By the time she reached Symon - if she reached him - she would be so bone-weary exhausted she wouldn't stand a chance. But there was no other choice. She couldn't afford to lose. Two worlds were counting on her. Batting the mask aside and exposing her face to the mob, Sam fought on, dodging a second swing of the 2x4, and stabbing the man in the throat with an almost contemptuous motion.

"Sam?" The voice was deep and shocked, but she couldn't pinpoint the source as she swirled through the crowd, blades slicing through Unborn flesh. A pair of arms grabbed her from behind, crushing her shoulders painfully inward and cutting off her mobility. A giant of a man appeared in front of her, grinning with the few teeth remaining in his cruel mouth. Sam struggled to free herself but the grip was too tight. The giant man's fist buried itself in her abdomen, knocking out all of her air and making her eyes pop.

He reached back to punch her again when his jaw suddenly exploded in a spray of bone and silver liquid. The man holding her was shocked enough to loosen his grip, which gave Sam enough opening to twist and draw her blade across his throat. A fist caught her in the shoulder, knocking her off balance. Her timing had been enough to avoid getting slugged in the face, but her knees buckled slightly as she tried to regain her balance. A foot caught her ankle, tripping her. In an instant, she felt as if she were drowning as the mob all scrambled to reach her as she lay prone on the street.

The top of a skull burst as a second bullet tore through one of the convicts. Another man screamed in pain as he fell to the ground, a slug burying itself in his shoulder. A man near her feet stumbled backward, then collapsed with a yelp. Sam hurried back to her feet in time to see as an arm reached around another man from behind and spun him around. A moment later the second man dropped to the ground as well.

"Sam!"

Hearing her name, she turned to her left and gawked. Calmly standing there as if he weren't surrounded by a tumultuous mob, wearing a sly smirk, was Gibson. "What the hell are you doing here?" Sam yelled over the barbaric noises that filled the street.

"Sam!"

Her heart skipped a beat. She would recognize that voice anywhere. Looking to her right, she saw him immediately, his face standing out like a sunbeam in a thunderstorm. All the ferocity, all of the survival instincts, the constant mental note to trust her body to keep her safe, everything faded out of her, out of the world. Out of every world. Standing in the middle of the chaos was Jack, a thick scar running down his cheek. Sam's lip quivered. She ran toward him almost blindly, her vision clouded by tears that streamed freely down her cheeks. She almost made it.

*　　*　　*　　*　　*

Gibson had no idea what was going on. Why was there a full-scale riot going on in the city? Why was Sam battling the small army that streamed toward her? How was she surviving? Why was she traveling with a Dybbuk? None of it made any sense. The one thing he did know was that the man who had been pushing through the crowd from her other side to reach her must be her husband. Through the crowd Gibson saw occasional flashes of the man's face as he punched, kicked, and clawed his way closer toward Sam, becoming frantic when she hit the ground. Gibson had been choosing his targets carefully, as opposed to spraying bullets blindly into the crowd. He still wasn't sure what effect the bullets would have on Sam, but her husband certainly wouldn't survive.

Gibson couldn't help himself and he yelled her name. When Sam's eyes met his, he gave her his most insolent grin, and a jaunty little wave with the hand that held the pistol. The next second, her husband called out to her. And that was when everything went to hell.

*   *   *   *   *

Sam was buffeted from all sides, the hands of the mob clawing at her as she ran toward Jack. She barely noticed until she lost her balance and fell again, smacking her chin into the pavement. Blood pooled in her mouth, but the impact was enough to bring her back to her senses. There would be time for Jack later. Right now, she was in the fight of her life. Her body ached from head to toe but she forced the pain away ruthlessly. There would be time later. She spat blood onto the street, the hot iron taste on her tongue hardening her resolve.

The Dybbuk appeared at her side as if by magic by the time Sam scrambled back to her feet. It looked up at her, then on the ground where the blood had splattered. Sam watched in confusion for a moment as her blood began to move, to pull in on itself instead of pooling outward, forming a flattened ball. "Your blood rebels against this world," Glen's voice echoed in her head.

The fox demon rubbed a frail claw through the blood momentarily, scratching an odd shape in the ichor before scooping crimson to its mouth. The Dybbuk lapped at its talons, feeding greedily. She knew the creature consumed the life force of other things as sustenance, but watching it made her feel queasy. Sam averted her eyes as it reached for a second helping, which enabled her to see a fist flying toward the side of her head. She dodged and struck out with her elbow, striking home with a sickening crunch as she caught the man in the solar plexus, dropping him to the pavement.

A man she hadn't noticed hooked the heel of her foot and brought her to the ground for a third time. Sam was able to get her hands in front of her to brace against the impact and protect her bloody face from smacking into the ground, but her back was exposed to the mob. A guttural howl came from above her, along with another pair of gunshots and screams of pain. She rolled to her side as quickly as she could, but Sam was so far beyond the point of exhaustion that she could barely keep from thudding her head on the pavement. A boot caught her in the small of the back and she shrieked in agony, blood spurting out from her mouth as spittle flew onto the street.

A busted hand leaking the silvery blood of the Unborns grasped at her wrist and she flailed, trying to push it away. "Sam!" Jack's voice again. She looked upward and saw her husband looking down at her, consternation etched upon his face. She realized it was his hand trying to grab her wrist. Allowing herself to be pulled to her feet, Sam stared into Jack's eyes.

"We really don't have time for a family reunion, Bloodwalker," grunted a voice next to her. She turned to see Gibson standing next to her, looking over his shoulder and flashing her a quick grin with his pistol pointed into the crowd. "In case you didn't notice, a lot of people want to kill you for some reason."

The deep, vacuous voice of the Dybbuk came from nowhere, and everywhere. It bellowed wordlessly, the sound far too loud for its diminutive body. Sam gasped. The Dybbuk was towering over Symon's mob, a two-story red-brown figure radiating waves of darkness. Despite a short cuff of hair covering its body, Sam could see powerful muscles flaring across the creature's torso and down its arms. Where the fox demon smashed down a door-sized fist, men screamed. One man, extremely brave or extremely stupid, grabbed the white flair at the tip of the Dybbuk's tail. Sam had never seen the tail before and assumed the creature had been keeping it hidden beneath the tunic. The monstrous Dybbuk roared as it felt the pull at its tail. Sam watched in amazement as the tail coiled around the man, engulfing him around the waist like a python. In moments, the man fell to the street in two distinct halves, severed by the pure strength of the Dybbuk. Sam thought she might be sick. It was one thing to fight for her survival but quite another to watch as a man's flesh and bone were torn asunder.

Sam noticed a tall man in a white suit climbing a streetlight to get a view over the crowd. His blond hair ruffled in a slight breeze before dropping down to partially obscure one eye. Sam's heart clenched. She knew who that man was, though she had never seen him before in her life. He watched and shouted orders as the Dybbuk unleashed its fury on his followers. Symon.

The Dybbuk's rage had captured everyone's attention. A gentle hand on her shoulder made her turn her head away from Symon. In her head, Sam imagined an hourglass, the sands flowing toward her confrontation with Symon. "C'mon, Bloodwalker," Gibson whispered in her ear. "Regroup." He gestured toward the wall of the nearest building, where a concrete stoop marked the entrance. Sam nodded. Jack was still watching the Dybbuk with his mouth hanging open. Sam grabbed his hand and pulled him toward the landing. Jack flinched in surprise at her touch but smiled as he looked at her. Sam's heart ached. They had so much to talk about. She hoped they would find the time soon.

Backs to the door, Sam, Jack, and Gibson watched the Dybbuk as it mauled the crowd, an unstoppable monster determined to destroy everything. Sam noticed the two men occasionally shot furtive glances at each other, like strange cats dumped into a box together. With the Dybbuk the center of the mob's focus, they enjoyed a momentary respite. She sighed and made brief introductions. The two men acknowledged each other with nods.

"Gibson," Sam said tersely. "You can apologize to me later. Right now, there's a man out there in a white suit, with blond hair. His name is Symon. Do you know him?" Gibson shook his head. "He's the one who caused this mess. If he turns toward us, tell me."

Sam turned her attention toward her husband without waiting for Gibson's acknowledgement. "Jack," she began, "I was told you were under Symon's control, like you were hypnotized." She gestured toward the swirling chaos encircling the Dybbuk. "I'm here to stop him."

Jack's eyes went wide. "Stop him?" Sam nodded, keeping her jaw firm. "Everything is hazy." Jack said, looking from her to the riot, to her blood-soaked clothing and bruised hands. "I don't remember you being violent, Sam."

"Long story," Sam replied, squeezing his wrist affectionately, careful to avoid his bloodied knuckles.

Jack was silent for a moment before continuing. "He has some kind of power, some kind of control over people. It was like being surrounded by fog, with a voice telling you where to go to get out of the fog, but in reality, the voice was pulling you deeper. Until I saw your face. I saw your face and suddenly I was myself again." He smiled at her briefly before asking, "Where did you learn to fight like that?"

Sam ignored the question, feeling her stomach churn. She was having a harder time staying focused on what she needed to do now that she had her husband in front of her, now that she was living the moment she had thought about for so long, though she had never imagined their reunion would be such a bloody one, with a rioting mob as background ambience. "What happened to you, Jack? You were supposed to come home to me, and then the doorbell rang and you were..." Sam trailed off, unable to finish her thought while she was looking into his eyes. She averted her gaze and saw that Gibson was keeping watch on the battle. The Dybbuk roared again but Sam trusted Gibson to get her attention if the mob turned its attention back toward them, and she needed to hear what Jack had to say.

"I don't remember all of it," Jack said slowly, his tone distant and muddy. As he continued, he met her eyes. "I remember leaving work. It was overcast, starting to rain. I remember swerving to avoid hitting a deer. Or something like that. Some sort of animal. Then I woke up here."

"They said," Sam cleared her throat. Her heart raced, pounding in her chest faster now than it had while she danced with the blades. "They said you weren't alone in the car, Jack. They said you..."

Gibson knocked the thought out of Sam's mind as he shoved her and Jack hard to her right, pressing them against the metal bar that served as a railing. Gibson yelped in pain as a knife clattered against the stonework, having passed through the space where Jack had been standing a split-second earlier.

Sam saw Gibson clutching at his left arm, where a deep gash had sliced through his sleeve and tore through his skin. Gibson was panting heavily. "Your friend Symon is here," he groaned, wincing as he gingerly touched the wound.

Sam turned to see Symon on the street a dozen paces away, grinning at her broadly, surrounded by six of the most terrifying men she had ever seen in her life. Two were lithe-like, quick and deadly. Three of them were average height but muscular, the kind of men who expected to always get their way, with force if necessary. The last man was standing behind Symon, and was the largest person she had ever seen, a towering giant with broad shoulders and thick arms. The giant saw her jaw drop and smiled wickedly, showing as many teeth present as missing. Sam's heart thudded, threatening to burst free of her chest. The Dybbuk was still crushing anyone who was foolish enough to get too close to it, but it had been lured down the street by half of Symon's mob. The other half were visible to her left, fighting against what she assumed were police officers, judging by the flashing blue and red lights. When had the police arrived? She had been so lost in her battle she hadn't noticed.

Only a moment passed before Jack and Gibson were standing at her sides. Gibson was barely moving his left arm, but he held the pistol with a firm grip in his right hand. Sam had never known Jack to be the kind of person to get involved in physical confrontations, but he stood solid and firm. The two groups stared at each other for what felt like an eternity, motionless as the failed challengers of Medusa.

It was Symon who broke the silence, a faint English accent tingeing his high-pitched words. "Who are you? I don't like unknowns in my world, and you, my dear, are most definitely an unknown."

"It's not your world," Sam answered darkly. "I know all about you, Symon. Release these people!" Sam gestured at the mob overflowing the street.

Symon screeched a laugh. "Release them? Why would I even consider your request? I saw you slicing and dicing my friends here, twirling your deadly ballet. I wonder why you are even involved in this experiment of mine." Symon tapped at his chin with a long, bony index finger.

If nothing else, Sam thought, *this madman certainly had a flair for the dramatic.*

Symon's eyes shifted and he focused on Gibson. Sam's muscles tensed when his eyes drifted toward Jack. "You," Symon said, waving his hand dismissively toward Gibson, "you are clearly some hired tough with no value beyond your pistol." Gibson growled but didn't answer. "But you," Symon continued, pointing directly at Jack, "you, I do not understand. It's obvious from your clothing that you came from The Jar with the rest of my friends, but why are you over there," another gesture toward Sam and her companions, "instead of over here?" A grandiose flourish of his hands seemed to encompass every place in the world that was not the concrete landing to this unknown office building. "Tell me: what is your name?"

Jack's fists were clenched as he took a step forward, placing himself slightly in front of Sam. "Jack Nightshade!" he roared, staring daggers at Symon.

Symon curled an eyebrow, then cocked his head at an odd angle, like a dog trying to understand. Suddenly, he straightened and grinned broadly. "I remember you!" Symon declared, cackling in that mad, high-pitched voice, pointing at Jack with a bony finger. "You know, people used to call me Jack, too. Sometimes." Symon laughed again, tilting his face toward the clouds with insane mirth at a joke only he understood. Abruptly, his voice became deep, more akin to the growl of an ancient predator than the sound of a man. "I remember ripping you APART!"

Symon lunged forward with the speed of a viper, a sudden and violent movement sending him hurtling toward them faster than Sam could have imagined, his bodyguards rushing behind him. Gibson's pistol roared twice, striking one of the heavily-muscled guards in the shoulder and chest. He fell in a writhing heap, screaming in agony, but the others ignored their fallen comrade. Sam darted to put herself between the men and Jack, flipping the knife in her right hand backward, so that the blade was pointing behind her. Trust your blood.

She hurtled headlong to meet the pack, catching the closest man across the ribs with a wide arc of her dagger before utilizing the momentum of her swing to tuck and roll. Unfurling, she hamstrung one of the thinner men. To Sam, time slowed, each breath lasting minutes as she resumed her dance with renewed vigor and ferocity. She heard a strangled shout from Gibson but couldn't understand his words. Casting a furtive glance in his direction, Sam saw he was grappling with another of the muscular men, but the injury to his left arm was obviously inhibiting his struggle. Jack was driving his fists into the man's side to no apparent effect in an attempt to help Gibson. Sam needed to trust they would be able to handle that man, or at least keep him occupied until she could help. This was her fight to win.

The man with the severed hamstring was trying to reach her, crawling awkwardly on the ground. Sam barely looked in his direction before stepping on his hand with one foot and kneeing him on the bridge of the nose, sending him limply to the street.

Symon and his bodyguards came to a near standstill a few paces away from her. Sam noticed for the first time that Symon wore a look of uncertainty instead of arrogant madness. He squinted at her quizzically before asking again, in a tone that bordered on impressed, "What are you?"

She didn't answer. Symon was straight ahead of her, the gigantic man a few steps behind, looming like a distant volcanic mountain. While one of the thinner, more agile men was motionless on the ground, the other stood to her left, twirling a small makeshift club, a broken chunk of metal, in his hand as he shifted his weight from side to side. A larger man was far to her right, edging slowly to try to get behind her. One to the left, one to the right, and two in the center. Her fingers itched to get at Symon and end this, but her instincts urged her toward the man on the left, even if that would expose her back to the other three. If she went right, she was afraid the faster man might reach her with his blade before she could dispatch with the thick-shouldered goon. In an odd counterpoint to the stillness surrounding her, the final of Symon's bodyguards was still grappling with Jack and Gibson, though they finally seemed to be getting the upper hand over the lone man.

Sam feinted right for a half step before darting to the left as quickly as possible, the blades in each of her hands glinting with silvery blood. The thin man spun to avoid her charge, narrowly avoiding a desperate slash that passed through the air where his neck had been a split-second earlier. A flashing thrust with the other blade was deflected by the thin man. The resounding clash of metal on metal echoed in the air. Sam knew she had only moments before Symon and the two remaining rioters would reach her. She needed to make her move now so she could face them head-on.

Twisting her hips, Sam slid her foot out and caught the man on the side of the knee. He barked in surprise as he staggered sideways. The momentary lack of balance was enough for Sam's blade to find home, burying itself in the man's gut. His eyes widened in shock. Sam ripped the dagger free and shoved him backwards, using his body as a springboard to bounce off of him and roll, putting the felled man between herself and Symon. As she turned toward the muscular man who was rushing to meet her, Sam hurled the knife in her right hand at him. It was a risk to throw one of her two remaining blades, but she needed the edge. It scored a direct hit, lodging itself into his Adam's apple. A gurgling scream bubbled from his throat as he clutched at the hilt. A moment later he fell motionless to the street.

Sam ran toward the fallen man to retrieve her blade before skidding to an awkward halt halfway. The grinning face of Symon abruptly filled her field of vision as he stepped in front of her. She took an involuntary step backward and thumped into a brick wall. No. Not a brick wall. The giant man. With surprising speed, he grabbed her wrists and pulled both of her arms across her chest, as tight and restrictive as a straitjacket. Her final remaining dagger clanged on the ground as he squeezed her wrist hard enough where she felt her bones rubbing painfully together.

"Now you," Symon said slyly as he stepped closer to her, "you are an extraordinary specimen. In a previous life, well..." the mad grin was so wide it engulfed the entire bottom half of his face, "let's just say in other circumstances, I would have had a lot of fun with you." Sam struggled against her captor but knew there was no possible way she would be able to extricate herself from the grip of the colossal bodyguard. "Now, now, my dear," Symon waggled his index finger at her. "We have plenty of time to figure you out."

A roar of anger came from Sam's right. She struggled unsuccessfully to face the sound, knowing what she would see, a pit of ice forming in her stomach. Jack came running into view, heading directly toward Symon, who turned toward him casually. "What do *you* want? I already killed you once. Do you really want me to do it again?"

Sweaty and red-faced, Jack glared at Symon. "Let go of my wife," he growled, fists balled up at his sides.

"Your wife?" Symon asked, surprise in the words. "How intriguing!" An insane cackle erupted from him. Sam pulled with all her strength at the enormous man's grip. He didn't even react. Sam wanted to scream with frustration.

Jack looked past Symon for a moment, meeting her eyes, boring into her soul. "I love you, Samantha," he said, his voice firm and steady. Unafraid. Before she could respond, Jack charged at Symon, his right fist cocked back.

And then everything seemed to happen at once.

227

Chapter 18

It took all her willpower, but Sam relaxed her muscles, going limp in the massive man's grasp. The sudden change of pressure made him stumble, and that was all the opening she needed. Sam stomped his foot as hard as she could, creating just enough space to be able to mule-kick him in the knee. She felt the pop of his kneecap as it dislocated before she felt the crunch of it shattering under her heel. The giant toppled over with a deep bass roar of agony. Sam didn't waste any more time on him. She grabbed her knife from the street and raced toward Symon's back. Ten feet away.

Jack was grunting loudly with effort, swinging wildly with both fists, desperately trying to connect with any part of Symon. For his part, Symon only dodged Jack's punches, taunting her husband. Seven feet away.

Sam could hear Symon's crazed giggles even over the blood that pounded in her ears. Jack launched another wild haymaker that flew past Symon's head. Four feet away.

She heard the unmistakably wet sound of parting flesh at the same time she saw Jack's eyes bulge in shock. With a shriek of agony and rage and a thousand other raw emotions, Sam drove her knife through the back of Symon's neck with a single upward stroke, burying the blade to the hilt alongside his vertebrae.

Sam felt something curl between her legs and screamed again as her flesh ripped. She looked down and saw a thick, serrated bone-like tail where it had erupted from Symon's body, twisted around her calf, and rose upward behind her. The tail thrashed wildly, scoring her skin with blind aggression. She gasped in surprise as the tip of the tail buried itself in her back before going limp, its final death throes exhausted.

Sam sagged forward, exhausted and bleeding badly, groaning as the tail's tip ripped free from her flesh. She heard a voice as she fell but couldn't decipher the words. The street rushed up to meet her face, or maybe it was the other way around. It was so hard to think. So hard.

Something stirred deep inside her, something primal and ethereal. She tried to turn her head to see what was happening, but she had no eyes.

She reached out with hands that no longer existed. Everything was brilliant and white, stretching in every direction. Had she still possessed a mouth she would have gasped. She was the light, a steadily pulsing source of brightness. Was she dead? What would happen if a living person died in the world of the dead?

A tiny speck of darkness appeared on the horizon, regardless of which direction she focused. The darkness was so small she ignored it at first, still reveling in the sensation of being part of everything. The darkness grew, and before long it was no longer possible to ignore. Deep within the darkness were flashes of light, sudden and violent, like lightning in a storm. As the darkness expanded, so did Sam's sense of foreboding. It followed her everywhere, growing, threatening, looming. It was evil, and it was inevitable.

Now that she knew there was no escaping the darkness, she became drawn to it, fixated on the dichotomy between the clouds and the lightning. She approached it, watched its edges spread, coal-grey wisps of smoky fog licking at the light, infecting and corrupting it. The larger the darkness grew, the faster the lightning flashed. Up against the edge of the darkness, Sam pushed against it with her mind, her essence, and found it impossible to pull away. Panicking, she tried to flee, but there was nowhere to go. The darkness had surrounded her and was closing in.

At the last moment before the darkness overtook her, Sam took a deep breath, insomuch as a bodiless, lung-less entity could take a deep breath. Heart thudding in her chest, the darkness swelled and accepted her. Her light wasn't engulfed by the darkness: they merged. The moment it happened, Sam finally understood. She wasn't the light, or the darkness. She was both. She was her own universe, her own person, and she had good and evil inside of her, just like everyone else did. The lightning flashing in the darkness was no different than a cloud blotting out the sun on a summer day; they were simply different perspectives of the same thing.

Sam reflected on her life, both in the world of the living and the world of the dead. She had spent so much time waiting for something to happen to her, instead of making it happen for herself. She had been a follower, a person standing passively in the background, never confident enough in herself to step forward. When she met Gibson, she followed him blindly because he told her to, because she didn't know what else to do, how else to survive. She didn't begrudge him that; he was simply trying to help a stranger who needed help. She was grateful for his kindness, his willingness to put himself in the line of danger for her sake, but she never learned how to stand on her own two feet while accepting his kindness. When he pushed her away, it was for her safety, and she left because he had told her to leave. She had even become reliant on the Dybbuk, on its ceaseless guard of her when she slept. Always a follower. Until she met Assemblist Kratha.

Kratha had given her back her memories, had opened her mind to her past, and Sam could have simply fallen back into her habit of being a follower. The Assemblist – and Glen, against Kratha's wishes - had also told her to let her blood sing, to trust her instincts. Kratha had seen into Sam's essence and knew she would do as she was told, but Kratha knew Sam would never be a follower again. She was a Bloodwalker, and for the first time in her life, she believed in herself.

*　*　*　*　*

Robert Webb was having a very strange day. He had only been a member of the Fourth City's police force for a short while, but he expected he might never see another event quite as strange as this one. The only times he had seen legitimate riots were on TV. Battling back a horde of escaped convicts in the afterlife was not something he had ever considered as even a remote possibility. It had been a brutal fight at times, wave after wave of onslaught, but the strangest thing was when every single one of them suddenly clutched their heads and fell to the ground screaming. He had stared at the street, full of prone men, for several minutes before looking over at his partner. "What the hell just happened, Jacob?" Webb asked, stunned.

"Not a clue," Jacob shrugged, looking disappointed. "I was just getting warmed up." He had scratches on his hands and arms and a large welt forming around his left eye, but he appeared otherwise uninjured. When the convicts had gotten close enough, Jacob had rushed into the fray. Webb hoped the younger man would grow out of his hotheaded attitude

230

before it got him killed. Webb wondered if his attitude had been what got him killed in the first place.

The convicts were eventually hauled to their feet and handcuffed. None of them resisted. They all seemed to be in shock, expressing confusion about how they got there and what had happened. Webb could relate.

A few blocks past the front lines, Webb saw her, unmistakable even from a distance. It was like a punch to the gut. The ground around her was practically glowing with the silver blood of the dead. "What the hell just happened?" Webb repeated, this time to no one in particular.

*　*　*　*　*

Sweat poured down Gibson's face, stinging his eyes. He was an investigator, not a gladiator. He would forever be grateful to Sam's husband. There wasn't a chance he would have survived that battle without the man's aid. Jack's foot connecting with the groin of the attacker was the opening he had needed to pistol whip the man. While Gibson was trying to catch his breath, Jack had run off to help Sam. Gibson didn't have the energy to immediately join in the fight. Looking over at the man who had sacrificed himself for his wife and seeing him staring blankly at the sky, Gibson felt another surge of guilt and regret.

"Focus," Gibson muttered to himself. "Focus."

He had turned Sam over as gingerly as he could manage, trying to keep her back from scraping along the street. Not knowing what else to do, Gibson put pressure on the worst of the wounds and cradled her head, whispering comforting things to her. He wasn't sure she would recover from her injuries. Her breathing was faltering and hesitant, but he didn't know what else to do. "It's over now, Bloodwalker," he whispered. "You did it. You won."

Epilogue

"Bloodwalker."

Sam opened her eyes, surprised to find herself sitting at a long wooden table, much like the ones in Old Town, in The Cupboard. Assemblist Kratha sat on the opposite side of the table, a small smile on her face.

"You've done well, Samantha. You have surprised the Assembly with your determination and efficiency," Kratha said gently. "Surpassed our every expectation."

Sam's head ached. "How did I get here?" The last thing she remembered was being surrounded by Symon and his bodyguards, Jack and Gibson fighting one of them on the steps to some office building.

"You're not really here," Kratha answered. As if to emphasize the point, the table vanished and the ground became clouds, with the pair of them each sitting on their own bench as if there was nothing at all out of the ordinary with their surroundings.

Sam gasped. "Where am I?"

"I don't know. This is a dream, Bloodwalker." Kratha shook her head. "We haven't been able to locate you yet."

Both women were silent for a time. It was Sam who spoke first, the questions tumbling from her lips like a waterfall. "What happened? Where is Jack? Where is Symon?"

An expression of solemnity crossed Kratha's face for an instant. "You confronted Symon and killed him. You saved the living world and the world of the dead, but you were badly injured in the process. Your husband..." Kratha trailed off, refusing to meet Sam's gaze. "He sacrificed himself to save your life, Samantha."

The memories of the battle on the streets of the Fourth City crashed into focus. A pained scream tore through the clouds, obliterating the fragile vapors. Sam didn't realize she was the one screaming. Everything she had gone through, all of the pain of losing him, the frustrations of trying to return to him only to discover he was dead, their temporary reunion: everything felt like a waste. She knew she was on the edge of hyperventilating. In the back of her mind she knew she should be proud for saving two worlds from Symon's madness, but at that moment, altruism was not enough.

Kratha did not watch Sam scream and cry, for which she was grateful. It seemed to go on for hours, days perhaps, but only when Sam had finally exhausted the last vestiges of raw emotional pain and fell to a sputtering stop did Kratha look back at her. "I know it's not what you want to hear right now, but your husband sacrificed himself because of his love for you, and his decision led to your victory. You should understand just how great of a task you have undertaken, and how much this world is in your debt."

Despondency hit her hard, but Kratha was right about one thing, at least: she didn't want to hear about Jack right now. She had already lost him once in the living world, then relived the agony when The Assembly helped her get her memories back. Losing him for a third time was more than she could bear. Desperate to distract herself, she blurted out, "Is Symon gone now?"

"Yes," Kratha answered immediately, clearly pleased to move on to a different topic. "After you confronted him, we were able to hold his spirit in temporary abeyance, parsing it before it dissipated. We found many answers there, even as the process and the discoveries curdled our stomachs. Symon had always been chasing eternal life, which is why he had killed when he was alive," Kratha said quietly. "He targeted women, believing that as the bearers of children, they were also the key to opening the path he sought." There was a pause and a sigh before the Assemblist continued. "He cut out their organs when he killed them. He would experiment, brewing concoctions and testing them on himself, attempting to create a formula to extend his life. There were stories about Symon, back when he was alive. He was never captured, but he became known as Jack the Ripper."

Sam gasped. Jack the Ripper? "Are you serious? That's..." she trailed off, unable to find a word to properly express her thoughts.

Kratha nodded. When she continued, it was in a voice heavy with regret. "After he died, he came to us, as I told you before. He charmed many of the Assembly and developed unnatural skills. After he escaped the chaotic rift he caused in Old Town, his experiments became even more sinister. Eventually, he discovered a way to alter his body into something not of this world, or hopefully any other world."

"The creature he became protected his essence inside of its shell, allowing him to pass into the living world. Once he had achieved that feat, he became reliant on the consumption of human flesh to extend his time in the living world. Perhaps it was destiny that during one of these voyages to the living world he encountered your husband. Symon had passed into the living world and was still in the creature's shell when your husband veered off the road on his way home to you, which in turn set you on the course to arriving here and existing as a Bloodwalker." Kratha offered a small, sad smile. "If only we could have seen these things when he came to us the first time."

The heavy silence fell again. Sam held her head in her hands and looked downward, watching as the tops of the clouds collapsed and reformed, minute changes curling lazily by the second. She wondered if some of those changes were caused by the tears silently sliding from her face into the formations below. Kratha cleared her throat quietly before softly adding, "For your husband's sake, I hope there is another world after this one. For everyone else's sake, I hope there isn't, or else Symon will rise again."

Questions bounced around in Sam's mind, jumbling together haphazardly. Finally, she blurted, "How did I get to this world in the first place? We went to the séance and something grabbed me. Then I woke up in an alley in Purgatory."

"I don't have all of the answers, Bloodwalker," Kratha said, not unkindly. "I saw your memories when I removed your block, but what I saw then was not something I had seen before or since. It would appear that something from between the worlds answered the call of the séance, but that is, unfortunately, just speculation."

Something from between the worlds? Sam had never considered what might be living in the spaces in between beyond the Void Hunter, that horrific creature from the subway station that forced its victims to forget. The thought made her shiver. "Do you know how-" Sam cleared her throat and started again. "Do you know how Jack ended up in prison?"

Kratha sighed. "When we examined Symon's spirit, we saw many disturbing things. Most of it was warped and twisted, like coiled, malignant tumors. His mind was as evil as his actions. As I said, he had just arrived in the living world when he encountered your husband, and was full of dark energy. You see, he hadn't shifted back into his human form yet, and those transformations required a great deal of energy. When Symon attacked your husband, whether intentionally or not, he implanted some of his own darkness into Jack. That darkness latched onto your husband and dug its barbed teeth into his heart, corrupting it. Somewhat. After your husband awoke in the world of the dead, he was filled with rage and confusion, and he lashed out."

"I can't imagine Jack acting that way."

"He was not himself," Kratha answered softly. "He was corrupted by Symon's evil, and would have remained in Symon's control forever, had he not seen you. The mere sight of you, Bloodwalker, was enough to free him. In an instant, his love for you overwhelmed Symon's poison. His love for you is why you are still alive."

"Am I still alive?"

Kratha did not answer, and Sam kept her focus on the clouds, unable to look at her. The almost casual movements were so simple, so peaceful. After her battle with Symon, she wondered if maybe she should try to be more like the clouds: soft, distant, forgettable, unassuming. As the thought crossed her mind, though, she also thought of thunderheads and hurricanes, of dark, dreary monstrosities the color of iron with the ferocity of a wrathful god. She was light and she was darkness. Everyone had within them the power of creation and destruction. An hour passed. Maybe a day. "What happens next?" she finally asked.

"Next?" Kratha laughed, then smiled at her. "Next, you wake up."

Sam's eyelids fluttered open momentarily, but she shut them as quickly as she could. Why was she staring at the sun? She groaned in pain; everything hurt. Carefully, Sam turned her head slightly to the side and opened her eyes to bare slits. Not the sun - an intensely bright overhead light. Her brain was fuzzy. She tried to scratch an itch on her forehead but couldn't move her arms. That made her eyes open a little wider, her mind to focus a little more. Looking down the length of her body, Sam saw a pair of thick leather straps restricting her movement. She was wearing a thin, light blue hospital gown.

A woman's face was suddenly hovering over Sam's, eyes wide with shock. Or fear. The woman looked away and an instant later Sam felt fumbling hands pulling at the wrist straps. "You need to get out of here," the woman said in a clipped, breathless voice.

"Who are you?" Sam croaked. Her mouth and throat felt dry, unused, like they had never held moisture.

"I'm a nurse," she said, not looking at Sam. "You've been unconscious for months. Sedated. They've been running tests on you." She cast a quick glance at Sam before darkly adding, "Using your blood for tests."

Months? What was happening? The nurse saw the confusion on her face. "You were transferred here about seven months ago. This is the hospital wing of a government facility, in the outskirts of the First City. The doctors injected a formula made from your blood into mice at first, poor things." The nurse was loosening the final ankle strap. "Eventually the doctors tried the formula on Unborn cadavers. Nothing happened at first, but the doctors were impatient. Dumped the bodies back in the morgue and went back to redesign the formula. The first set of cadavers – the doctors took to calling them Cads - they awoke after five days, but they were changed. Scared the hell out of the guy working his shift when they suddenly started moving, that's for sure. They weren't alive, but they weren't really dead anymore, either. They were like a new species, mostly human but..." the nurse grabbed Sam's hand and pulled her upright, "changed. They could… do things. Move objects without touching them. One day I walked by the room they were kept in and I saw one of them floating a foot from the floor, standing there in the air as if it were the most natural thing in the world."

"Why are you telling me this?" Sam gasped, trying to fight back the bout of lightheadedness that swept over her as the nurse helped her sit up. She coughed out a thick curl of her own hair that had somehow managed to find its way to her lips. Surprised, Sam ran her fingers through her hair, feeling its length.

"The Cads broke free," the nurse said breathlessly, panic etched on her face as she swiveled her head to look around the room. "Destroyed almost everything in their path. I locked myself in an observation room and hid in a cupboard for three days. I don't know if they knew I was in there or not, but I wasn't taking any risks. Not after I saw what they did," the nurse swallowed loudly, "to the doctors."

The nurse made sure Sam was steady on her feet before rushing over to a tall wooden dresser. She pulled out a plain white T-shirt and black sweatpants. "This all happened a few weeks ago. I haven't heard anything from the outside since. I stayed here, praying you would wake up."

Sam pulled on the clothes, trying not to grimace at the sting that stitched across her back, where Symon's barbed tail had burrowed into her flesh. It must have healed during her time in the hospital, but atrophy had made the scars painfully stiff. "Why are you helping me?" Sam asked as the nurse handed her a pair of thinly-soled shoes.

"Why?" Confusion rippled across the nurse's face, battling with the panic that had been there since she had first appeared next to Sam's bed. "Because you're a Bloodwalker. You're Patient Zero. Because you're the only one who can stop them."

MY ENORMOUS GRATITUDE to the many friends and family members who have encouraged and supported this work. Whether you provided critical feedback and editorial suggestions or simply allowed me to talk myself hoarse about the project, I am incredibly grateful. The list of people, both real and fictitious, who helped to inspire this book is far too long to include here, but please know that you have my thanks. That being said, I would be remiss not to mention Gomez and Morticia Addams, specifically their portrayals by John Astin and Carolyn Jones, who taught a young, aspiring writer that love can come in many forms and that challenging circumstances can be overcome with enough passion and commitment.

To you, fair reader, I sincerely hope you have enjoyed this novel. If nothing else, Sam is a character who exists to remind me to believe in myself, and with that belief comes extraordinary strength, and I hope that she can be a similar beacon to you.

Finally, thank you to my two children, in whom I see such glorious potential and creative inspiration. Thank you for always making me want to be a better human.

-A.E.
June 3rd, 2025

ALEX EMERSON lives in New York with his wife, two children, and a particularly enthusiastic dog who I swear is going to knock the front window out of the frame one of these days. Mr. Emerson is frequently daydreaming and plotting out the latest tale to be told and has also written a short story collection, titled *Nightmares and Dreamscrapes*. He is also an avid gamer and can be found bumbling through a variety of video game content on YouTube. Visit him online:

www.alexemersonbooks.com
BlueSky: @alexemerson.bsky.social
YouTube: https://www.youtube.com/@AlexIsgAEming